SHADOWSHAPER LEGACY

SHADOWSHAPER CYPHER
BOOK 3

DANIEL JOSÉ OLDER

SCHOLASTIC PRESS / NEW YORK

For Anika, brave and brilliant

Text copyright © 2020 by Daniel José Older
Map copyright © 2017 by Tim Paul
Frontispiece copyright © 2020 by Nilah Magruder

Library of Congress Catalog-in-Publication Data
Names: Older, Daniel José, author. | Older, Daniel José. Shadowshaper cypher ; bk. 3.
Title: Shadowshaper legacy / Daniel José Older.
Description: First edition. | New York : Scholastic Inc., 2020. | Series: The shadowshaper cypher ; Book 3 | Audience: Ages 14 and up. | Audience: Grades 10–12. | Summary: A war is brewing among the different houses, some of Sierra's shadowshapers are still in jail, and the House of Shadow and Light has been getting threatening messages from whisper wraiths, and even though one spy was exposed Sierra is not quite sure who she can trust — but the deal with Death made by one of her ancestors has given her power, and she will need to control it and confront her family's past if she has any hope of saving the future.
Identifiers: LCCN 2019030317 (print) | LCCN 2019030318 (ebook) | ISBN 9780545953009 (hardcover) | ISBN 9780545953016 (ebk)
Subjects: LCSH: Magic — Juvenile fiction. | Puerto Ricans — New York (State) — New York — Juvenile fiction. | Puerto Rican families — Juvenile fiction. | Paranormal fiction. | Brooklyn (New York, NY) — Juvenile fiction. | CYAC: Magic — Fiction. | Occultism — Fiction. | Puerto Ricans — New York (State) — New York — Fiction. | Brooklyn (New York, N.Y.) — Fiction. | LCGFT: Paranormal fiction.
Classification: LCC PZ7.1.O45 Sj 2020 (print) | LCC PZ7.1.O45 (ebook) | DDC 813.6 [Fic] — dc23

10 9 8 7 6 5 4 3 2 1   20 21 22 23 24

Printed in the U.S.A. 23
First edition, January 2020

Book design by Christopher Stengel

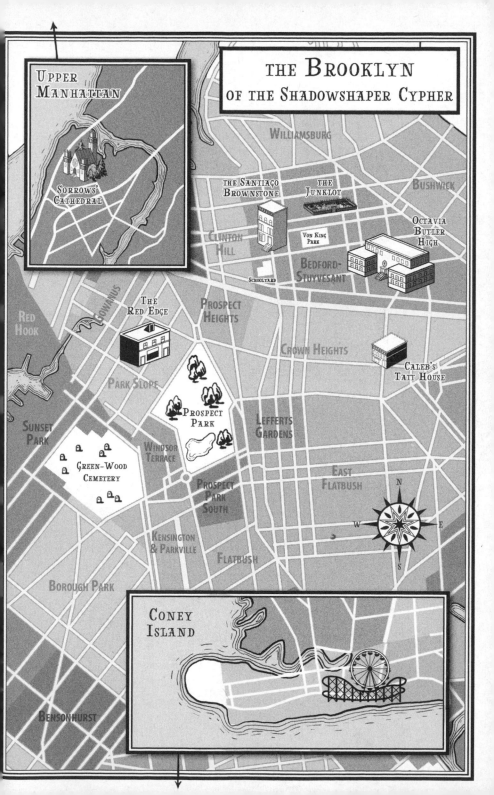

OUR LADY OF
SHADOW & LIGHT

KING OF IRON

FORTRESS

LA CONTESSA ARAÑA

THE DECK OF~ WORLDS

BLOODHAÜS MASTER

THE EMPTY MAN

THE RIVER

THE REAPER

Once, a very, very long time ago, when the stars seemed so close and the trees and soil still sang songs of that first act of creation, a girl within the walls of a great palace made a deal with Death.

I know what you're thinking: These things never go well. And you're right — they don't. In some ways, this one was no exception. But of course, the truth is in the telling, and it all depends on whom you ask.

She was a small child with brown skin, curly black hair, and dark eyes, and she was fierce — the eighth-born and most unexpected child of a magnificently gaudy and extremely powerful sorceress, who also happened to be a countess.

Of the seven who had come before her, three had died — one turned to stone soon after being born; one was too curious, scaled the palace tower when she was only five, and plummeted into the forest below; one went rooting around in La Contessa's potion cabinet, and they never even found the body.

But the reason this eighth child was so unexpected, you see, was that her father had died horribly two years before she was born. This of course meant that he wasn't her father at all, no matter how many times La Contessa insisted he had been to the guests at her lavish dinner parties.

The truth, which everyone around knew and almost no one dared to say out loud, was that one of the indentured servants, Santo Colibrí, was the real father. Santo Colibrí was a man known far and wide as a healer and one of the greatest singers of all time, a man whose voice could call forth the gods from the heavens and persuade the trees to lower their branches when he passed so they could get a better listen to those sweet, sonorous melodies.

His grandparents had been taken from the Congo, but they escaped when they reached this faraway island and found their freedom in the mountains.

No one was surprised that Santo Colibrí had made a baby with the powerful widow in the palace. Everyone was surprised that she'd let the baby live.

Ha!

Let the baby live. As if it were up to her.

The truth was, she'd done everything possible not to, but all her immeasurable powers, and they were great indeed, proved not to be enough to take on this small girl and her famous singing father.

Well, let's expand that circle a bit, shall we? They may have been the final line of defense, but it was really the other servants — two cooks, a gardener, and one of the guards (of all people!) — who had sabotaged the first, oh, six or seven attempts. You see, Santo Colibrí had a good handful of lovers and more than a few close friends on the palace grounds, and once it became clear what La Contessa was up to, which is to say, once she missed her first monthly, well, everyone got to work.

Selena the cleaning woman, also quite an herbalist in her own right, switched out the potions in La Contessa's cabinet that she would've used to abort the fetus for ones that would help it gain access to the mother's powers.

When La Contessa sent scorpions skittering into the newborn's nursery, Parada, the gardener, picked them off one by one, and it was El Tuerco, one of the palace guards that La Contessa had brought all the way from Spain, who fought off a local drunk that had been paid to break onto the grounds and strangle the young girl in her bed.

On and on it went, and as the botched infanticides added up, La Contessa became enraged and paranoid (to be fair, she had every reason to be — at least half her staff was working against her). (To be even fairer, they had every reason to be — she was, after all, trying to murder her own daughter.)

The dinner parties became strained events, as La Contessa rattled on and on somewhat incoherently about vague goings-on in political events back in Europe — mostly failed assassination attempts and coups in places no one was sure really existed. One by one, all the high-society expatriates stopped making the trek out into the woods to visit, and the palace became a kind of deserted hideaway, haunted by La Contessa; her three strange, pale daughters; her one unmurderable brown daughter; and the servants.

Of course, the townspeople made up stories about the palace: that it was cursed, that monsters lurked within, that those strange lights in the tower were La Contessa sending out signals to other witches around the world. Most of them would become true eventually, even if they weren't at the time.

But La Contessa was not one to give up easily. Or at all, really. Her tenacity and wit had earned her a place in the high court back in Spain, and that same tenacity and wit had gotten her exiled and nearly beheaded, and either way, she had no intention of stopping now. She'd been alive for a very long time, much longer than her moderately middle-aged appearance belied, and she'd studied under some of the greats, and she still had a few tricks up her ridiculous, puffy sleeves.

She stormed up to the tower one night in a fit of impatience and rage. At this point, it wasn't even about saving face or keeping secrets no one believed anyway — it was the principle of the thing. How dare a mere child resist death so many times, when death was La Contessa's will! It would not do to have her powers so challenged by one so small. The girl was six now. She had made friends with everyone in sight except her own sisters, and she seemed to be charmingly oblivious to her powers.

There was, perhaps, a small seed of admiration in La Contessa's grim and twisted heart as she entered the tower room and set about her sorceries.

If the girl refused to die, then perhaps Death himself would have to be summoned to handle the matter. It was downright unnatural, after all. Who better to right such an egregious wrong?

It was a windy night, and everyone knows Death loves the wind. La Contessa prepared everything, and then waited till the clocktower in town struck midnight. Then she began to conjure, to pull, to sing and carry on with such a frightening cackle and howl that townspeople all over El Yunque looked around in terror and held their loved ones close.

Of course, nothing happened.

Not at first anyway.

You don't just call up Death. Even if you're a wise and powerful sorceress — Death isn't one to just come when called. He's not some common street dog, after all. He's Death.

But La Contessa was, as you've seen, arrogant, and unwieldy, and probably more than a little bit lost in her own sauce by this point, if we're being honest. She didn't just believe the rumors about herself, she'd started most of them.

As the night wore on and on and on, and it became increasingly clear that not only was Death not coming, but none of his mighty denizens or fang-gnashing servants were either, well . . . you can imagine. An even more terrible clamor emerged from the tower, echoed through the valley over the treetops, and ricocheted across the forest-covered mountains, all the way to Aguadilla and as far east as Ceiba.

Then, because as anyone who has lived and died knows, Death has a sense of humor, as the sun began to rise over La Contessa's groveling, weeping form, a cool zephyr whipped through the room at the top of the tower. La Contessa looked up, and she must've appeared something like Death herself — makeup smeared, her face twisted into an almost inhuman scowl of disappointment.

But there in the still gray twilight stood the towering empty visage of Death himself, that rictus grin just visible beneath the drooping cowl.

Please, La Contessa said, but it was really a demand. *Please, take that foul creature who is my daughter! I beg you. I have been your devoted servant for so long, I remain so today. I ask only this of you, Death. Complete the work that I have started.*

Death, being Death, said nothing, only nodded very slightly and then was gone, with what La Contessa could've sworn was the slightest chuckle.

That morning, when La Contessa walked wearily down from her tower, the nursemaid Altagracia, one of the few palace servants who'd remained loyal, came running over in tears. It was Angelina, La Contessa's firstborn child — she had died in her sleep.

La Contessa sunk to her knees, raising both hands over her head. She ordered that the corpse be dressed in her finest gown and laid in state in the chapel, and then she stood, turned around without another word, and marched back up to the tower.

One must be specific when speaking to Death. La Contessa knew this. She had let her frustration and the long night get the best of her. She had made a terrible mistake. But that only strengthened her resolve. She would figure out what to do about Angelina later. Now she needed revenge.

She spent the day preparing and mixing up new potions, and when midnight came around once again, La Contessa commenced another night of awful howling and carrying on, and the whole island of Puerto Rico trembled and looked off toward the dark rain forest and wondered.

Many nightmarish tales were conceived in those two terrible nights. Most of them would become true eventually, even if they weren't at the time.

Death seemed somehow proud of himself on that second daybreak. That smile seemed just a little wider, his back a little straighter.

La Contessa ignored it. What good would it do, getting mad at Death himself? None. The mistake had been hers, and hers alone.

La bastarda, La Contessa said. *Take her.* And then, because she knew the power of names and what they could do, she closed her eyes and whispered the words she hadn't spoken since the child was born: *María Cantara. Take her.*

When she opened her eyes, Death was gone, and the sun had just peeked over the tops of the palm trees. La Contessa allowed herself the slightest of smiles before beginning her slow descent to her living quarters.

Death came to María Cantara the next day at that yellow-blue hazy moment when late afternoon becomes evening, right as Old Salazar was making his rounds lighting the flickering lanterns throughout the palace.

It was María Cantara's favorite time of day; she loved to watch the forest grow dark and listen to the night birds begin their festivities. She would gaze out from one of the balconies and make up fantastic stories about the different creatures that lived in El Yunque. Most of them would become true eventually, even if they weren't at the time.

When Death appeared, María Cantara didn't fright or even cry like most people did. She smiled.

Death smiled back, but Death was always smiling, so that was neither here nor there.

Have you come to take me away? the little girl asked.

Death, ever smiling, nodded.

What if I don't want to go?

That empty stare was, even María Cantara had to admit, a little chilling.

What would it take for you to leave me?

Death, being Death, didn't talk, but he did raise one hand, palm up, as if to say, *And what do you have to offer, child?*

My mother, María Cantara said, and Death very nearly burst out laughing. That would never do, though. Too easy. And powerful as this young one was, if things came so easily for her, she would never come to learn the deeper secrets of life and death. He would've enjoyed complying, but it wasn't the way, it wasn't the way.

What, then? the girl said, a little stubborn pout on her face.

Death, being Death, didn't talk, but he did slide three words in an icy whisper through María Cantara's mind: *Your firstborn child.*

Done, she said, with such finality and firmness that even Death himself was taken aback. She was, after all, only a child, and had little to no concept of what a firstborn was. Still . . . the speed with which she said it — the clarity — it was almost like she had something up her own sleeve.

Intriguing.

Death nodded once more, but then found that he wasn't quite ready to leave yet. The whole interaction had caught him off guard, and he wasn't used to feeling that way. He wasn't used to people looking him in the eye, or not crying and carrying on. And he hadn't spent any quality time with a flesh-and-blood mortal in a very, very long time.

So he stayed, and when María Cantara turned back to the darkening woods around them, she felt the icy presence of Death like a gentle breeze beside her, and together they stared out into the shadows and made up stories of all that may have been and would probably soon come to pass.

PART ONE

ONE

The last streaks of a strange, greasy sunset slipped into darkness as night stretched across the cold New Jersey skies. Sierra Santiago grinned through chattering teeth and pulled her maroon hoodie up over her fro against a chilly breeze that swept across the field toward her, rustling the tall grass and sending tiny waves through a nearby puddle of murky water.

"You ain't nervous?" Bennie stepped up beside her.

"Excited, honestly," Sierra said.

She didn't have to look to know her best friend was rolling her eyes. "Okay, girl."

So much work had led up to this one moment, and Sierra was mostly relieved it was finally going to happen, regardless of how wrong it might go for them. Anyway, it had reached a point where it *had* to happen: It was simply, undeniably time, and if she'd tried to maneuver or predetermine the outcome any more than she already had, it would blow up in her face.

"You don't think they'll be mad that we, you know, lied to them and shattered the fragile peace and all that?"

Sierra smirked. "What peace? Ain't no peace that I can see." Since inadvertently destroying all but one of the Sorrows and becoming the House of Shadow and Light a month and a half earlier, Sierra's crew of shadowshapers had been getting threatening messages from whisper wraiths, catching strangely shaped figures that stalked them through the streets of Brooklyn, and fending off halfhearted attacks from random spirits. Clearly, someone was trying to rattle them. Old Crane and his House of Iron was probably behind it somehow, but he'd pledged neutrality until things calmed down and had even sworn to protect Sierra's brother Juan, her crush Anthony, and Izzy while they were in lockup. Still: No one could be trusted. That much Sierra had learned. Bloodhaüs was on the rise, clearly vying to knock the House of Shadow and Light out of the way so they could take over dominance. And allying with Old Crane on the low would be just the way of doing it.

Anyway, the Bloodhaüs was a bunch of raging skinheads, so regardless of whether they were behind the attacks, as far as Sierra was concerned, they had to go.

"You right," Bennie said. "I just mean . . . no one can prove it was Bloodhaüs that was coming at us."

"Ha."

"And they still gonna be mad."

"That only matters if they can do something about it."

Bennie shivered. "That mask you been painting on . . ."

"What about it?" Robbie had drawn it for her the first time. Halloween night, when everything had changed and she'd finally embraced her role as Lucera, Mistress of Shadows. It had felt right, and not just because everyone else was dressed up too. That face paint had saved her life when she'd squared off with the Sorrows later that night. It had been there for her when she'd needed it most, a form of art to channel spirits through, and ever since then it had felt like donning armor every time she applied the grinning skull over half her face.

"Gives me the chills," Bennie said, raising her eyebrows. "But I guess that's the point, huh? You only paint it on when some shit's about to go down. What *are* you planning, Si?"

Sierra just let her grim smile speak for her.

It was a fair question, though, and usually she preferred having her people know the full score of what was gonna go down. But tonight was different. First of all, she wasn't totally sure how things would play. If Mina's intel was right, Bloodhaüs was every bit as ruthless as they'd projected themselves to be. And even if they were less powerful than the shadowshapers, they were more experienced and more desperate. They would play dirty, Mina had assured everyone at the planning meetup.

That's fine, Sierra thought as Big Jerome rose from his position in the tall grass and signaled that someone was coming. She nodded at Bennie and then crouched out of sight.

She had no intention of playing clean.

"Took y'all long enough," Big Jerome said from somewhere up ahead.

"You talk too much," a sharp voice cut back. "Where's your leader?"

Good, Sierra thought, still crouching amidst the weeds. *Goad them. Make them mad.* She closed her eyes, let the spinning world open up around her. Her spirits spun a slow circle around the field. She let them lift her consciousness, carrying her mind's eye into a gentle glide. The Bloodhaüs representatives stood uneasily in an open area facing the shadowshapers.

There were six of them — five not counting Mina. Two men and three women against Big Jerome, Bennie, Caleb Jones, and Robbie. Easy enough to take, especially once Mina blew her cover and messed with 'em from the inside.

But nothing was ever easy. Farther back in the field, three more Bloodhaüsers waited beside barrels of some kind. Probably full of blood, knowing these creepers. That was fine. She had another move or two up her sleeve as well.

"On the way," Big Jerome said.

"A likely story," a woman snarled.

"Did you want to talk seriously or not?" someone else said. "Because we don't need to be here."

"If you didn't need to be here, you wouldn't be here," Caleb said. "You don't trust Crane, and rightfully not, and even if you did, you know you'd have to put him down somewhere along the line if you want to get on top, yes? So why not get him out of the way now while you have a common enemy in power?"

"Yes," sneered the first voice — a woman who sounded a little older than Sierra; the one Mina said was called Axella, probably. "We've all heard about how he strung you along and then nearly destroyed you, Caleb." It sounded like there might've been the tiniest hint of sympathy in that rebuke, but that didn't seem likely.

Easy, Sierra thought. Crane's betrayal had been a sore spot for Caleb, and it probably always would be. The old man had been a keeper of a lot of the lore behind shadowshaping and the Deck of Worlds, and even Sierra's grandparents had trusted him with their deepest secrets. He'd been playing them all along, a House of Iron spy amongst the shadowshapers.

Caleb wasn't about to be baited, though. His voice was steady: "Did you bring what we asked?"

"Slow down," the second voice growled. That would be Krin, probably. Mina had said he acted like the leader but was probably just posturing, or a decoy. "How do we know you're not hiding body paint, hm? All those layers."

"It's cold, you pervert," Bennie said.

"Dake, Mina," Krin barked. "Check them."

Sierra exhaled. The Bloodhaüsers had insisted on meeting way out here, miles away from any graffiti-covered walls or sculptures that Sierra's crew could 'shape a spirit into and weaponize against them. The House of Shadow and Light had agreed on the condition that no weapons be brought at all. Even with Mina on the inside, no one was really sure how their blood magic worked, and the *Almanac of the Deck of Worlds* said that they were notorious for stockpiling arms for some forever-imminent apocalypse.

"Assholes," Sierra whispered, closing her eyes as Mina and Axella made their way across the open area between the two houses. At least they sent Mina to check the girls. Bennie, Caleb, Jerome, and Robbie all rolled back their sleeves and pulled their pant legs up, lifted their shirts to show paint-free tummies.

"Easy, jackass," Bennie growled, shoving Mina back.

"Hey, hey!" a few of the Bloodhaüsers yelled.

Mina just shook her head and stepped back, staring down Bennie. "She's clean. No drawings."

"Alright, alright," Krin said. "Dake?"

The boy searching Caleb and Robbie had to be about seventeen. He'd slicked his sandy blond hair back against his head and wore a busted military jacket over jeans and combat boots. In Brooklyn, he could've been mistaken for a hipster. Sierra wondered if he was one of the high-ups — the Bloodmage or Sanguine Berserker.

Robbie and Dake exchanged icy glares as the Bloodhaüser finished his search and moved on to Caleb.

"If Lucera didn't come, what was even the point of this parlay?" Axella demanded.

Everyone wants to flush everyone else out, Sierra thought. *Well . . .*

"Did yours?" Robbie asked.

"Of course," Axella said. "We keep our word. You don't need to know who that is, but they are here." They'd been cagey about who was running things, even once Mina had won their trust enough to get initiated. As the House of Shadow and Light's resident spy, she'd been able to be initiated into the blood magic without them knowing about her other powers. But they still hadn't taught her how to use it or shared their organizational secrets with her.

"What good is having your leader here to negotiate with us if we don't know who it is?" Bennie said. Something rustled behind Sierra. Her eyes sprang open and she whirled around, but the tall grass revealed nothing. Had it been the wind?

"Seems we're at an impasse, then," Axella said. "I guess we'll be leaving."

A bluff, Sierra thought, but she couldn't concentrate on the talks and scan the area for danger at the same time. Sure, she had backup farther out in the weeds, but how would they know she was in trouble if she couldn't make a noise without revealing her position? Without making a move, she called on the churning forces of shadow and light within her.

"And risk us picking you off one by one or getting crushed outright by the House of Iron?" Caleb said. "I don't think so."

"Or we could just wait around till you two decimate each other and then swoop in and clean up the mess."

There it was again, just off to Sierra's right and a few feet away. Not the wind. And then another one to her left, rustling toward her. If she used her powers, if she even moved too much, she'd be revealed, and she wasn't ready for that yet. Whatever they were, they seemed small — neither rustle was very loud, more like a gentle scurrying. Still, Sierra didn't like it.

Sierra. Vincent's voice, an urgent whisper. *Something's happening.*

Vincent had become Sierra's top lieutenant on the spirit side of things. He was Bennie's older brother, and he'd been cut down in a hail of NYPD gunfire when he was sixteen and Sierra and Bennie were eleven. Then he'd gone on to form a cadre of like-minded spirits who'd been killed by the state — the Black Hoodies — and they'd joined forces with Sierra's shadowshapers.

And now he was one of the shadows circling this weed-strewn New Jersey field in the middle of nowhere, and while he was always pretty serious, he sounded downright upset.

"What kinds of things?" Sierra whispered. "I got movement around me down here."

Yeah, we see that, but we can't make out what they are. 'Bout a dozen of them moving toward the crew from different directions. They converging.

The rustling had moved past Sierra now, and she was glad she hadn't given up her cover. But still — a dozen?

"Where you going?" Caleb demanded, and Sierra realized maybe the Bloodhaüsers hadn't been bluffing at all. Or maybe the whole meetup had been a bluff.

She stood, opening her mouth to give the command to bum-rush them, when she realized everyone was looking at someone barreling toward them from the other side of the field: Tee.

TWO

Tee strode through the tall grass, trying to calm the tiny earthquakes that wouldn't stop rattling through her. She felt immeasurably badass and immeasurably terrified at the same time. Plus, she was freezing. She wasn't built for this cold-ass weather, dammit. She was supposed to be on some island, speaking French and sipping colorful drinks out of coconut shells with Izzy.

But Izzy was still locked up — her untamable temper had caused them to revoke bail — and Tee was here: storming through a nasty, windy field outside Jersey City toward a bunch of nazi blood wizards as creepy little unidentified creepmongers rustled creepily through the field around her.

Dammit.

Somehow this was all Sierra's fault. Except it wasn't. Sierra was maybe the only one keeping things together. She wasn't sure whose fault it really was, except the blistering December night wind, the slowly creaking gears of the universe, or maybe — probably — that unspeakably vast and irritating little stack of cards called the Deck of Worlds, which seemed to have thrown everything out of whack.

And even though it also wasn't properly the Bloodhaüs's

fault either, that's where she was about to direct all her rambling anger.

"Hey!" one of the Bloodhaüsers yelled. "What's going on! Who's that?"

"I knew they were pulling something!" a woman said, backing away.

Good, Tee thought. *Run from me. Fear me.*

She raised her arms to either side and caught the flicker of shadows swarming to her, felt that gentle susurration of their touch as they embraced her like a breeze and slid along her skin.

That would be little Tolula Brown, one of the Black Hoodies. She'd zipped suddenly to where Tee had been posted up, teeth chattering, as the prickly tête-à-tête prattled along. Tolula didn't speak, but Tee could tell she was shook.

And before she'd been able to make sense of what was going on, that rustling had erupted from the grass on either side of her — a rustling and a kind of horrible, rattly breathing sound, and Tee had had enough.

Whatever was happening, Sierra couldn't be the one to reveal herself — they'd immediately throw everything they had at her, and then who knew what would happen? Which meant it had to be Tee. And so here she was, storming like a terrific jackass across a dingy field at dusk, both ferocious and terrified, toward these leather-clad magical fascists.

One of them held her ground as the others backed away, and that was the one Tee would take out first. It was like any street fight — you find the tallest, meanest-looking, most vicious one and kick him as hard you can in the nuts and then bust the rest up while they're still in shock. Or, run for your life if they're armed.

Tee wasn't sure if they were armed — they definitely weren't supposed to be, not that that meant anything, really — but she knew who the toughest one was. She set her sights on the tall white woman as her step became firmer and Tolula's shadow tendrils locked with the sharply edged abstractions Robbie had painted along Tee's arms earlier that night.

Tee was coming in from the side, so she could see the full spread of shadowshapers and Bloodhaüsers squaring off across from each other. In range now, she felt the swirling body paint activate, a cool thrum against her skin, and was about to fling both hands to hurl it forward on the shrill momentum of Little Tolula's ferocity when the woman in front of her raised one hand and squeezed it into a fist.

A dilapidated smudge blitzed through the air in front of Tee's face. "What the —" she said, slowing her stride. Another one hurtled past from somewhere nearby. They were gray-brown and covered in tattered, matted hair. The grass rustled, and Tee spun, hands outstretched, just in time to see a gaping maw and two claws lurching up toward her.

"Gah!" She unleashed all her paintings at once, sending Tolula's full force bristling off her arms in a dash of yellow and red and smashing into the creature, which flew backward into the grass and disappeared. Up ahead, the shadowshapers were glancing around warily as snarling, crusty beasties flung in shambling arcs through the air past them.

The Bloodhaüsers had stopped their retreat and were now venturing closer and closer.

This was about to get nastier than they'd planned for. Tee had panicked. Whatever that thing was, unloading both her arm paintings onto it was overkill. Now she was left with the paintings on either leg and one elaborate one on her back. Not bad, but she couldn't afford to freak out. Tolula's small form twirled up toward her, and then Tee felt that flush of contact. She raised both arms above her head, breaking into a jog toward the Bloodhaüs woman again. The painting on her back split into two vicious, spiky wings. It looked like some kind of angry M.C. Escher crab, she'd thought, when Robbie finished and she was left to gaze into the mirror at her wide form, the folds of her naked back that she'd come to love, in part through Izzy's caress.

Now Tolula locked with the whole image and then divided it and herself within it into two, barreling forward along each arm and then careening out into the sky as Tee broke into a full-on run.

"Back!" the woman yelled, and another furry creature leapt from the grass between them. The thing caught one of the colorful projectiles full-on and squealed toward the ground. The other one splattered across the woman's face and sent her stumbling. Tee followed up with a full-body tackle, bringing them both down in an aching tangle of limbs.

"Get it off!" the woman screeched, shoving a hand sloppily into Tee's face. Tolula swerved that spiky paint across her neck and into her scalp. Nearby, something snarled and rustled along the ground toward them, and Tee heard the sounds of approaching boots.

"Protect the queen!" someone yelled. *Well, there's one pressing question answered*, Tee thought, but she knew any minute Bloodhaüsers would be on her, pulling her off, and frankly, who their queen was wouldn't matter much if Tee ended up stomped to death.

"Grahhh!" a sturdy, deep voice yelled from behind her, and then Caleb's massive form swung into view and collided sharply with one of the approaching Bloodhaüsers. Tee let out a sigh of relief and then concentrated on holding this woman's failing arms down.

"Protect the queen!" The call echoed across the field, and it sounded like there were more of them than Tee had originally thought. They must've had troops hiding out in the tall grass too. Then a snarling bleated out to Tee's left, and something hairy collided with her and dug its teeth into her shoulder.

"Ahh!" Tee yelled, scurrying off the woman and ripping the thing off herself. It came apart in her hands — just frail bones and tattered fur and the dusty remnants of insides — and mostly fluttered away in the breeze. The bite hadn't gone too deep, probably didn't even break the skin, but still . . . "Ugh! What the hell?" She looked up to see the woman getting to her feet and pulling something shiny from her jacket.

"Gun!" Tee yelled, diving for the weeds, and then bright purple light spread across the sky.

THREE

Spirits flooded toward Sierra as she stood. They were young and old; some felt downright ancient, from a whole other era of human history. Didn't matter. They were with her, like she knew they always would be. She'd called them, and they'd come in droves, and now they swirled in a shadowy, glowing tidepool around her and slid through her with that chilly tremble one by one. They filled her, as they had once before, found the pools of light and shadow within her and then ignited, fusing and then unfurling outward through the purple streaks Sierra had painted along her arms.

The lines splashed out and upward like bright lava that didn't give a damn about gravity. A purple glow lit up the night and still the spirits poured through her, bolstering the strength of wavy spills extending from each arm.

Up ahead in the field, everyone froze. *Good*, Sierra thought. She could just make out the awestruck faces of her friends and enemies, all locked in combat. And there was the woman who must be Axella — the one they'd called their queen. She held a pistol in one hand and the other was raised above her head, palm out, now clenching into a fist.

"Si, watch out!" Tee called from where she lay on the ground.

Four blurry shapes flung toward her out of the weeds. Sierra swung one arm forward, and the massive purple streak came swooping out of the night like a huge burning wave. It flushed through each of the attacking creatures, leaving only a few wisps of fur and dust in its wake.

Before anyone could grasp what had happened, Sierra swung her other arm, and the second purple streak flicked across the field and smashed into Axella's gun hand, knocking the Bloodhaüser over and the pistol into the grass.

"Get her, Tee," Sierra said, turning her attention to the others. The Bloodhaüsers had given up fighting and were scurrying to get away. "Stop them, y'all."

Caleb simply backhanded the one nearest to him — the tall guy called Crevil — crumpling him. Mina, who had managed to stay out of the way for the most part, just dropped to her knees, hands raised, and made a pretty good show of sobbing. A third woman, who'd been fighting with Robbie, made a dash for it. Sierra flung one streak then the other out into the night, smacking the woman's feet as she ran and sending her careening into the mud.

"Bring them to me," Sierra said. "I want them to see this."

She squinted out into the darkness as the shadowshapers grabbed up the Bloodhaüsers and returned to the field with them.

Someone was missing.

Dake! The boy who'd searched Robbie and Caleb for body paint.

Spirits, Sierra thought, but they were already on it, spinning cool, wide circles in the sky above. She closed her eyes, letting the purple streaks gather gradually back into her arms.

There.

The boy was hiding in a patch of tall grass nearby, his whole body heaving up and down with each breath. Ever so slightly, Sierra smiled as the semblance of an idea took root in her mind. *Make sure he doesn't go anywhere*, she thought. Vincent grunted an affirmative and circled closer.

"Don't you dare lay a finger on our queen," the woman who'd tried to run whimpered. Mina just cried quietly, and Axella sent a defiant glare at Sierra.

Crevil scowled at her. "Shut your face, Enta." He turned to Sierra. "What are you going to do to us?"

"Whatever I want." Sierra walked slowly toward them. "That should be obvious."

"You do know," Axella said smoothly, "that as an ascendant house of the Deck of Worlds, we are protected and have rights, especially as prisoners. You can't just murder us in cold blood."

Sierra stopped walking. Something glinted up at her from the dirt. "Is that so?" she said pleasantly, bending down to retrieve the pistol. "Then why would you bring this to our meeting?"

Axella shrugged. "We knew you couldn't be trusted, and obviously we were right."

Sierra felt the pistol's cool heaviness in her hand. She'd held a gun once before — her godfather, Uncle Neville, had meticulously taken all the bullets out of his Glock and handed it to her along with a stern warning to either never touch a gun or learn everything about it before she did. Then he'd taught her as much as he could about his and taken it back, his face uncharacteristically clenched. "I mean it, Sierra. These are

26

world-enders, is what they are. Only time you need to use one is to end the world."

Now Sierra passed the weapon over to Caleb's waiting hand and felt the whole of Bloodhaüs let out a breath. *They're more afraid of me than they are of big ol' Caleb*, she realized. *And it's probably not just because of the face paint.*

"Let us go," Enta pleaded. "I'm sure we can make a deal."

Sierra shook her head, eyebrows raised. "Making a deal was the point of *this* meetup, and look how that went. Nah. Dealmaking time is over." She took a step toward Axella. The other Bloodhaüsers flinched collectively. She was their queen indeed, then.

Sierra was done playing. She stood eye to eye with Axella, took in the woman's tight face, her threaded eyebrows and sleek bob. She had a whole other life, surely. A day job, maybe — a corporate executive or a lawyer — or perhaps she was a housewife. She might have a family, Sierra realized. Kids tucked into bed and waiting for her in some suburban enclave, blissfully ignorant that their mom ran with a dangerous white supremacist supernatural gang.

Axella didn't flinch when Sierra placed one palm against her pale forehead, but her eyes went wide when understanding dawned on her. This was what the whole meetup had been about: This was the point. Bloodhaüs had set a trap — they couldn't help themselves.

All Sierra had done was make sure they would only ensnare themselves. And now they were at her mercy.

What Sierra was about to do would reverberate all through the Deck of Worlds. It would tremble from the Iron House to all the nascent groups trying to get on top and reach all the way to the mysterious Hierophants to La Contessa Araña herself. They would feel the shivering coils as the Deck rearranged itself around the total collapse of Bloodhaüs, and they would understand: Sierra Santiago did not adhere to their ridiculous little rules. The Hierophants would finally show their faces — they'd have to, since they arbitrated the Deck and were supposed to maintain order — and then she'd figure out how to get them out of her way too.

"No," Axella whispered. "Anything. I'll give you anything."

All Sierra could feel was the cool rush of spirits spilling through her arm. The blood magic churned, a majestic pool deep within Axella. Sierra's spirits decimated it in seconds, sent tiny flickers of it spiraling out into the ether as they trundled through.

"What's she doing?" Enta moaned. "What's happening?"

And then it was done. A sudden silence. Sierra stepped back and Axella slumped forward and then fell to her knees, face buried in her hands.

"Listen carefully," Sierra said. "As of tonight, consider yourselves vanquished and Bloodhaüs annihilated completely."

"That's over a century of tra —" Crevil started, but Caleb backhanded him again and he quieted down.

"Understand," Sierra went on, "that the woman who you once called queen is now nobody. She has no power." Axella let out a quiet sob. "And understand this too: We see you. We know who you are now, we know where you live, who your families are, what your routines are. We are the shadows. We are the spirits of the night. We're everywhere. If you try to meet up with each other or anyone else from Bloodhaüs again, we will know. And we will make you suffer." She made eye contact with each of them, managing not to smile when she got to Mina. "We are everywhere." She turned around. Shook her head. "You are each to head in a different direction and never let us see you again."

A moment passed; the whole sky held its breath. "Now go," Sierra said.

And they did.

The last footfalls of the now defunct Bloodhaüs faded into the night, and then there was the faraway rush of traffic down I-95, the random clicks and whispers from the field around them, the gentle shush of water tinkling somewhere nearby.

Sierra realized everyone was staring at her.

"What?"

She tried to flash an innocent grin but then remembered half her face was a skull. The dim forms of shadow spirits began to emerge out of the darkness around them.

"That was a lot," Bennie said.

Vincent stepped forward beside her and lowered his hood. *Dake.*

Sierra hadn't forgotten, but Vincent was right — he didn't need to see whatever conversation was about to happen. They'd have to have it later. Sierra turned to Tee, who, always meticulous about her looks, was wiping the field grime from her slacks.

"What?" Tee asked, eyes wide with . . . was that fear?

Sierra realized she had been about to give a command, softened instead. "That Bloodhaüs boy is out in the weeds behind me," she said quietly. "Can you go get him?"

Tee nodded, headed off. Sierra turned back to find the rest of the shadowshapers were still gaping at her.

"What?"

FOUR

"Shit," Tee mumbled, stumbling through the darkness and weeds.

For not the first time (never the first time, when *had* been the first time?), she felt too big for herself, too big for her bones even. Just an ungainly walking disaster in pants, and even her pants, which she was positive had fit perfectly when she'd put them on earlier, seemed to cinch tightly against her skin and shove her belly out farther. "Dammit."

It wasn't Sierra's fault. It wasn't anyone's fault but her own. Somehow, in the midst of tangling with those ridiculous nazi (now ex) blood magicians, she had just become a bumbling mess. She didn't even know when it had happened; she'd felt mostly just annoyed passing all that time hidden in the damn grass. And then mostly terrified as everything seemed to go so suddenly south and she had to intervene.

It was too dark to see where this peevish little muskrat would be hiding, and she was in no mood to get ambushed by some baby fascist in his last-ditch-effort, lost-cause bullshit. She scowled and squinted into the waving grass ahead of her. Took a step forward and felt her foot sink into first mud and then water, murky black water.

"Dick."

Forward or back, forward or back? There didn't seem to be any right answer, and to top it off, this kid could jump out at her at any moment. Or send one of those roadkill demons her way, if that was one of his special blood powers. "Ass." She took a step back and with a sucking, slurping pop, felt her penny loafer yanked off her foot. "Aiino," she whisper-yelped, splashing her now socked foot into a nearby puddle as she leaned forward to snatch her shoe.

Her fingers grasped it, but now something was rustling just ahead of her, and whatever it was — might be evil possum meat or an evil teenage boy and it didn't matter which because both were equally as bad, and dammit — she was going to have to leave her shoe behind. So she did, cringing and cursing, and flung forward into the muddy underbrush as Little Tolula swam gracefully through the sky nearby.

"Is he there?" Tee whispered, but of course, Little Tolula didn't speak, and anyway, it didn't matter. He was, popping up suddenly — his pale, shocked face taking in Tee for just a moment before he turned and bolted.

"Ass! Dick! Crap!" Tee yelled, barreling after him through the mud.

He was long and lithe, and he seemed to just fade off into the night like a ghost, but she could still hear him panting and sloshing around up ahead, and she'd be damned if she was going to go back empty-handed, especially after seeing Sierra turn into a supervillain and eliminate a whole house from the Deck in one fell swoop.

"Tolula," Tee called, and the child spirit spiraled into view above her. "Let's do this." Tolula swan-dove downward, and

Tee felt her swoosh through as the paint on her leg began to tingle and swirl.

She was clenching her fists and squinting up ahead, running out of breath, feeling enormous and somewhat pathetic, when a great big rustling and snorting erupted to her left. She leapt away with a really, really embarrassing squeal — if that was one of those roadkill creatures, it was a huge one, like they'd've had to have found two or three wild boar carcasses and stitch-them-together type situation.

The gigantic rustling snorting thing veered closer to her and then burst ahead, still concealed behind the waving grass. Out in the darkness, Dake gave a scream that made Tee feel a little better about her own yelp. And then a shape seemed to launch out of the field and take over the entire night, like an all-black plane had suddenly decided to take off from beneath the mud.

"Cojo!" Tee shouted, finally catching her breath and pumping a fist.

Cojones the junkyard dog let out a massive snarl and, judging by the shriek that came next, landed directly on top of Dake.

Tee hurried over, wondering if she'd find only body parts left.

"Help." The boy's whimper reached her before she got to him, and then she stepped into the clearing, and sure enough, there was Cojones, looking very pleased with himself and preening slightly on his haunches, a deeply defeated Dake squished underneath.

"Walk," Tee demanded, once she'd managed to coax Cojo off and Dake had calmed down some.

"Just . . . just . . ." He shook his head, wide eyes blinking at where the slobbering hound stood glaring at him out of the darkness. "Just keep that . . ."

"Yeah, yeah," Tee snapped. "But did you die? You didn't. He didn't even bite your ass, kid. Now walk."

Dake turned his gaze to her, and Tee felt a little chill run down her back but refused to show it. His eyes were auburn with long lashes and on a less nazi-ish kid would've been beautiful. His cheekbones looked like they'd been sharpened, and he had a little flush of acne running along his neck where he probably pretended to shave every morning, even though he had no facial hair to speak of. Had he been there that night upstate when the Bloodhaüs had almost wiped out Tee, Izzy, and Uncle Neville? It was all a blur: Everything had happened so fast. And then a mysterious and amazing woman known only as R had let loose with some kind of machine gun and sent the fascists scattering for cover.

Tee couldn't put her finger on it, but something flickered in this boy's eyes that let her know he wouldn't give a second thought to strangling the life out of her if he got a chance. It wasn't just rage. Rage was a fiery thing, and it could fuel a reign of terror, for sure. But even rage could be reasoned with, dampened. Defeated. What Tee saw there in Dake's eyes was something different: hate. She was barely human to this kid, something more like prey.

"Cojo," Tee said, without looking away.

Dake threw his hands up. "I'm going! I'm going! Just . . . okay!" He started marching through the grass, hands still raised. Tee followed, then Cojo came loping along behind.

"And if you curl even one finger toward making a fist, Imma make sure Cojo has a Bloodhaüs sandwich to nosh on, ya hear? I saw what your queen did with her little hand motions."

"Bloodhaüs doesn't exist anymore, remember?" Dake grumbled.

"Oh, damn," Tee said. "And here I am without my tiny violin to play for you." Tee snickered to herself as the sound of their footsteps filled the night. She'd stopped cringing so hard at every single step with her bare foot, gotten used to it, she supposed, and she was pretty sure Izzy would've loved that sweet little zing she'd just delivered.

Aaaand just like that her momentary good mood was ruined.

Izzy.

The absence of Izzy, which felt a hundred times bigger than Izzy herself, like the negative space she'd left behind kept inflating and inflating and would one day become the whole world: a never-ending emptiness.

But she wasn't gone forever, not really, just shoved away in a cell behind a hundred layers of concrete and steel. And she was protected, supposedly. The Iron House couldn't break their word, it was said. Unlike all these other scumbags.

"Look who the huge satanic demon hound dragged in," Bennie snarked as they made their way into the clearing.

"You have no idea what you've done, do you?" Dake said.

Bennie looked Tee up and down. "Where's your shoe, girl?"

"I don't even want to talk about it," Tee said, still trying to ignore the overwhelming lack of Izzy expanding around her.

"Who wears loafers to a secret parlay anyway?" Caleb said.

Tee does, Izzy would've barked, and then everyone would've laughed. Tee felt like crying.

"Tee does," Sierra and Bennie said together, and everyone except Dake laughed. Tee allowed herself a chuckle and then silently berated herself for being so caught up.

"Fair enough," Caleb said. "That one you still got is pretty sweet."

"Thanks," Tee said, not even pretending to sound pleased.

"Maybe we'll find the other one when we're done with this guy." He nodded at Dake.

"You . . ." Dake seethed, staring at Sierra. "You . . . don't know . . . all the history . . . all those years of work and toil that we've done, building up, passing on the legacy . . . the legacy!"

"Yeah, yeah," Sierra said, stepping forward to face him. "Calm ya nuts."

"You don't even —"

"Bloodhaüs isn't gone," she said.

"Uh?" about five people said at once.

Tee finally snapped out of the Missing Izzy Cocoon enough to catch up. "What do you mean it's not gone?" she asked.

Dake looked like he didn't know whether to spit at her or burst into tears. "You said —"

"I said it's over, yes," Sierra allowed. "But all I did was take out your queen, really. You still have your blood magic, don't you, *Dake*?" She spat his name out like it had gone sour in her mouth.

"Don't! Don't you dare take my —"

Sierra shook her head, massaging the spot between her

eyes. "No one's taking your magic, man. At least, not if you cooperate."

"Cooperate? I could ne —"

"Just listen for a sec before you make melodramatic declarations that you're going to have to backtrack on anyway."

Dake got quiet.

Tee — all the shadowshapers, really — stared at Sierra with barely disguised awe. Everyone knew she'd had it with running away, with barely catching up, with being a newbie in this deadly game of magic and mayhem and not even really knowing the rules. But they'd never seen this side of her. This was something new.

Tee wasn't sure if she liked it or not.

Sierra let a moment of silence pass, eyebrows raised, and then continued. "You are — or were, I should say — the Bloodhaüs's spy, correct?"

Dake just stared at her.

"Okay, cool," Sierra said, raising her hand to his forehead and closing her eyes.

"Wait, wait, wait," Dake pleaded. "Yes. Yes, I'm the Crimson Agent."

She took her hand away, smiled. "Is that what you guys are calling it? That's cute. Alright, well, we need use of your services."

"Huh?"

"I need you," Sierra said, "to infiltrate the House of Iron."

Now it was everyone's turn to say, "Huh?"

This was bonkers. "Si," Tee said. "How can we tru —"

"We can't," Sierra said, still blessing Dake with a serene smile. "But we don't have to trust him when we know that he knows that his whole beautiful century-old legacy will be wiped out completely with just a few quick strokes, right, Dake?"

"I . . ."

"With the Bloodhaüs Master eliminated and no way to get a new one, since they don't have the Deck, all anyone has to do is take out a few more of their initiates for the house to be eliminated completely. Isn't that right, Caleb?"

Caleb nodded. "You know it."

"And I'm sure Dake does too. So . . ."

Tee watched as Dake looked up at the night sky, let out a long, steamy breath. Closed his eyes. Finally: nodded.

She didn't like any of this, but she knew Sierra had a plan and had already outmaneuvered one of the oldest, most powerful houses out there. At least, it seemed like she had.

"Good," Sierra said. "Thank you. Get home safely."

Dake looked around, taking in each of their faces. Tee didn't like that steely auburn glare of his. It spoke more of vengeance than any kind of acceptance. And of course it did: He was a damn Bloodhaüser. There was no taming him, no trusting him. Not even with the upper hand.

Dake nodded once, cast a weary glance at Cojo, then walked off into the darkness.

FIVE

"Guys! Guys! Guys!" Sierra yelled over the din of everybody yammering at once. "Just chill for a sec! Please!"

Caleb was guiding the Culebramobile along the scattered night traffic of the New Jersey Turnpike. Up ahead, the cold, twinkling towers of Manhattan seemed to sneer out at them.

Sierra caught Caleb's sharp, inscrutable eyes in the rearview mirror for just a second before he looked back at the road. He was the only one who hadn't had something to say about what had just gone down, and that somehow made his opinion the one Sierra wanted to hear most.

She let the tinny pop jam on the radio and Cojo's heavy panting take over the car for a few blessed moments. Then she let out a deep breath and said, "Okay. I know that was a whole lot."

"It was more than a whole lot," Bennie pointed out. "It was a *whole* whole lot."

"Right," Sierra allowed. "It was. I know that. And we all knew going in that it was gonna be."

"We knew it was gonna be an unpredictable shitshow," Jerome said. "But we didn't know you were going to turn into the Joker on their asses."

Sierra felt her spirit drop. She'd done everything she could to protect them and wrap this whole ugly chapter up, and all they saw was what she'd kept from them. "I just —"

"Bloodhaüs is annihilated," Tee said. "And okay! I admit it was badass. But you did the most, Si!"

"I thought it was pretty cool," Robbie said quietly. Everyone turned to the back of the van, where he sat in the darkness beside Cojo.

"I mean . . ." Bennie said. She didn't have to finish the sentence — everyone knew Robbie had been Sierra's kinda-sorta boyfriend at the beginning of this whole shadowshaper business, had given her her first lesson in shadowshaping, in fact, but then he'd stayed aloof, couldn't figure out how to commit or even really take a moment to just be with her, and she'd slipped suddenly away from him and directly into the arms of Anthony, the tall and delicious bass player of Sierra's brother Juan's band, Culebra. And almost immediately, Anthony and Juan had ended up locked away along with Izzy, and Robbie had resigned himself to sticking around and just trying to be friends. And all that history hung in the quiet after Bennie's voice trailed off.

"I agree," Caleb said. "That shit rocked."

"But we didn't know about any of it!" Bennie complained. "We didn't even know Cojo was there! How did you even get Cojo there without us knowing?"

Sierra shrugged. "I brought him out earlier today with Uncle Neville."

"And just *left him* in the field?" Tee said.

"He was fine!" Sierra said. "Weren't you, boy?"

Cojo barked appreciatively, and they all heard his tail thump a few times against the rear window.

"That's not the point," Jerome said. "The point is we had no idea all that was gonna go down."

"I barely did either," Sierra said. "I mean, I had some of it in my mind, obviously, but it was all a bunch of different possibilities depending on how Bloodhaüs reacted to us. Half the time, I was making shit up as I went along!" Why was she yelling? Sierra wondered to herself. But also, why were they ganging up on her? "I was just trying to be ready, and I'm sorry if me not telling you every detail of my plan hurt y'all's feelings, but —"

"It's not that our feelings are hurt," Tee said in that somber voice that probably meant she was right about whatever she was saying, "it's that we could've died out there. The situation was out of control. That woman pulled a gun, Si."

"Exactly!" Sierra said. "Y'all let yourselves get searched for body paint but didn't bother searching the evil blood nazis? The ones who love guns? What was that?"

They'd entered the Holland Tunnel and hit stop-and-go traffic, and Sierra wanted to be anywhere but in the damn car. Well, no, not anywhere. She wanted to be wrapped up in Anthony, taking in his sweet smell and feeling him all around her. And since she couldn't have that, she wanted to be alone in the dim embrace of her room, clacking another letter to him on her typewriter. Yes. There she would make sense of all this somehow.

"That was sloppy," Caleb admitted. "And here's something else that was sloppy" — his eyes darted away from the road and glanced back in the mirror again — "we got a leader, guys. Like it or not, agree or disagree, that's what it is, and Sierra is that leader. And y'all welcome to have all the disagreements you want here in the van, away from all those eyes out there, feel me? But when we in the field, when we in a fight, or a negotiation, or *anywhere* else besides with just each other, you do what the general says. Period. You don't question her in public, and you definitely don't question her in front of the enemy." He paused, nodded his head twice at his own words. "Feel me?"

"I feel you," Jerome said. "It's like" — he hunched over and let his bottom lip droop, then said in a halfway decent Marlon Brando voice — "What's wrong with you, Michael? Never tell anybody outside the family what you're thinking again."

"Exactly," Caleb said. "Except he says it to Sonny, not Michael. Michael never woulda done that."

"Isn't it Michael who says it to Fredo?" Tee said.

"He does later," Caleb says. "That one's: Don't ever take sides against the family."

"When he gets to Vegas!" Jerome yelled.

Sierra had had enough Godfather trivia, but she kept her mouth shut. Caleb had stood up for her, and he was right. She wondered if Bennie and Tee agreed, though. Or whether it even mattered.

The truth was, beyond all the bullshit that was going on with everyone else's opinion of what had happened, deep down Sierra felt amazing. She felt like something had unraveled inside her that had been squinched up and tucked away for . . . well, for her whole life, probably.

She'd figure out whatever she had to with her friends; tell them more if that's what it took to make them feel included. But she knew that that thrill, the thrill of battle and, even more, the thrill of victory — that was hers and hers alone to cherish, and she'd earned it. Earned every second of it. And no postmortem or group dynamic would take it away.

SIX

Forty-five minutes later they'd all had some time to calm down, pass out, listen to the same handful of corny pop songs on the radio several times through. Caleb pulled up in front of Jerome's apartment building on a mid-gentrification block of Lafayette and turned down the radio. "Y'all good? Got real quiet back there."

Sierra had spent the time staring out the window, alternating between daydreams of Anthony's smile and going over and over what had just happened. Beside her, Bennie looked up groggily from Sierra's shoulder and rubbed sleep from her eyes. "What year is it?"

"Yeah, those car naps will do that," Jerome said, packing up his stuff.

"Listen," Sierra said. "Before we start splitting off for the night . . ." Everyone looked at her. "I just . . . I'm sorry y'all felt uninformed. . . ." That didn't sound right somehow.

"Try that one again," Tee said.

"I'm sorry I didn't inform y'all about everything."

"Better," Bennie said.

"It'll do," Jerome agreed.

"But also —"

"Here we go," Tee said.

Sierra ignored her. "But also, there's gonna be some shit that I can't tell you sometimes, and I need you guys to trust me that I know what I'm doing and if I don't tell you something, it's not just cuz I want to be coy, you know? I got reasons. And —"

Bennie cut her off. "But then why didn't you just —"

"Because," Sierra said, "I don't always know how to explain those reasons. Even to myself."

"I hear that, Sierra." Jerome made his way out of the van and then poked his head back in. "And we still rolling with you. I'm just saying, that could get one or all of us killed."

So could telling you, Sierra wanted to yell, but it didn't make sense and she was empty of fight. "I'm doing my best," she said, meeting Jerome's eyes.

He nodded once. "I know." And then he was gone.

———

"How'd you know anyway?" Bennie asked. They had been sitting on Sierra's stoop for almost an hour, letting the chilly night ease them back into regular everyday life after the thrill of all that had happened and whatever would come next. Cojo lay sprawled out, taking up the whole top step and one or two below it, snoring gigantically and sometimes twitching, his big ol' wrinkly face smattered with a ravenous smile.

Sierra hugged her jacket closer to herself, blew out a steamy breath. "Know what?"

"That ol' auburn eyes was the Bloodhaüs spy."

"Oh." She smiled. "It was a hunch at first. Then it just

really *felt* true, if that makes sense. And then he went ahead and confirmed it." She chuckled to herself.

"You know you still have the half skull on, right?" Bennie said. "So when you do that little creepy laugh you look extra, extra double creepy."

Sierra shrugged. "I'll be that."

"Do you . . . do you know what the next move is?"

Sierra leaned back, resting her head on Cojo's rising and falling flank. Dake would be trying to figure out a way to betray them and get his house back, that much was certain. He could try to team up secretly with the Iron House while pretending to infiltrate them. But without the Deck, they wouldn't be able to do much at all. The Deck of Worlds had five cards for each house: the Spy, the Sorcerer, the Master, the Hound, and the Warrior. Once a house emerged as ascendant, they appeared on the pages of the *Almanac* and on the Deck itself, but members of the house couldn't take on their roles and step into their powers unless they touched the card that matched with them.

Up until two months ago, the Sorrows of the House of Light had always had the Deck in their possession, and they portioned out powers to different emergent houses who came and paid tribute to them in that creepy cathedral hideaway uptown. But now Sierra had the Deck, and she had no intention of giving her enemies any more ability to come after her and her friends.

"I guess we gotta do like Wu-Tang says," Sierra finally said, putting her hands behind her head. "Protect ya Deck."

"Sierra, it's ne —"

"I know, dammit! Let me have my pun!"

44

Bennie shook her head. "It's not even really a pun if —"

"Shh!" Sierra hissed. "I'm appreciating the sound of my own sense of humor. Since no one else will."

"Seriously, though." Bennie stood up. "It's a school night. And I'm sleeping in your bed."

Cojo blinked up at her like she'd just cursed out his mother, then stretched, kicking Sierra in the head with one paw.

"Ow!" Sierra said. "Watch it!" The junkyard dog rolled onto his front and then stood and let out a massive yawn. "Alright, alright, I'm coming."

Bennie opened the door, and Cojo bustled ahead of her to get inside. She stopped, blocking the entrance.

"We going in or what?" Sierra said.

Bennie looked her in the eye. Sierra gulped. "You have it somewhere safe, right?" Bennie asked.

"What, the Deck? Of course."

"Do you really think it's a good idea that no one else knows where it is? What if something happens to you?"

Sierra didn't like where this was going. Her friends were already targets. If they were captured, they could be tortured, worse . . . And with all these supernatural shenanigans floating around, some rando magic creep might get it in his head to try and extract the information somehow. It was dangerous. But then, everything was dangerous. And Jerome was right, what they didn't know could get them killed just as easily, if not more so, than what they did.

"I do. But . . ." She looked around. "Alright, come with me." She walked in, the sudden, overpowering heat of her family's brownstone wrapping around her like an old friend.

"*Here?*" Bennie hissed, following her and locking the big

wooden door behind them. *"You have it in your house?"*

"Have what in our house?" Dominic Santiago said from the easy chair in the front room, where Cojo was perched like a furry, slobbering mountain on his lap.

Sierra froze.

"Oh, hey, Bennaldra." Dominic narrowed his eyes at Sierra. "Would you please inform your pet that she is not a lapdog, oh daughter of mine."

"Cojo, down boy," Sierra called. The panting beast lowered himself gently to the floor, curled up at Dominic's feet, and promptly passed out.

"And, uh, Cojo's a he, Mr. Santiago," Bennie said, forever unhelpful.

Dominic didn't take his eyes off Sierra. "What do we have in our house?"

Sierra stared at him for what felt like a tiny eternity. "Something important," she finally said. "And private."

"Sierra." Another excruciating moment passed. "When I told you that I understood and was alright with you and your friends . . . and your mami . . . having a whole secret woo-woo world that was beyond my capacity and quite frankly outside my pay grade to really comprehend, I'm pretty sure I was clear that my leaving the whole thing alone was conditional on it not bringing any kind of messiness or danger to anyone in this household. Correct?"

"Well . . ." Sierra hedged.

Dominic raised his eyebrows.

Sierra felt herself soften, wasn't even sure why. She was doing everything she could to keep the danger away, but wishing and hoping wasn't gonna do it. "I'm trying, Papi."

"She is," Bennie put in.

"That doesn't sound good enough."

"I'm not sure if it is," Sierra admitted.

"You know I have some people we can call," Dominic said, "if things get . . . you know, out of hand."

Sierra tried not to scoff. Her dad might've run the streets one day many, many years earlier, but that was all ancient history. "Who, Uncle Neville?"

Dominic looked mildly offended. "Some of his folks, yeah."

Sierra chortled and leaned over Cojo to give her old man a kiss on the cheek. "Thank you, Papi, I'll keep that in mind."

"I'm serious," he protested, picking his newspaper back up with a harrumph.

"Good night, Mr. Santiago," Bennie said with a giggle.

"Mmhmm."

In the kitchen, Sierra sucker punched Bennie's shoulder.

"Ow! Damn, Si!"

"You gotta watch your mouth, Bennie," Sierra whispered, pulling the cafetera out from the cabinet. "I'm serious."

"I know!" Bennie moaned. "I'm sorry! What are you doing? It's like midnight, Si. We gotta —"

Sierra shot Bennie a shut-it look, and she did.

The water shushed into the basin and the fine-ground café went into the filter and they all screwed together with the top part and went on the burner, which roared to life with a *click-click-click fwoom!*

Sierra turned to Bennie, found there were tears in her best friend's eyes. "B, what is it? What happened?" She crossed the tile floor and wrapped her arms around her friend without giving her a chance to answer. "Tell me. Who I gotta kill?"

Bennie snorfled a laugh. "No, no, it's just . . . sorry . . . something about this kitchen and . . ."

Juan.

Of course.

Bennie and Juan had known each other for damn near their whole lives, and Juan had always been the annoying older brother who acted like a younger brother, and Bennie had always been the nerdy best friend, and they'd probably barely ever blinked twice at each other until a few months ago when they apparently managed to fall irretrievably in love at almost exactly the same time without the other knowing, and they didn't even realize it until the night Juan got arrested.

"I'm sorry," Sierra said. "I know it's hard."

"I know you know," Bennie sniffed. "That's why I feel kinda bad making a big deal out of it all. I mean, we didn't even have a chance to kiss! At least you and Anthony —"

Sierra held Bennie at arm's length. "Girl, get that bullshit narrative out of your head, please. Anthony and I had y'all beat by like twenty-four hours at best. Ain't no kinda head start. And sure, we went further, but that doesn't necessarily mean it's harder for me than it is for you. We're talking about feelings, not bases."

Bennie scoffed and looked away, blinking.

"Aw, B." Sierra pulled her back into a hug and squeezed.

"And anyway, he's your brother. So you got a brother and, you know, *friend* or whatever we callin' it in there."

Sierra laughed through some tears of her own. "It's not a competition, dummy. I'm not keeping score. And look, just cuz I'm struggling doesn't mean you're not."

The cafetera let out its urgent burble as steam poured out the lip.

"If you don't tell me who this coffee's for . . ." Bennie warned.

Sierra poured a generous portion into a tiny elegant cup and placed it on a matching saucer. She threw in two heaps of sugar, stirred it, winked at Bennie. "Follow me!"

They stopped on the second-floor landing, and Sierra gave Bennie a hard look. "This stays between us, clear?"

Bennie nodded and snapped a salute. "¡Ándale!"

Sierra rolled her eyes. "I'm dead ass, B. No accidentally letting it slide in front of my dad, por ejemplo."

"Damn, Si. Alright."

"C'mon."

They walked up another flight, past the hipster's rented apartment, and then made their way up to the fourth floor.

"I knew it," Bennie whispered. "Lázaro's old place."

Sierra's grandfather Lázaro had been the top-dog shadow-shaper for a while. Well, top dog besides his wife, Carmen, Sierra's grandma, who held the all-powerful role of Lucera even after she died and became a spirit. Then she passed it on to Sierra over the churning waves off Coney Island. But Lázaro's apartment always had a kind of sacred glow in Sierra's imagination.

A faint light could be seen under the crack of the door as they approached, but it had nothing to do with Grandpa Lázaro.

"Wait," Bennie said. "It's not ol' Lázaro in there, is it?"

Sierra smiled and shook her head. He'd been dead almost

two months now, but of course that wouldn't stop him from showing up and haunting his old apartment.

"Cuz that'd be wild."

Sierra opened the door and a bright golden light filled the dim stairwell, sending both the girls' shadows flying against the wall behind them. "Brought you your cafecito, Tía Septima."

Bennie boggled. "Mama . . . Who now? Isn't Septima the last surviving . . ."

An ancient, crinkled face glared up at them from inside the room.

"Sorrow!" Bennie finished.

Ay, m'ija, Septima drawled irritably. *Took you long enough.*

SEVEN

¡Ahh! the Sorrow crowed, hunching even closer to the *Almanac of the Deck of Worlds*. Sierra had never seen her in such a cheerful mood. In fact, Sierra had never seen her be anything but moody and mournful about how her sisters had been destroyed and the House of Light was no more and ay dios mío que barbaridad, etc. etc. . . . . *¡Pero mira qué interesante!*

"Sierra," Bennie whispered. "What the hell is going on?"

They stood on the far side of Septima's small wooden table. The cityscape spread out in a beautiful nighttime canopy on all sides of them, buildings rising and falling, the twinkles of the late flights sailing smoothly across the starstrewn sky.

Pero siéntense, chicas, the glowing spirit insisted, barely looking up. She indicated two folding chairs in the corner that Sierra had brought up a few weeks earlier. *No tengan pena.*

"I don't know," Sierra whispered back as they walked over to collect the chairs. "She been a miserable asshole every other time I've been up here, even after her cafecito. It's really weird how excited she is."

"That's *not* what I'm talking about," Bennie growled. "And you know it. *Why* is there a *Sorrow* in your attic?"

"Long story?" Sierra tried.

Bennie glared at her as they walked back with the chairs.

They sat. Across from them, the Sorrow continued dithering away in Spanish at the *Almanac*. Sierra sighed. "Alright. Septima survived the collapse of the House of Light because when I attacked her with my shadowshaped face paint after they initiated me, some bit of shadow magic fused with her essence, so she had both shadow and light in her and —"

"So now she's part of our house," Bennie finished.

"Errrm, something like that," Sierra admitted.

"Ugh!" Bennie slapped her hand against her face. "How did this . . . Really?"

"Anyway," Sierra said, trying to keep the conversation moving, "we needed someone to keep an eye on the Deck and —"

"The Deck is *here*? With *that*?"

Entonces. Septima chortled to herself, fully oblivious to the girls' conversation. *Quiere decir que tenemos algo totalmente nuevo pasando aquí. ¿Puede ser? Puñeta . . .*

"I mean . . ." Sierra said.

"You have the most powerful sacred object in this whole dirty war in your grasp, Sauron's ring pretty much, and you basically gave it to a Nazgûl and were like, *Yo, hold this for me?*"

"First of all," Sierra said, "this apartment is impregnable. I mean, the whole house is protected — I made sure of that — but this floor up here? Extra double-duty ridiculous-level lockdown. She can't get out, no spirits or entities or anyone can get in without my permission. So let's start with that. It's more like, I had two things that needed safekeeping, right? The Deck and the Sorrow, and so they ended up in the same place. It's not like I've entrusted her with its care and she's just out and about, wandering around, brokering mad deals with rando house heads. She's as much a prisoner as a guest. And anyway, she knows shit. Shit we need to know."

"But what makes you think she'll be straight with us, Si?" Bennie demanded. "This is like the umpteenth sworn enemy you've entrusted our survival to this week alone!"

Chicas, the Sorrow said, looking up suddenly. *This is very interesante. Lo que está pasando en el Almanaque.*

"She said something interesting is happening in the *Almanac*," Sierra whispered.

"Thank you, Duolingo," Bennie harrumphed. "I took French, but I'm not a complete goober."

Sierra rolled her eyes and turned her attention back to the Sorrow. "What's happening, Tía Septima? In English, please, so Bennie can understand."

"*Tía?*" Bennie hissed.

Sierra elbowed her.

Septima turned her slow, dilapidated gaze to Bennaldra for the first time. She seemed to regard her for a moment and then nodded her approval and glared back down at the *Almanac*. *You have all but wiped out the Bloodhaüs*, she said. *See?*

She spun the ancient tome around so it faced Sierra and Bennie and indicated with a crooked, near-skeletal finger where the five cards of the Bloodhaüs had faded to almost nothing. *They are on their knees, eh?* She chuckled. *If we're being honest, nobody liked those guys anyway, not really. And they were, in a way, the opposite of the Shadowhouse, hm?*

"I always thought —" Sierra started.

Septima cut her off snappily. *Jes, jes, of course the House* of Light and Shadowhouse were always at odds and shadow versus light, jes, jes! ¡Pero! Este . . . *the power of shadow-shaping is, always has been, one of the spirit, no? Of death, hm? El alma — the soul.* She looked at Bennie. *¿Sí o no?*

"Uh . . . sí," Bennie said.

Eso. And the Bloodhaüs, it is a magic that is corporeal. Of the cuerpo, the body, hm? That is why —

"That's why they be flinging around roadkill!" Bennie moaned. "Ugh."

¡Eso mismo! Entonces, the spirit and the body, they are different, hm? Opposites, even. And you see, there are many different levels to this Deck in whose grasp we exist, jes.

"I never thought of it like that," Sierra admitted.

Anyway — Septima took a thoughtful, excited sip of coffee, closing her ancient eyes in appreciation — *un poco más azúcar next time, hm? The King of Iron only kept them around in case he needed to play them against us in the House of Light, I'm sure. But we were all ready to knock them out at any moment if need be.*

"Wow," Bennie said. "It's like the *Behind the Music* of the Deck of Worlds."

Not that what you have done isn't tremendous, young Lucera, tremendous. A vast accomplishment, hm? Jes, jes.

Sierra couldn't help the odd flush of pride she felt at the compliment. "Well . . ." she started.

Of course, Septima snapped, *you shattered one of the most sacred rules of engagement of the Deck of Worlds.* Sierra had been waiting for this. She nodded, solemnly.

Bennie boggled. "We did?"

"I did," Sierra said. "The two cardinal rules of this whole

thing are: You're not supposed to kill other members, and, even more importantly, you're not supposed to take away the head of another house's powers."

"These guys were going around killing shadowshapers like it was going out of style!" Bennie sputtered. "What about Manny?"

The Sorrow raised one bony finger. *Point of clarification: At the point that Dr. Wick went on his killing spree, he had already broken from us and was functioning on his own. However, I will also add that —*

"And why is the killing one *secondary* to the taking-the-powers-away one?"

"Killing is not the same as taking powers away," Sierra said.

Eso, Septima agreed.

"Since folks show up as spirits with all their powers still. Sometimes."

Bennie shook her head. "Okay, that's messed up. But also, didn't ol' boy in Park Slope try to take your powers away? That creepy guy we had to administer a fade to outside the club back in September?"

"Yeah," Sierra said. "I'd been wondering about that too." She shot a look at Septima, who suddenly seemed very interested in the *Almanac.* "Especially because Mina told us he was doing it on behalf of you House of Light creeps."

Ah, see, es que, este tipo es especial . . . Septima's voice trailed off.

"What's so special about him?" Bennie demanded.

This is what I am trying to tell ju. Septima seethed. *If you break the rules, there are consequences.* She started flipping pages. *You have to be discreet, you see. This man who attacked you may have been doing so on our behalf, hm? But he was not a member of the House of Light.*

Sierra rolled her eyes. "Discreet isn't really my style."

Well. Septima sighed, then turned to the first page, where the five Hierophant cards stood out against a black, tattered background that seemed to have tiny veins that pulsed with gold crisscrossing it: the River, Fortress, La Contessa Araña, the Reaper, and the Empty Man. *Then this is what you will have to deal with.* The illustrations showed a flowing rush of water in the outskirts of a distant city, a fortified tower, a huge spider with an old woman's face, a hooded angel of death, and a blank-faced man staring through a window at a happy family dinner.

Our mother. The Sorrow pointed to La Contessa Araña. *Your great-great-great-grandmother, Sierra. She created the five Hierophants as a balancing factor, to keep things in order, in case one House gained too much power. They were originally not supposed to have allegiance to any one side, but of course . . . not so much. But they are also the regulators. If a house gets out of line or* — she gestured at Sierra with what might've been admiration — *breaks a cardinal rule, then the Hierophants are allowed to take sides with opposing houses.*

"But also the old b —" Bennie caught herself. "Uh, your mama made herself one of them. So that's hardly fair. And didn't she come up with House of Light?"

Originally, Septima said sagely, *there were no houses, no need for houses. There was just the power of light, hm. And yes, La Contessa brought this power from the old world when she voyaged to the island of Puerto Rico and took up residence in a castle deep in El Yunque, which she inherited after her husband died suddenly from too much bleeding from the mouth, ears, and anus, lamentablemente.*

"That's an interesting way to die suddenly when there's an inheritance on the line," Sierra muttered.

Bennie shook her head, blinking. "Girl."

She anointed her four daughters as the Sorrows, Keepers of the Light. In her benevolence she included her youngest, María Cantara, la bastarda. But María Cantara was indolent and ungrateful. She stole off into the forests and joined forces with her father, a well-treated servant who also escaped, and together they created the power of shadowshaping, and they declared war on La Contessa and all that is good and light and beautiful in the world. That is when she became the first Lucera.

For a few moments, Sierra and the old woman stared across the table at each other. Sierra had learned to laugh off Septima's ridiculous spins on the family history; she spent her energy trying to figure out what the truth was beneath all that bullshit. But it riled her, deep down, that the only voice telling her about her own roots and legacy was that of a sworn enemy. And tonight was no exception. Still . . . she'd never mentioned the Hierophants before. And the Sorrow's whole demeanor was so suddenly different now; it felt like something else was coming.

Of course, Septima said slowly, deliberately, *that is all ancient history, hm? But now that you have broken this cardinal rule, the Hierophants are in play, as you shall see. . . .* She turned to the section about the emergent houses: Bloodhaüs, now faded, and, on the next page, instead of the different suits that the other houses had, all five images were identical to that of another card: the hooded man with a scythe known as the Reaper.

Sierra boggled. "What the —"

"Isn't that one of the Hierophants?" Bennie asked.

The Reaper is the most powerful Hierophant, the most mysterious. We say he, pero . . . the truth is, he's more of an it. Nobody really knows. He's like a virus, hm? When he appears así, taking over a whole house, it means great, catastrophic change is imminent, no matter what. This is what has been unleashed by your actions, Lucera.

Sierra felt her whole heart sink. Every time she felt like she had a handle on this whole Deck thing, it seemed to switch up on her. She'd already done so much, made so many moves, and it all seemed like some impossible, ever-changing puzzle anyway.

"Great," Bennie said. "So you've pissed off the power brokers and the Angel of Death is coming to kill us all."

Something inside Sierra steeled. She shook her head, standing. "Good. Just means we have to fight all the harder. We brought the Bloodhaüs to its knees. If the Hierophants want to come for us, we'll take them out too."

Once, a very long time ago, as the tide of disease and bloodshed swept across the Caribbean amidst armadas, freighters, and sugar plantations, a new power was born from the ashes of a very old one.

It was winter, and decades of chaos followed by a blockade had kept supplies low on the island, even for the supremely wealthy expatriates like La Contessa.

She had, in the not too distant past, done something she'd never done before in her entire, blessed life, and that was give up. After the death of her firstborn and the realization of how clearly inextinguishable her lastborn was, La Contessa realized she, for now at least, had somehow met her match, and took comfort that it was at least a member of her own family that had managed to outdo her, albeit a child.

And so, she brought María Cantara more or less into the fold of her other three daughters.

Three? you say, concern and curiosity etched on your young face. And yes, you have counted right — there should have only been two other daughters after Death so unceremoniously swiped Angelina from existence.

But that was one fight La Contessa hadn't given up on. In fact, she took her frustration over not being able to murder her youngest and directed it toward finding a way to bring back her oldest. And of course, it worked, up to a point.

Angelina returned to life as a shimmering golden wraith, not quite dead and not quite alive either, trapped forever in that not so sweet in-between, and even more inelegantly frightening than before.

But, you know, beautiful, if you're into that sort of thing.

Now, with war raging through the jungles around them

and the vast imperial armies sapping resources and making life in the palace very basic and irritating indeed, La Contessa gathered her four daughters in the tower room.

El Yunque spread out in a beautiful, bright green canopy on all sides of them, mountains rising and falling, great cloud castles sailing smoothly amidst them like towering metropolises of the sky.

From far, far away the cannonades could be heard, echoing through the valley.

My children, La Contessa said grimly, with a nod at each one. Angelina was impossible to read: Those dead eyes glared out from her shroud of gold and they gave away nothing. María Cantara managed to make herself almost as much of a blank slate as her somewhat-resurrected sister, but that was nothing new. The girl simply showed up, did what she was told, and then vanished back into her strange, dark world.

The other two, Veinalda and Septima, looked terrified. For the first time in their overprotected little lives, the outside world was encroaching on their faraway paradise, and La Contessa realized she had completely failed at preparing them for this moment.

The truth is, I had planned to do this much later on, you know, when you had all fully matured.

Veinalda made a small, terrified squeal. La Contessa ignored it. That one was born early and tiny and had remained a pathetic, insolent brat ever since, so it was no surprise that a mere notion warranted concern from her.

But, as you have seen, the events of this cruel and broken world have necessitated that we step forward as one, that we, the powerful, join together collectively to increase our powers and use them for good, for the triumph of light, for the advancement of civilization in this new place, yes?

All four sisters nodded. La Contessa wondered if any of them truly understood the depths of their struggle though, or what it meant to fight for one's survival. They didn't, of course, except maybe little María Cantara, and she was still just barely a teenager, incapable of really understanding anything.

Still: She was easily the most powerful of the quadrangle, even if her powers were a little unsettling. And she'd behaved herself, hadn't made a fuss about who her father was, or gone traipsing around the nearby villages with languid chisme. Sure, she disappeared for long periods of time into the shadows of the forest, but she always made it back for supper and just shrugged when pressed about what she'd been up to.

Anyway, they needed her. If this was to work, it would be her power that lifted them from being merely a close coven of light-wielders to something much more extraordinary. The other sisters had their magic, to be sure, but even combined, it wouldn't be enough to really bring them to the next level.

None of them needed to know all that though. Especially not María Cantara. She would get cocky, become a problem. Perhaps a very grave one indeed.

Together, La Contessa said, *we will bring an end to this brutal war, and our power and influence will spread across the island and then this region and then the world, an empire unto itself. As individuals, you each labor endlessly toward mediocrity. As a singular whole entity, you four will become something more powerful than the sum of your parts.*

She closed her eyes. They wouldn't understand, couldn't,

not for a very long time still, but it didn't matter. This was the beginning: In this room, in this tower, on this day, as the low rumble of cannon fire rippled across a sun-soaked sky over the mountaintops and forest canopy.

Join hands, my children.

This is how it would all begin. Light, unstoppable, pure, ferocious as fire, light poured through La Contessa and into the four girls standing hand in hand in that room at the top of the tower.

PART TWO

EIGHT

"No, no, emphasis on the four! Try again! Hold up, everybody." The clackity disaster that was the signature sound of Brass Monkey ground to a halt. Juan Santiago was pretty sure he'd never enjoyed silence so much as during the rehearsals of his prison band. If you could even call it a band (you couldn't).

"Six-eight means emphasis is on the *one* and then a slightly lesser one on the *four*, y'all." He waved his hands like a conductor. "*One*, two, three, *four*, five, six. Yeah? Not —"

"But then why not just do it in three-quarter time?" Beezo asked, lowering his trumpet.

"Urk," Juan said. It was a perfectly reasonable question, and Beezo wasn't trying to be a dick as he stared with those wide blue eyes at Juan. It was just that, these days, even perfectly reasonable things felt utterly insufferable: one of a million cracks that seemed to rupture through him all over again every morning when he woke up in a cage, and then over and over again throughout the day until he lay down and closed his eyes and tried to make all the cracks fall away, at least long enough to let him get to sleep. And then it began all over again.

Everything was steel and concrete and bright unforgiving

lights and buzzes and hums and clanks. Everything was shouts and threats and the reek of body odor, blood, and grease. Everything was hoping he would give up, fall apart, crumble, and crash. He wouldn't crash — he had to keep it together for Anthony if nothing else, and he had to be okay for his family and Bennie when he got out — but he couldn't help the cracks from splitting through him, tiny lightning bolts of desolation that grew with each day.

He wondered if the cracks would ever go away, even after he got out.

If he ever got out.

"Uh, what does *urk* mean?" Brayson asked. Brayson didn't play an instrument, but he liked to hang out at Brass Monkey practices because, he said, music made him hate himself a little less ("even y'all's wackity wack little jams").

"It means," Juan said, sending up a tiny prayer for his own patience, "that I don't have a clear answer, I just need you guys to understand that in this time signature, in this song, you gotta throw the heavier emphasis on the one, and the lighter one on the four, and none whatsoever on the five, which is where it keeps ending up. Which is just weird."

"Wow," Gerson said from behind his still raised triangle. "Music snob much?"

Juan rolled his eyes. Where was Anthony? He'd stopped coming to rehearsal a week or so ago. Juan couldn't remember the last time he'd seen his friend smile. Everything felt dire. Nothing had happened, and Juan believed his sister when she said they were safe under the Iron House's guarantee of protection, but still . . . sometimes he thought he would prefer it if they had to deal with some imminent attack — at least it would break up this feeling of slow, rotting death.

"Alright, kids," Officer Grintly said, looking up from a decade-old issue of *People* magazine. "Time's up. You still suck, alas."

"Thanks a lot," Gerson said. He *pling*ed the triangle one last time, and even that note was somehow off-key, like the whole cursed island just radiated some off-kilter vileness that bent any note into dissonance.

"We'll try again tomorrow," Beezo said, always so tragically hopeful.

"Yeah." Juan sighed. "I guess so."

"Don't you get tired of it?" Officer Grintly asked as the last couple kids cleared out of the cramped practice room.

"Making bad music?" Juan said. "Every day. But what other choice do I have? Bad music is better than no music." He knew he used to think that; it was definitely something he'd said before and meant. But it felt less and less true every day.

Officer Grintly laughed. He had bright red hair and an Elvis cut and no chin whatsoever. And he sweated, a *lot*. Faded tats of naked ladies and dogs with born and died years underneath them ran the length of his arms. "The other thing. The shadows."

"Oh." Juan had figured out pretty quickly that Officer Grintly was one of the Iron House's people on the inside. It was obvious somehow, and he'd intimated as much one day early on when he'd sat down next to Juan in the mess hall and whispered, "Old Crane says not to worry. You're in our protection as long as you're on the inside." Then he'd walked away without another word.

It was the *as long as you're on the inside* part that worried

Juan. What would happen when they were out? What had been happening all this time on the outside? For all he knew, a whole war had broken out between the House of Shadow and Light and the others, whoever they were. Juan had never kept up much with the whole spirit side of things, even though (or was it because?) Grandpa Lázaro had let him in on the secrets of shadowshaping at a very young age. But now . . . now it all seemed to be demanding his attention, and his sister had had to pick up the mantle and save everybody's asses, and here he was locked up and kicking himself for being so aloof and behind on his own family's spiritual legacy.

And, worst of all, he was away from his instruments. So he couldn't even strum the regret and uncertainty away the way he would've if he was free.

"Santiago?" Grintly's croaky voice interrupted Juan's space-out. "You there?"

"Yeah, the shadows, ah no? What do you mean?"

"I mean" — Grintly heaved himself up onto a file cabinet and sat there with his legs dangling off like a little kid — "you shadow folks mess with the dead, right? That's what those shadows are, really. And, okay, that sounds like it might get pretty tiring, honestly. The dead. That's a lot. Especially for a young person such as yourself."

It was hard to take Officer Grintly seriously because he said everything with a slight buzz of incredulous sarcasm. But Juan was pretty sure he was being sincere just now, so he thought it over and then shook his head. "Nah, the dead are really alive, when you get to know them. That's how my sister explained it to me once, and I realized she was right. They died, but there they are, still moving through this world and interacting with each other and us and art and all this stuff. And the deeper in you get, the more you understand them, so they're not just like woo-woo spooky shadows, you know? They're like . . . people? Just people who happened to have died already, is all." At least, that's what Sierra had said it was like. Juan hadn't really gotten close enough to them to figure it out, even for all those years he'd been a shadowshaper. The truth of it — that negligence — was like an ongoing cringe.

"That's kinda deep," Grintly acknowledged. "I'm just saying, iron is the truth."

"Huh?"

"That's just a thing we say: Iron is the truth. Like a motto? That's one of our basic principles. That's why we can't lie. It's foundational."

"Oh. You can deceive, though, right?"

Grintly shrugged, which Juan took to be an extreme yes.

"When we say iron is the truth, though, it also means we're unbending; we are who we are, deep down, on the surface, whatever, wherever: the truth."

"Sounds like something a corny dude would caption his shirtless photo with on Instagram, to be honest."

"Oh, the Iron House doesn't have a social media presence. That's where snakes and charlatans run rampant."

"Probably for the best," Juan conceded.

"Alright, shadow kid," Grintly said, hopping down from his perch. "Let's get you back to your cell."

"Yeah." Juan felt suddenly exhausted. He hadn't done much at all today, but it didn't matter really. Just existing took its toll with all those bars caging you in.

They made their way through the bright unfriendly

hallways, clanging metal doors and jeers echoing through the building around them. Then Grintly let Juan into his cell, nodded once, and walked away whistling.

Anthony didn't even look up. He was sitting on his bunk, bare feet on the cold floor, staring at his hands.

"Uh, you okay, man?" Juan asked.

"You ever wonder what the hell was wrong with you that you once found prison rape jokes funny?"

"Wha —" Juan sat down next to his friend and put an arm around his shoulder. "What happened, Pulpo? You okay?"

Anthony blinked. "Huh? Oh, yeah, no, nothing happened. Sorry." He shook his head as if coming out of a trance. "I'm — I was just thinking, is all. Just . . . when we came in, and then the whole time we've been here, right? I've been so afraid that could happen, because you hear stories and you hear jokes, and then I thought, wow — I've, like, *laughed* at those jokes. Like, somehow that was funny to me."

"I mean, it's funny to a lot of people," Juan said, trying to remember if he'd ever laughed at one.

Anthony shot him a shrill look.

"Not defending them! Just saying you weren't alone in laughing at them."

"Right," Anthony said, turning back to his thoughts and scratching his close-cropped haircut. "That's what I mean. Like, it's sociopathic, really, if you think about it, to think something like rape is funny. It's completely evil. But, like, we do, we're told that's just cool, haha, wow . . . It's just gross to me, and I'm mad it took me being in a position where I was worried about it actually happening for me to take it seriously. What kind of a human am I?"

Juan looked his friend over carefully.

Anthony had lost weight since they'd been inside. He'd come in tall and fit, like almost ridiculously fit, bulging muscles and a six-pack and all that. Now you could see his ribs through his T-shirt and the skin seemed to just hang off his arms — not flabby, just lethargic — like it had given up. Like he had given up. Even his skin, usually a rich dark brown, seemed to be slowly turning gray somehow. Or maybe that was just the lighting in this god-awful pit. Juan had lost all perspective.

"You're a really amazing human," Juan said.

Anthony looked up, opened his mouth to say something.

"— in a shitty, shitty world," Juan finished. "That teaches us how to be monsters. And we're locked up in the wickedest heart of this shitty world, and so our only job right now is to make it out of here without becoming the monsters they've been trying to make us into our entire lives. Feel me?"

Anthony nodded.

"And if we can do that, well . . . that'll be something else. Nothing short of amazing, really. But even the fact that we've made it this far, that you've made it this far, and here you are becoming an even better human being instead of doing the opposite, well . . . that's what matters, man."

Anthony looked away. Juan couldn't help but feel like there was something his friend wasn't telling him. His face had been strained the past few days, even more so than usual, like he was heaving around some great weight. And being locked up was plenty heaviness for anyone to lug, but this seemed different. They'd always told each other everything, *everything*, but Juan had no idea how to ask what the feeling of this sudden distance between them was about.

"You're right," Anthony said. "Feel like my brain keeps looking for a way to blame me for everything wrong with the world. Especially these days."

"Of course it does. Look where we are. It's trying to make sense of why we're here. But there ain't no good reason for it, man. None at all. And the sooner we both get that, the better off we'll be."

He nodded.

Juan eyed him. "Hey, you feeling like . . . you know?"

Anthony rubbed his face and scowled. "Nah. I'm alright." He stood up, shook it all off. "Just overthinking is all."

He hadn't had an anxiety attack in a while — two weeks, maybe? — and when he did have them, they'd somehow always happened when it was just the two of them in the cell, thank God. Still: The threat of it seemed to pulse through every moment while they were imprisoned. Knowing the guards here, any of them could take Anthony freaking out as an excuse to try and beat his ass. And sure, they were supposedly protected, but how much could Busted Elvis really do for them when push came to shove?

"I'll be alright," Anthony said. "Just gotta . . ." His voice trailed off, because there wasn't much he could do, really, and both of them knew it.

"Santiago! King!" a gruff voice called from the doorway.

Juan looked up, heart beating double-time for no reason he could name.

"You're free to go. Let's move."

Juan blinked. "What?"

NINE

Tee whirled around in her chair and glared at Bennie and Sierra. "She has a *what now* in her attic?"

Sierra rolled her eyes and put her head down on her desk. "It's not an attic, it's my abuelo's old apartment."

"Feel like that's aggressively beside the point," Tee said.

Bennie just shook her head.

"Didn't the Sorrows, like, try to kill us? Like, a month ago?"

"A month and a half," Bennie said. "But yeah!"

"Bennaldra," Mr. Cruz said. "You with us?"

"Hydrogen!" Bennie called without looking up from their conversation.

"Very good."

"How do you do that?" Tee grumbled, turning back around.

"It's what I do," Bennaldra said.

Nothing made sense and Tee wanted to scream. How could Sierra be keeping a Sorrow in her house? And the fact that she hadn't told anyone about it until now made it even worse. Especially after last night.

She was pretty sure Izzy would've agreed with her that it was messed up, but she was also pretty sure it was ridiculous how much she thought about Izzy and tried to guess what she would or wouldn't be doing. The truth was, Izzy was unpredictable, and that's what Tee loved most about her. Even when it caused static between them. Like the time they got into a yelling match over whether the BET Awards should have a country music category. ("Country music comes from *black* people!" Izzy had screamed on the downtown 2 train, scaring all the gentrifiers. "So it's *black* music! It's ours!" She'd glanced around, challenging anybody to disagree. Only Tee took the bait, and another round erupted that only ended with Izzy admitting that even though she was still right, a good bit of her passion on the topic came from the worry that she wouldn't get any recognition for her inevitable country-western album because the black people awards shows didn't have the category and the white people ones were all racist. They'd kissed and made up, and then made out, further freaking out the entire train car.)

"Trejean." Mr. Cruz's voice shattered Tee's sweet memories.

"Hydrogen!" Tee yelled. Everybody laughed. "What?"

"Ah . . . what?" Mr. Cruz made a show of looking confused. Someone always had to be the class clown, but it usually wasn't the teacher. But Cruz was adorable in a fatherly/chipmunk kind of way, with that gallant little mustache of his and those round glasses, and all his jokes were cringeworthy but harmless, so everyone pretty much rolled their eyes and gave him a pass. "I was asking, Trejean, what people's plans are for Christmas break. But if hydrogen is your plan, then so be it."

Everyone laughed some more.

"Oh," Tee said, then, "Man, I'm just trying to make it to Christmas break, to be honest."

Cruz blinked a few times, then said, "Yikes. Well, see me if there's anything an old science teacher can help with." He nodded once, as if to assure her he wasn't joking, and then moved on. Tee thought it was pretty sweet, but she'd been burned by well-meaning teachers who opened their door only to slam it in your face and then get you locked up in Woodhull's psych ward, so she had no plans on ever revealing anything important to one again. Well, not anytime soon anyway.

"Alright, kids," Cruz said. "See you ne —"

The electronic bell blurted out overhead. Cruz gave up and waved everyone off with a chuckle. Out in the hallways, a hundred doors burst open and the entire student body of Octavia Butler High spilled out and began the hustle and bustle to next period's class.

"See," Bennie said, nudging Sierra and nodding at Tee as they maneuvered through the crowded corridor. "This is what I mean. You literally having cafecitos with the enemy and none of us the wiser."

"But —" Sierra started.

"I ain't done talking," Bennie said, dead serious. Sierra shut up. "I ain't saying you shouldn't have ol' girl up there or that you messed up, even, so don't get defensive. I'm saying, you need to be checking in with us more. Not so we can, like, tell you what to do, but so we can do this shit together and —"

"I mean —"

"And! That's why I told you you gotta clue in at least one other shadowshaper on the situation." She reached across Sierra and passed an imaginary mic to Tee. "And now it's Tee's turn to speak, ay!"

"Hey!" Sierra yelled.

"Tee got the mic!" Bennie yelled over the din of someone's busted cell phone speakers blaring out a hot new bop. "Nothing I can do about that! Tee got the mic. Kick it, Tee."

Tee held the invisible mic up to her lips, felt ridiculous, tossed it behind her shoulder like a long-lost lightsaber some random girl had shown up on the mountainside with. "Look," she said. "Imma break it down best I can, Si. I get you got schemes, and I bet they hot schemes."

"Internal rhyme," Bennie pointed out in hype-man voice. "What *what*!"

"Bennie," Sierra growled.

"Tee got the mic still! What *what*!"

"Then why do *you* keep talking?" Sierra demanded. "Never mind. Yes, Tee?"

"I'm saying, maybe Septima has reformed. Maybe she does want to help us. Maybe she's being honest, or playing with a full deck . . ."

"Pun intended!" Bennie yelled, still in hype mode.

They both ignored her. "But if she's not, and there's a good chance she's not, then that could easily bring us all down. And the only way we gonna figure it out is if we do it together. Like, if you have us to bounce off what she's saying so we can help see what's what."

Sierra shrugged a grudging nod. "I see . . . what you're saying . . . there."

"And maybe Caleb, because he knows everything about the Deck and all that."

"Wait, aren't we in the AV room today?" Bennie said. "Why are we going to the third floor?"

"Ugh," Sierra grunted. "I was following you, young genius."

"Oh no," Tee droned. "We'll be late for part seven hundred of a movie about black Civil War soldiers starring Matthew Broderick."

Sierra and Bennie cracked up. The hallways had almost cleared entirely, just a few scattered stragglers, mostly ninth graders with those backpacks twice their size. For a moment, Tee imagined they were just normal teens, debating normal teen things, whatever that was — BET Awards for country music, she supposed — and not dealing with some deadly supernatural warfare that was breaking out all around them.

She shook away the thought. This is who they were, what they'd decided to become. She had no choice but to accept it.

"I get what y'all saying," Sierra said. "And I know you're not trying to gang up on me, despite Bennie's insistence on being Lil Jon."

"YEAH!" Bennie yelled way too loud.

"And I'm gonna try to keep y'all in the know more."

"Not good enough," Bennie said, suddenly serious again.

Sierra sighed. "I'm gonna keep y'all in the know more. BUT!"

"No buts!" Bennie said.

"Not *but* as in, *but really I actually won't do it at all*," Sierra clarified. "But as in: There's something else we have to discuss too."

"Oh?" Tee said.

"The Hierophants."

"Oh," Tee and Bennie both said at the same time. The halls were empty now, and their squeaking sneakers echoed up and down them, amidst the muffled voices of teachers getting their classes settled behind closed doors.

"What about them?" Tee asked. The Deck of Worlds had five cards that transcended any house— the Hierophants: the Reaper, La Contessa Araña, the River, the Empty Man, and Fortress. They were like super-powerful jokers, the way Tee understood them, and they played some mystical, completely unclear role in how the whole machinery of the Deck functioned. The only one whose identity they knew for sure was La Contessa Araña. She was Sierra's great-great-great-grandmother, Doña Teresa María Avila de San Miguel, a freaky old lady (apparently a spider?) who had created the Deck of Worlds and the House of Light by turning her three (wicked annoying) daughters into the Sorrows. She'd also made her fourth daughter, María Cantara (Sierra's great-great-grandmother), whom she'd had with a "servant," into a Sorrow, but then María Cantara had run off and formed Shadowhouse out in the wilderness, declaring war on the House of Light. And La Contessa had created the other houses as backup and the Hierophants as wild cards, and so the whole mess began and went on to explode and unravel over generations.

At least, that was the best anyone could figure out based on Decklore and what the Sorrows had said.

Whatever the truth was, though, the Hierophants gave Tee the heebie-jeebies. She didn't like how little anyone knew about them or that they could be literally anyone, or the creepy pictures on the cards. (The Empty Man was a guy with no face staring, somehow longingly, into a window at a family eating dinner together, and it just felt all kinds of wrong.) She would've much preferred bugging Sierra about how she had a Sorrow in the attic.

"We gotta find 'em," Sierra said, and both Tee and Bennie groaned.

"I know, I know, but if we're gonna . . . win this thing, if we're gonna survive it even, we can't afford to let them just be wandering around or allying with our enemies, ya know?"

"But . . . how?" Tee said, not wanting to know the answer, knowing it anyway.

"See," Sierra said, "that's why I'm talking to you two!"

Another simultaneous groan.

"My two best shadowshapers!"

Grumbles.

"My favorite people in this whole wide world not counting people directly related to me!"

"And Anthony," Bennie pointed out.

Sierra shrugged. "I love you guys the most. Period. Hoes before bros. Even fine-ass, sexy, vibrato-singing, bass-playing bros."

"Wow, thanks," Tee said dryly. "I hardly know what to say."

"Look —" Sierra started, but she was cut off by a rattle of drums and the sudden shredding screech of an electric guitar coming from her pocket. She glanced around guiltily, then pulled a phone out.

"Sierra!" Bennie gasped. "We're supposed to turn in our phones when we come through the metal detectors!"

"I do," Sierra said nonchalantly. "I turned in one of Anthony's old burner phones." She blinked at the screen. "Why is my mom calling me right now, though?"

"But how do you get past the metal detector with it?"

"I think you guys forget I'm lowkey dating the dude that used to sell weed to all our security guards. There are methods." She put the phone up to her ear. "Hey, Mami, my love! Wassup . . ." Sierra stopped walking. "What?"

A moment passed. Tee could make out María Santiago's excited voice on the other line, but she couldn't quite tell what she was saying. It sounded like she'd gone full Spanglish.

"When?" Sierra said, sounding the opposite of excited. "How?"

She shook her head as another barrage of Spanglish poured out. *"Wait,"* María's voice said, suddenly very clear and very loud. *"Why do you have your phone at school, m'ija?"*

"Oop, time for class!" Sierra said, and hung up. She looked at Bennie and Tee, backing slowly down the hallway. "We gotta go. We gotta go now."

"What?" Tee yelled.

Sierra had broken into a run. Tee and Bennie started jogging along behind her. "What happened?" Bennie asked.

"Desmond Pocket called my parents," Sierra called over her shoulder. "Said Juan and Anthony have been released or are about to be! He doesn't know why, he's trying to find out now."

Tee thought she might pass out from the suddenness of it all. Did that mean . . . was Izzy free too . . . and if so . . .

She looked up to see Sierra holding the phone out toward her like they were passing the baton in a relay race. "Call Desmond," Sierra panted. "Find out if Izzy is getting out too, and if she is . . . you gotta . . . we gotta . . . we gotta get to them."

"Why?" Bennie asked. "What's going on?"

They rounded the corner together and started down a

stairwell, footsteps ricocheting wildly across the cavernous building.

"The House of Iron's guarantee of their safety only counts for when they're locked up," Sierra explained. "And we just took out Bloodhaüs. So . . ."

"Say no more," Tee said, and ran harder, dialing as she went.

TEN

"You know . . ." Anthony said as they walked down a long, echoey corridor.

"Go on," Juan said.

Neither of them looked anywhere but straight ahead. Their shoes squeaked against the floor. Behind them, the corrections officers' boots clomped along, their keys jingling, their clubs brushing against their uniform pants. One of them could just swing back and clobber either Juan or Anthony at any moment. Sure, the security cameras would catch it, but who would care, really, when the footage disappeared and the other guard testified that they'd been attacked, that it was self-defense, that Juan and Anthony were monsters, animals, that had to be put down. It's how plenty of people saw them anyway; how hard would it be to convince a grand jury of it? If it even got that far, which it wouldn't. They would die unavenged and maybe unmourned; and the state would try to enforce amnesia like they always did, bury the memory of who Juan and Anthony really were under the weight of all those lies, just like they'd lied on Bennie's brother Vincent, and so many others.

"Juan?"

Juan had his fists clenched, his whole face tightened. He

tried to release them, but the truth, the rage of that truth, kept charging through him, clamping his synapses and muscles into impossible knots. He'd waited and waited to be released, and kept everything in, and in, and in — he had agreed to stick around to make sure Anthony made it through okay, and he wouldn't let himself fall apart. He'd been protected, after all, they both had been, and that meant it was a matter of waiting, nothing more.

So Juan had girded himself and buckled down and waited. He'd missed everyone; he'd mourned the sky and sun, which he now barely got to see, and his family, but he knew he'd see them again. So he waited. When sorrow came, at first blindingly intense, he let it in once, one late night when Anthony was asleep that first terrifying week — sobbed as quietly as possible, and then he'd sworn to himself that would be it, he would deal with the rest when he got out. That meant the rage couldn't come either, and he'd held it off all this time, but now, walking down this hallway toward either freedom or certain death, it surged and surged through him, relentless.

A sharp pain erupted through Juan's back — the shove of a nightstick. He'd stopped walking, lost in memories and burning anger. He spun, arms ready to rise and release a beatdown, but found his friend's longer, stronger arm, holding him back.

"We're so close, bruh," Anthony whispered. "Don't do this."

Juan blinked. The white man staring back at him was breathing heavily, one hand on his security belt. A dare. *Go 'head*, his young face challenged. *Catch this bullet.*

Juan held eye contact for a good couple seconds, panting, feeling Anthony's chest rise and fall, his heart pounding through his arm. He thought about Sierra, about Bennie, about all who had come before him and all the music there was still to play.

And then he noticed something. The officer wasn't looking at him anymore. He was looking at Anthony. Juan turned, saw Anthony's eyes glued to the officer's.

What was happening?

And then the moment passed: The officer backed off; Juan turned around. They all kept walking as if nothing had happened.

But something had definitely happened.

Juan looked at his friend. "What was it you were trying to tell me?"

Anthony shook his head. They turned into a doorway that led to a small office with a bulletproof walk-up window. "Nothin'. Tell ya later."

"Wait here," the officer said, and disappeared into another door, then came back a few moments later with two trash bags that he placed at their feet. "Your stuff. Make sure everything's there."

"What if it's not?" Juan asked.

"Then that sucks."

Juan rolled his eyes and started fishing through the bag. They'd been arrested on Halloween night, playing a spontaneous gig to protest Sierra's arrest, and Juan had been dressed like Fred from the Scooby Crew: blue bell-bottoms and one of his dad's polos. But the shirt had been sullied when the cops rushed the stage and threw Juan in the mud. The memory of being tackled and held down pounded once more through him.

"We'll give you a moment to change," the officer said, and they both walked out.

"Who would've thought," Juan muttered under his breath as they took off the orange jumpsuits and started dressing, "that the day we've been waiting for would be so nerve-racking."

"What do you mean?" Anthony pulled on his ripped jeans and then the old tank top he'd been wearing at the protest. Their wallets, keys, and cell phones (both long dead) were stuffed into manila envelopes inside the trash bags.

"Remember I told you how we're protected as long as we're in the system, by that group that I kinda was vague about, but I swore that they'd keep us safe even though they're kinda the bad guys?"

"Yeah," Anthony said. "About that . . ."

"Well, we're about to be out of the system."

"Juan."

"And we know at least that weird crimson Elvis guy is on their team."

An aggressive banging sounded from the door. "Hurry up in there!"

"Juan," Anthony said sharply. "I joined the House of Iron."

"WHAT?"

The door swung open. "Alright, boys," the guard yelled. "Time's up, let's get you moving."

ELEVEN

"Can you possibly drive any faster?" Sierra urged as the green cab she was in chugalugged grudgingly through Queens.

"This is the Jackie Robinson," the driver, a middle-aged cat with Panamanian flags draped all over his dashboard, shot back. "People die being in a hurry on these curves. And I'm not going to be those people. And neither are you, and you can live to see your sixteenth, thanks to me. So you're welcome."

"I turned seventeen last month," Sierra informed him. "And people might die if we're *not* in a hurry, sir, so please."

Bennie just shook her head and tried Caleb's cell again with a growl.

Sierra normally would've tried to catch a ride with Uncle Neville, but there was no time, there was less than no time, and even though the cab from the middle of Brooklyn to Rikers was going to empty her out, there was no other way. And every passing second felt like another moment that could seal Juan and Anthony's fate.

How could she have not seen this coming? Of course the damn Iron House would retaliate against her for knocking out their one potential ally against the shadowshapers. And Crane's people had three shadowshapers in their protective custody, which meant that they'd be the easiest to get to. Sierra ground her teeth and glared at her phone, which stubbornly refused to produce more information about how Tee's progress was going getting to where Izzy had been locked up, a facility in south Brooklyn.

"Anything?" she asked Bennie.

"Caleb says . . . wait." She put her phone to her ear. "What's going on, C?"

The other shadowshapers were all still in class and completely unreachable, so Sierra had had to rely on only the adults for once. Her mom had opted to step back from all of what she called "the exciting stuff" after everything that happened Halloween night, so Sierra called back to tell her not to bother picking up Juan, then had to get off the phone quick to avoid eight billion rightfully suspicious questions. Then, as Tee and Bennie tried and failed to flag down taxis, she'd called Uncle Neville — it had gone to voice mail — so she'd tried Nydia Ochoa, a librarian at Columbia who had studied the shadowshapers for years before becoming one. If Neville was anywhere, he was probably with her, and the two of them were a pretty unbeatable pair when they teamed up.

But Nydia's phone had gone to voice mail too, and then Bennie finally snagged a cab, and they were off, and Sierra was stuck with a pounding terror inside and the echoes of her own terrified voice leaving desperate messages for both of them.

Culebra's reckless intro riff zipped her back to the present tense, where a soggy rain had begun sloshing against the taxi windows. "Nydia!" Sierra almost sang, putting the phone to her ear. "Where you guys at?"

"We're heading to Rikers now," she said. "Neville's driving."

"Hey, girl!" Neville's voice chimed in from farther away.

Sierra had to fight off tears. That meant they'd be there first, no matter where they were coming from. At least some-one, no, two someones — a badass probably gangster and a fierce shadowshaper — would be there to protect the boys when they got out. "Thank you," Sierra said. "I . . ."

"Stop," Nydia said. "You already know. I'm just sorry we didn't get your first call. We were —"

"None of my business!" Sierra yelled. "Just thank you, is all."

"Alright, lemme go — I'm trying to paint some evil machinery on my body while Speeds McGee goes Mach ten on the FDR."

"Tell him to go Mach twelve!" Sierra called, and then hung up with a long exhale.

"Caleb says they're outside the detention center and don't see nothing," Bennie reported.

"Hey," the cabbie called, locking eyes with Sierra in the rearview. "When you said people might die if you don't get there in time, that wasn't just some teenage girl drama, was it?"

"It absolutely the hell was not," Sierra said. "And I'll have you know —"

"Say no more," the man chuckled, and gunned it.

TWELVE

"What did the lawyer guy say?" Caleb asked.

"Desmond. He hasn't been able to find anything out so far," Tee said. "Keeps getting the runaround from his sources."

Caleb shook his head and took another swig of coconut water. "Yep. Sounds like some Iron House bullshit."

"What do you mean?"

They'd spent the past twenty minutes standing against a bodega around the corner and across the street from a concrete park that was near the fortresslike detention center. Twenty-foot-high walls topped with barbed wire encircled the place, and American flags waved cornily in the early afternoon breeze. Caleb hadn't said much up to this point, except to make sure they were as far enough away as possible from the building itself while still being able to see the entrance.

Tee could never tell if he was actually mad at something or just had a surly demeanor. Or both. But either way, she liked Caleb, dark cloud and all. He'd shown up just a few minutes after her, ready for action. And the man struck her as someone who would fight hard for people he loved and always tell the truth, even when it hurt. He was also a legendary tattoo artist, and she hoped he'd do one for her someday. Maybe a matching one with something Izzy got. Not like their names or anything so obvious; something mysterious and intriguing that only they knew the meaning of. Izzy already had a few, at least three of which were extra cheesy and she already regretted.

Izzy.

She would get out of this alive. Both of them would. Tee transformed her desperation into a rugged determination, and that sustained her for the otherwise nerve-racking moment.

"House of Iron is in the prisons, right? For obvious reasons."

"Because there's so much of their favorite element there."

Caleb nodded. "Exactly. But also, their whole thing about telling the truth and all that. To hear them tell it, that strict adherence to honesty makes them the house of justice, so to speak. So they got guys entrenched all throughout the criminal justice system, supposedly. Lawyers, judges, corrections officers. All that." Caleb's whole demeanor seemed to warm up when he was explaining something — a born teacher. It was like he forgot that he was supposed to keep up the vexed façade.

"But it was House of Light who had that corrupt lawyer working for 'em, right?"

"Well, yeah, House of Light is — was — all about power and control. So of course they'd get a lawyer embedded. Plus, they'd been gunning for Sierra since before she even knew what a shadowshaper was so that was how they figured they'd keep tabs on her."

The detention center doors swung open, and Caleb and Tee craned their necks around the corner to get a better look. A family — two little kids and a mom — came out. The mom was crying into her cell phone, trying to keep the kids from waddling off, fishing in her purse for some tissue.

"Anyway," Caleb said, turning back away, "that whole justice thing is what I mean by *Iron House bullshit*."

"Why?"

"Because a lie of omission is still a lie. A deception is a lie. You can't just pretend the words you speak are what matter when it comes to honesty and then call yourself all about the truth. Makes me sick."

"You thinking 'bout Ol' Crane, huh?"

Back when Crane had been alive and posing as a shadowshaper, the old man had taken Caleb under his wing and taught him about the Deck of Worlds and various assorted magics. Caleb had taken care of him, spent endless hours at the St. Agnes Home keeping him company, given him his trust and respect. And then Old Crane had betrayed all the shadowshapers — revealed himself to be not just a part of their rival house but the Iron King himself. One of his henchmen had badly wounded Caleb with some kind of chain weapon that left a permanent scar running like a sash across the tattoo artist's chest and annihilated some of the spirits who had been deeply woven into the fabric of his body art.

"I deeply, extremely, bottomlessly *hate* that guy," Caleb said after a pause. "I'm not one of those people who don't use the word *hate* much — I use that shit when it's true, which happens to be every now and then to semi-regularly — but . . . but it doesn't even fully do justice to how deep my dislike of Old Crane is. I hate him more than I hate Facebook. I think I like cancer better than I like that rotting vulgarity of a creature."

"Well, shit," Tee said.

"If I ever figure out how to kill a spirit," Caleb rumbled, "it's curtains."

"It's weird though, right?"

"What's that?"

"It was that creepy priest guy that hit you with the chain, right? But how do you feel about him?"

"Oh, that guy?" Caleb shrugged. "He's a soldier. He was doing what he was told, protecting his king. I'da done the same, so I can hardly be mad at him. If I saw him in the street, he'd just be another dude in the street, no love lost."

Tee made an unconvinced face.

A group of corrections officers rounded the corner at the far end of the square, coming back from their lunch break probably. They all gawked and guffawed at something on a cell phone screen one was holding up for the rest to see.

"It's the hypocritical thing that kills me," Caleb said. "Yada, yada, Iron is the truth, okay cool, and then go around stabbing cats in the back."

"Cats being you."

"Me being cats. Truth is, since we're talking about the truth, I just want this whole thing to be over so I can go back to being a regular shmegular ol' tat artist, not some henchman in an ancient spiritual battle. No offense."

"None taken," Tee said. "I feel the same. We didn't ask for this. I just want to shadowshape and hang out with my girlfriend all day."

"Yeah. Exa —" Caleb cut himself off, and then his mouth dropped open, his eyes glued to something across the park from them.

"What is it?" Tee asked, trying to get a look past the slow-moving traffic.

"Remember when I said if I saw the guy that chain-smashed me in the street, he'd just be another dude in the street, no love lost?"

"What, like five seconds ago? Uh, yeah."

Caleb took off at a fast pace toward the detention center. "I lied."

THIRTEEN

"Man, I hate that damn place," Neville said, chewing on some kind of flavored twig they sold in the halal groceries, and scowling across the channel to where Rikers Island rose out of the water like some evil wizard's lair. "That's the devil's dungeon."

He spat once, then put his arm around Sierra and pulled her close as they watched another ferry pull off from the prison dock and head their way. "I don't remember ever having to take no boat there though."

"The bridge is under construction," Sierra said. "According to their website. I was trolling it last night for any info we might need. Didn't come up with much."

"Is it actual construction or some sus Iron House ploy?" Nydia asked.

"As far as I'm concerned, *everything* is a sus Iron House ploy until proven otherwise."

Neville nodded. "I've taught you well, grasshopper."

"Get ready," Bennie said from Sierra's other side. Nydia squeezed Neville's shoulder once and then rolled up her sleeves. Around them, Vincent and a few of the other Black Hoodies spread out into battle formation.

Sierra stepped forward. The December wind slathered tiny frozen rain shards against her face like the kiss of some giant phantom dog. Around her, a few other people waited for their newly freed loved ones: an elderly woman with flowers, a young couple, a guy in blue postal service trousers holding a shiny balloon. Corrections officers milled about on the landing, looking surly and ready to pop off at any moment if someone got out of line. No one Sierra recognized from their run-in with Iron House, but all she'd met were Crane and his Iron Knight, a tall, slender man dressed like a priest who carried a huge chain. Any of these fools could be on his side, really.

The ferry got closer, seemed to be taking forever.

"What's the plan?" Bennie asked, and it was a good question, but Sierra once more didn't have a good answer. She couldn't just yell, *Improvise!* with a whimsical chuckle and think everything would be alright. But that's all she really had at the moment.

"Just gotta keep our eyes open and then get 'em out of here quick," Sierra said, feeling like it wasn't nearly enough. Bennie nodded once, apparently satisfied.

Neville chimed in, speaking Sierra's heart with an authority she couldn't muster: "Times like this — extractions — any plan gotta kinda depend on whatever plan we up against, to some extent. And we really have no idea what we're up against in this case, right, Sierra?"

"If there even is one."

"Right. Which means we gotta stay light on our feet."

"Alice," Sierra said softly, and one of the Black Hoodies stepped beside her and lowered her cowl, a tall girl with raised eyebrows. "Can you see if they're on that boat? And see if any Iron-types are with them."

Alice nodded once and flushed out across the water along with two other spirits.

Sierra felt a bristling in the air, like the sky itself was recoiling somehow. Then a murmur rose among the shadow spirits, and finally, the telltale off-key crystalline jangling that meant Old Crane had arrived.

She took one last look at the approaching ferry — Alice and her small crew had just reached it — then turned slowly around. The shadows had formed into a tight ring around Sierra, Bennie, Neville, and Nydia. A BMW idled in the parking area just beyond them, and a white woman in sunglasses and a pantsuit stood in front of it. Sierra cocked her head to the side, waiting.

Sure enough, the jingle-jangle grew louder, and then the shadows spirits all took one step back as a hunched-over figure made from dangling silverware appeared. He carried a scepter staff and wore a rusted crown, and he was shaking his old head, sending even more dissonant tinkles out into the gray winter sky.

All the other people had moved to another part of the waiting area, surely sensing something indescribably off in the air.

"Crane," Sierra said.

Young Lucera, the old man's croaking voice shivered through her. *It seems you've played an unusual hand, I must say. You are more . . . aggressive than the last Lucera. I admire that.*

"What do you want?" Sierra said.

It is collection time, I believe.

Sierra made a show of a patting her pockets. "Damn, and here I am with nothing to give."

Oh, I don't think that's true. I gifted you something when we met on Halloween night. An early birthday present, you might say.

"The Iron Knight card," Sierra said. "That was really sweet of you."

It's time for the card to come back to its rightful owner.

"So you can . . . use it to destroy the shadowshapers? Why would I do that?"

Because, Crane rasped in his foul whisper, *we have something you want, mm?*

Sierra narrowed her eyes, tried to calm her rising pulse. Had this all been another distraction? When she'd parlayed with Crane on the rooftop on Halloween, he'd delivered the card alright, but the whole thing had also been a ruse to keep Sierra occupied while the House of Light made its play. She glanced around for some imminent attack, saw nothing. Some of the shadows had spread into a wider circle, enclosing them all in a well-guarded perimeter. Others stayed close, Sierra's personal protection unit. Neville and Nydia kept sharp eyes on either side; Bennie stared down Crane.

"Go on," Sierra said.

Crane just chuckled. Behind him, the woman by the Bimmer whispered into her cell, looking unimpressed. She leaned forward, whispered something to him, and the old ghost shook his shimmering head, sending a pitchless cacophony cascading out.

Sierra. It was Alice, returned from the boat, which was

now slowing as it approached the docks. *Something's wrong.*

Sierra turned, scanned the choppy waters, the devil's dungeon beyond them, the pale sky.

Your brother and Anthony King are there. There's a guard with them who's definitely Iron House; it's all over him.

"And?" Sierra whispered.

Something's off with Anthony.

Sierra's eyes went wide; her fists clenched and the light and shadow in her began to rise, sending tiny tremors through the arrows she'd lined her forearms with in thick black ink. *What is it?* she thought to Alice.

I don't know. He has powers now. I'm not sure what.

The gangplank dropped, and three officers marched off first, followed by some people Sierra didn't know who must've been just set free as well, and then she caught sight of Anthony's dark, beautiful face above some little white kid's head.

Alice was right, but Sierra couldn't put her finger on what it was that was different. He'd lost weight, for sure. Even from far away, she could tell his cheeks were sallow; his neck seemed longer, thinner somehow. He wore that same tank top he'd had on Halloween night — of course, that's all he had — but now it hung off him loosely like excess flesh on a starving man.

It was a chilly December afternoon, but Anthony didn't seem to notice. Beside him, Juan marched, eyes straight ahead. The two friends wouldn't look at each other. After all they'd been through together . . . what had happened?

Sierra blinked a few times — everything felt like it was moving very slowly. Anthony stepped off the gangplank, nodded once at the guard behind him, and walked right past Sierra and the others without even a glance. Sierra just stood there with her mouth slightly open as the boy she'd come to love — yes, love — slowed his stroll ever so slightly beside Old Crane's shimmering visage, bowed his head once, and then got into the waiting BMW and was gone.

Crane vanished; the BMW pulled off. Sierra turned around to find Juan staring after them. "Juan," Sierra said, and she was so happy to see him, finally, but everything felt like some terrible dream too, and they hugged, but all he could do was shake his head, blink away tears, and no matter how much they talked, or cried, or laughed, the brisk air around them still filled with the endless dissonant jingle-jangle of Old Crane's cackle.

FOURTEEN

"Caleb, man! Wait!" Tee pleaded in a hissing whisper. She caught up with him halfway across the street, yanked his arm so hard he spun around with a surprised look on his face, then softened, exhaled. "We gotta . . ." Tee started, suddenly breathless. They'd been waiting for what seemed like hours, and before that she'd been waiting for weeks and weeks, and now everything was happening so fast — way too fast, and if they didn't move right, Izzy would get snatched away and be gone all over again, this time much worse, which hardly seemed possible. And Caleb of all people had to understand that. They couldn't let this whole thing shatter.

"We gotta . . ." She tried again. "We gotta watch. If we jump ol' boy now, the whole thing could go to hell — they snatch Izzy and and and . . ." She felt a wave of panic rise up in her at the possibility.

Caleb nodded once, whatever sudden hatred he'd been pulsing with dissipated, and they ducked behind an SUV parked beside the open area. "I'm sorry," he said, and Tee could tell those weren't words the man spoke with any regularity. "I gotta get a handle on that. You're right." He looked her in the eyes, possibly for the first time. "How do you want to play it?"

"They can't snatch her while she's in custody, right?" Tee said.

Caleb nodded. "Them's the rules."

She peered through the SUV's window, across the park, to where the priest — he was the Iron Knight, if Tee remembered correctly (the dick) — sat smoking a cigarette on a bench with his back to them. Still no sign of Izzy, but those massive doors could swing open and vomit her out into the Iron House's clutches at any moment. "And you got the Culebramobile still?"

"Parked around the corner, yeah."

Spirits started to gather around them, summoned, Tee imagined, by the imminence of action. They could probably smell it on her a mile away, all that love and ferocity she burned with, all Caleb's rage, all that was about to happen. Tolula zipped through the air nearby and Tee allowed herself a tiny smile. "So . . . we snatch her before they can."

Caleb nodded again. "I like it. I'll swing the van into position, keep it idling on that corner. If the Knight is in place already, it won't be long, so even if they peep me, it'll hopefully be too late for them to do anything about it."

"Bet," Tee said, blinking through the rising urgency of the moment, the panic that it would go horribly wrong, grasping for some sense of determination, of hope, beyond it all. "I'll get her to you. And these guys" — she glanced at the growing crowd of spirits gathering around them — "will run interference."

Caleb smiled. "You're trembling."

Tee shrugged. "I'm terrified. I love her."

He held out his fist. "I know. We got this."

Tee dapped it. "Hell yeah."

———

"This is happening," Tee said to herself, stepping forward into what felt like a war zone but was actually, for the moment, a quiet Brooklyn street that happened to be in front of the detention center. "This is happening." She knew she was speaking, but her words felt a million miles away, washed and faded beneath her pounding heart, each impossibly loud breath, her rising terror.

No.

She would step up. She had to. For Izzy. "For Izzy," she whispered to herself, a shivery mantra. "For Izzy."

She knew it was happening because the spirits had started swarming, Izzy's name slithering from their wispy shadows like a zephyr: *Isake . . . Isake . . .* the way they always did when one of the 'shapers was in trouble. And a Lincoln Town Car that had been idling by the park suddenly lurched forward and in front of the facility.

That was when Tee stepped out from the corner she'd been peeking around.

"For Izzy," she said again, louder now, as the screech of the Culebramobile's tires sounded from behind her, Caleb gunning the engine, roaring forward. "For Izzy."

The priest — the Iron Knight — was standing now, saying something frantically into his cell phone, stepping into the street in front of the double-parked Lincoln. That massive door swung open, and Tee broke into a run toward where she knew Izzy was about to be, the shadows swirling and sprinting along with her like an unstoppable tide, some blitzing ahead and swooshing past the priest, who must've felt that ill breeze and spun, eyes tight and suspicious.

Caleb revved the Culebramobile past Tee down the street, sideswiping the Town Car hard into the boxy sedan parked beside it with a metallic wrenching. Tee kept running. The priest had followed the spirits a little down the block; now he spun around at the sound of the crash and gaped.

Izzy stepped out of the door into the chilly December air, free, finally free, her concerned gaze landing on the damaged cars, and then Tee smashed full-on into the girl she loved, and the van door opened in front of them. "What the hell!" Izzy yelled. And then they were inside the Culebramobile, and Caleb was already screeching off — the street a jumpy blur outside the slowly closing van door.

"We in!" Tee yelled, although Caleb clearly had gathered that much. "Go!" (He already was.)

"What the hell!" Izzy yelled again. "Seriously, guys! I don't —"

"Hold tight," Caleb called, swinging hard around a corner along the side of the detention center. Tee and Izzy both went flying into the side of the van. Tee looked up just in time to see a tall man in all black step into the street up ahead: the Iron Knight.

"This dude," Caleb muttered.

The priest held both hands up, and something long and black came zipping toward them out of one, then the other.

Chains.

"Ahh!" Caleb yelled, swerving to the side but still catching the first one full-on with the windshield, which cracked but didn't give. The second one blasted straight through it, past Caleb, past Tee and Izzy, and smashed out the back window. The windshield hadn't shattered though, the chain had somehow burrowed its own hole with a spiderweb of tiny cracks splintering off it. "This . . . dude . . ." Caleb said again, veering away from the row of parked cars he'd been shredding and back into the middle of the street.

Up ahead, the priest had retracted his first chain and was lifting his arm to send it out again. Instead, Caleb gunned it. The Iron Knight realized what was happening a second too late. Tee saw his face go from stone-cold killer to holy shit, and then a tremendous thump sounded, and he was just a long sprawling figure flying upside down into the air.

"Oh my God!" Tee gasped.

"What the hell is happening!" Izzy yelled, still trying to right herself and catch up to what was going on.

Tee glanced out the back window just in time to see the priest land on a parked car and slide off into the street.

Caleb slowed to a halt at the corner. "He down?"

"Yep," Tee reported.

"For the count?"

"Ah . . ."

Izzy crawled up onto the seat beside Tee and looked out the window. "Sure looks like it."

The priest lay in a muddled heap, moving ever so slightly. Then he rolled over.

"Wait," Tee said.

He got up on his knees, shook his head, and stood.

Izzy grimaced. "This Terminator ass motha —"

"Hell no," Caleb said, throwing the van into reverse.

"You're going back?" Tee said.

"We finishing this," Caleb said, but another car swung around the corner before he could accelerate. It was a black SUV, and it was moving fast.

"Careful," Tee cautioned.

Caleb twisted around and squinted at the street behind them. "Are they about to —"

The priest turned too, caught the full force of the SUV's front grille, went flying forward this time — not up and back like before — and rolled about a hundred times. "Ahhhh!" everyone in the van yelled at once. The SUV kept coming, faster now, and then swerved slightly as it approached where the Iron Knight lay crumpled. It had adjusted, Tee realized, so the tires lined up directly with the man's head. She squeezed her eyes shut just before it hit, heard Izzy go, "Ughhhh!" and Caleb mutter something under his breath. And then the van's engine growled, and they lurched forward and screeched off as the sounds of sirens grew louder around them.

FIFTEEN

Juan Santiago was having trouble expressing himself.

That was nothing new, really — he'd always been better with rhythms and melodies than he had with words — but this felt like a whole new level of complete uselessness. The gray sky filled the windows of Uncle Neville's Cadillac, and occasional flecks of slush speckled them and the traffic heading back toward Brooklyn. And the strains of some song on the radio and the strange warmth of people around him who loved him, people who wouldn't hurt him, mingled with the gnawing shock of his best friend's betrayal. It was all one — a million different dissonant pieces came together to form this impossible moment, and none of them made sense, none got along. It was like trying to write a song with a bunch of random notes — no key or chord sequence, no bass line: just chaos.

Worst of all, this was a moment when Juan needed to make sense, maybe more so than any other time in his life.

"I still don't understand," Sierra was saying, reeling from a whole different angle of the same betrayal as Juan. She'd been saying some version of that refrain for the past fifteen minutes as they inched along the Jackie Robinson, with graveyards stretching out to either side and the towers of Manhattan in the distance. And Uncle Neville and Nydia exchanged concerned glances in the front seat. And it all just seemed like a blur, like Juan was very, very far away or it was happening behind some filthy glass that he could barely see through. "I don't know," he kept saying, or he thought he was saying it over and over. "I don't know how to explain it."

The pounding rage still simmered through him from before, but now it was a mess — didn't know where to point itself, because the pain of being betrayed had mixed with the pain of being locked up, and neither made any sense. And through it all, a strange, incongruous joy kept surfacing, because in spite of it all, he was free, he had made it, and there was a sky overhead and people who loved him and —

A dark brown hand slid on top of his, sent a tingling warmth ricocheting through Juan's whole body, through even his dimmest thoughts.

Bennie.

She had waited for him. Had come to visit him. Had written him. She admired him, she'd said, and he couldn't believe this beautiful woman who he'd known all along but somehow, like an ass, never truly seen, this brilliant, wise woman *admired* him. He'd done something noble, she'd said, staying along with Anthony to make sure he was okay. And then thoughts of Anthony and the Iron House tumbled back in, sullying the moment.

"Hey," Bennie said, her face close to his, her breath against his cheek. "Hey, hey, hey."

He blinked up at her, felt the pain and confusion swirl within him, put his head down on her shoulder and sobbed.

Hands rubbed Juan's back, Bennie's, and then Sierra's too,

and then even Nydia reached from the front seat and patted his shoulder, and he was surrounded by love, soaked in it; they wouldn't let him fall.

He snorted and shook his head, lifting it away from Bennie's shoulder, hoping he hadn't snotted all over her puffy jacket. Accepted the tissue someone passed him and horked into it a few times, finally allowing himself a chuckle and then glanced around.

"I wish I could make sense of it," he said.

"Did he mention the letters?" Sierra asked, immediately back in detective mode now that he'd calmed down.

"What letters?"

"The letters I wrote him? On the typewriter Neville gave me for my birthday. I wrote him like a damn book on that thing."

"Uh . . . no."

"That's weird," Bennie said, back on the case too. He could see her turning over possibilities and theories in that scientist brain of hers. He wished he was half as smart as she was. Wondered if she could really be with a guy like him.

"What'd you write about?" he asked, trying to at least act like he was able to stay focused.

"I told him," Sierra said, looking pretty shell-shocked herself. "I told him everything."

"*Everything?*" Bennie asked.

Sierra nodded her head to the side, as if the entire sprawling past six months of her coming into her own as a shadowshaper and then the head of Shadowhouse and then creating a whole new house from the ashes of two old ones was just hanging in the air around her. "Everything."

It was pretty incredible, Juan marveled, what his sister had done, what she'd become. He'd realized it over and over while he was locked up — how rare and amazing a person she was, how he needed to tell her more often that he was proud of her. This wasn't the time, though — it would just seem like he was delirious and overwhelmed, which, to be fair, he was. He'd wait till some moment when she would really hear him and let it sink in.

"Did he respond?" Bennie asked.

Sierra half shrugged. "Kinda? I mean, he wrote back, yeah, but he never really said much about all the shadowshaper stuff. Like, he acknowledged it, but didn't . . . really . . ." She slowed down, probably about to realize something crucial that everyone else had overlooked.

"What?" Juan asked, impatient. People should just say what they were thinking as they thought it, not make everyone else wait till they had it all figured out, dammit.

Sierra shook her head. "No, just . . . it didn't really bother me that much, that he didn't mention it, because I knew it was a lot to lay on him in a letter, you know, and there was no way to really feel out where he was at about it, but like . . . it is odd, right? Like, someone drops this whole epic story about how they're part of a magical crew dealing with dead people and moving murals, and you're just like, okay, cool. I guess I kinda figured you were filling in the gaps, Juan."

"Me? Ha, no. I never mentioned it, and he never asked, so . . ."

"That *is* weird," Bennie said. Her hand still rested on Juan's, and he was more grateful for it than he knew how to express. It felt like he'd float away if she let go, out into the chilly gray sky, and never be seen again. And folks would just shake their heads and say, *Ah, Juan — he just floated away. . . . All that mess at Rikers was too much for him, even when he got free. . . .*

"I thought one of the things you liked so much about Anthony was that he wasn't all enmeshed in the whole thing," Nydia said.

"Yeah, well . . ." Sierra shook her head. "Obviously that backfired."

A sullen silence took over the car.

"Shit," Bennie said. Everyone looked at her. "Crane said he had something we want, right? And then everything with Anthony happened, but like . . . Anthony's not a hostage."

"Not if he went to their side," Juan said with a low growl in his voice.

"Not if he did it by choice," Sierra pointed out. "We don't know . . ."

"Either way," Bennie said.

"Izzy!" Sierra, Bennie, and Juan all said at once.

"Tee hasn't checked in," Sierra said, glancing at her phone.

"I'm already calling Caleb," Nydia reported from the front seat. "It's ringing." Juan heard the tattoo artist's muffled voice at the other end of the phone. He sounded out of breath.

"Wait," Nydia said. "Slow down, man. What? *What?* Is Izzy out? Is she okay? Yes?" She nodded and gave a thumbs-up to the back seat, and everyone erupted into cheers.

"Wait, wait, wait! Guys! Quiet down, I can't . . . *what?*" Everyone got quiet. "Ah . . . let me put Neville on. This sounds like his department." She passed Neville the phone, shaking her head.

Juan, Sierra, and Bennie looked back and forth at each other with furrowed brows.

"First of all," Neville said, tucking Nydia's cell between his shoulder and his ear while he drove. "Don't say anything about what happened. Not one word. Clear? I don't want to know, and I definitely don't want to say it over the phone. I just need to know what you need right now, and then I'm gonna tell you how to get it. And you better write it down on a piece of paper, yes, like a caveman, because the next thing I'm probably going to tell you to do is get rid of that phone you're using."

"What happened?" Sierra whispered.

Nydia shook her head. "Didn't say, but Nev's right, it's better we don't know. All I know is, they were in some kind of, ah, car accident? But they're okay. And they need to get rid of the Culebramobile."

Juan blinked at her. "Like, keep it out of sight for a while, right?"

"Ah, no," Nydia said. "Like, lay it down in its final resting place. Probably with gasoline and a big fire."

Juan rested his head back on Bennie's shoulder and tried to make the whole world go away around him.

SIXTEEN

"Got it. . . . Okay, yeah. . . . No, I'm writing it down — my memory sucks. Yes, on paper. Alright, Uncle Neville. I promise."

As Caleb talked in the front seat, Tee held Izzy's face in her hands and took her in like a deep gulp of a delicious drink after a drought.

"Yes . . . I swear. Is that Bushwick? Okay, yeah. We can make it there."

They were nestled in some shadowy corner of Prospect Park, far away from the sirens and screeching tires and cops and freaky priests being hit by cars. They were alone, almost. And Izzy was alive. She was alive and okay.

"I don't think there's any way to do a quick paint job before we go, no. But I promise I'll stick to quiet backroads and avoid high-traffic areas. . . . Sure. Yeah, I think so too. . . . No doubt, no doubt."

Izzy's face looked tired, her eyes more sunken-in. Or was that just Tee's imagination? It didn't matter. She was okay, mostly. In one piece anyway. She was real, and she let herself be held and gazed at and drunk in. Tee would take care of her;

she'd nurse her back to being okay; she'd scare away the night-mares; she'd make it better, whatever it was. Or she'd try anyway. And she'd be there beside Izzy to keep her company even if she couldn't fix what hurt. She said as much, in a des-perate, tearful whisper, and Izzy nodded, tears streaming down her face, eyes closed, taking it in. Taking it in.

"And this, ah, associate of yours, he know we're coming? He's . . . okay, okay, cool. Not a problem. Gotya. And look — tell the others for me that it seems like there's, um, someone else in play. No idea who, but he, er, he doesn't like the Iron House much, let's put it that way. . . . Yeah, anyway, I'll keep you upda — don't? Okay, no worries. I'll just . . . yeah. Okay, talk to you la — hello?"

Still caressing Izzy's face, Tee dug her cell phone out and handed it over to Caleb as he turned around.

"Girls, I need your — oh. Thanks." He took it, looked at Izzy.

"Hers is dead," Tee said. "So it shouldn't matter."

Caleb nodded, turned back around. "That dude is no joke," he muttered, popping out the battery and SIM card of Tee's phone.

Isake, Isake, Isake. Tee let her girlfriend's face become everything for just a few more breathless moments. Soon they'd be back out in the cruel, impossible world again, and who knew what would happen? They could be torn away from each other, killed . . . it was too much to think about. But right now, in this moment, Tee had Izzy, and Izzy had Tee, and Tee'd be damned if she was gonna let whatever terror lay ahead ruin that.

"Come here," she whispered, pulling the smaller girl into a tight hug and feeling her body rock against her with sob after sob. "Come here. I got you."

It had started to rain — one of those nasty winter rains that can't decide if it's sleet or hail or what — and it sent an ocean of tiny shushing taps against the leaves and branches overhead and danced little pitter-patter patterns across the roof of the Culebramobile.

Up front, Caleb rustled around in the glove compartment, scribbled something on a scrap of paper, looked out the window for a few moments, breathing heavily.

"Girls," he finally said. "I'm sorry to —"

"No, it's okay," Tee said, looking up from Izzy. "I know. We gotta move."

"Yeah, this is gonna be dicey at best." He turned the key, and the Culebramobile's engine sputtered to life.

"We gotta get our game faces on," Tee said. "Can you do that with me, babe?"

Izzy nodded, wiping some of her tears away. "Alright," she said. "Alright."

Caleb started backing them out of the shady grove they'd been hidden in. "Look, Uncle Neville said the best thing would be for us to drop off Izzy somewhere."

"I'm not leaving Tee," Izzy said.

"Babe," Tee said.

"He also said you probably wouldn't agree to that, and I wouldn't feel right about it either, but then again, I don't feel right about bringing her along."

"It's just Bushwick," Izzy said. "We can make it there from here without getting stopped."

Caleb eased them out onto the main road circling the perimeter of the park. "Thing is," he said, then he shut up as a police car appeared behind them, driving slowly with its emergency lights on. "Shit. Already?"

"Let it pass," Tee said. "I think they just always have their lights on when they drive in the park."

Caleb drove slow — probably too slow — but the cruiser swerved around them and kept it moving, and all three let out long exhales.

"What I was saying," Caleb said, "is that probably, whoever that was in the SUV was someone in the game, so to speak. Some other emergent house's hit man, most likely. Maybe a Bloodhaüser that didn't get the message the other night or doesn't care. Either way, they're probably going to clean up after themselves, is what I'm saying. I don't see someone who killed that intentionally leaving a body behind, unless they had to. It would call too much attention down on all this."

"Right," Tee said, still blinking away the memory of that long man stretched out on the concrete just being run over. They pulled out of the park and circled Grand Army Plaza, then headed up Eastern Parkway, past the library and Brooklyn Museum, toward Bushwick.

"So they're looking at destruction of property, most likely. Problem is, there are cameras everywhere, especially around prison facilities and such. But *if* we end up pulled over for any reason, Neville said the story is this: Y'all flagged down an unregistered one — Tee, you wanted to surprise Izzy when she got free."

"She did that alright," Izzy said, and flashed that old mischievous smile of hers that made Tee melt a little bit.

"And the cabbie — that's me — got a little wild on his way outta there. And that's it. No harm, no foul."

"But won't they —" Tee started.

"Don't worry about that," Caleb cut in. "It's Neville. He can sort it out, if it comes to that. Between him and the lawyer guy y'all got. But what we don't need, what y'all don't need, is a newly released Izzy being shoved back in the system. Not under any circumstances. Right?"

"Right," they both said emphatically.

Izzy sniffed and rubbed her nose. "Thank you."

"Bah." Caleb waved the notion away. "What wouldn't I do for my favorite rapper, King Impervious?"

Izzy chuckled a little bit through her tears and then looked out the window as Tee put an arm around her and they both watched the city slide by.

SEVENTEEN

There was a notion.

It kept flickering at the back of Sierra's mind, teasing, vanishing. Almost clear, still somehow indecipherable.

What was it?

The car had descended into a sad silence by the time Neville pulled up in front of the Santiagos' brownstone. They'd dropped off Nydia and Bennie, and no one really knew what to say — everyone was sorry his homecoming wasn't happier and wished things hadn't gotten so messed up, and that was all there was to it.

For now anyway.

But that thought, that little dancing maybe, kept dancing, slipping away, sizzling along.

"Alright, kiddos," Neville said, turning to the back seat and not even bothering to smile. "Juan, I'm glad you're out. You ever need to talk to someone 'bout what it was like and how to readjust, you know where to find me. I been through it, more than once, though it's different for everyone."

Sierra had a hard time picturing him reaching out for help, but who knew, really? She'd learned about sides of her brother she'd never imagined before in the past couple months.

"Thanks," Juan said. "I will." He shook his head. "I know I gotta . . . I gotta talk about this stuff." He landed a determined stare on Neville. "I'm gonna give you a call. We'll grab coffee."

Neville nodded. "Good man. Don't keep it bottled up. The important thing," he went on, "is that you're back now, and you can start the process of healing. Don't rush it. Trust it. And we'll deal with all that other stuff soon enough, don't you worry." He winked, tipped his hat, and then punched Sierra on the knee. "Be careful. We'll talk later, alright?"

She nodded. "Hit me up. And you be careful." It seemed like they floated out the car, through the freezing rain, up the stairs and into the house, where Dominic and María Santiago stood waiting, eyes already wet with tears and arms open to finally embrace their son.

The whole house felt alive with their love. María had cooked, and the joyful warmth of all that garlicky steam filled the first floor, seemed to ease Sierra's aching muscles and pulsing mind. A big pot of habicheulas burbled on the stove, and an orange glow emanated from the stove, where chicken baked within. The whole family glided in a little cumulus cloud of hugging, laughing, crying, abrazos, and besos toward the table, where Juan was made to sit while hands returned to stir the beans, scoop Bustelo into the cafetera, and retrieve dishes and silverware from cabinets and drawers.

And all the while, that something, that nagging, churning, cackling *something* kept right on, and on, and on. It felt like it lived in the base of Sierra's skull, right where her spine reached to, and like it would never go away and never be fully there either.

She looked at Juan over plates of steaming food, saw that his smile was real, his revival in this epicenter of familial love was a true one. And she breathed a sigh of relief. Of course, nothing was solved, and his journey to healing would be a long one, but at least in this moment, right now, he could be present and enjoy what he'd been deprived of for weeks and weeks on end.

"And now for dessert," María Santiago announced.

"Mami, I'm so full," Juan complained, laughing.

Dominic stood up. "This dessert is not food, though."

He stepped out into the hallway, and Sierra heard a scratchy, faraway, familiar voice say, "Ready, Papi?" and her dad made a shushing noise. Sierra put down her coffee cup.

"Is that —" Juan said, and then Dominic walked back in, his face illuminated by the gray glow of the laptop, which he then turned around, and there was Gael, a million miles away, a million zeroes and ones, scratchy and blurry and barely there, but still there, there, there, and smiling and squinting at his own monitor somewhere in Afghanistan.

"I can't . . . Is that you guys? You there, little bro?"

"GAEL!!" Sierra and Juan both yelled at the same time. Dominic set the computer down on the table, and María just sat there looking proud of herself, and the image resolved, like magic, and Gael was even more there, smiling out at them.

"Look, I'm sure this connection won't last, and y'all know I can't talk long, but hey! Juan! Welcome home, buddy. I heard about what you did, and I'm proud of you, man. You're a real hero. You really made me proud, kid, you know that, right?"

"Thanks, big bro," Juan said, looking somewhat lost and wistful. Both he and Sierra had always been about as different as possible from their older brother — he was so straitlaced, such a dudebro — but they'd also adored him since they were babies, followed him around the house, bickered for his attention and approval.

"And you," Gael said, glaring at where Sierra must've been on his monitor.

"What'd I do?" She laughed, threw her hands up defensively.

"Stay in school or something, I dunno! Did you pick a college yet?"

"Junior year practically just started, Gael. Relax."

"Do you even know what you want to study?"

"I mean, accounting, obviously. Have you met me?" She'd barely finished the sentence before everyone burst out laughing. "Wow, jeez, okay, so supportive, thanks, guys!"

"I miss you guys," Gael said. "A lot."

"No shit," Juan said. María slapped his shoulder. "Ow! I mean, we miss you too, man! Can you come home soon?"

Gael made a face. "Eh . . ."

"That's top secret, isn't it?" Sierra said.

He nodded, shook his head. Shrugged. The doorbell rang, and Cojo could be heard skittering to his feet in the living room and then letting loose a monstrous barrage of raspy, baritone threats. "Holy crap," Gael said. "You got a dog?"

"I'll get it," Dominic said as María started gathering up plates and bringing them to the kitchen.

"They didn't give you the pupdate?" Juan said.

"Not just any dog," Sierra said.

"Doesn't sound like just any dog."

"Juan!" Dominic called from the front room. "Mrs. Middleton and the kids stopped by to welcome you home! Come say hi real quick."

Juan scooted back his chair and ran off. "Be right back!"

Sierra couldn't remember the last time she'd been alone with her oldest brother. If this even counted as alone. And she had no idea what to say to him now that she was. There was so much — too much to ever be able to explain over a blurry Skype call, and anyway, someone would walk in at any second, so what was the point. There had been a time, though, years ago, when she had told Gael everything about her life and known that anything she said was safe with him, that he wouldn't judge her but wouldn't hold back from telling her if she was messing up. He was safe.

"He doesn't look so hot," Gael said.

"Yeah, well . . ." Sierra squinched up her face. Where to even begin?

"There's a lot going on over there, huh?"

"You have no idea, man."

"Keep an eye on him, Si. Promise."

She tried to make eye contact, whatever that meant over these dots and lines, stared into the camera as hard as she could. "I'll do everything I can to keep him safe," she said.

"¡Sierra! ¡Los platos!" María called from the kitchen. "I don't remember this being your party, young lady, so you better get moving!"

Sierra rolled her eyes and stood as Juan came back in. "Later, big bro," she said with a mock salute that she knew would drive him nuts.

The notion came back to her as she headed upstairs later that night, her tummy full of delicious food and mind buzzing with coffee. It still danced just out of sight, but she could feel it getting closer. She'd paid it no mind for a few hours and it had resolved itself accordingly. There were so many other things to worry about: what had happened with Tee and Izzy, for instance, which she still had no idea about, and what other entity had come into play. And what the House of Iron was planning. And whether Dake would do her any good or just figure out some way to betray and destroy.

She stopped on the second-floor landing. She was too wide awake to go to bed. And she needed answers. She walked up another flight, past the sad strains of an arrhythmic acoustic guitar coming from Terry's apartment, and then climbed to the top floor.

Septima's faint glow lit a golden line at the crack under the door.

She wasn't sure if she missed her grandfather or not. He'd gotten her into this mess, partially. Kept the family secret from her and opened up a rift with his own wife, Carmen, when she'd initiated Sierra as a shadowshaper against his direct orders. But Carmen was Lucera, the most powerful being in the shadowshaping universe; instead of fighting, she'd disappeared to a hideaway out in the ocean, amongst the spirits, and then, when Sierra followed the clues she'd left behind and discovered her, Carmen had passed on the mantle of Lucera to her granddaughter and vanished forever.

Lázaro had died a few months later, and sure, he'd said

sorry over and over in one of his rare lucid moments, but it had always felt like an apology more for his own benefit than something he actually meant. He had almost brought total destruction on the shadowshapers — a tradition he helped bring to Brooklyn — *of course* he was sorry. Fat lot of good it did anyone.

He'd probably never gotten a chance to apologize to his wife for being such a crusty old fool. Sierra wondered if Carmen had ever forgiven him.

But really what she wondered was whether she'd ever forgive Anthony, if what it looked like had happened had really happened.

Are you going to stand outside my door all night? Septima's voice rasped. *Or are you going to come inside and keep me company with your insidious and pathetic teenage melodrama?*

EIGHTEEN

"Yeah, so," Tee said, "we're being followed."

"Dammit! Shit! Dammit!" Caleb yelled from the front. "Is it a cop?"

"Worse," Izzy said.

"Worse than the cops? How —" Tee saw him glance into the sideview, and then his eyes went wide. "Goddammit."

The black SUV had been following them since somewhere in the middle of Bed-Stuy. At first, Tee hadn't thought much of it — probably just a coincidence. There were tons of black SUVs bopping around Brooklyn at any given moment. But then Caleb took a series of random turns, driving almost too carefully the whole time, and whoever was driving stayed right on their tail, like they weren't even trying to conceal the fact that they were tailing them.

Now, as Caleb took them along a bumpy stretch of Broadway under the train tracks, the SUV clung so close to their back bumper that Tee and Izzy could *almost* see inside the slightly tinted windshield.

"Dammit, dammit, dammit!" Caleb growled again, and revved them forward suddenly.

"Uh, remember we're still trying not to get pulled over," Tee called.

"The spot is just up ahead," Caleb said, swinging hard around a corner and gunning it again. "We're almost there!"

"You up to 'shaping?" Tee asked.

Izzy made a dubious face. "It's been a minute. The House of Iron had some kind of lock on the facility that kept spirits out, so I was shit outta luck for practicing." While most of the other shadowshapers used visual arts to send spirits into, murals and drawings usually, Izzy's skill was lyrical. The shadows would gather around her and solidify in the air on the strength of her rhymes, clobbering attackers out of the way with the same ferocity Izzy used to drop verses.

Tee nodded, not feeling so hot. "Okay, great." She had Sharpie marks up and down her arms, and Little Tolula was probably somewhere nearby, plus a few others she usually rolled with. But they had no idea what they'd be up against or even how many. And whoever was in that SUV, they'd taken out the Iron Knight without a glint of hesitation.

"And here we go," Caleb said. They turned into a driveway that led to a nondescript warehouse with a big grate front entrance. "Um . . . it should be open?"

A tall, brown-skinned man with a bald head and goatee strolled up to the window like this kind of thing happened every day. Caleb lowered it and the man leaned in, suddenly flashing a huge smile. "You Neville's people?"

"Yeah," Caleb said, "but —"

"I'm Rohan. You can trust me. If Neville sent you, then you're our people, and you're safe. Who's in the SUV?"

"That's what I was about to tell you. We don't know, but they took someone out earlier. Well, after we did, I guess."

Rohan seemed to think about this for a moment. "Wait. You took him out . . . with this van, right? That's why you need the —" He made some hand motions that Tee figured must mean they were going to dispose of the vehicle forever. "And then he wasn't fully taken out, so this asshole finished the job?"

"Right," Caleb said. "But we don't know who he is. Plus, he followed us. Can we come inside?"

"I like your style," the man said. Tee thought his accent might be Guyanese, maybe. "Took the dude out with the van. That's a good move. I'm gonna remember that."

"Can we —" Caleb tried again, but the man silenced him with a held-up hand.

"This man has followed you all the way here. And now he's —" He pulled a sharp-looking pistol out of his jacket and held it up, tapped his earpiece. "C — we got a situation, eh."

Tee stayed low but poked her head up just enough to see that the driver's-side door of the SUV had swung open. A slender, sallow-faced white man in a grayish-blue suit stepped out, both hands raised. "Hey, hey, hey," he said. "I'm a friend. I come in peace and all that." That grin said otherwise, though, Tee thought. About as trustworthy as a cornered snake. His black hair was slick and greasy, and he had a few days' worth of stubble lining the bottom half of his face.

"Cool," Rohan said, pointedly not lowering the gun. "Except these are our people and you're not, but you've been trailing them and acting wild suspicious, my guy. You got something to say, say it."

The guy laughed a few times, and it was not the laugh of a man who felt threatened. Even empty-handed and staring down the barrel of a gun. "I need to talk to the people in that van." His face went suddenly serious. "I give my word I won't hurt them."

"Seeing as I don't know you," Rohan said, "your word don't mean shit to me."

"Look, my name is Mort. I'm a friend. I mean, clearly! You guys . . ." He stepped forward, caught sight of Tee, and locked eyes with her. Tee felt herself tense inside. "You saw me take out the Iron Knight, didn't you? You think people just go around dropping major players in the Deck of Worlds for shits and giggles? No. That was a gift."

"Do you guys know what the hell he's talking about?" Rohan asked.

"Yes," Tee said, unlocking the side door and sliding it open.

"Tee!" Izzy said as Caleb yelled, "What are you doing?"

"Ah," Mort said. "Here's a brave soul. I wonder which card chose you, hm?"

Tee just stared at him.

"That's good, that's good," Mort mused, his squinting eyes giving only condescension and disdain. "Keep that stuff close to your chest. No one needs to know. Now, look: I'll be quick. Lucera knows who I am. We squared off over the summer and she won. Maybe she mentioned it."

"You're the guy the House of Light hired to come after us," Tee said, taking a step back. "She mentioned you alright." Mort's hands could deplete someone's power away, Sierra had said. She had only barely managed to get away, and it had taken Bennie's help in the form of a solid ass-whupping.

She hadn't been sure what kind of entity this guy was, but the whole thing had been some ploy of the House of Light's to come after them and wipe out the shadowshapers, and Mina had been involved, back before she'd defected from the Sorrows to Shadowhouse and brought the Deck of Worlds with her.

"Yes, only nice things, I'm sure. Point is —"

"We're not interested," Tee said.

"Point is," he repeated, this time with a slight growl in his voice that sounded somehow feral. But then, instead of getting to the point, he looked up and his eyes went wide. Was this some trick? Tee didn't want to be that jackass who turned her back on an enemy and ended up clobbered on some obvious shit. Then she heard what sounded like an entire battalion's worth of automatic weapons clicking and clacking bullets into their chambers.

She risked a quick glance and there was indeed a small army behind her pointing an array of very serious weaponry at Mort. A beautiful woman in sweatpants and a hoodie stood in the front, rifle steady at her hip, smile slightly askew and 100 percent delectable. Behind her, a few other gunners surrounded a short, thick, and very irritated-looking man with small eyes and close-cropped hair. He wore a simple tan jacket and slacks, and it was clear that every single one of the heavies standing there would've taken a bullet in a heartbeat to keep him alive. The guy didn't even have a damn gun, but from the look of him, he simply didn't need one. Tee felt absolutely certain that those thick hands had ripped more than one life away without the benefit of a weapon.

Tee had never been on the wrong side of so much firepower

before, but she felt somehow sure that their aim was impeccable. Still. She peeked over at Izzy and Caleb, both of whom just blinked out from the van with slightly open mouths.

Mort raised both hands and smirked. "Hey, now . . ."

Rohan let out a little chuckle. In fact, all these folks seemed to be unabashedly pleased with themselves, except for the man in the middle, who just stood there looking irked. "My name is Charo," he said. "And you're in my house."

"Listen —"

"I wasn't done talking," Charo said. "So no, I will not listen." He glared at Mort, challenging him. Mort kept his sneer intact and his mouth shut. "You are in my house, and these are my people you are threatening. If you think you're going to call the police, understand that here? On this block? We are the police. And if you reach for your phone, you'll be paste before you can illuminate the screen. Do you understand?"

"I do," Mort said, finally sobering up. "And I would never bring the police into an internal matter such as this. I just want to —"

"Leave," Charo said. "This is not a negotiation."

Mort locked eyes with Tee. "Tell Lucera I have an offer for her," he said quickly, stepping backward. "The Iron Knight was a gift, to prove my sincerity. I have something that she wants."

The man radiated power in a way Tee couldn't put words to or fully understand. It wasn't just that he was so unimpressed by the nearness of a gory death; there was something else about him, an energy that felt like a deep vacuum and seemed to seep outward in every direction, like the man was a black hole.

And then she understood. "You're a Hierophant," she whispered.

Still looking her right in the eye, Mort's smile grew slightly wider.

Then he turned around and walked back to his SUV, got in, and drove slowly away.

Something was on the ground where he'd been standing. A business card. Tee crouched down, picked it up without even thinking. *MORT* was written in typewriter type letters over a phone number.

"What's that?" Izzy called.

Tee pocketed the card, unsure why, even more unsure of what she was about to do next. "Nothing."

NINETEEN

Juan lay in bed and there was no music inside him, only noise.

Cell doors slammed and voices cried out — terrified, mocking, anguished.

A reckless tangle of Christmas lights barely illuminated one corner of the bedroom he'd slept in his whole life. His favorite metal bands glared and screamed from posters on the walls. It was inordinately tidy, consequences of being away for so long, to the point that his half almost looked as drab and boring as Gael's, which they'd left untouched since he deployed. Ugh. Juan threw an old T-shirt on the floor to reclaim the space some and then went back to staring at the ceiling.

There was no music inside him, only noise.

Boots squeaked on cold hard floors, the squeaks flung outward like phantoms and bounced cackling off the walls, back and forth and back and forth as footsteps approached and then fell away. Clubs clanged against bars, the gurgling complaint and then final *fwoosh* of the toilet, the gradual drip and then steady stream of cold water from the shower. The chaos of voices in the yard, yells rising, bucking against each other, and then the slap and clap of flesh against flesh, more yells, then boots on gravel, cocking guns, and urgent bleats over the intercom.

There was no music because there was no room for music in lockup. Each sound took up too much space, refused to sort itself into any rhythm whatsoever, defied logic or story. Worst of all, beneath and between everything, the never-ending ambient drone trundled on, an insidious vacuousness that only served as a constant reminder that this soulless facility still functioned.

And even though Juan's body wasn't in lockup anymore, its musicless jumble was all he could hear when the rest of the world went still.

His guitar leaned against the far wall, abandoned and dejected. Juan didn't even want to look at it. He didn't want to look at anything, but when he closed his eyes, all he saw was his cage. He would've called Anthony, but Anthony had betrayed him, and anyway, he didn't want to trigger him into an anxiety attack on his first night of freedom, even if he was a traitor.

But this clanging and banging, this impossible absence of music, this wouldn't do. He sat up, suddenly sweaty. *What if it never came back?*

He couldn't remember a time when the music hadn't been there for him. Even when he was actually in Rikers, it seemed to be just a few deep breaths away, waiting to swoop in and bring that sense of calm, however temporary, however fragile. A rhythm would start up, chords gradually simmering to life around it, giving it shape, momentum.

But now . . . nothing. And if he didn't have any more music inside him, did that mean he'd never be able to shadowshape again? It seemed absurd how much the thought terrified him — he barely knew how to 'shape as it was, so what difference would it make if it was gone? — but somehow the family legacy loomed large, and more than anything, Juan was acutely aware of needing to be able to defend himself in these cruel, magic-infused streets.

He didn't think too hard about it as he opened his laptop and powered it up. He knew if he overthought it, he wouldn't do it, and he had to do something. Sierra had snuck out about an hour earlier. He'd heard the creaking of floorboards as she tried and failed to be slick about leaving late at night — their parents sleeping cluelessly through it as always.

She was surely off getting into who-knew-what kinda mess, but she could handle herself, that much was abundantly clear, even if things were spinning way out of control.

And with Sierra gone and Anthony bad, that left one person for Juan to reach out to.

"Juan?" Bennie's sleepy face squinted out at him, dimly lit by her own screen. If Juan had any lingering doubts that he'd only fallen for her because of the sudden divine revelation of seeing her in that brightly lit, fully feathered, skanty Carnival outfit before the West Indian Day parade earlier that year, they were wiped out by the way she took the floor out from under him in just a bonnet and plaid pajamas. For a few seconds he blinked at her, breathless.

"You okay?" she asked, cocking her head to the side. "What is it?"

"I . . ." He shook it off, tried to collect himself. This didn't feel like the time to be waxing poetic somehow. Still: the shape of her face, the glimpse of that collarbone, even the small platter of sleep crusties she was now trying anxiously to wipe away as she glimpsed her own image in the pull-away window.

"Juan, talk to me, dude."

"I just." More than all that though, if he was being honest, it was the way she looked at him. There was concern on her face, but she knew to keep it light, knew how to be gentle with him and still let him know she took him seriously. She had kept in touch with him while he was inside, and while they'd barely had a chance to tell each other how they felt, she'd managed to let him know, without ever really saying it outright, that she wanted him, felt him, craved him, and that when he got free she would be there, ready for him.

Normally that kind of ambiguity, however sweet, would've raised one of his eyebrows and then the other, but with Bennie it just made him even more sure they were on the same page without ever discussing it. Any outright declarations would've felt out of place in the midst of trying to make it through his ordeal. If they were going to express deep things to each other, Juan wanted it to happen far away from his cage.

Bennie finally just laughed. "Okay, man, talk to me when you're ready." She perched her chin on her hands, elbows on a pillow, and batted her eyelashes. "I'm right here."

See? he thought. *Even that. Even that.*

"How did you . . . when did . . ." He took a deep breath. "How did you come into your own as a shadowshaper?" he finally said.

"Oh, let's see." Bennie sat up, folding her legs beneath her, and adjusted the screen so she was still on camera. Laughed at her own memory, shook her head. "I was in the lab at Butler after school, tinkering."

Juan's mouth dropped open. "I am shocked."

It took Bennie a half second to catch up, and then she

narrowed her eyes. "I'm glad your sarcasm is still intact, Juanisimo."

And just like that, he felt the slightest bit normal again; the slamming cages and approaching boots fell further into the background of his mind.

"Why you smiling so hard?" Bennie asked. "It wasn't *that* funny, buddy."

"Nothing, nothing," Juan said. "Keep going."

Bennie shot him a suspicious look, then complied. "And I felt the spirits there. It was the first week of school; I was modifying one of the school telescopes cuz the ones Butler has are absolute booty and not the good kind of booty. Booty like stinky-butt-booty booty."

"Okay, I think I understand your point here."

"Just trying to be clear. Anyway, yeah, I felt the spirits. This was before Vincent had shown himself to me, and *that's* a whole other story for a whole other night, thank you very much."

Juan knew there had been some messiness with Bennie's murdered brother appearing to Sierra before Bennie, but he didn't know the details. He did like the sound of *a whole other night*, though. He liked it a lot.

"So they just looked like the tall glowing shadows, you know? And they were longstepping around the place, all intense and excited, and I was scared at first. It was like they wanted something but couldn't tell me what, and of course I had no murals handy to 'shape them into; no chalk. But I did have the instructions for the 'scope. And I thought, *This is a form of art, isn't it? It might be a technical drawing, but someone still drew it, yeah?* And, like, who really knows the exact parameters of what can and can't be used to 'shape a spirit into, ya know?"

"Ah, true, true," Juan said, stroking an imaginary goatee sagely.

"What's that accent you're doing, bro?"

"Huh? That's my scientist accent, B. *Obviously.*"

"You sound like a porn star playing a sexy German nun."

Juan boggled at her. "What kind of porn have you been watching?"

"Ugh, never mind!"

"I mean, whatever it is, I support you. I am kink positive. But also, whoa."

"Any . . . way . . ." Bennie growled, putting her face in her hands.

Juan pulled the sheet over his head and wrapped it under his chin so just his face poked out, and when she looked up, he whispered, "Ah, Fräulein! How do you solve unt problem like Bennaldra?" and wiggled his eyebrows suggestively.

They both fell out laughing for a good five minutes, then Bennie had to run off to the bathroom, and when she got back, they were both getting sleepy and agreed to finish the story another night. "You good?" Bennie asked, suddenly serious, almost sad.

Juan nodded. "Thanks."

After they logged off and he lay back down in the darkness, the clangs of cages had faded even further away; it was their laughter that filled his mind now, and somewhere, very faintly, the slightest hint of a melody.

TWENTY

The freezing rain had tapered off, thank God, but the tempera-
ture plummeted as the night grew deeper; an icy wind flushed
across the rooftop and invaded all the tiny openings in Sierra's
winter jacket, her hoodie underneath it, and her coal-black jeans.

She hardly noticed.

Down below, Anthony's family was finishing up their own
welcome-home dinner, dishes were being put away and coun-
ters wiped down. She could make out figures moving back and
forth behind the slim curtains on the front window, a warm
light emanating from a warm house that wrapped around a
family, Sierra suspected, as full of love and heartbreak for their
newly freed son as her own was.

Anthony lived on one of those streets a few blocks off
Eastern Parkway that couldn't decide if it was a quiet suburban
enclave or a bustling city market. Massive prewar apartment
complexes — one of which Sierra was standing on the roof
of — loomed over two-story Victorians sandwiched between
fruit stands, cell phone outlets, nail salons, a dollar store. And in
another few years, it would probably all be Starbucks and glossy
hipster high-rises.

The bedroom at the back of the house was Anthony's.

There was a small yard. In another hour or so, she'd be standing in those shadows, and her spirits would slide smoothly along the outer walls of his house, into his window. They'd be formed into thick, razor-sharp arrows that would surround him before he could make a move, and then she'd be inside, and he'd be at her mercy, and she could get some damn answers.

Sierra's phone vibrated inside her jacket pocket, and she answered without taking her eyes off the King house. "Yo."

"Sierra?" Robbie's voice. She felt a twinge of — what was that? Guilt, probably — and rolled her eyes. Residue from having hurt him in the messy transition between a kinda-sorta relationship with Robbie to something much more sudden and beautiful but still unclear with Anthony. And now she was here, stalking the one she'd chosen, because he'd betrayed her, and talking to the other. Had it all been a mistake? "Where you at?"

It hadn't, she decided, firmly putting the brakes on that whole line of thinking. Even if Anthony was a traitor, Robbie couldn't commit until it was too late, and she'd rather be with no one than someone she had to walk away from to find out his true feelings. "Er . . . out and about."

A pause. She didn't want to lie to him, but she wasn't really comfortable explaining herself either.

"So, getting into trouble. Need backup?" It was a sweet offer, made, she thought, more on the strength of the friendship they were still trying to make work than anything more.

"I think I'm alright. Did Bennie update you?"

"Yeah," he said. "Anthony and your brother are free, but Anthony joined the Iron House while he was locked up and didn't tell Juan? A mess."

"Pretty much."

"And Tee and Izzy are lying low with Caleb because of something that went down when they were scooping her up, but we don't know what."

"Yeeeah."

"And a new entity of some kind is in town."

"You got it."

"And you're at some undisclosed location doing something suspicious. Sure you don't want backup?"

"Ha — keep your phone on just in case."

Another pause, and Sierra found herself grinding her teeth. Why did everything have to be so complicated?

"Sierra?"

"Yeah?"

"I'm okay, you know. I'm not . . . I'm not here waiting for you to come to your senses or hoping you'll come around. You don't have to feel . . . you know, awkward around me."

She exhaled, not sure whether she resented him making assumptions or the fact that his assumptions were right. Either way, she was relieved.

Sierra, came Vincent's warning just as a footstep sounded on the gravelly rooftop behind her. "Gotta go," Sierra said, hanging up with another slight cringe and then spinning, whipping one hand out wide as she did and flicking it forward into the darkness behind her. A black arrow flung through the air, powered by spirit and the shadows that churned within, and found its mark against the face of a hooded figure standing in the shadows about ten feet away.

"Ah!" a voice yelled as the person stumbled backward and braced themselves against the doorway leading back into the building.

"Got more of those if you're interested," Sierra growled.

The figure shook it off, then stepped forward into the light and lowered their hood. Dake. Sierra tightened her fists. "Sneaking up on me is a bad idea, Dake."

"I honestly didn't think I'd be able to get the drop on you," he said with a self-satisfied grin. "Guess you got some training to do."

"In what possible interpretation of the last ten seconds are you the one that got the drop on me?"

He shook his head as if it was all so obvious. "I mean, I made it all the way up onto the roof without you knowing."

"I'm not the one with a brand-new arrow-shaped shiner on his face, bruh. I wouldn't be feeling too good about myself if I were you."

"Whatever." He walked up to where she was and gazed down to the street below. "Find out anything juicy about your boyfriend?"

"He's *not* my boyfriend." Sierra had to restrain herself from arrow-slapping the shit out of him once again. "Did you come here for any particular reason or just to get your ass handed to you repeatedly?"

"How about, *Thank you, Dake, for giving me the heads-up on an impending move against my team, even though you're a brand-new member of Iron House and only there because I blackmailed you into being my spy?* How 'bout that?"

Sierra shrugged. "Saying *thank you* would imply that I'm grateful." She turned her attention back to Anthony's house, where the figures behind the curtains were now moving back and forth rhythmically . . . the Electric Slide, Sierra realized. Quite a homecoming.

"So saucy," Dake said with what might have been a flirtatious smirk. Sierra aggressively hoped it wasn't.

"Did you bring me any intel?"

"Intel." He shook his head. "You really believe your own hype, huh?"

"So that's a no, then. Cool."

"What makes you think I can be trusted?"

"Why would you think I trust you?"

"You put a lot of responsibility in my hands, sending me undercover like this after you decimated my crew."

Sierra blew out a steamy breath of air and rolled her eyes. "I guess. Can you tell me what you've found out now?"

"They believe him."

"Who believes what now?"

Dake nodded down at Anthony's house, and Sierra halfway wished the nod would've thrown him off-balance and sent him tumbling to the street below. "The Iron House, they believe your boyfriend really did come into their ranks."

"He's not my boyfriend. And, I mean . . . didn't he?"

Dake raised his shoulders and scratched his head. "Who am I to know? I'm just a spy in the House of Iron myself."

Sierra snorted. "Did you come up with that all yourself?"

"I'm just saying, they don't suspect him. And they know a lot about a lot, from what I can tell. And I can tell you this: He came into the house of his own accord, not under duress or any threat."

"What makes you think that I think he's anything besides what he's declared himself to be?"

"It's a cold December night and here you are on a rooftop outside his house, probably getting ready to ambush him with your little Sharpie demons and have a good little heart-to-heart about what's really going on."

She rolled her eyes. "That's not my style."

"Well, infiltrating an enemy house clearly *is* your style, and what I'm trying to tell you is that if you did send him in as a spy, you might want to be worried that he actually crossed over, at this point."

"Maybe you should worry about whether they believe *you're* a spy or not and less about what they're thinking about my" — she caught herself, but just barely — "friend."

The truth was, they'd never named what they were. It left her out of breath and elated all over when she realized it was happening and that her childhood crush felt the same way about her. And he let her in in a way no boy ever had, opened up to her like his worst fears and deepest secrets were a precious flower that only bloomed in the depths of a cave that only she was allowed to venture into.

"Oh, please," Dake scoffed. "I'm the Crimson Agent. Deception is what I do."

Sierra rubbed her eyes. "Do you ever listen to yourself, Dake? Like, really listen?"

"Alright." He turned to go. "Well, I've said all I had to say."

She held up her hand. "Wait."

"Hm?"

"What's the ritual for entrance into Iron House?"

"Huh?"

"What do they make you swear?"

"Oh, you know — the basics. That you'll uphold and

honor the truth at all times because the truth is iron and iron is the truth, all that bullshit."

"And?"

"And you will defend Iron House from any other house and lift them up into supremacy for the whole world to see their glory."

"Yikes. That sounds right up your alley."

Dake gave a vague nod. "I guess. Doesn't bode well for your boy, though. If he swore that and can't break an oath, you know . . ."

"I just asked about the oath, Dake, not your relationship advice."

"I thought you weren't in a relationship."

"Leave, Dake."

He stood there for a moment, and the wind whipped between them, and Sierra imagined and discarded several different ways of hurting him as cars rolled past in the street below; the lights had finally gone out in Anthony's house.

Dake walked away, probably smirking.

Slowly, gingerly, as if she'd been injured, Sierra lowered her tired body down onto the cold rooftop gravel and dangled her legs over the side. She felt the spirits gather behind her, that gentle susurro, something like a zephyr in the chilly night. They had been there, keeping an eye on things all along, making sure he didn't make a move. And now they were worried about her, felt that sudden sadness she'd been holding back radiate off her in heavy waves.

Alice's voice rose from the soft murmur: *Lucera?*

"Not right now," Sierra said, the thickness of oncoming

tears heavy in her voice. She let out a long breath that rose in a steamy cloud into the darkness.

The spirits signaled their understanding in quiet, faraway whispers and widened their berth around her — giving space but not leaving entirely.

Sierra put her face in her hands and sobbed.

TWENTY-ONE

A Hierophant.

Tee sat at the beat-up plastic table in the second-floor office area of the Medianoche Car Service and sipped the coffee she'd been given from a paper cup. And pondered. Izzy had knocked out on the couch and was snoring loudly. Caleb was downstairs watching the Culebramobile get turned into scrap metal. Some tinny bachata song tinkled along on a radio somewhere. The place smelled like carpet cleaner, Florida water, and car grease.

Well, Sierra had said she wanted them to find the five Hierophants, Tee thought. She probably hadn't expected one of the Hierophants to find them, nor for it to be someone they'd squared off with in the past.

The dude was sketch, that was obvious. He looked like a greasy pencil-thin evil car dealer in a cheap suit and was somehow too old and too young for his own face at the same time. Plus, he'd tried to end Sierra. But he'd also literally murdered the most dangerous fighter of their enemy house. And he'd tracked them down with an offer of some kind. That wasn't the kind of thing one did lightly, even in the cutthroat battleground of the Deck of Worlds.

There was something . . . enticing about the whole situation, Tee had to admit. With a Hierophant on their side, they could surely wipe out the other houses and bring this whole ridiculous war to a close. Hell, considering they'd just ended the Bloodhaüs and now the Iron House was Warriorless, they might not even have to make another move at all once word got out they'd recruited Mort.

She stood up. Wouldn't that be something . . .

Izzy snored away on the couch.

On the garage floor below, Caleb and the crew chatted back and forth about tattoos and assassinations.

¡Me engañaste! some brokenhearted Dominican dudebro wailed on the radio as a high-pitched guitar riff circled back to the one over a vicious club beat. *Me mataste . . . lentamente y con cariño . . . me mataste . . .*

Tee put her hand on the doorknob, ever so slowly turned it. The door swung open with a squeak, but Izzy didn't stir, and then Tee was in the stairwell, and at the bottom was a corridor that opened out to the garage on one end and led to a door marked EXIT at the other.

The Hierophant's business card felt like something alive in her pocket. It churned, beckoned her.

Caleb's laughter echoed through the garage along with a few other voices — Rohan's and the woman in sweats. Tee could go to them. Join their circle of idle, easy chatter and let the impossible, grotesque day fade from her pulsing mind. It would be simple. She could go back upstairs, slide onto the couch alongside the girl she loved madly and wrap around her, whispering her back to sleep and then close her eyes and dream of their life together.

Instead, she scowled and headed out the back door into the chilly night, cell phone already in one hand, her other hand fishing through her pocket, pulling out the card, trembling fingers punching the number as Bushwick trundled past in the form of hipsters heading to a party, the gradual grind of midnight traffic, an old aching man limping home from the bodega, trying to light a cigarette with shaking, arthritic hands.

"That was quick," Mort said with what was surely a smirk.

"Yeah, well," Tee murmured, but didn't have anything to follow up with. It *was* quick, and maybe that was her first mistake: seeming too hungry for whatever he had to offer. Maybe the whole thing was a mistake. Probably. But still, the temptation of ending this all in one fell swoop called to her like a siren song. It would not shut up, she knew that. If she didn't try, the possibilities would follow her around, keep her up at night, dancing endlessly through her head as more bodies dropped, more chaos erupted.

No. She could end it — not now but soon. She knew that. She felt it.

"Are you still at the gangster's car lot?"

"Right out back," Tee said, and her voice sounded small somehow, childlike.

"I'll be there in five."

"Okay," she said as the call went dead. "See you then."

"See who when?" Izzy's voice demanded from behind her.

Tee spun around, heart pounding. "I . . . I just —"

Izzy looked so tired and tiny in the sharp light over the door. Tee wanted to crumple to the ground and beg her forgiveness. She wanted to sweep her up in her arms and tell her everything would be alright. She wanted to burst into tears. Izzy held up one finger. "You suck at sneaking around" — then the other — "and you suck at lying, babe." She shook her head. "So just . . . don't bother."

"I know," Tee said. "It's that . . ."

"You were calling the creepy white dude."

"He's a Hierophant, Iz. He could . . ."

"He could what?" Izzy stomped one foot. "He could kill you is what. He could trick you, kidnap you. He could lock you up, just like . . ." All that fierceness suddenly emptied from her face, and she blinked a few times.

Tee crossed the bit of sidewalk between them and wrapped Izzy up in a hug. "I just want this to be over. And I want to do my part."

"But, Tee," Izzy whispered. "I just got free. We just saw a man get his head crushed by an SUV, like, a few hours ago. And now you want to get into the SUV that crushed him."

Tee nodded. "I know."

"This guy tried to empty Sierra of her powers. He almost did. Who knows what he could do to you . . ."

Tee heard the sound of a large vehicle pull to a stop behind them. It idled loudly. Pretty soon the window would whir down, and Mort would yell something obnoxious out at them. Or maybe he'd just drive off and the opportunity would be gone forever.

Tee stepped away from Izzy, rubbing her face. "I'm sorry,

Iz. I have to . . . I have to try. I don't want this to be our lives. I don't want this to keep going."

Izzy could've yelled out, or cursed her, or said some passive-aggressive shit, and that would've sucked plenty. Instead, she just nodded sadly, like she'd never see Tee again, and turned away, and that was a thousand times worse.

TWENTY-TWO

Down through the darkness, past frosted windows, chipped concrete façades, and dim streetlamps, past building entranceways and parked cars, and then the concrete met Sierra's boots as the spirits deposited her gently beside a small hill of trash bags.

She used to thrill at the sensation of being carried along in the gentle embrace of those shadowy tendrils. That weightlessness. That freedom. Now everything felt far away, like all her emotions were happening in another room, behind a closed door.

No.

She wouldn't let Anthony's betrayal, or whatever this was, dampen her whole world. She refused. The wind whipped some errant raindrops across her face, and she shook her head, pulled the hood back up, and crossed the street. Slipped easily over the small fence around the King property and then, silent as a shadow, made her way alongside the house until she came out at the backyard. A nearby streetlight cast an orange haze over the drooping vines and fronds of their garden, mostly bare and scraggly for the winter, but the rest of the small plot was empty. The house loomed above her, dark.

Sierra took a breath, felt the spirits gather. *Enter?* Alice asked, stepping forward on a long shadowy leg.

Sierra took in a deep breath of fresh winter night air. Anthony lay in bed. Tossed a thousand possibilities through her mind.

The Iron House believes his vow, Dake had said. Claimed. And they knew what they were talking about.

And did she really know Anthony? Sure, he'd been friends with her brother since they were kids, but that didn't mean he hadn't been dealing with some other entity on the side all along. Wick had been close with Grandpa Lázaro and still managed to betray and almost destroy him. That had been different, sure, but . . .

None of it added up.

Worst of all, it was Sierra's own heart, with its distant pitter-patter, that refused to make sense of this mess. That was why she was second-guessing herself. That was why this whole thing was such a big deal. It was her heart that kept sending tiny images up like distress signals: Anthony's face close to hers; Anthony struggling his way through an anxiety attack; the way his body felt cocooning hers; when, finally calm, he'd fallen asleep, each slow breath lifting her head up and then letting it gently back down; the splash of fireworks in her own chest when she thought about him.

Sierra let out a low growl, then said, "No."

Alice glanced at her: a question.

"I don't . . . I don't know what to do," she admitted.

Alice nodded. *Neither would I.*

They stood there in silence; behind them, the other spirits faded back into the night.

I don't remember my life, so I don't remember who I loved, Alice said. *But the feeling is one that I still carry in me, even though I don't have a face to go along with it or any moments I can thread together to help me make sense of it. It's just like a giant flame that I carry in me, and sometimes I think maybe that's just what love is — not something you feel for another person, necessarily, but just something so gigantic that it's impossible to keep inside you, and so when you find someone else you think you can trust, you have to share it with them, otherwise you'll explode.*

"That sounds about right," Sierra said. "But what do you do when the person you thought you could trust turns out to work for the enemy?"

Alice swooshed gently in the breeze. Said nothing.

Sierra took a long breath, and something inside her resolved. One way or another, she'd have an answer.

And there it was: a simple kind of peace seemed to sweep in, sloshing away all that roiling anxiousness. She would find out what she needed to know, and that meant she could make a move. And more than anything else, it was the tiny paralysis that was killing her.

She nodded once, and around her the chilly night air suddenly became alive with the dead.

TWENTY-THREE

"Are you scared?" Mort asked with a slippery note of laughter in his voice.

"That's an obnoxious question," Tee said, keeping her gaze focused on the dark streets slipping by out the window. They'd worked their way through a series of quiet residential blocks in Bushwick, passed beneath the expressway, and were now navigating the industrial back roads in or near Queens. She'd only just managed to calm herself down enough to think somewhat coherently, now that all the possibilities of a horrible death had cycled through her head a few times and, perhaps, gotten bored. "But no," she finally added. "I'm not scared. Are you?"

Mort let out a soft chuckle and then sighed and pulled the car over by a rocky embankment between two warehouses. Moonlight shimmied among pale glints of the city along the dark river up ahead. He cut a sideways glance at Tee. "Stay in the car."

"What is this?" Tee demanded. "I came along. You owe me some answers."

Mort smiled, and it looked something like death. Then he got out, said, "I owe you nothing," and closed the driver's-side door.

Sierra picked up on the second ring and whispered something unintelligible. Mort was making his way through the darkness toward the river, his back to Tee. No one else was around, as far as she could see.

"Sierra?" Tee said quietly. "What did you say? Why are you whispering?"

"Why are *you* whispering?" Sierra hissed. "This is, uh, not a great time to talk. Where are you? Is Izzy okay?"

"Yeah, she's with Caleb," Tee said. "And I'm . . . No time to explain. I don't know how long I have. It's the guy, Mort, you told us about who came at you last month."

"What?"

"I know," Tee said. "I just —"

"Tee, get out of there." Sierra's voice was a shrill, desperate whisper. "We beat the crap out of him, and he's extremely powerful and probably wants revenge! Get out now!"

Tee scowled. "He said he has an offer to make us. I'm going to hear him out. I just wanted to — I wanted to check in, is all."

"Tee, go! Get away! Nothing he'll say is on the level. You're not safe!"

Something moved in the shadows a little down the block. Tee lowered herself down in the seat and squinted through the tinted windows. "I think he can help us, Si," Tee whispered. "I promise I'll stay safe."

"Where are you?" Sierra demanded.

Tee hung up. Sierra was right to be worried — of course she was! But this made sense in a way Tee couldn't explain, at least not with Mort about to show up again at any moment and creepy things sliding through the darkness. She put her phone on silent and tried to find whatever had moved, but the night was perfectly still around her.

There! A figure slid along the sidewalk, almost gliding. It crept between the two buildings nearby and was gone. It looked like a regular person, maybe, but . . . taller. And ganglier. And maybe just a shadow? Tee shuddered. This day had already been extremely long and terrifying — she'd seen a man crushed to death, for crying out loud, and even if he had been someone who would've probably killed her without hesitation . . . it was the first time she'd seen someone die. And Izzy was out and already mad at her and . . .

Someone walked down the street toward her, but she couldn't make them out. Another figure, this one short, hunched over. Swathed in black cloth, it looked like. What was happening? A chill came over Tee and she had to fight the urge to just get out of the car and make a dash for it.

But then it would've all been for nothing. She'd lose track of Mort, and this whole situation would spin even further out of control. If only she could track him somehow even after she left, if she ever did leave.

If only . . .

The idea wasn't even fully formed when she'd finished pushing the CALL button beneath Izzy's name. It rang once and then went to voice mail. There were three missed calls from Sierra. Everything was shit. Tee called again.

"I want you to know," Izzy said, "that we're fighting right now, and I'm only picking up because you might be in mortal danger and I don't want to live the rest of my life with the burden of having missed your final call as a living pers —"

"Okay, okay, okay," Tee snapped. "I get it — we're fighting. Shut up a sec and listen to me."

Izzy growled but shut up.

"Remember when we went through that really obnoxious codependent period and we got that app that allows you to know where the other person is at all times?"

"I — Stalkr?"

"Yeah, that one. Do you still have it on your phone?"

"I mean . . . I feel kind of attacked right now."

"Izzy!"

"Yeah, but only because I never delete anything. And it can't track you unless I turn it on and you turn yours on and —"

Now someone was running, yes, definitely running, toward her from the rocky embankment. It was definitely Mort.

"Turn it on," Tee said, and hung up. She found the app and clicked it open. Cheerful blue letters splayed out across a white background with a little twinkle of sunlight around them: *STALKR!* followed by the emoji of two curious-looking eyes. Mort was a few feet away, glancing behind him.

"Come on," Tee whispered. "Come on."

He'd stopped running and was fishing for something in his pockets, still looking back toward the river.

The home screen appeared and a message box popped up asking Tee if she wanted to activate the app. "Yes, goddammit," she snarled, clicking the button. An excited star popped into a confetti drop, and then the little icon signifying Izzy's account materialized on her screen. "Thank God."

Mort had turned back toward her and was sprinting to the SUV, face stricken.

She let her phone slide to the floor and then kicked it under the seat just as Mort pulled the door open and threw himself in.

Had she silenced it? Tee felt her heart rate surge. Mort, panting, threw the car into gear and screeched off.

She had. She definitely had. Right? Yes.

She glanced out the window at the dark street and the even darker river as they peeled away. Nothing was coming. Nothing that she could see anyway.

"Are you scared?" she asked.

"Ha," Mort said dryly. "Terrified."

TWENTY-FOUR

Sierra pocketed her phone and growled inwardly.

Tee wouldn't pick up. Sierra had no way of finding the girl, and she sounded alright somehow — excited even. Which didn't mean she was, not by a long shot, but there was nothing Sierra could do about it. And Tolula was probably with her, and . . . anyway, the night was crisp, and the spirits deployed, and the whole world, each molecule and passing breeze, seemed ready for Sierra to make her move. Finally.

So she would.

Anthony's house seemed gigantic in front of her, his room a million miles up. But it wasn't. It wasn't. She closed her eyes. Nodded. Felt the spirits slide into place around her, felt the night hold its breath (or was that her holding her breath?), and then felt the ground fall away from her feet as her tummy turned one somersault. She would have her answer, she thought, as she rose into the sky and the markings on her arms tingled and prepared to strike.

Anthony's room was on the fourth floor, her reconnaissance spirits informed her, and there was a window, sure, but she wasn't about to bust in that way or even just show up knocking like some freaky vampire. That was too dramatic, honestly, and he would probably scream, and the whole thing would go to hell.

No, Sierra would act like a slightly more normal person and come in through the hallway window. That made sense. More sense anyway.

The spirits brought her there and she paused, peering into the darkness within. Breathed in and out, and then placed a hand against the cool, rain-speckled glass and sent a spirit-guided shard of ink down along her arm and directly into the lock. Why was her hand trembling, though? She'd faced down horrific foes in combat. She'd destroyed the House of Light *and* Bloodhaüs. She was unstoppable and she damn well knew it, so what was this shiver and why wouldn't it go away?

The lock gave with a tiny click, and ever so slowly, Sierra opened the window. It made more noise than she would've liked, but the house remained silent as she slid inside and stood panting in the third-floor hallway.

"Okay," she whispered to herself. "Okay. I got this."

Sierra! Alice's voice cried over the soft sound of feet rushing up stairs.

"Got what, bitch?" a voice said behind her. Sierra spun around just in time to see a figure swinging through the dark hallway toward her.

TWENTY-FIVE

"You gonna tell me what that was all about, now that you've gotten some heart-attack comfort food in you?" Tee said. "Or nah?"

Mort shoved some more fries in his mouth and managed to look somewhat remorseful. He was unpredictable, she had to give him that.

They'd driven in silence all the way through Williamsburg and Bed-Stuy, and then Mort had parked on a dark street in Prospect Heights and led her to a brightly lit late-night diner where everyone seemed to know him. He seemed to be legitimately shook, Tee realized, so she'd decided to give him the grace period and let him eat in peace, but now he'd decimated that "California Burger" disaster and she was fed up not having answers.

When he didn't offer any up, she took a pointedly loud slurp of coffee and continued staring at him.

"Agh, teenagers," Mort finally said with a roll of his eyes. He looked tired: face sallow, that half-moon of stubble reaching down his neck. Was he aging right before her eyes? "And people think Hierophants are a pain in the ass."

"You *are* a Hierophant!" Tee whisper-shouted. "I *knew* it!"

"Keep it down, kid," Mort said, furrowing his brow.

"It's not like anyone really knows what that is," Tee pointed out. "Or cares."

"Yeah, well, you never know, ya know?"

"Not really."

"Point is, yeah, I am, and I was trying to make you guys an offer tonight that would've really helped turn the tide, if you can believe that."

Tee squinted at him. "Huh?"

"Yeah, I know. Doesn't seem likely. I accept that. Your buddies did beat me unconscious a few months ago, true, and by all rights and means I should probably want to kill you."

Tee just stared.

"And I could kill you, just FYI."

She knew it was true, but it didn't sound very convincing when he said it out loud. "Okay."

"Point is, ah . . ." He shook his head and sportled up the last dredges of his chocolate milkshake. "Point is, I'm sick of this shit. And I don't care much for you guys, but I care even less for the other guys, if we're being honest, and anyway, you destroyed the one house that used to give me any play, really, so now I'm just . . . I'm just out here, and I just want this all to be over. Problem is, I tried to do it the right way, talking to the others about it — well, two of the others. No one knows where the Reaper is, ever. Or what even. And La Contessa's always holed up in her palace, so . . . it was just me and the River and Fortress, as always."

"Didn't seem like it went very well."

Mort made a tragic kind of smile. "Ah, no. But look — this little war you guys are fighting? I'm gonna let you in on a secret,

Trejean. It's about to not be going well for you, okay? The Hierophants are pissed. The other ones, I mean. Well, some of them. And when the Hierophants are pissed, well, there's not much that can stop them, you know? And yes, your boss lady might've laid some mean hands on me and toppled my whole shit, I'll give you that, but when I say she's no match for what's coming? I'm not just making shit up, okay? I know these guys. Hell, I am these guys. And it's not gonna be pretty. She shirked the rules, and that means all bets are off. No hostages, no prisoners, no mercy. Understand?"

He never raised his voice, but people were starting to stare anyway. That low rattle of danger swirled through the diner, raised the hackles of a table full of EMTs nearby.

"I . . ." Tee said, shaking her head. "I guess?"

"What I'm saying is, you need an ace. And I'm offering you one. There's only so much I can do, and . . . and I'm really done, quite frankly. Let's get out of here. I'll take you back to the lot. You have twenty-four hours to decide, and then I take my business elsewhere."

"How are we supposed to decide when you haven't even said what you're offering?" Tee growled.

Mort stood up, dropped a fifty on the table, and walked out.

TWENTY-SIX

"Wait!" Sierra hissed, blocking the first kick and dodging the second. "Hold up!"

It was a girl, Sierra realized, raising her arm to ward off another blow as she backed down the hall. Her age, maybe a little younger. She wore Batman pajamas and had her hair tucked into a bright green headwrap.

"Get the hell out my house!" the girl yelled.

Anthony's little sister. Of course! A half second after the pieces came together, Sierra caught a socked foot directly in the face that sent her hurling backward into a wall.

"Whoa, whoa, whoa!" a voice boomed from down the hallway. Anthony, Sierra thought, trying to steady herself for the next onslaught. "Carmela, chill!"

He came running past Sierra, blocking his sister's next attack and holding her off.

"Who this trick, Anthony?"

"That's Sierra, Carms! Juan's little sister! Chill!"

"Why she in our house, man?"

Sierra's face throbbed — that kick had not been the work of an amateur. She rose, steadying herself against the wall. "Where'd you learn how to do all that?"

Carmela blinked at her, caught off guard, but her eyes stayed narrowed, fists clenched. "Why do you care?"

"She does capoeira at the rec center," Anthony said, glaring at his sister. "And obviously she takes it a little too seriously. Carms, go get an ice pack from the freezer and bring it back up here for my —"

"For your *stalker*?" Carmela damn near spat. "No problem." She whirled around and stormed off in a huff.

"Wow," Sierra said. "I've never seen someone look so vindicated while wearing Batman pj's."

"I heard that," Carmela yelled from the next floor down.

Anthony just blinked down at her. She'd forgotten how tall he was, how all his clothes seemed to fit just right and accentuate all the right parts, how it felt to be standing this close to him, even if he was . . . whatever he was.

"Sierra, what are you doing here?" Anthony hissed.

"I could ask you the same question." It halfway occurred to her that that probably wasn't the best comeback as she was saying it, but the words came out anyway, and she tightened her face and just went with it.

Anthony let his stern face do the talking, and they ended up just staring at each other for a good couple seconds, which left Sierra feeling queasy in her stomach. All she would have to do was get on tiptoes and she could reach his lips with hers and they could just clear this whole thing up the right way. But no. Anthony was the enemy now, and that was that.

"I live here," he finally said, but it was almost a whisper, defeated, instead of the triumphant shattering clapback it could've been.

"I know," Sierra said.

"You shouldn't be here." His voice was still low; it sounded more like a warning than a threat.

"I decide where I should and shouldn't be, thank you very much."

They were still staring. Sierra had no idea what to do with her body, because any move she tried to make might turn into hugging him, and that was *definitely* not the right thing to do.

Carmela's soft footsteps could be heard making their way up the stairs toward them. Sierra hated this moment, but she didn't want it to end, because at some point she'd have to get to the bottom of why Anthony was with the House of Iron, and bad as this uncertainty was, whatever came next was surely worse.

"I miss you," she whispered, and Anthony closed his eyes.

"Ice pack," Carmela said from the top of the stairs. "But I can't believe you made me go get this after I successfully defended the house from an attacker." She was smiling, Sierra noticed, and she'd wrapped the ice pack in paper towels, which was thoughtful. "How'd you get this high anyway?" Carmela asked, walking over to them.

"You're not the only one with secret ninja skills," Sierra said.

Carmela tried to scoff, but it was really more of a laugh. "No, c'mon, for real. That's like forty feet, girl. You got a grappling hook?"

"I told you she was magic," Anthony said quietly, and at first Sierra thought it was a joke.

Carmela didn't laugh or roll her eyes, though. Instead, she

quipped back, "Yeah, but I just thought you meant it like in a gross lovey-dovey-type way, not in a shows-up-at-the-fourth-floor-window-like-some-Dracula-stalker-freak-type way."

"I meant it both ways," Anthony said, still looking at Sierra. Sierra's heart gave a frustrated lurch, but somehow it felt like it did in her stomach instead of her chest.

"Okayyyyy, then!" Carmela said, handing the ice pack to Sierra with wide eyes. "I'll just be going now! Bro: I'm glad you're back and mostly okay, but, um, for real, yell if you need anything. And you." She shot a smirking glance at Sierra and raised one eyebrow. "I got my eye on you. I kinda like you, but that doesn't mean I won't kick your ass from here to Riverdale if you hurt my brother, feel me? Especially after all he's been through."

Sierra liked her too, in spite of being on the receiving end of her capoeira skills. "I feel you," she said. "And, uh" — she rubbed her face, where there was probably a nice black-and-blue making its way to the surface — "nice moves, for real."

"Yeahhh," Carmela said, backing away. "Sorry 'bout that."

She disappeared down the stairs. Sierra went to speak, but Anthony held up a hand and rolled his eyes. "I can hear you listening, Carms!" he called.

"Fine, fine, fine," Carmela grumbled from the third floor. "Going to bed for real now."

Anthony tilted his head, closed his eyes. "Carms!"

Sierra lingered somewhere between cracking up and bursting into tears.

"Okay! Sheesh! I'm out! Ain't nobody interested in your weirdo love life anyway! Damn!" Finally, they heard her footsteps retreat and a door slam shut.

"Why don't we go in my room and talk," Anthony said.

Sierra clenched her jaw. "I don't know, man."

"You came all the way here." He waved a hand at the stairs. "You got past my crack security team. I assume you have some questions."

"You're damn right I do," she said, the anger flushing back through her. How dare anyone even consider betraying her? She was Sierra María Santiago, and she was Lucera, dammit. The spinning center of the shadowshaper universe, the Lady of Shadow and Light, conqueror of the Sorrows, the mysterious Dr. Wick, and the Bloodhaüs. First of her goddamn name.

So why was she shivering inside?

"Fine," she managed curtly. "Lead the way."

TWENTY-SEVEN

"Don't forget," Mort said as the tinted window whirred closed over his weird grin. "Twenty-four hours."

Tee stood in the rain for a moment, watching him drive off through the night. Then she turned around and ran to the doorway. *None of this is going to go well*, she thought, ringing the buzzer over and over. *None of it*. But the worst of it all would be Izzy. She would probably never forgive Tee for running off on the same night of her release, and she'd be right. Tee was an asshole for running off into certain danger — and that much maybe was okay, or at least the right thing to do in some weird reckless version of the world — but she'd tried to do it on the sly, which would've left Izzy waking up alone and confused — and *that* was the real asshole move.

Damn.

No one was answering, and Mort was getting farther and farther away, and maybe Izzy's app didn't work or connect right, and even if it did maybe Izzy would be so mad she wouldn't let them use it and —

"Ay," Rohan's gruff voice said as the door cracked open and the muzzle of a Glock peeked out.

Tee stepped back. "Whoa, man."

"Who goes there and all that."

"It's me. Tee. I have to speak to Izzy. Now."

Rohan's stern face replaced the gun. The door remained ajar. "Last I heard you went running off with the very dude I firmly instructed to leave you the hell alone earlier tonight, or am I mistaken in that?"

"Yes, but . . . man, listen: I *have* to speak to Izzy, okay? And Caleb. It's urgent!"

"I need to know why you were running with the enemy, little sister. That's all there is to it. Security of this place is currently in my hands, and it's feeling very compromised right now, if you know what I mean."

Tee nodded, gulping. At least he'd taken that gun out of her face once he'd seen who she was. She couldn't just piledrive through this, no matter how rushed she was feeling to get this fight with Izzy over with and track down Mort. She took a breath. "Reconnaissance," she finally said.

Rohan quirked an eyebrow, and she knew she'd said the right thing. "Go on."

"That dude, Mort, right? He's a power player in this situation we're in. You could say, he holds some of the cards. And he made an offer to give me information tonight that I had to look into."

"Sounds like a classic disinformation campaign," Rohan said. "But go on."

"Well, that's what I thought too, right? Because clearly the dude's bad news."

"I smelled that on him from a block away, to be honest. All

the charm of a dead fish wrapped in yesterday's newspaper, as they say."

"Right. That's why I linked up my phone to Izzy's with this app that lets you know where the other phone is at any time."

Rohan's eyes went wide. "Now that is some stalker shit right there. You guys might want to look into, I dunno, counseling or something, if you think that's healthy in a relationship. I mean, maybe it is! I don't know, but —"

Tee waved her hands around. "No! Man, I know! We know! We tried it for like three seconds and then got freaked out and deactivated the app! Anyway, I had her turn it back on, and then I hid my phone in his car."

Rohan took a split second to put all the pieces together, then perked up. "Mort!"

"Right!"

"Oh, shit! Tee! We gotta let Izzy know! Come on, girl!" He flung the door open and hurried off down the hall. "Close the door behind you!"

This is gonna suck this is gonna suck this is gonna suck this is gonna suck.

Tee shuffled down the hallway and out into the wide-open garage, followed Rohan through the fleet of fancy Town Cars and past one of those huge Access-A-Ride vans that looked like it had been repurposed into a partymobile.

This is gonna suck this is gonna suck this is gonna suck this is gonna suck.

They crossed an open area where a few guys in coveralls

gathered around the charred remains of a motorcycle, picking at its innards gingerly like neurotic buzzards over a kill.

This is gonna —

"Tee!" Izzy's voice rang out, and Tee cringed as her girl-friend came running out of the office area at the far end of the garage. Caleb was behind her, and he seemed to sigh with relief and then took off on her heels. Tee couldn't read her girl-friend's expression clearly, but it definitely wasn't happy. She braced herself as Izzy ran up and then almost crumbled to pieces when those two slender arms wrapped around her neck and the full weight of Izzy, all hundred and five pounds of her, smashed directly into Tee, followed by a hundred kisses.

"Whoa, whoa, whoa!" Tee yelped.

"Shut up and get these kisses," Izzy whispered.

"Wow," Rohan said from somewhere nearby. "I'm just going to update Caleb over here because clearly you two need a minute."

"I thought, I thought, I thought," Tee stammered.

"Shut up, I said." Izzy laughed, still kissing her.

"I just."

"Woman," Izzy growled.

Tee shut up accordingly, and then suddenly she was sniffling — there was a sob in her for sure, trying to break out, but she wouldn't let it, no way, not here in the middle of all these cars and killers and not now in the middle of everything going on.

"Okay," Izzy said after a bunch more kisses on Tee's face and neck. "Now you can talk." She still held Tee in a tight embrace.

"I thought you were gonna kill me?" Tee said, half laugh-ing, half maybe-crying, but not really either.

"I thought about it," Izzy admitted. "Decided I'd miss you too much. And then I was just worried. And while you were wrong for trying to sneak off — most of all for thinking you'd be able to." She got up in Tee's face with her finger, but, somehow, sweetly. "*Never* underestimate me again, Trejean." Tee nodded. "I mean it."

"I wanted to apologize about that," Tee said.

"Yeah, yeah, I accept," Izzy said, finally letting her go. "But yo — about that tracking situation."

"Yeah," a gravelly voice said from the doorway Izzy had come out of. "About that."

A figure stood there, backlit by the sharp fluorescents of the office. She was slender and dapper as shit.

"Is that —" Tee gasped into Izzy's ear.

"The one and only," Izzy whispered.

"Well, damn," Tee said. "Shit just got real."

TWENTY-EIGHT

Being intimate with Robbie had never really made much sense. It was like their bodies didn't quite speak the same language, or more to the point: Robbie didn't seem to know what he wanted. Things would get all hot and heavy, and then just as suddenly they'd cool but not in a way that felt natural or smooth, they just seemed to be following whatever strange conversation Robbie was having with himself in his own head. Which made sense, because that single dynamic did a pretty good job summarizing the whole non-lationship, and that's why Sierra had finally spun all the way away.

The strong, silent thing was cute from a distance, intriguing even, but once push came to shove, it turned out being with someone who knew how to express themselves, to say out loud what they wanted, were worried about, ashamed of, what brought them joy — that mattered, made all the difference in the world, in fact. And while Sierra couldn't have put her finger on it at the time, that's what ultimately let her know that she and Robbie, at least Robbie in his current form, weren't going to make it as a couple. Or a semi-non-whatever couple. Or anything besides, hopefully, good friends who shared a deep understanding of a magical world almost no one else knew about. Which wasn't the same thing as romance or love, as it happened, although it certainly had felt like what she imagined those things to feel like, at least for a while.

Anthony, though.

Anthony.

That boy moved with Sierra like he was born to. It wasn't just that he knew what he wanted and knew how to ask for it, both with his eyes and his words. He also knew how to listen. Sierra could feel Anthony's body respond to the tiny trembles and directions of her own, could sense his attentiveness and care in how he touched her, the patience with which his hands found hers, and the gentleness with which he moved his body against hers. Anthony knew how to take his time, and somehow that had meant that even in the short time they'd spent together, Sierra had felt seen in a way she hadn't felt from a partner before.

And maybe that was why, standing there in his bedroom with what felt like the world spinning recklessly around them, with two warring houses poised to crash mercilessly into the empty space between them, Sierra couldn't stop trembling. She managed to keep it hidden inside herself, so that was something. But even if Anthony couldn't see it, *she* knew it was there, and it bugged her. That's not how she did things. Boys didn't throw her off her game. They annoyed her. They caused some strife and headaches, sure, but they didn't make her feel butt-ass naked when she had all her winter clothes on. This wasn't part of the game.

"Are you gonna go first or should I?" Anthony asked. He was sitting on the bed, looking directly at Sierra like maybe she had some of the answers to all this mess. She didn't, though. This wasn't how it was supposed to go. She was supposed to

have him pinned and caught off guard with a hundred shimmering shards of spirit-powered ink arrows pointed at his neck
for the kill shot, and then he was supposed to spill his guts
about whatever bullshit had happened to cause him to betray
her, and then she'd be done with it and curse him out or
threaten him if he crossed her again or whatever and be on her
merry way.

Instead, she stood before him feeling exposed and nostal-
gic for a relationship that had barely existed.

Instead, she had no idea what to say. Or what she wanted
to hear.

"Neither?" she said softly.

He flinched a little. "Then do we just . . . just sit here?"

It seemed nice, but she knew she didn't have that luxury.
She closed her eyes, silently called on the churning darkness
and light deep inside. Breathed. "I came here to threaten you,"
she said. Within her, the light rose; the shadow rose. "You
were going to wake up to my spirit soldiers surrounding you,
and you were going to tell me *why* —" The word came out in
a guttural half sob and Sierra paused to collect herself. The
shadow and light spun and sputtered like competing lava lakes.
If she was just slightly reckless, if she tilted too far one way or
the other, it would all come spilling out, and Sierra didn't know
what that would mean. "Why you swore allegiance to a house
that you know is bent on my destruction."

"Si —"

"Stop." She felt something fierce flicker through her. That
slight pleading sound in his voice. She wouldn't tolerate
excuses. Anthony couldn't lie to her, not as a sworn soldier of
the Iron House, but he could bend the truth to something that

made him look good, and she would know, and she would hate him. "Think carefully about what you say next."

He nodded. Stood. Sierra steeled herself, looked up at him defiantly.

"I read your letters," Anthony said, all hints of pleading gone. "I read them over and over." He shook his head, eyes far away. "Besides Juan, that was the only thing I had to cling to. That's what grounded me. When I felt an attack coming, when my mind tried to overthrow me, when all that panic crept in: I would reread one of your letters, then another, until I had them all memorized so I didn't have to pull them out to read them, I could just do it in my head."

Sierra kept her face stern, but inside, all she could think of was Anthony fighting off wave after wave of anxiety inside that hellpit of an island, surrounded by steel and men who hated him, far from his family, from her.

"I don't want to say you kept me alive," he said, "because that's not a fair burden to put on you, and anyway it's not totally true — there were letters from my family too, and the thought of what Carmela would've done if I'd . . . if something had happened to me. And your brother. And whatever . . . there were a few things that kept me close to this world, but your letters — you, Sierra — most of all. For whatever reason. Well, because of how I feel about you, that's the reason."

He paused, gulped, shook his head.

"Go on," Sierra said quietly.

"When the House of Iron guy started talking to me, it was clear what he wanted from jump — he was there to recruit me, and it was obvious why too. They'd read your letters, of course, and they knew what I meant to you. They wanted to use me as a weapon."

Sierra scrunched up her face, blinked away a few tears, but they came anyway.

"That's how scared they are of you," Anthony said with undisguised awe. Then he scowled. "And that's how dirty they are. So when Grintly — that's the guy Iron House has on the inside, or one of them anyway — when he started talking me up, I just listened. Peeped the game and listened. He told me all kinds of stories about how Iron House came to be and this guy Old Crane who'd infiltrated the shadowshapers while secretly building his own crew on the side, and how we grew even more powerful in death Obi-Wan Kenobi style, etc. etc."

Sierra groaned and motioned for him to go on.

"Exactly. Grintly kept talking about how the Iron House is the one true path and the only way forward to peace and how their reign will end this silly age of warfare between the houses, and look, I've read enough American history textbooks to know when I'm being fed a pile of propaganda garbage dressed in shiny golden bullshit, and I know how to look impressed, so I played along, played along until —"

Somehow the truth of what had happened had been creeping through Sierra's mind all along, at least this possibility of it, but now that it was turning out to be true, it terrified her more than she'd realized it would. "Until they made the offer to initiate you into House Iron."

He nodded. "Between the letters you wrote me telling me about your life and the shadowshapers and everything else, and this guy's crooked version of the world, I put the pieces together and had a pretty clear idea of what might be coming down the pipes."

"So you accepted?" Sierra's whole body thrummed. He didn't know what he'd gotten himself into, and he'd done it for her? It was too much. Way too much.

Anthony raised his eyebrows. "They swore that this was the path to peace, and —"

"And you *believed* them?" Sierra seethed.

Anthony scoffed. "Of course not! I mean, I know they can't lie, but I know their version of peace involves you being out of the picture."

"But . . ."

"But *mine* doesn't."

Sierra cocked her head at him.

"I made Grintly go over what the ceremony would entail, step by step. What I'd have to say, what I'd have to swear to. All that."

"And?"

"And I never lied to them. I will do everything it takes to protect the Iron House and bring peace to the warring factions of the Deck of Worlds."

Sierra closed her eyes, knew what was coming. Loved and hated it with equal ferocity. "And?" she whispered.

"And that means I will do anything I can to help you overthrow the King of Iron and destroy anyone that gets in the way of us forging a true peace between Iron House and the House of Shadow and Light." Sierra looked at him, and finally, for what seemed like the first time in ages, Anthony let his big, brilliant, unstoppable smile shine through. "And I'll do it from the inside."

Sierra shook her head. "Why?"

"I already told you: You saved my life. Least I could do is

try and infiltrate the assholes who are trying to take yours and burn them to the ground."

She laughed, crying a little too. *It won't work,* everything inside her screamed. *They'll use you as a hostage, and as soon as I make a wrong move they'll still use you against me, only you'll pay the price for my recklessness. They'll break you and then use you to break me.*

She shoved the voices away, stepped forward into Anthony's open arms, then put her hands on either side of his face and brought it down to hers.

TWENTY-NINE

"What'd you say this app thing is called?" R said in her tobacco-stained voice. "I gotta get me one of these. Can just follow along out of sight and you don't have to worry about losing the trail!"

"Stalkr," Tee said. She still couldn't get used to the idea that this unstoppable force of a woman was driving them nonchalantly through the streets of Brooklyn. Tee and Izzy's first encounter with R had been at a creepy upstate campsite; they'd tracked a killer priest up there with Uncle Neville and then gotten themselves hemmed in by some Bloodhaüs goons, and then R had shown up, guns literally blazing, and scared off everyone, saving their asses and inspiring hours and hours of what was basically glorified fan fiction as Tee and Izzy wondered over and over who Uncle Neville's mysterious friend was. He wouldn't give up any answers, not even a name, so they had to be content with making shit up.

And now the mysterious Ms. R was just sitting there next to Tee like it was no big deal, maneuvering her Crown Vic through the shadows like it was some kind of steel-cased shark with tires. R was probably in her fifties but moved like she had been a dancer in another life, that simple grace and ease, and

Tee knew those hands had taken more than a few lives. "And this character we're tracking, what's his deal?"

"He's like a . . ." Tee fumbled around for the words.

"He's like an underboss," Izzy said from the back seat. "But he's a top dog. A power broker. One of five, and they're supposed to be neutral or maintain balance or whatever it is powerful people convince themselves they're doing when they're clearly tipping the scales in their own favor."

"And it seems like whatever is in Mort's favor is maybe in ours too," Tee added. "Emphasis on *maybe*. But he did take out one of our enemies for us — their main muscle, in fact."

R cocked an eyebrow. "Take out?"

"Literally crushed the dude with his SUV," Izzy said.

"And then backed up to finish the job when the homey got up," Tee put in. "It was disgusting."

R nodded, clearly impressed. "That's a friendly gesture and all, but still. I don't trust him."

"Good," Izzy said. "Neither do we."

"Hence the little phone maneuver," R said. "Got it. Speaking of which . . ."

Tee checked Izzy's phone. The blinking light had finally stopped moving. "He parked!" she announced. "Or he got killed or something. Either way, just across the bridge in Queens."

"Call your big red-haired friend and tell him to get Rohan to meet us there," R said. Then she narrowed her eyes and floored it.

Five minutes later, the Crown Vic rounded a corner onto a dark industrial block near the Fifty-Ninth Street Bridge and slowed to a simmering halt. Tee and Izzy let out a breath of gratitude that they had survived what felt like seventeen brushes with death all at once. Up ahead, Mort's SUV idled beside a huge old graffiti-covered factory building with boarded-up windows.

"He in there?" Tee asked.

"Someone's in the driver's seat," R said.

"Now what do we do?"

R smirked. "We *could* go in there guns blazing."

"Ooh," Izzy chimed.

"But I'm pretty sure I'm the only one here who's armed, and anyway then you wouldn't find out what you need to know, and I'm guessing right now reconnaissance is more important than snatching souls. Plus, our backup isn't here yet."

Tee nodded. "Makes sense, makes sense."

"I just wanted to see R take some fools out," Izzy admitted. "You right, though."

"I've done this kinda thing once or twice," R said dryly. "Well, not exactly this, because you kids are clearly into some out-there disaster play."

"Facts," Izzy said.

"But you know . . ." R flipped her hand back and forth a few times and shrugged to indicate más o menos.

"Soooo . . ." Izzy said.

"So we wait."

Tee imagined the breaking dawn might find them there still, in a blinking stupor, but it ended up only being a few minutes before Mort stepped out of his vehicle and looked around. He rubbed his face, seemed to be talking himself through something. Started to get back in, then shook his head, and finally closed the door and walked up to the warehouse entrance.

"Your guy seems stressed," R noted.

Tee closed her eyes. She knew what would happen next anyway: Mort was going to do some sweet magical maneuver to jack the lock and get inside. And she had backup of her own to summon.

The air grew thick around them as spirits emerged one by one. When Tee opened her eyes, the warehouse door was indeed open and Mort gone. R hadn't seemed to notice the floating shadows in her car. "How the hell did he pull that off?" she muttered. Izzy's lips were moving in time to a silent beat — she was preparing her own soldiers for whatever was about to happen.

"Did you guys see what he did to that lock?" R asked. "This really is some otherworld shit. I gotta be honest, I'm not sure how much help I'm going to be for you two."

"It's alright," Tee said, opening the door. "We'll take it from here."

R made a face. "I don't like any of this. Rohan and Caleb should be here any minute. You have my number. If you call it, I'm coming in heavy, so get out the way. Clear?"

"Damn," Izzy said, sliding out of the Crown Vic behind Tee. "Now I just wanna call it and see that shit go down."

R shot her a look. Both girls nodded and crept along the street toward the warehouse amidst a cadre of spirits, ready for battle.

Well, well, well, an icy voice sounded out across the shadowy, trash-strewn warehouse amidst the off-key tinkling of wind chimes.

Tee froze. Old Crane, the King of Iron. And he must have realized they were there. Should they attack? She glanced at Izzy, who shook her head.

Another Hierophant has decided to step into the fray.

Tee exhaled. They must've been talking about Mort. Sure enough, his voice sounded a moment later from up ahead: "Greetings, Iron King. And greetings to your assorted courtesans and fools."

That Hierophant shit must be a hell of a drug, Tee mused. Mort sounded legitimately cocky — that same easy drawl and general unimpressed shrug of an existence Tee had come to know him for. Yet here he was walking all alone into the heart of a house whose head soldier he'd mercilessly killed just a few hours earlier. And he was being an outright dick at that. She wondered how much of it was an act.

A few murmurs of disapproval and mock offense rang out.

Tee and Izzy kept close to the wall, crept at an achingly slow crawl toward the far room, where a gentle glow sent long shadows of rusted machinery stretching into the darkness.

You come to my court, the Iron King's voice boomed, *insult my guests, after what you've done today?*

"I have no idea what you're referring to," Mort said with mock innocence. "If you have a complaint, you're welcome to take it up with the lady in charge. Good luck reaching her, though. I hear the wi-fi is terrible in that old castle of hers."

A massive chaos of gears and pulleys filled the area between one room and the other. Tee motioned Tolula and the spirits to stay back, out of sight, and made her way close enough into the rusted mesh to be able to see through to the other side.

"If they find out we're here," Izzy whispered, creeping up beside her, "all that guy on the throne has to do is snap his old dead fingers and this whole situation here is gonna be our enemy."

Tee conceded the point with a nod, and they extricated

themselves some and slid alongside the gears, managing to get a glimpse of the room beyond.

That shimmering visage — all those dangling, tinkling pieces of silverware in the shape of an old bent-over man — sat at the center of the far end of the room on an intricate, rust-covered throne made from huge gears and old car parts, like some kind of steampunk Westeros monarch. He clutched a long metal staff and shook his head back and forth slowly, sending hellacious chiming jangles out into the air amidst the growls and laughter of the men and women around him.

This had to be the upper echelon of the House of Iron. There were about ten of them. They were mostly white and middle-aged, wore nondescript clothing and had nondescript haircuts. All except one — a young man whose shaved head was just beginning to grow back in: Dake stood a few feet to the left of Old Crane, arms crossed, face tight. He must've done something to gain their trust so quickly that he was even allowed in the room at all, let alone so close to the King. Probably made a big show of wanting to destroy the House of Shadow and Light now that his own precious Bloodhaüs was gone. Tee doubted any of it had been an act, though.

Mort stood facing them all, his back to Tee and Izzy, his hands at his sides.

"You must want to die, coming here like this," one of the men said.

"Oh, the King of Iron is mighty and audacious indeed," Mort droned. "But I don't think even he would be so audacious as to take out a Hierophant in his own court."

Mmm, perhaps, Old Crane mused with a chuckle. *But I doubt these two would mind much.*

Someone stepped out from behind the huge metal throne. At first, Tee thought he was on stilts, the guy was so tall. He wore clothes that were soaked through, and water seemed to steadily trickle from his fingers, pooling around his massive drenched boots.

Tolula appeared beside Tee; she was trembling.

The man wavered where he stood, like he might collapse at any moment. A long, filthy black beard hung down from his chin, and his skin was a sickly off-white. Thick brows creased his long wide forehead as he glowered down at the world around him with pupilless eyes.

Another figure stepped out from behind the throne, this one not quite as tall but wide and burly. Utility belts were slung across their chest and in overlapping crisscrosses around their waist, and they wore dusty black military fatigues and a strangely shaped gas mask that seemed somehow ancient and futuristic at the same time.

Now Tolula was motioning Tee frantically. It was time to leave.

But they couldn't just leave. Not with whatever was about to go down being about to go down. And anyway, Tee was pretty sure they wouldn't be able to get out with nearly as much stealth as they'd gotten in.

"River," Mort said. "Fortress. Imagine meeting twice in one night. And so far from home, Fortress."

The other two Hierophants, Tee realized. That tall one, River, she presumed, must've been who she'd seen slinking through the shadows earlier.

"Dog," River said, his seething voice low and crackling with some faraway frequency, like someone crinkling up paper.

"Dog of the shadow children. You shouldn't be here."

"Oh, but they already have an actual dog," Mort scoffed. "And it's Shadow and Light now, as I'm sure you know. But anyway, speaking of dogs, I'm not the one who was cowering behind the throne, waiting to be beckoned by my master." There was an uncomfortable pause, then he finished quietly, "Like a little bitch."

"*We* only came tonight because of what *you* did, dog!" River's voice seemed to crackle as he spoke, infused with some distant storm. "But never mind. You've always been impatient, Empty One." He bowed his head forward. The air thickened.

A cacophonous shiver of bells sounded as the King of Iron rose in his throne. *River!* his voice rasped out. *What are you —*

Something dark and shiny seeped out of the shadows across the floor, spread. Tee's eyes widened. Black water pooled around her feet. She traded a glance with Izzy. She knew how much her girlfriend hated getting wet, and they had every right to make a dash for it now that they had a chance.

Izzy's eyes were determined though; they matched Tee's. With the slightest of nods, they turned back toward the panicking court as dark water gathered at their ankles, as the burly Hierophant in the gas mask took two steps and then broke into a headlong charge, as Mort bent his knees and extended his arms, bracing himself for the oncoming attack.

"Now!" Tee yelled, and spirits rushed forward around them.

THIRTY

Slowly, lovingly, the world returned to Sierra as her breath came back to normal, her pulse slowed, and with it, all the chaos and sorrows she'd managed to leave behind for those blissful — she checked the clock — hours!

Well.

That managed to bring her a slight grin as she gazed up at Anthony's smiling face.

"Ay," he said.

She scooched herself up and draped herself over him, letting her mass of hair tumble all over his face until he giggled, and then laid her ear against his bare chest. "Can we do this?"

He nodded, pulling her up even closer, and kissed her. "Yes."

She raised her eyebrows. "So cocky."

He shrugged. "Asked and answered. Next question."

"Tell me the part about how I saved your life so the least you could do is —"

"Infiltrate the assholes who are trying to take yours and burn them to the ground?"

She nodded, enjoying it all at a whole new level now that she already knew what he was going to say. Enjoying even more his fingers brushing up and down her spine as his chest rose and fell beneath her. "That was a good one, my Iron Prince." A tiny firework went off inside her. She sat up. "Oh shit!"

"What's wrong?"

"Iron Prince!" she yelled, pulling on a pair of his sweats. They were way too big. She yanked the drawstring into a tight knot.

"Who's the Iron Prince?" Anthony sat up, brow creased. "And where do you think you're going dressed like me?"

Sierra forced herself to slow down. "Nowhere, I just . . ." She glanced around the room, snatched her shoulder bag from where she'd draped it over his chair. Sat across from him on the bed and put it between them. "Listen." She let a few moments slip past as she caught her breath.

To his credit, Anthony didn't make any corny *I'm listening* jokes; instead, he sat there, content but curious.

"You're not scared?" she asked, reaching into her bag.

He scoffed. "Of you?" Then tilted his head in concession. "Okay, yeah, some, but I know you're not gonna hurt me."

"Good," Sierra said. She pulled out the Deck of Worlds, shoved her bag on the floor, and placed the Deck on the bed in its place. "But I meant scared of what we're about to do, the House of Iron, this whole ridiculous world you've just thrown yourself into."

"Ah. I mean, yeah. But that doesn't mean I'm not committed."

Sierra nodded her approval. She liked that he didn't try to force his bravery or pretend this was going to be easy. The cards slid easily over each other in her hands. She'd shuffled them so many times now, knew the weight of them and their tiniest inconsistencies.

"The Deck," Anthony said with an appropriate measure of awe. "When I tell you those Iron guys are going bonkers trying to figure out where you've stashed that . . ."

Sierra wiggled her eyebrows. "Mmhmm, I'm sure. The Deck is how a house completes its crew. There are five face cards for each house, yeah? The Master, the Hound, the Warrior, the Spy, the Sorcerer."

"Like Dungeons and Dragons on crack," Anthony said.

"Basically, plus with LARPers that take it way too seriously. But anyway, once you touch the card that you match with, it clicks with you and grants you the powers of that entity. The power to track for the Hound, strength for the Warrior, the ability to hide what house you really belong to for the Spy, the ability to initiate for the Sorcerer."

"And the Master?"

Sierra let a smug smile shine through. "We can do allathat. And more. But the Iron House already has a Master, as you know. Sorry. They have a Warrior too, this freaky priest guy."

"Ah, Father Trucks," Anthony said. "Heard about him. They love that guy. Sounds like a creep."

"He is. Hit our man Caleb with some kind of weaponized chain that obliterated half Caleb's tat-spirits. Anyway, we don't know what else they have. Which means —"

"They might have a job opening, which means —"

She did a little shimmy with her shoulders. "It's a long shot, but who knows? It might be you."

"It might be me," Anthony said slowly.

They looked at each other for a few moments, and Sierra fought the urge to curl up into him and let the night guide them toward whatever bliss they could find. They didn't have that luxury, not yet. But he was right there. All she would have to do was —

"Should I, like, kneel in front of you or something?" Anthony asked.

Sierra's eyes went wide. "Huh?"

"Aren't you going to knight me or something? I dunno. Seems like what they do in movies."

"Oh! Right." Sierra's pulse wouldn't slow down no matter how hard she tried to soothe it. "Right, right. Movies."

Anthony tilted his head. "Sierra?"

"Never mind. Dirty mind. Ignore me."

"Wow!" Anthony said, nodding approvingly. "Rain check. In the meantime . . ."

Sierra blinked, rubbed her eyes. Stood. Shook it off. "Yes! But for now, kneel, Sir Anthony. Kneel platonically before me."

Anthony pulled the sheets off himself, stood, and stretched.

Sierra cringed. "On second thought, put on some pants first, maybe?"

"Oh, my bad. You're wearing mine."

"Surely you possess more than one pair of pants, you nudist."

Anthony rolled his eyes, heading to the closet. "You're no fun." He came back in a pair of gym shorts and went down on one knee before Sierra, lowering his head.

"Ugh, how are you still so tall when you're kneeling? This is ridiculous."

Anthony shrugged a snort-laugh.

"Whatever." She unwrapped the Deck from its mantle and that eerie glow filled the dim room.

"Why does it do that?" Anthony asked.

Sierra raised one shoulder. "Dunno. I just figure it's cuz it's magic or whatever. Magic shit glows, right?"

"I guess? You had that with you that night at your house, huh? After Lázaro's wake, when we brought Juan's drunk ass home. That glow . . . I remember it."

Sierra nodded. The memory felt so far away somehow. A whole other time. She'd lied to him clumsily about what it was, and then she'd lied some more and almost lost Anthony because of it. These cards, this damn Deck. All it did was reap lies and destruction wherever it went.

No more. She wouldn't let those lies tear her and the ones she loved apart.

Anthony looked up at her. "You okay?"

She nodded, her gaze removed. Tried to snap back to the moment. The moment which was glorious, which was more than all she'd hoped for, even if the future and past seemed dim around them. "Just got caught up thinking about my crap attempt to explain away the Deck that night."

"A *wake gift*," Anthony mimicked unconvincingly. "Roooight."

"Ay!" She swatted his arm, but the truth was, joking about it with him somehow made everything a little better. "Sorry about that, though. For real. I . . . I just didn't want to involve you. I know we already duked it out over lies, but that was later, and I just —"

"Sierra," Anthony said. "It's the past. The past is the past. You barely knew me then. And whatever, right now, we're here, and my knee is starting to hurt, so, you know . . ."

"Right, right! Okay!" She shuffled through the Deck until the Iron House cards showed up, separated them, and stashed the rest back in her bag. "The Iron Sorcerer!" she announced in an appallingly British-accented baritone. She held up the card: A bald-headed white man stretched his hands to a storm-torn sky. He wore mechanical battle regalia — all gears and pipes over metal breastplates and leather cuffs — and his weathered face clenched into a constipated fist.

"Yikes," Anthony said.

Sierra hushed him. "You make the role into what you need it to be. Don't worry what the card says. You shoulda seen mine."

"Fair enough."

"Head down." She laid the card on his dome and waited a beat. "Feel anything?"

"Early-onset arthritis, maybe."

"Ugh." She put the card back with the others and took out the Iron Spy. A black-haired woman who looked like she'd been drawn by a horny thirteen-year-old Goth — all clumsy sharp angles and boobs bursting out of a skimpy leather top. She carried a formidable battle ax and looked like she'd never returned a text in her life.

Anthony made a meowing sound and Sierra brapped him unceremoniously with the card and then realized what she'd done. "Shit! I meant to — dammit. Did you feel anything?"

"I felt you swat me upside the head with Elvira."

Sierra slid the card away and pulled the Hound of Iron out. "One more to go. If you get this, um, creature, you can track down anyone in the other houses. Theoretically." It looked like a steampunk gargoyle, this metallic monster snarling at a distant cityscape from the top of a clocktower. She placed it on Anthony's head.

He frowned. "Nada."

"Damn." She replaced the card. The Iron Knight was next, but that was obviously already taken. She frowned at it. Still . . . on a whim, she held it out to Anthony as he stood.

"Whoa!" Anthony jumped back, shaking his hands like he was trying to dry them. "What the hell?"

Sierra gaped at him. "Are you joking?"

He shook his head, eyes wide. "What was that?"

"The Iron Knight, my dude. Aka you, apparently."

"Shut up."

She held out the card. He took it gingerly, then squinted at the picture of a medieval knight riding into battle astride a fierce warhorse. Nodded approvingly. "Well, shit."

"But . . ."

"What happened to Father Trucks?"

"What indeed," Sierra muttered, scrambling for her phone. "But more importantly, what happened to Tee? She was up to something with this guy Mort earlier and then wouldn't take my calls." She pulled it out and lit up the screen. "Holy shit."

"What?"

"Shit, shit, shit." She had about a dozen missed calls, most of them from Caleb, and thirty frantic texts.

THIRTY-ONE

"King takes knight / that means we got you for ya priest," Izzy rapped as four shadow spirits marching on either side of her solidified into something much more physical. *"You a yard sale still-life / I'm a ma-ma-masterpiece! / Beast-mode, battle toad / now we coming down the road like ready, set, go!"*

Tee watched the solidified spirits launch into the fray, where Mort nimbly dodged another of Fortress's lurching attacks as the Iron Housers groped at the floor, frantically trying to seal out the encroaching river water with their metalwork. Only Dake seemed to have his attention elsewhere: He was bent low like the others, but his gaze stayed fixed on Mort.

Tee scratched three more chalk spears onto the plaster pillar she'd been ducking behind. She'd already sent a cadre of spirited-up shards into Iron House ranks, mostly to cause confusion and keep everyone off her and Izzy's back while they figured out what to do next. Now she wanted to be sure Dake didn't get a chance to make good on whatever it was his crafty little nazi brain was plotting.

River! the King of Iron bellowed from his throne. *You'll rust us all to pieces! Stand down this deluge!*

With a snarling glance, the River hurled a thrash of dark

water into Old Crane. The old ghost's howls seemed to fracture the whole night as his spectral shards flung in all directions. Everyone looked up, astonished. He wasn't gone — Tee could tell because that agonized screech kept shuddering through the air around her — but he'd been shattered and humiliated on his own turf.

Izzy's tall spirits had taken advantage of the sudden pause to swarm Fortress, who swatted them away with slow but unstoppable swings of those monstrous arms.

"Mort!" Tee yelled. "Come on!"

He looked up, then growled: "What are you kids doing here? Get —" The River's cruel tide leapt up suddenly and soaked Mort, who spluttered backward but managed to stay standing. Fortress — ever ready — barreled full-on into him, and they both went tumbling into the knee-deep mire.

"No!" Tee yelled. She and Izzy launched toward the thrashing Hierophants. Across the room, Dake had broken into a run as well and was closing fast. *What was he up to?*

Tee hadn't messed with the whole light part of Shadow and Light that much — she was still trying to master shadowshaping, honestly, and adding a whole new power into the mix didn't seem to make much sense yet.

But.

But she'd felt that power inside herself. Had seen Sierra and Mina blast those brilliant flashes outward like thunderclaps when need be. Had sworn she was gonna get the hang of it soon.

Maybe soon had come.

And anyway, she felt it rising in her, that light, like a time-lapse video of sunrise. All she had to do was — she felt a dull thud on her shoulder and looked down, her run slowing to a jog. Up ahead, Mort was beneath Fortress, coughing and gasping, and Dake was still hurtling toward them. But something was sticking out of Tee. A metal rod, rusty and corroded. And now bloody, right at the part where it had torn through her T-shirt and entered her flesh.

Tee tried to take another step but ended up splashing to her knees as Izzy yelled something unintelligible at Dake and the spirits around them swarmed into a frenzy.

Then a sharp pop broke the air, and then many, many more as something pinged off a nearby gear. A bullet. That's what had pinged. Everyone ducked and the air seemed filled with tiny, whistling shards of death. The shots sounded like they were coming from everywhere at once, but when Tee looked back (that water lapping up against her waist now, like she was sinking, slowly sinking, or maybe it was the river rising, quickly rising, even faster than she'd thought it could), Ms. R and Rohan were standing in the doorway, both with a gun in each hand, their faces calm as they laid down a steady, even blanket of fire: *Pop, pop, pop, pop.*

Holy shit.

She looked down, everything seeming to slow even further, and sure enough she was still impaled somehow. She wondered if the metal rod was sticking out the other side of her, and then Izzy was heaving her up into a broken kind of run, and Mort was with them, coughing still and soaking wet and badly bruised but definitely alive. And a wave of water crashed around them as they all made their clattering, disastrous way toward the exit, where R's car would be.

Tee was probably bleeding out. Or she would be when they

pulled that rod from her shoulder, which she was pretty sure Dake's sorry ass had heaved with his brand-new goddamn iron skills. And then Tee would probably die, and one of the shittiest parts about that would be that she'd have been bested by a pathetic little nazi douchebag and wouldn't even have the chance to get him back for it.

Maybe one of those many bullets had found his ass, and that would be something, at least.

As they passed where Ms. R and Rohan were waving their now silenced pistols back and forth like sentries, Tee glanced back at the drowning factory. The Iron Housers were scrambling and splashing through the dark water. Old Crane had managed to reemerge, but only as a barely visible, trembling echo of the regal phantom he had been just a few minutes earlier. He stood amidst the mess, waving those jangly arms around and howling.

That prick Dake was nowhere to be seen — hopefully he'd drowned.

But the damn gigantic Hierophant was making a damn move, stomping toward them with humongous strides that displaced tidal waves of river water.

"Back!" Ms. R yelled, and then both she and Rohan let loose with each hand, tiny explosions lighting the darkness as pop after pop sang out.

Fortress didn't seem to care. Each bullet found its mark but barely slowed them down.

"Get out of here!" Rohan hollered, but Tee wasn't even sure where here was anymore, or where they were supposed to go. The water in front of them churned, and then a great metal gear swung upward and stopped in front of them, blocking the door.

Tee let out a gasp. She'd thought she might at least make it to the car, where she could die in peace surrounded by her friends. Now it looked like she might have to die along with her friends. A surge of adrenaline spiked through her, breaking that eerie trance state being impaled must have put her in. She glanced around. There, across the hall, was another doorway, although she didn't know what would stop the Iron Housers from blocking that one too. Izzy had already seen it and was dragging Tee that way with Mort sloshing along in their wake.

Behind them, Ms. R and Rohan had leapt out of the way as Fortress came crashing into the gear and spun around. The Hierophant's masked face turned to where Tee, Izzy, and Mort were hurrying away.

Spirits swooshed through the air all around them. Ahead, the water vomited up a metal crossbeam that Izzy had to swerve to keep from hitting. They sloshed past it.

Fortress growled and stomped toward them.

Then stopped.

A bright green shape splattered across their gas mask and spun into action, whipping across the giant's thick body in an electrified sizzle.

"Go! Go! Go!" Up ahead, Caleb stood at the door, arms outstretched toward Fortress. Izzy, Tee, and Mort rushed toward him as another one of his tats went whizzing past and found its mark on the Hierophant.

Tee felt the world begin to spin out of control. Pain lanced outward from her shoulder, like her body had finally caught up to what had happened. She tried to breathe deeply, only managed to cough a few times and make things worse.

"Hang on, baby," Izzy growled. "Hang on."

"I'm okay," Tee tried to say, but it mostly came out as more coughing, and suddenly she couldn't seem to find any air, no matter how hard she pulled.

A blast of dark water smacked into Mort just as they reached the doorway, and for a second he disappeared beneath the swirl. Izzy kept dragging Tee, right through the doorway and into the front room. Tee glanced back just in time to see Fortress, still writhing from the onslaught of those tattoos, heave themselves toward Caleb. And then Mort popped up with a gasp and a splash and limped to the door.

And then the world whipped into a vicious spin cycle as Tee tried to inhale and could only barely manage it.

"Stay with me I said!" Izzy yelled, pulling her toward the far door. Tee stumbled along, falling apart, falling down, clambering back up. The water wasn't as deep here, and the Iron Housers seemed to be too concerned with their flailing king to bother with anything else. Old Crane's cries still filled the air amidst the slosh of water and yells.

And then they were outside, and Ms. R was behind them, along with Mort. "In the car," she said in a raspy whisper that sounded like it took all her self-control to make sound calm. Izzy pulled open the door of the Crown Vic and turned Tee so she could lie back across the seat. Mort limped toward them, still panting and looking in every way like shit. But at least he wasn't impaled, Tee thought, as Izzy helped her sit. Rohan and Caleb burst out of the factory in another gush of dark water, Rohan facing away from them and still letting off pop after pop.

Tee found she could actually lie all the way back, which

meant there wasn't a whole other part of that metal rod poking out of her back, so that was . . . something.

Then more people were yelling, and car doors slammed and the pops got farther away as tires screeched and the world outside the windows whirled into a dark spin cycle of shadowy buildings and spiraling streetlights.

<hr />

"Tee."

Izzy's voice.

"Tee, babe! Stay . . . stay here, babe."

Izzy's voice and the vomitous hurl of motion. And then the hurl of actual vomit speeding up her throat. Tee turned her head and let out a gush of blood and bile.

"Tee, babe, please, babe," Izzy chanted. She didn't sound mad anymore, like she had in the factory. She sounded terri-fied, anguished. Like Tee was already dead. But Tee wasn't dead, she was pretty sure. Dead people don't vomit, right? She was still in the back seat of Ms. R's Crown Vic, though, which meant she'd just ralphed on the nice leather seats and may be dead soon enough if she survived being impaled.

"Not the hospital," someone was insisting. Mort, she thought.

"What do you —" Ms. R growled, and then Izzy yelled, "Goddammit, Mort! She has a goddamn rod sticking out of her!"

"I know, I know, I know, just . . ."

"This isn't the time for —" Ms. R said.

"Let me do something!" And then Mort's face appeared over Tee. He looked even paler than usual and the passing streetlights flashed over his furrowed brow, the dark bags under his eyes. That deep frown. "Hi, Trejean."

"I still d-d-don't t-t-trust you," Tee said through chattering teeth. She could still only kinda pull oxygen into herself, but she must've been able to breathe somewhat, otherwise she'd be dead. She was pretty sure that made sense.

"Do what you're gonna do!" Izzy yelled into Mort's face.

He nodded, undaunted, and placed one hand on Tee's forehead. Then another on Izzy's.

"What the hell?" Izzy said, but she didn't move.

"What's going on back there?" Ms. R demanded.

"What's going on is, do *not* take any of us to a hospital," Mort said in a no-nonsense growl. "No matter what happens!"

Izzy's eyes looked glassy, calm, her tense face relaxed. "Ahhh," she said, more of a sigh.

"What are you d-d-dooo . . ." Tee heard the sound of her own voice trail off, become a gentle song. The orange streetlights kept sailing past overhead, Mort's face squinted into a determined grimace; beneath it all was a song. It was still Tee's voice singing it, but the whole world seemed to be singing along. It rose up from Tee's lips and circled around her, a luminous serpent, a trembling vine. It became smoke, became fire, it roared, simmered, then spread.

"How," Tee whispered as the spreading song covered everything in a dewy, shining dapple of frost. "Whoooo . . ." Once again her word slid long, then echoed and extended and unraveled across the dusky air in the back seat of Ms. R's Crown Vic. The song that Tee's word had become found Izzy and wrapped around her. And then it pulled.

Tee didn't know if she had made it do that or if it did it on its own; didn't matter, really. All that mattered was that she wanted Izzy with her and there Izzy was, slumping genially forward onto the car seat beside Tee. There wasn't really room for both of them, so Tee kind of nudged over some and Izzy slid between her and the backrest part, and then they both lay there breathing, and the night was a song, the world was a song, and above them Mort's face finally went slack, and maybe he even smiled, just a tiny bit, before he blinked and collapsed backward in what seemed like slow motion.

And then there was the wide-open darkness of the sky and the swish of lights and passing cars and Ms. R's urgent voice; and Izzy there all the while, her breath and her pulse merging with Tee's, her almost weightless, limp body alight with the song of both their voices as it cascaded outward and outward and covered the whole world, and both their mouths filled with the marvelous taste of something spicy and sweet like ginger; and they smiled, finding each other's eyes in the darkness of that back seat, because they knew, somehow they knew, they knew what no one else knew, and that, amidst everything else, was enough.

Once, a very long time ago, when the wars raged between those who had once roamed freely across the land and those who came to steal and plunder and destroy, a girl broke free from her greatest enemy, her own mother.

A Spaniard had come to visit the palace, and María Cantara could tell from the haughty, over-authoritative way he carried himself that he was terrified.

And well he should be, although probably not for the reasons he imagined.

La Contessa assembled her four daughters at the far end of the grand front hall, amidst tapestries and stained-glass windows and all beneath the swirling, grandiose decorations of that magnificent, over-the-top dome. The servants lined up in rows facing each other, and even though by now almost all of them (except ever-faithful, nosy old Altagracia) were conspiring to destroy La Contessa in one way or another, they formed an imposing gauntlet to stare down from the doorway.

Even more imposing still: La Contessa's elite guard stood shoulder to shoulder before the door. In a fit of paranoid rage following the tragic mix-up with Death, she'd maimed them, depriving each of a different sense, supposedly to heighten the other four senses. It was unclear whether this was designed to inspire terror or loyalty or some creepy combination, but either way, they remained ever by her side. Well, all except Frantico, who died of an infection soon after having his skin flayed off.

That left four: Terrizo, whose nose she'd had chopped away; Quisombo, the eyeless; Peyton, with just pale scars where his ears once were; and El Tuerco, who remained desperately in love with María Cantara's father, Santo Colibrí, and somehow had kept his treachery and amorous pursuits a secret all this time. Still: La Contessa had had his tongue removed, and he was all the more committed to her destruction, as far as María Cantara could tell.

The four guards parted their crossed spears as the Spaniard and the Taíno boy carrying his luggage entered the hall.

This man was an ambassador, María Cantara decided. He carried scrolls and wore an insignia on his uniform with the symbol of the crown on it. He was an ambassador and he knew La Contessa from back in her pre-exile years.

The Spaniard bowed low when he reached the feet of the four sisters. La Contessa stood behind them, her glare stony as ever.

I bring the good wishes of the King and Queen of Spain, my countess, the man said elaborately.

La Contessa laughed and then spat on the floor beside her, and the man looked up in horror from his bow. *Rise, clown*, she said sourly. *Your pathetic demonstrations and protocols mean nothing here. This is very simple. You have need of us, mm? Otherwise the royal fools wouldn't have come crawling back. You are short supplied, and the French, British, and now the Americans are kicking your royal backsides all over the Atlantic Ocean. Mmmm . . . what a tragedy. . . .*

Pathetic demonstrations was a pretty apt phrase, María Cantara figured, because that's exactly what La Contessa herself was engaged in. She'd spent the past three weeks preparing for this visit, which the few loyal spies she had left in Madrid had helped engineer. But whatever. She would do what need be to get what she wanted. And María Cantara would then make sure to unravel it piece by piece.

Surely, the man stuttered, *you would set aside your wounded pride for the good of your —*

Don't tell me about pride! It only took those words, that outburst, which was really a cue, and the sisters fell into formation, clutching hands and letting the light pour through them in a collective roar. The whole hall flushed with that sudden surge, and for a few moments, no one could see anything.

These are my daughters, La Contessa said as the flash began to fade and the ambassador looked around, blinking and terrified. *The Sisterhood of Sorrows. Keepers of the light, a quadrangle of power whose wrath you do not want to incur, believe me. Together with my own magic, it is they who will defeat the native insurrections you face and keep your slaves from rebelling. That is* all *that will stand between you and utter annihilation, hm?*

María Cantara quieted the seething that erupted inside her. *Soon*, she thought. It wasn't time yet, but soon it would be, and then she'd never have to perform this base charade again. And then she'd be free.

But, Contessa . . .

And in return, your regurgitated motherless King and Queen will reinstate my position in the courts and make me Regent Commander of this island, hm? You must think on it, yes? Check in with your superiors. Fine. Take one of my servants with you as a gesture of my goodwill, and when you have decided to grant me what you know I deserve, return him with the good news.

She motioned to Parada, a gardener, and María Cantara felt a cringe in the pit of her stomach. Parada had saved her life more than once, and he'd trained her to recognize and cultivate plants, to understand their subtle wants and needs, to harvest and nurture. He knew the secrets of lilies and azaleas, understood the quiet music of the trees. Plus, Parada was part of her and her father's grand plan to topple La Contessa, and him being gone indefinitely would require them to rework everything.

But, Contessa, Parada complained, *my wife has just given birth, and without me here, who will tend to your lush gardens and harvest fresh fruits and vegetables for your dinner?*

Are you not my servant? La Contessa seethed. *To do as I please with? Fine. You, Santo, go.*

No! María Cantara knew she had made a terrible mistake as soon as the word left her lips, but it was already too late. In just that tiny moment, everything had come undone.

La Contessa snapped her head at the girl. She understood.

And it was over, just like that. All their planning, all their patience: dashed, because María Cantara had let loose that single word, and in so doing, smashed the delicate veneer of distance and obedience she'd worked so, so hard to create all this time.

Santo Colibrí saw it all too, saw his daughter's disappointment in herself, saw the tragedy that was about to unfold, the unwinnable battle that lay ahead. La Contessa raised her arms, eyes narrowing at María Cantara, light gathering around her.

Attack! Santo yelled, and the world seemed to slow as bodies burst into motion around him.

The three Sorrows who weren't María Cantara clenched hands and sent blast after blast of pale flashes of light into the hall, stunning and singeing and charring everyone in their path.

¡La bastarda! La Contessa yelled, and the three sisters

turned against their own, brightness gathering. But María Cantara had been backing away slowly, her own powers swirling in an ever-brightening tornado.

Santo Colibrí watched in horror and admiration as his daughter seemed to catch fire within a blast of heavenly light while arrows and spears shrieked through the air. And then, with a magnificent burst, the burning spire around her unleashed and boomed outward, and the sound of crumbling walls, pounding feet, and screams took over the world.

Ven a los cuatro caminos, a los cuatro caminos ven . . .

The song a gentle whisper in her mind, and then her own voice singing sloppily on top of it, the lyrics and melody muddled.

Donde los poderes se unen y se hacen uno.

She was no longer within the palace; the warm, musty smell of soil let her know. And somewhere, not far away, garlic simmered in oil.

Mira cómo mis enemigos caen.
Mientras mi voz de espíritu grita.

When she opened her eyes, though, it wasn't the sunlight cutting through the cool forest canopy that greeted her.

Hello, she said to Death. *I haven't seen you in a while.*

Truth was, the girl and the towering collector of souls had

spent many, many nights side by side at the balcony, gazing out at the dark forest. But once María Cantara had allowed herself to be initiated into La Contessa's Sisterhood of Sorrows, Death had simply stopped showing up. María Cantara didn't mind — she'd more or less known it would happen, and she figured that once she completed her sabotage and stole off to the wide world, Death would come back.

She just never expected it to be so soon.

Those robes gathered in languid, almost fluid folds, like the slow drip of molasses, and they expanded ever outward: Everything was darkness except the stark glimpses of bone grinning endlessly beneath the cowl.

My child.

Am I? María Cantara wondered out loud.

Death replied with only one word, a name: *Lucera.*

María Cantara nodded, accepting it.

I have saved you on this day, and in saving you I have claimed you, and in claiming you I have named you. But none of these are my true gift to you.

She just blinked up at him. Death had never had so much to say at one time.

My true gift to you is power. My power.

I can take any life I want? María Cantara asked, maybe a little too excited. She can be forgiven though, I think. She strongly suspected that La Contessa had survived the melee in the palace, and she was also pretty sure a lot of other people hadn't. She simply wanted to finish what she'd started.

A terrifying throaty ripple of sound erupted within María Cantara: Death's sordid chuckle. *My power is much greater than that, as you will see, m'ija. Well worth the price you have paid.*

Price? María asked, even as darkness swept over the grinning skull and she sank back into a senseless sleep.

———

Now she was sure she was dreaming when she awoke again, this time into a nightmarish world stricken with sharp blasts of pain every time she moved and then even more pain when she winced. And, as she blinked awake with a moan, two dozen half skulls turned their worried (half worried?) expressions toward her.

A bright searing burn ripped through her as she tried to scuttle away from the deathly horde.

M'ija, a voice said, but it wasn't Death, it wasn't a whisper within. It was her father. A man stepped forward, half skulled like the rest of them. No, it was paint. Why had they all so grimly decorated themselves?

She shook her head, tried to squint, blink away tears, and more blistering anguish erupted.

It's me, Santo Colibrí said. *You saved us, my child.*

Why . . . She tried to finish her sentence, but only gasps of pain came out.

Come, let me give her some more ointment, hm? another familiar voice said. *The poor dear.*

How . . .

You've been asleep for almost three weeks, m'ija, her father said. *The rebellion has begun. We paint our faces like this in your honor, because of what you did.*

I don't . . . "understand," she was going to say, but then, very suddenly, she did understand. The price that Death had spoken of. She didn't have to reach up and touch her face to realize that half of it had been seared clean away in the blast of light she'd unleashed to fend off her sisters. She didn't need a mirror — why would she? At least twelve reflections of herself were looking right back at her.

Somehow, even through the pain that screamed inside her with each tiny movement, Lucera looked up at the family that had always been there for her, had saved her life and now were saving it again, those that would die to protect her and those she would die to protect too, and she smiled.

PART THREE

THIRTY-TWO

Juancito.

Juan Santiago tried to sit up, but the hand he'd put down to steady himself missed the bed entirely, and he followed it in a yelping tumble over the side.

"Aha!" He jumped to his feet, glanced around. "What?"

He was in his room. For real for real. He was safe. No bunks. No prison guards. No mean fluorescents burning out his retinas. No sign of imminent death clomping down a cold metal corridor toward him.

But who had just said his name?

He was in his room, by himself, and there was Gael's familiar anal-retentive side of the place, everything annoyingly tidy and where it belonged under threat of violence until he got back from Afghanistan. But more importantly, there on the wall were all Juan's metal posters, and there was the unruly mess of wires under his desk that led to a bunch of random electronics, and outside the frosted window the first soft signs of daybreak were whispering into existence over Brooklyn, not the choppy waves of the harbor.

It was still dark, but he was pretty sure no one was lurking in the corners, and anyway, it had sounded like . . . it had sounded like a spirit voice. And they'd used the Spanish diminutive version of his name that the damn ancestors always insisted on calling him, as if he didn't already have a complex about being shorter than his younger sister.

"Hello?" he said to his empty room, feeling somewhat like a dick.

Nothing.

The truth was, even though Grandpa Lázaro had taught him about shadowshaping when he was just a kid, and he'd grown up seeing those tall, long-legged shadows shimmering in the corners of his eyes and sometimes just walking up to him — he'd never really taken the time to learn that much about what it all meant. He just knew they were protecting him and they showed up at his gigs (hell, sometimes they were the only folks that showed up at his gigs, in those impossible early days of Culebra) and that was that.

Then Sierra had suddenly turned out to be the top-dog shadowshaper, and Juan had felt super weird about having hoarded that knowledge to himself without really meaning to, and then things really came to a head at a gig in Park Slope during the West Indian Day parade, when some creepy white dude had accosted Juan outside the club and drained almost all his powers.

Waking up from that nightmare, Juan had felt empty in a way he'd never known he could. The spirits were far away from him, and it was like someone had removed a layer of his skin — something he'd just never thought about that much and always taken for granted was gone, or mostly gone, and all he knew was he needed it back.

In the cab heading home that night, that familiar warmth

of feeling spirits close to him flooding back through his body, he'd sworn he'd get his shit together finally when it came to shadowshaping. He had to. And then he'd got that regular gig at the Red Edge, and he got busy and then, just like that, he was locked up, and the House of Iron had made sure no spirits were getting into Rikers under any circumstances; so there he was empty again, and he swore when he got out he would for real for real get it together, and he meant it.

And now he was out, barely a day, and already they were whispering into his dreams. At least it made some sense.

He looked at his phone.

Six fourteen in the damn morning.

That ridiculous rigorous prison routine had really infected him, even in that short time.

Still . . . he felt lowkey amazing, as long as he didn't think about Pulpo being a traitor. The spirits had woken him, even if in a kinda-not-there creepy way, and he'd been half the night Skype chatting with Bennie. Life was kinda incredible, in an off-center sort of way. If this was what it felt like to wake up early, then maybe he should do it more often.

The smell of French toast greeted him as he opened the door to the hallway. And beneath it, that gurgle of the cafetera and the clatter of silverware on dishes. His mom had clearly anticipated the early rise — she didn't even look surprised when she turned around from the stove at the sound of his socked feet descending the stairs.

"¡Desayuno!" she said with a wide grin. She was already fully dressed in a pantsuit and jacket, her face made up, hair perfect. "I'm so happy you're home, m'ijo."

He jumped down the last few steps and snuggled into her

arms. "Me too, Mami. I thought school was out for Christmas break, though."

"Out for the kids. The teacher's work is never done."

"Ugh."

"Meetings and more meetings." She ruffled his spiky hair. "I was really worried, you know."

"I know, Mami. I'm sorry I scared you."

"It's okay." She held him at arm's length, looking him up and down with sharp eyes. "I know you did it for a good reason."

"Yeah, I thought so too . . ." He slumped into a chair by the counter and made a face. Pulpo's frown kept popping back through. He'd gone to lockup for his best friend, and his best friend had decided to join up with the enemy. None of it made sense.

María cocked her head at him. "¿Pero?"

He shrugged. "I don't wanna talk about it. The coffee's ready?"

"Claro que sí, m'ijo."

He poured himself a cup, settled back into his seat as María Santiago threw another chunk of butter onto the sizzling pan.

Culebra was done with, that much was for sure. The very thought brought its own kind of devastation, but Juan had started to make peace with it. The two boys had come up with the name and whole concept behind the band one epic night when they were twelve. They'd gone to a concert at the Prospect Park bandshell — some old-school salsa group. There was a coffee truck there, one of those fancy hipster ones, and they'd each ordered something called a Frosted Midnight Death

Special of Eternal Bliss & Damnation. They had no idea what it was, but the name alone was enough. It turned out to consist of about eighteen espresso shots swirled into a frothy, frozen cappuccino icy-type thing and topped with cinnamon, an orange peel, and gooey chocolate gumballs. It lived up to its name, in other words, which was an impressive feat on its own.

They'd stood there in the trees, back a little from the dance floor, watching some couples cut it up a little *too* perfectly, those ones you could tell had been to every single salsa class possible in a desperate grasp for some flavor, while other couples clearly had no idea what they were doing but were having a blast anyway. And then those occasional — usually elderly — ones who just seemed to glide effortlessly amidst the struggling masses, nailing every step like they had been born in frilled skirts, guayaberas, and dance shoes.

And then Pulpo's cell had rung — he had one of those fancy ones with the extra loud ring, so it blasted this death-metal song called "GARANGA" (all caps or death) straight out across the field — and for a single blissful moment, the metal ruckus had blended with the jangle of those piano notes and timbales.

"Ugh, this chick," Pulpo had said, declining the call. "What's wrong?"

Juan was just standing there, blinking. "Why did you . . . why did you make it stop?"

"She's mad annoying, man. I'm not trying to talk to her, and I've told her that from jump but —"

"No, no," Juan said, still staring off at some distant star in the darkening sky. "Why did you make the music stop?"

"What, my ringtone? Juan, what's wrong with you, man?"

Juan raised one hand and whispered, "Listen," as he took out his phone and called Pulpo without looking at it. "Just listen."

That second time the chaotic mash-up of thrash and suave charanga played, Pulpo stood up very straight and looked down at Juan. "Holy shit."

They kept calling Pulpo's phone until one of the dancers complained and they got kicked out, and then they walked all the way back to the Santiagos' Bed-Stuy brownstone, yammering the whole time about time signatures and chord changes and who they could bring in and what they should call it. And the planning session had gone on straight through the night, thanks to the Frosted Midnight Death Special of Eternal Bliss & Damnation and despite multiple threats of grievous bodily harm from Sierra down the hall.

"Juan?" María's voice pulled him from his memories. "Why are you clenching your fists, mi amor? Talk to me."

He shook his head, grunted. The truth was, he really didn't want to lose his best friend, and it made it even worse that he was totally clueless as to why it had happened. And he was going to have to do something about it. He had no idea what, but sitting on all this sadness and anger wasn't an option. Normally he'd put it into a song and bring it to the boys, but . . . "No, it's just . . . I dunno."

María rolled her eyes, making sure he didn't think she was actually convinced by that, and put down a plate stacked with steaming, butter-and-syrup-soaked French toast. "You don't have to talk to me about it, but you're going to have to talk to someone to figure it out. Now I have to go to these *meetings*." She said the word like something disgusting had just died in her mouth. "Enjoy your breakfast and —"

A deafening explosion of Cojo's barks blasted away whatever María was about to say next.

Someone was at the front door. Or many someones, maybe? Sneakers squeaked and stomped amidst the sounds of motion and . . . struggle? Juan jumped up, hurried out into the den along with his mom as Cojo's barks charged through the air once again.

"Who is —" Juan said, but then the front door flew open and Sierra backed in with something — no, some*one* in her arms.

"Juan!" she yelled, heaving the top part of Tee's unconscious and bloodied body through the door. "A hand?"

Juan rushed forward, grabbing her waist. Caleb, sweating and panting, had her legs.

"¿Pero qué . . . ?" María gasped, jumping in to help too.

"No," Sierra said, leading them toward the staircase. "Stay and help —"

"Coming through," someone yelled from outside.

"— them," Sierra said.

An enormous brown-skinned dude with no hair and an audacious goatee ducked into the house with Izzy slung over his shoulder. María looked up at him with wide eyes, hands raised to help. He looked down at her, panting. "Oh, no, I got this, thanks, mama. Where to, Sierra?"

"Upstairs," she said between pants. "Fourth floor."

"Damn," the man said. "Maybe I do need a hand."

"I definitely do," a raspy voice called from behind him.

María glared at her daughter. "Sierra, ¿qué carajo pasó, coño?"

"I can't . . . not right now, Mami, I'm sorry! Juan, help with Mort. We'll get started on the stairs."

"Who the hell is Mort?" Juan asked, walking over to the doorway. Then he froze. A tall, slender guy with the hood of his hoodie pulled low over his face was hauling yet another unconscious person in the door. Except Juan knew this one too. It was the random creepy white guy who had knocked him out and almost drained all his shadowshaping power the night of the West Indian Day parade. Juan whirled around, ready to demand Sierra explain what this . . . this *fiend* was doing in their house. But Sierra was already clambering Tee up the stairs with Caleb.

"Can I get a hand?" a familiar voice asked. Pulpo stepped inside and pulled the hood away from his face.

THIRTY-THREE

The door to Lázaro's old apartment slammed shut, and for a few blessed moments, everyone just stood there panting.

Tee, Izzy, and Mort had been laid out on the bed beside each other. Rohan had dropped off his load and made a hasty, mumbling retreat.

That left Juan, María, Caleb, and Anthony, who now formed a small half-moon around Sierra.

Here it came.

"What is this traitor doing here?" Juan demanded, just as Caleb growled, "Where the hell were you?"

María got up in Caleb's face just in time to cut off Anthony. "Don't you come into my house and talk to my daughter that way, jóven!"

"Yeah," Anthony said, over her head.

"You don't get a say in this, iron boy," Caleb snapped.

"Hey!" María grabbed Caleb's pointing finger and pulled it down to her face like she was about to bite it off. Caleb flinched. "I am espeaking to you!"

Caleb threw both his hands up, took a calming breath. "My apologies, Mrs. Santiago. It's just that —"

"I still want to know why this traitor is allowed in this house!" Juan wailed.

"I'm not a traitor," Anthony growled, whirling around, but there wasn't much fight left in him.

"Sure look like one from where I'm standing," Caleb said.

"Jóven." María menaced, backing Caleb up. Then she turned to Sierra. "M'ija. What is happening?"

"I'm not a damn traitor!" Anthony yelled this time, just as Sierra said, "He's not a traitor."

Everyone looked at her. "He's a spy."

Caleb eyed him, fists still clenched. "Oh word?" he muttered.

"I don't believe you," Juan said, staring down Anthony with wide, watery eyes. "I don't believe you."

Who's a spy? a creakily old voice tingled as the bathroom door flew open and a gold light poured out into the dingy fourth-floor apartment.

"Oh, here we go." Sierra sighed. She'd completely forgotten about Septima.

"Sierra María Santiago," María seethed. "Why is there a Sorrow in my house?"

Suddenly nobody had a damn thing to say, not even Septima.

"Ah," Sierra said. "Thing is —"

"Sierra María Santiago," María said, reeeeeal slow and quiet, and Sierra knew at that moment she was basically dead. "Let me rephrase that question."

"Hoo boy," Juan whispered.

"Why is one of the vile desmadrosas hijo de puta

comemierda de la sinvirgüenza chocha de la pinga hermanas de mierda en quien me cago hasta la muerte" — she smiled sweetly, then snarled — "in my goddamn house?"

Technically, I am also a member of this fa — was all Septima could get out before María pulled off her shoe and hurled it across the room, then launched after it in an unstoppable tornado of *coñazo* and *puta madre*s.

The shoe caught Septima smack in the forehead, a direct hit, and to Sierra's surprise, it sent the Sorrow hurling back as everyone else jumped into motion to hold off the oncoming slaughter.

"¡Jamás! ¡Pendeja hija de la gran —!" María was yelling when Juan, Caleb, and Anthony finally got their hands on her and pulled her away from where Septima was cowering.

"Mami!" Sierra yelled. "Mami! Listen to me! Jeez! Just —"

"No, you listen to me, Sierra! I want her out! Now!"

"Seriously," Caleb said, stepping between María and Sierra like a man who didn't mind dying. "This woman tried to destroy all of us."

"She unleashed Dr. Wick on this family," María said. "The reason your grandfather was in the state he was in, and you have her up in this very room, Sierra? The nerve!"

Sierra felt a tiny part of herself crumble. She knew how it looked, she knew it was dangerous, but the truth was, she hadn't considered that little tidbit of tragic irony. Mostly because, if she was being honest with herself, it didn't matter that much to her. Lázaro was dead, and his ghost certainly hadn't shown up anywhere, so he didn't care, and even if he did, Sierra was long past giving him a say in things.

And anyway, Septima had more information than anyone else about how the Deck of Worlds and the houses worked, and that took precedence over everything else.

Still, she hated hurting her mom.

"Look," Sierra said calmly. "I'm sorry that —"

"No apologies," María said. "I don't care. I know that tone, young lady. You're about to apologize but try to explain something to me about why it's necessary, etc. etc. And I don't care. She goes. She goes, she goes. Que se vaya. She cannot —"

"No," a voice said from the other end of the room.

Everyone looked to the bed, where Izzy was sitting up eerily straight, blinking rapidly. "No," she said again.

Caleb reached her first, then Sierra. "Iz, you alright?" Sierra asked as Izzy used Caleb's arm to help herself stand.

She looked . . . different, but Sierra couldn't place what it was. Neither of the other two on the bed stirred at all.

"No what, Isake?" María demanded shakily.

"No, she doesn't go."

"And what makes you think you can tell me who stays and who goes from my own house?"

"Because we need her on our side if we want to win," Izzy said. She stepped forward, away from Caleb and standing on her own in the middle of the room. When she looked up, her eyes flashed with a strange kind of fire. "And believe me, we want to win."

Coño, Septima whispered. *She's a Hierophant.*

THIRTY-FOUR

A smooth line, curving around and looping back up.

"I still don't like her being here."

"No one likes it, María."

"But if I have to, then I have to."

"Well, I don't like him being here."

Then small scratchy lines along the inner coil, giving it depth and girth.

"Juan, I told you, I'm not . . . I'm sorry, man. I'm so, so sorry. You have to understand —"

"I don't have to do anything, Pulpo."

"Hey, both of you. We gotta focus."

Then a wider line ranging around the first one's circumference and stretching above and past to wrap down and outward into a jagged nozzle. More scratches along the inner wraps, growing longer toward the center.

"Look, nobody's happy about any of this, okay? But like Izzy said, we have to . . . we have to . . . Argh! This is ridiculous!"

I would just like to say that I am pleased with the outcome so far.

"Shut it, Septima. Nobody asked."

Desgraciado.

The gas mask was coming together. Sierra added a thick splotch of a line along the top to give it some shine and then sketched a quick, heavy body beneath it and wrote: *FORTRESS.*

"That what — he? she? they? — Fortress looks like?" she asked Izzy.

Izzy, her back against the wall beside Sierra, arms crossed over her chest, appraised it with narrow eyes, nodded. "We have no idea what gender Fortress is, but yeah. Give them straps and utility belts and big galoshes. It's part of the whole getup."

"Cool." Sierra drew in the gear and then moved on to the spot next to them. "And you said the River's like a tall Rasputiny dude, yeah?"

"Mmhmm. No pupils. Narsty-as-shit-type beard. Sallow cheeks."

Sierra got to it.

"I don't even know what we hope to solve with this. It's too many enemies in one place, too much distrust."

"We don't have much of a choice."

Sierra's mind slid into that sweet trance state she loved so much as the tip of her Sharpie described the River's long gangly arms and scraggled beard. Drawing was peace. That was all there was to it. There could be a whole battle royale erupting around her — there basically was — and she'd still manage to be there drawing away with a pleasant smile on her face. There, with a marker in her hand and the quiet joy of an anchor to keep her mind focused just enough so that it could wander freely through her thoughts without trying too hard — Sierra greeted bliss like an old friend.

"I just worry . . . I don't know. How will we —"

"We wait to see what Izzy has to say, and then Tee when she wakes. That's all I got. Then we figure out what the move is. Feel me?"

"I guess."

Everyone else's conversations rattled on like the rumble and howl of a distant train passing in the night. Sierra knew eventually she'd have to face whatever they were bantering about, but right then, there was nothing to figure out except how to show the way the River shoved forward his liquid weapons with that sorcery of his. It was corny, but she switched from black to blue and drafted waves flushing out to either side of his towering frame.

"Who that, Moses?" Juan asked, suddenly taking his attention away from being mad at Anthony just in time to razz Sierra. "Moses a Hierophant now? That's wild. We're really screwed, huh?"

"It's the River, jackass," Izzy scowled, and Sierra was relieved to hear her friend sound a little bit like her old self again. She'd been on that straight-up faraway ethereal trip since she woke, talking like she was receiving dictation from some long-gone phantom, and Sierra hadn't liked it one bit. Everyone had started yelling at once when they realized what Izzy was. It was chaos, and Izzy herself had remained uncharacteristically chill throughout it all. Hauntingly chill. Now, twenty loud minutes later, she seemed to be getting back to baseline Izzy, at least a little.

Sierra had finally given up trying to calm everyone down and gone to her room to get a huge roll of white paper she'd borrowed (stolen) from the Butler High art studio. They didn't need it, not really, and anyway, it was for students, right? And what was she? Exactly. No harm, no foul.

She'd come back up and had Anthony help her cover one whole wall of Lázaro's old apartment with the paper. Then she'd popped the cap off a Sharpie and gotten down to it, mapping out all the information they had about the Deck of Worlds and the Hierophants in quick sketches and interconnected lines.

It was the only way she knew to make sense of all this mess, and anyway, she couldn't be bothered to waste time arguing with anyone anymore.

She didn't like hurting people's feelings, but the truth was Izzy was right, and Sierra was just glad someone else had said it, someone with the newly invested authority of being a Hierophant, no less — they wanted to win. Needed to, really. It was a question of survival. And if that meant that feelings got hurt, well, better that than people getting hurt.

She would do what she had to do to get them over the line intact. To win. She'd already made peace with the fact that it was impossible to do that without anyone getting hurt. She just had to figure out how to protect her loved ones as much as she could and come at the Iron House with all she had. And then see about taking apart the whole damn thing.

"You ain't mad at me?" she quietly asked Izzy as the conversations bristled and flowed around them.

"Mad? For why, Si?"

Back to the black Sharpie and filling in the errant bristling hairs of the River's narsty beard; Sierra exhaled and raised her eyebrows. "Cuz I wasn't there when shit went to hell. Caleb was pissed, before you woke up and everything got weird . . . er, weirder. And I get why."

"Why? Because you're supposed to be perfect?"

"Uh . . ."

"Didn't you call Tee back like forty-seven times? She said you probably were mad after she called you and then hung up and then ditched her phone."

"I mean, yeah. I could've —"

Izzy shook her head. "Si, stop. Sure, we coulda gotten wiped out, no question. But that's not on you. That's on the corny metalheads who tried to wipe us out. And those two Hierofreaks."

"Are you, like, allowed to talk that way about your fellow —"

Izzy scoffed. "I just did, didn't I?"

The River done, Sierra wrote his name underneath and then wrote *LA CONTESSA ARAÑA* under a blank box she'd drawn beside him, and then *THE REAPER* beside that.

"Do you know how, ah, how it all works yet?"

She shrugged, her eyes still glistening with that strange faraway fire. "Nah, give it time, I said."

"How much time do we have? Before the other guys get their shit together enough to wipe us out completely."

Izzy gave a noncommittal shrug. "Wish I knew. Not much."

Sierra drew another empty box, looked at Izzy. "Got a name, Hierophant?"

Izzy opened up her wide Cheshire Cat grin. "Just call us Air."

"Oh? I like it." Sierra scrawled it in elegant handwriting. "Wait, us?"

Izzy nodded over at where Tee was still knocked out on the bed. "Just wait till my better half wakes up, boyyyy."

"Okay," Sierra said, stepping back from the messy little galaxy she'd etched across the wall. "Let's see how things are looking."

"Looking like you're trying to catch a serial killer," Big Jerome said. He'd shown up with Bennie and Nydia a few minutes before they'd all settled down to get started and Caleb had done his best to catch them up while Sierra finished the drawings. "Which might not be so far off from the truth."

Sierra snorted. He wasn't wrong. She'd lined up the five Hierophants in the center of the paper: Fortress, the River, La Contessa Araña, the Reaper, and Tee and Izzy, aka Air. She'd circled the *La Contessa Araña* in purple and written *Doña Teresa etc. etc.* beneath her and then *Sierra and Juan's great-great-great-grandmom*.

Then she'd drawn a brown-skinned girl with a big fro off to one side with a loose approximation of the House of Shadow and Light around her. Mina had the word *Spy* below her and a question mark below that. After tons of phone calls and texts, no one had any idea where the hell she was, and Mina didn't really have any friends that they knew of. She lived with her grandmother out in Staten Island, but that wasn't much of a lead.

A red line connected Mina to the tattered remains of Bloodhaüs at the bottom of the page, indicating that's where she'd been embedded.

On the other side of the page were Krin, Fraz, Bak, and Trank, all looking like the busted skinheads they were, and Axella with the word *Queen* under her and a big X over her face. Finally, Dake, who was connected by another jagged line to the top right corner, where the Iron House was looking appropriately surly and overconfident. Sierra had drawn Ol' Crane a mess of silverware in the middle and a picture of the priest with another big X over it. Then came Anthony, Officer Grintly (dressed in his corrections uniform), and a couple random folks that Izzy could remember from the night before.

"Sooo," Sierra said. "Let's start in the middle. What do we know about La Contessa Araña here?"

Everyone shifted in their seats so they could turn and look at Septima, who hovered in a far corner in her little golden haze. *¿Qué?*

"Your mother," Sierra said. "And don't hold out on us, Septima."

Hold out on you? I don't know what you're —

"Failed to mention that Mort was a Hierophant, didn't you?"

Ah, bueno, es que . . .

"Save it," Sierra said. "Just tell us about your mama."

Septima swooped in little half circles for a few moments, then conceded, shoulders slumped. *She lives in a crumbling palace in the —*

"Wait, hold up," Jerome said. "*Lives?* As in, is currently alive now and today?"

In a manner of speaking, jes.

"Is she a ghost?" Bennie asked.

In a manner of speaking, jes.

"Septima," Sierra warned. "No games."

No, it's that what she has become, from what I know, is not something that is so simple as alive or dead, ghost or not. Ask the Hierophant, she can explain.

Izzy rolled her eyes when everyone looked at her. "I know what she means, but I can't really explain either." She gave a dismissive wave. "She exists. That's all we need to know. Just keep going."

"She built the Deck," Sierra said. "And she did it to —"

Bring balance and order to a broken world! Septima insisted.

"Yes, the Deck and everything that goes on around it seems very orderly and calm," Caleb snorted. "No chaos at all."

Septima deflated some. *She did not know it would cause this much problems.*

"She felt the need to create order," Sierra said, sketching a quick arrow leading down and away from La Contessa, "because she was worried about" — she wrote *María Cantara* at the other end of the arrow — "my great-great-grandma."

Y su comemierda padre, Septima added.

"Don't disrespect my ancestors in this house," Sierra said before her mom had a chance to. "Name."

¿Qué?

"What was my great-great-great-grandfather's name, Septima?"

The glowing spirit seemed to almost fizzle out entirely before finally rallying. *Santo Colibrí.*

"Saint Hummingbird?" Juan piped up. "That's amazing."

"New band name," Anthony suggested. Juan looked like he was about to laugh but then remembered he was supposed to be mad at Anthony; he clammed up quick and crossed his arms over his chest.

"Bet," Sierra said, writing his name near María Cantara's. "So father and daughter ran off to the jungle together, right, built up a crew out there and founded shadowshaping, yeah. The first shadowshapers." She wrote it and made a few nondescript figures around them, along with some trees.

"Badass," Izzy said.

"And they had . . ." Sierra said.

"Mi abuela," María said. "Cantara Cebilín Colibrí."

"Who dressed however she damn wanted, right?" Sierra asked, remembering a photo her mom had shown her of Cantara dressed in a full three-piece suit looking as fierce and handsome as she wanted to and proud as hell.

"Ha," María scoffed. "She did *whatever* she damn wanted. She was unstoppable, hm?"

"And she had Mama Carmen, who had you, who had me and Juan and Gael," Sierra finished, drawing in quick sketches of each one as the arrows swooped up to connect the family to the current crew of shadowshapers.

"My thing is," Bennie said, "is we shadowshapers or is we House of Shadow and Lighters?"

"We both," Sierra said simply. "I'd been trying to figure all that out too, but something Septima said the other day made it make sense. Shadowshaping is a whole other thing, really. It's connected — that shadow magic is like a tiny piece of spirit that resides inside us and gets activated when we initiate, right? But shadowshaping is about connecting to the dead, to art, to the world. The shadow magic, the light magic, the two of them together — that's part of the Deck's powers that we draw on from within. That's how I see it."

"You right," Izzy said, standing and taking a green marker from Sierra. "Only thing you're missing here is this." She drew thick lines between each cluster of drawings and then other ones reaching outward from La Contessa.

"The Deck is a spiderweb?" Jerome asked.

"Basically," Izzy said.

"Oh, snap! It really is." Sierra circled the word *Araña* with her purple marker. "That's why she's the Spider Countess!"

Izzy nodded. "Mmhmm. She's the center of it all. The engine and the source. The way Lucera is the beating heart of the shadowshapers. And you know how the Deck and *Almanac* update to keep up with the changing events? Who you think doing that?"

Sierra shuddered. This ancient creature was holed up in some ruined palace in the deep forests of Puerto Rico and still somehow had her long fingers in the daily events here in Brooklyn. What a creep. And she had the nerve to be related to Sierra.

"And don't forget this," Caleb said, standing and grabbing the black Sharpie. "These guys" — he started drawing a line from the River and Fortress — "are in bed with these guys" — and led it directly to the Iron House. "And they coming for us."

"What do we do, Sierra?" Anthony asked.

Sierra took in the mess of lines and pictures, shook her head. "I have no damn idea."

THIRTY-FIVE

"You sure you're good?" Juan asked as his mom finished bundling up against the morning chill.

She turned around slowly and somehow looked very small and very angry. "I am not good," María said. "Not at all. But I will be. When this whole thing is over and that *thing* is out of my house. Because it will be over, Juan José Santiago. And she will be gone." She hefted a tote bag full of paperwork onto one shoulder, kissed Juan on the cheek, and headed out the door.

"Shit," Juan whispered. He hadn't seen her that mad since he'd dropped out of school to tour with Culebra. And she was right. And so was Sierra. And María probably knew Sierra was right, and that made it all the worse. Both were right, and nothing made sense. And they might be dead or otherwise obliterated any minute, apparently, so what did it even matter anyway?

And Anthony was either helping the creeps who were trying to destroy them, or he was spying like Sierra said, but either way . . . either way . . . Juan tightened his fists as he stared out into the gray street.

It started to snow — just a flake here, a flake there — and Juan had to admit it threw a lovely, peaceful kind of filter over the brownstones and parked cars and maple trees on his block. But still . . . the churn of anger persisted, his face as tight as his fists with each passing thought of Pulpo.

He shouldn't even be mad. Not really. Sierra knew what she was talking about. Even if she'd caught feelings, which she undoubtedly had, she wouldn't let them cloud her vision when it came to this. If she said Pulpo was on the level and, in fact, putting himself in harm's way by spying for them, that's what it was. So why was Juan still pissed?

The snow tapered off, started up again. Upstairs, they were probably still going over strategies and lore and trying to make sense of what they knew. Juan sighed, and then a dark brown hand slid around his chest, startling him at first and then calming him immeasurably. An arm followed the hand and Juan inhaled a deep fruit-laced breath of whatever girly body spray Bennie favored, felt her body press up against his. He smiled from the inside out.

"You know," Bennie said slyly in his ear. "We were all upstairs wondering."

"Oh no."

"Where in the world . . ."

"Don't say it."

"Is Juanmen Santiago! Ayy!'"

Juan closed his eyes and shook his head. "I bet you feel really original right now, huh?"

"How was I supposed to resist, man?" She squeezed him tight and he felt all fluttery and gross. Beautiful, really. But gross beautiful.

"Do you *know* how many times I've heard that joke? It's not even . . . It's Carmen Sandiego! Whatever!"

Bennie giggled and put her chin on his shoulder, which was unbearably adorable and still only kinda broke through Juan's terrible mood.

Flurries started winding their slow, flitting descent through the pale sky once again.

"You want to talk about it?" Bennie's voice soft, worried.

Juan shook his head, then bounced it from side to side. "There are so many things to talk about."

"Yeah," Bennie said. "But one's really bothering you."

"Do you believe that Pulpo's really on our side?"

Bennie took a good long minute to answer, which Juan appreciated. Meant she was really thinking it over, not just regurgitating what Sierra thought. "Yeah," she finally said. "Yeah, I do. I don't see him going over to the other side, not for real. But you know him best."

Juan snorted. "I thought I did."

"Ah." Juan could tell Bennie had just wrapped her head around the whole situation and figured out whatever it was Juan could just flail at. How did she do that? She'd just managed to get a better grasp on it than Juan had, and all he'd said was a handful of words. She was smarter than him and it was so sexy. Now all he wanted to do was stop talking about Pulpo and go make out somewhere, but that probably wasn't on the table. Not yet anyway.

"So what is it?" Juan said, instead of turning around and kissing Bennie full on the lips. "What's going on?"

"He hurt your feelings, silly."

"But —"

"Hey," a deep and familiar voice said from behind them. "Can I —"

"Oop, that's my cue," Bennie said. She kissed Juan's cheek and skedaddled with a quickness.

Great. From the best to the worst in just seconds. Juan kept looking outside, jaw clenched.

"I'm just gonna, uh, stand back here some, because I'm not supposed to be seen here, so . . ."

"I get it," Juan said.

"Look, I . . ." Pulpo's voice trailed off. He was probably shaking his head, waving his hands around. That's what he did when he didn't know what to say.

"You're sorry," Juan said for him. "Okay, cool."

"Well, yes, but clearly it's not cool. You won't even look at me. What's up, man?"

"Apparently, you hurt my feelings. According to Bennie."

"I can't imagine what gave her that idea," Pulpo said.

Juan growled.

Pulpo's laugh was nervous. "That came out wrong! And I'm not trying to laugh! I mean I'm not laughing at you! Or at this! This is not funny! I just . . . this is what —"

"This is what happens when you're upset," Juan said, feeling shitty about how cold his voice was. "I know." Pulpo was about twenty seconds away from a full-fledged panic attack. It often started with that giddy laugh that seemed as utterly out of place as a penguin at a disco. The laugh would dissolve into a hiccupy kind of sob, and then he would just melt down entirely.

"Look . . ." Juan was having trouble keeping his thoughts straight. The half of him that always took care of Pulpo when he was having one of his attacks was battling with the half of him that was still mad at Pulpo. He turned around. Looked into his best friend's eyes, saw how hard he was trying not to

240

freak out. Pulpo knew that would only make whatever they had to say to each other more complicated, near impossible. He was doing everything he could to hold off the flood of terrifying thoughts working their frenzied way through him.

Why was Juan so mad at Pulpo?

"You did hurt my feelings," Juan admitted, his voice still cold. "Because . . ." The answer came as he spoke, but he hated it. He shook his head, spat it out anyway. "Because you told Sierra and not me."

Anthony blinked a whole bunch and did some weird stuff with his face that meant it was still going on, but he was calming down some too.

"And I feel really, really, grr, childish about that," Juan said. "And I really don't like that that's what it is, but if I'm being honest, and I'm trying to be, then that's what it is."

Pulpo nodded.

"I realized it because I was still mad even when it turned out you're not a spy. And, yeah, you're not a spy. I believe you." Juan resisted the urge to apologize, wasn't even sure why it was there. It just was.

"I get it," Pulpo said. "I do." He breathed deep, eyes closed. Opened them again. Looked at Juan. "I totally get it. And it's not childish. You're my best friend in the world and you did something incredible for me. You sacrificed your freedom for me, and there's no way to ever repay that, but even if there were, I still went ahead and lied to you while you were busy saving me, and I'm sorry."

Juan nodded, scrunched up his face, hoping he wasn't about to cry.

"I'm gonna say this to explain myself," Pulpo said, "not as

an excuse. But it might make you mad all over again, and that'd be, ah, understandable."

Juan lifted his chin. "Who said I stopped being mad?"

Pulpo managed a slight smile, then got serious again. "The plan was not to tell anyone. Like, at all."

"Did you really think that was gonna work?" Juan demanded.

"I did, actually. Right up until your sister broke into my house and almost got her ass beat by *my* sister and then basically, like . . ." Pulpo looked away, cringing. "I pretty much just, you know, like, *had* to tell her."

"Uh-huh," Juan said, punching him lightly in the chest. "I bet you did."

Pulpo laughed awkwardly. "Point is . . . I wasn't going to lie to her, I mean —"

"You lied to me!" Juan said, getting all bothered again.

"No, I know, I know." Pulpo waved his hands around. "Because I could. I mean, because I had to! Juan, level with me! Do *you* really think you would've been able to keep it a secret? In those cramped quarters? With Officer Grintly breathing down our necks all the time? Quizzing us and bugging us and making small talk and shit? Really?"

"I mean . . . probably," Juan said, shrugging. "Wouldn'ta been easy, but yeah."

Pulpo sighed. "For me. For *me*, I'm saying now, because okay, that's not even fair, to put it on you and your big mouth —"

"Hey!"

"It is, though."

"You're not helping your case here, man."

"For *me*, I'm saying — for me to maintain the whole thing,

I had to believe it. It had to be true. Like for real true, not pre-tend true. If I'da told you, it woulda been a secret, a lie. Keeping it from you made it feel like I was really going over to the other side. That's why it worked."

For a few seconds, they just stood there looking at each other. Anthony's face was lit by the stark winter day. Behind him, the house was warm and cozy, and upstairs, all their friends were plotting how to take out some ancient evil that was tied into Juan's bloodline. And there were instruments upstairs, and now Pulpo was in on this whole magical world, even if he was on the wrong team. He got it. It didn't have to be a secret between them anymore. It hadn't ever weighed that heavily on Juan, mostly because he'd never bothered getting that involved before. But now he was going to, and he would have his best friend there to talk about it with when he did.

"I get it," he said, and it felt like the fist that had been squeezing his heart finally released. "I get it."

Pulpo let out the longest breath of all time. "Maaan . . ."

"You didn't have to act like I can't keep a secret from the stinking Iron House, though, damn."

"I mean . . ."

"Shut it. I'm trying to forgive you."

"Right, right. Okay, go 'head."

Juan nodded a couple times, considering. "I forgive you."

"Hey!" Pulpo smized.

"Don't do that, man, that's corny."

"Wow, Juan."

"But hold up: Carms beat Sierra's ass?" They headed inside. "I need details!"

THIRTY-SIX

Sierra stared down her crew.

Nydia Ochoa, Columbia University librarian, historian of the supernatural, a personal hero of Sierra's. Already a force of nature, now even more unstoppable. Plus, she'd somehow found her match in Uncle Neville, which was . . . a whole other story, really. She stood with her back to the wall, hands in her pockets. Ready.

Beside her, Bennie sat on the arm of the couch. Sierra's best friend in the whole world and something seemingly brand-new: a techshaper. She could use spirits to pick a lock, hardwire a car, reprogram a computer. Pretty much anything.

Her hand rested on Juan's shoulder. Juan who had suffered through a month and a half of Rikers for Anthony. Juan who had been there all along, who had decided to finally step up and enter the fray.

And Anthony sat on the couch next to him, quiet, calm, (beautiful), the Knight of Iron. Sierra quieted a swoon threatening to toss her focus out the window.

Big Jerome sat in the middle of the couch. He'd gone from being a total shadowshaping disaster to one of the best light workers in the squad, and Sierra had no idea how, she was just happy to see him thriving.

Izzy was next to him with her head resting on his shoulder. Sierra had no idea what this new Hierophant status would mean for her or what would happen whenever Tee managed to wake up. It scared her a little to think about, she had to admit, but they would just have to wait and see.

Robbie sat on the other arm of the couch, long and beautiful as always, with his locks all pulled back into a ponytail and his tats sprawled magnificently along his arms. Sierra had learned to get used to his strange quiet spells. He'd had a point on the phone the night before: Things didn't have to be awkward between them. But it didn't help that he himself was often a walking awkward moment. Still, he was one of the best shadowshapers out there. And he'd made the effort to be her friend even after everything they'd been through.

And finally, Caleb. The Sorcerer of Shadow and Light, looking surly as ever in the far corner, arms crossed, brow creased. He usually wasn't quite as pissed as he looked, but these days everything was so jacked up and out of control, Sierra had no idea. She needed to check in with him.

Septima hovered away from everyone else, over by Lázaro's old bed, where Tee and Mort still lay unconscious. It was probably for the best that Septima knew enough to keep her distance; Sierra wasn't interested in any more infighting or bullshit.

"Alright, listen," she said, quieting the anxious murmur of conversation. "We don't know when Tee will wake up. We don't know where Mina is, and we don't know what's coming at us or how. We have to work with what we do know and what we can find out. And" — she looked at her brother — "what we can change."

Juan perked up. "Huh?"

"The night you guys got locked up, a new house was born from the ashes of two old ones," Sierra said.

"Right. The House of Shadow and Light," Juan said. "I heard!"

"Juan Santiago, you're a shadowshaper. One of the originals of our generation, in fact."

Juan blinked a few times and gulped. "Uh, yeah. Heh."

"And now it's time for you to join us in this new house. Step forward." She managed to say it all without making it a joke, without acting like she thought it was corny — she just spat it out straight. Everyone else took her cue and stayed solemn. Juan stood up, adjusted his jeans, stepped forward.

"Sorcerer," she said. "Where ya at?"

Caleb walked up, nodded at her, stood in front of Juan, and placed one hand on Juan's head.

"I thought we'd be bringing Tee and Anthony into the fold today," Sierra said. "But for obvious reasons that's not happening. So it's you, mi hermano. Everyone, gather 'round."

Robbie, Nydia, Anthony, Bennie, Jerome, Izzy, and even Septima all crowded into a semicircle around Juan, who knelt and bowed, his eyes closed, a small smile on his face.

"Do you," Caleb began, "Juan —"

"José," Sierra said. "Accent on the *e*."

"Do you, Juan José Santiago, enter wholly, body and mind and spirit, into this union as a member of the House of Shadow and Light?"

Juan nodded. "I do."

"And do you swear to protect your fellow . . . housemates, as if we were blood?"

"I do."

"And do you join with us in the balance of shadow and light, and accept the powers of these two forces within you?"

"I do, I do."

"Fellow Shadow and Lighters," Caleb said. "Put your hands on his head."

Bennie, Jerome, and Sierra placed their left hands on Juan's crown along with Caleb's.

Juancito. The air grew thick and several shadowy figures appeared around them: Vincent, Alice, Tolula. A few others. Sierra acknowledged them with a small nod. They each placed hands on Juan. "And so it begins," Caleb whispered.

"Whoa!" Juan yelped. "I feel it! It's like a . . . wow!"

"Very nice," Caleb said, grinning for real. "You may step back, everyone. And, Juan, you may —"

"One sec," Sierra said as the others stepped away. "Stay down a beat. Thank you, Caleb."

He nodded and stepped back.

Sierra pulled the Deck out of her pocket, took out the top card: the Hound of Shadow and Light. "Lemme see something, Juancito."

"The ancestors get to call me that," Juan grumbled. "Not my younger sister."

"Uh-huh. I'm gonna check a card on you. You cool with that?"

"Bring it."

She placed the Hound card on his head, and he jumped backward. "Whoa, whoa, whoa!"

"Ladies and gentlemen," Sierra said with a wiggle of her eyebrows. "The Hound of Shadow and Light."

"Arooooooo!!" Juan howled, and it sounded a little too convincing.

"Damn, man." Sierra laughed. "And congrats!" Everyone closed in around him with hugs and back pats and shoulder punches.

"What, ah . . . what does that mean?" Juan asked.

Sierra shook her head. "Man. We about to find out, I guess. I need you to track down Mina ASAP. I'm not sure how it all works. I mean, I guess I got the power in me somewhere, but I've never used it and . . . ask Cojo?"

Juan guffawed. "I'll figure it out."

"Ah . . ." Izzy said, looking around, brow furrowed.

"What is it?" Sierra said. "What's going on?"

"That's what I'm trying to figure out. I . . . okay, I'll say this about being a Hierophant: I don't fully understand the powers yet, but I can feel . . . it's like we're more deeply connected to that web I told you about that bridges all the elements of the Deck."

Tee sat up straight in the bed, startling the shit out of everybody. Her voice sounded far away, off somehow. "Something's happening."

"Tee!" everyone said at once.

Izzy reached her first, but only because she shoved people out of the way. "Babe! Babe! How you feel? You okay?"

Tee scowled, rubbed her face, then nodded. "Yeah, but . . . I feel . . . something . . ."

"What is it, babe? I feel it too, but what is it?"

"I don't know . . . change? Something's shifting."

"What you want us to do, Sierra?" Jerome asked.

"We gotta find Mina and make moves," Sierra said. "Juan, that's you. Take Bennie. And please don't howl while you're out there tracking her, thanks." Juan looked jubilant and then crestfallen, but he nodded, saluted, and got himself ready to go.

Bennie shot Sierra a sweet smile, batting her eyelashes. "I'll see that he doesn't."

"Good," she said as Vincent stepped out of the shadows beside his sister and pulled back his hood. "What's up, Vincent?"

The spirits who've been trailing the Bloodhaüsers reported in just now.

"And?"

And they say the Bloodhaüsers are on the move.

"What? All of them? Where to?"

They don't know yet. But they've gathered at a parking lot in Paramus and are caravanning into the city right now.

Sierra squinted, as if whatever was going on would resolve itself as the rest of the world blurred. No such luck. "Stay on 'em?" she asked. "And keep me updated."

Vincent nodded, then turned to Bennie, who stood beside him. They passed a quick stare back and forth, then each held up a hand palm out to meet the other's. For a moment, their hands merged — Vincent's shining bluish one over Bennie's brown solid one. Then they both nodded and headed off.

"Stay safe," Sierra called. "Alright." She glanced around. Nydia, Robbie, Jerome, Caleb, and Anthony looked back at her expectantly. Izzy tended to Tee, who still looked dazed. "What are the Bloodhaüsers doing? Are they going to war? They know they're being watched, so whatever it is, they're betting everything on it. Are they —" The jangle of an old salsa song cut her off. Anthony boggled and took out his phone. He held up the screen so Sierra could see.

Officer Grintly.

"Everyone, shut up," Sierra whispered.

Anthony put the phone to his ear. "Hello?"

"Anthony? Where are you, kid?" said the voice at the other end.

"Uh, Brooklyn. What do you need?"

"There's a lot going on, son. You sure popped up at quite a time in our history. Iron House needs your help. All hands on deck. I'm gonna text you an address. I'll explain when you get here." He hung up.

A moment passed, in which everyone looked back and forth at each other. Then the rustle of people standing, grabbing their coats and bags, took over. "Nydia, take Caleb and Robbie," Sierra called over the din. "Anthony will text you the address he gets. Post up nearby and see if Neville and some of those taxi hoodlums y'all hung with last night can back you up. Who knows where this'll go."

"Taxi hoodlums," Robbie said, punching Anthony lightly on the shoulder. "New band name."

Anthony laughed, and Sierra allowed herself a tiny sigh of relief.

Nydia snapped a salute. "Aye aye, captain."

Sierra rolled her eyes. "I wish y'all would stop doing that."

"Yo, make sure Tony Stark goes out the back door," Izzy called from the bed.

"Who's Tony Stark?" Anthony asked.

"You are," Sierra said, covering her face and shaking her

head. "Iron Man. Welcome to the House of Shadow and Light and our corny-ass sense of humor."

Anthony gawked. "Whoa, that was a good one, Iz!" He threw up his hands. "And I know! I'm undercover. I was never here. I don't know any of y'all. I'm out!"

"And his name is Anthony!" Izzy insisted. "How was I supposed to pass that one up?"

Everyone started moving at once, pulling on jackets, talking briskly about what might be happening. Only Anthony and Sierra stood perfectly still.

"Be careful," she mouthed at him across the room.

He smiled, mouthed, "You too," and walked out the door.

THIRTY-SEVEN

Everything felt so different and somehow the same.

But nothing would ever be the same.

Every swirl of dust seemed so distinct as it spiraled through the stale air of Lázaro's old apartment. Tee could feel the gentle vibrations of people walking down the street four floors below, the tremble of a car passing, the shiver of leaves on the tree outside.

She blinked, tried to focus on what was right in front of her.

"Baby," Izzy said, concern in her eyes. Concern and love. Her hand reached out, found Tee's face, wiped a trickle of water away. "Babygirl."

Why was she crying?

She didn't know. Everything was simply so much. What had even happened? she asked Izzy.

Izzy shook her head, rolled her eyes. She was still Izzy. She glowed with a new kind of ferocity, some secret inner light charged her, but it was one Tee felt too. Felt but couldn't describe or make sense of. Not yet anyway. It was just there. And it was the same as whatever illuminated Izzy.

"So much," Izzy said, eyebrows raised. "So, so much."

"Wikipedia version?"

Izzy scoffed.

The room had cleared out pretty quickly after Tee woke up. Things had been really blurry and weird, like she was watching everything from inside a musty jar. She'd felt a sharp twinge pulse through her and it had shoved her unceremoniously awake and into a room full of her closest friends. All she knew was that something important was happening, something she was deeply connected to — so much so that she could feel it all through her body, that change. But there were no words for it, no explanations. Everyone had leapt into action, and now she and Izzy were the only ones left, except Sierra, who was staring at a huge sheet of paper covered in drawings, and the old spirit lady Septima, who hovered in the corner muttering to herself.

"What's the last thing you remember?" Izzy asked.

Tee moved her mouth from one side of her face to the other. "Hmm . . ." The night before crept back to her consciousness in sudden, strange spurts, like a preview for a movie she'd already seen. Scooping up Izzy from outside the detention center. The SUV crushing that man's head. The garage. Mort. The diner. The showdown at the drowning warehouse. And then . . . Izzy's eyes went wide as she patted her shoulder where the metal rod had entered her body. She flinched; still tender. "I got stabbed," she said.

Izzy nodded, face creased with worry.

"It was that emo nazi prick, Dake. I think. I didn't see him do it, but . . ."

"What else?"

"We were in the Crown Vic with Ms. R and Mort and . . ."

Mort had done something. Something huge. She sat up very straight. "What did he . . ." Someone was lying beside her in the bed. Tee gaped at Mort's unconscious body. "Izzy. What the hell happened?"

Izzy chuckled. "I was pretty out of it too, honestly, but not quite as much as you — pretty sure they brought us back to that garage where Ms. R has her crew. There was a doctor of some kind there, a Haitian woman. She checked you out and I remember her shaking her head a lot, but not out of worry — more like fascination. She checked me out too, but I was just . . . I could hardly talk. I was just barely there. Like I was hanging on by a thread to this reality."

Tee nodded. She knew exactly what Izzy meant.

A toilet flushed in a part of the apartment Tee couldn't see, then came the shushing of a faucet. Then a door opened and Jerome walked out. He smiled at her. "How you feeling, Tee-Cake?"

"A hundred bucks short of empty," Tee said.

Sierra got up from her musing and stood beside Jerome at the foot of the bed. "Hey, Tee. You want hugs or you want space?"

Tee hadn't realized she didn't want anyone but Izzy touching her until Sierra asked, and she was immediately grateful and felt a little guilty. She put her hand on Izzy's knee to make sure she didn't go anywhere, even though she knew she didn't have to. "Space, please." She looked down, then met Sierra's eye. Could tell from the way Sierra's own eyes widened a little, that same glint of fire that burned in Izzy's could be seen in hers too. "Thanks," she said. "For asking." She wanted to swear things would go back to normal soon, that everything would just be cool again, but it would've felt like a lie. And anyway, she wasn't sure that was what she wanted. She didn't know what she wanted.

"Cool," Sierra said, offering a gentle smile to let Tee know she understood. "We gonna hit the bodega and stoop sit for a minute to get our thoughts together anyway."

Jerome waved awkwardly, and they walked out. Septima had hovered off to another part of the apartment. It was just Tee and Izzy, and Tee felt like she'd been waiting for this moment her whole life, like she couldn't quite breathe right until it came. And here it was. They turned to each other, smiled, and closed their eyes.

THIRTY-EIGHT

"How is this supposed to work?" Juan asked, once they'd walked a couple blocks through Bed-Stuy, just turning random corners like Bennie had suggested.

She shrugged and looked up at the sky. "I mean . . . I was kinda hoping it would just click in by now and you'd run off barking and howling and stuff."

"Sierra said no howling! Do I get to howl?"

"Don't you dare!" Bennie snapped, in a playful way that made Juan want to kiss her. Focus! He had to focus! But how was he supposed to focus when Bennie was right there, being extra cute and kissable. And they hadn't even really kissed yet — not more than a kind of quick one in passing, and they hadn't admitted what they felt for each other, even though it was right there and obvious in plain sight, just waiting to be named and cultivated and to grow.

It was right there, wasn't it? Juan paused, suddenly overthinking everything. What if it wasn't, and she was just being really nice because he'd gotten out of Rikers and she'd said she'd had feelings for him before but didn't anymore but didn't know how to tell him and —

"Juan!" Bennie yelled into his face.

"Ah! What?"

She jumped up and down in front of him, her breath coming out in steamy puffs. "You're trying too hard!"

He gulped. "I am?" Shit. She really was just being nice to him.

"Yeah, man. You gotta just let it flow. You're the Hound of Shadow and Light, playa. It's inherent to you. It's not just that you got this — you *are* this. This is who you are, man. I know it's new, but this you."

"That was . . ." He blinked a few times. She *wasn't* just being nice to him.

She put her chin to her chest and looked up, making her voice all deep. "Yessss?"

"That was the best pep talk I've ever heard in my life."

"Bam! Bam!" Bennie punched the air twice, then spread her arms wide. "Wuuuut!"

"Seriously, you should be a motivational speaker for, like, weirdo supernatural people like us."

Bennie tipped her head thoughtfully. "Hmm, that's a, um, small target group, probably, from a marketing perspective, Juan, but okay, cool."

Sierra had made a terrible mistake pairing them up. That much was clear. Total newbie mistake, from a leadership perspective. She knew exactly all the seriousness between them, so she had no excuse! Bennie was just standing there blinking at him with her winter hat pulled back around her cute ears and her sparkly lip gloss and little blue swirls of eyeliner, and Juan was about to just politely, in a very gentlemanly way, take one step forward so they were close enough together to see the pores of each other's skin and then say something sweet and breathy and then —

"AH!" A fierce kind of awareness ripped through him, like the flickering awake of a new consciousness.

"What's wrong?" Bennie asked, her adorable face fraught with concern.

A brand-new knowledge. That's what it was. No, better: a new way of knowing. Juan knew where to go. Not just that — it was like there was an imaginary thread at some distant point and it was yanking him toward it. He *had* to get there. And anyway, he didn't want the trail to go cold. "Haha!" He blinked, glanced around. "Ahahaha!"

"What's so funny?" Bennie demanded. "Let a girl in on the secret."

"I think it's . . . I feel it." He looked around again, let the urgent pull bristle for a few more seconds, relishing what he knew was about to happen. Then he grinned even wider and took off down Gates Avenue at a run. "I feel it!"

"Wait up!" Bennie yelled, jogging after him. "Her ass better not be in Staten Island!"

THIRTY-NINE

"I'm starting a new house," Jerome announced as they sat on the stoop slurping icies and watching the random comings and goings on Sierra's block. "Just thought I should let you know."

"Oh God," Sierra groaned. "Here we go."

"It's only gonna be for married women."

Sierra shook her head. "And you're gonna call it House Wife. Brilliant."

"Sierra! Ugh! Why would you steal my glory like that?"

"Heh, glory. That's cute." She sucked the last bit of extra-saccharine, half-frozen blue gunk out of the plastic sleeve and then popped open the lid of her coffee.

"What about a house of only buckets?"

"You mean like the people can make buckets do whatever they want? Because, like . . . why."

"No, I mean a house where all the members are buckets. Only buckets."

"I need you to stop talking, Jerome. Just . . . take a time-out."

"I'm just saying. We could always have one that cooks flat sugary breakfast treats and has to have members from many different countries."

Sierra put her head in her arms.

"Hey, isn't that the kid who dropped out of our middle school in like the first week?"

She glanced up the block, already bracing herself, and sure enough, here came Little Ricky Tate, sauntering along like it was a lovely spring day.

"Hey, hey, y'all!" Ricky called once he got a few steps closer.

"Oh boy." Sierra sighed. Ricky had catcalled her over the summer, then been a dick when she'd told him to fall back. Then he'd apologized in October — the night of Lázaro's wake, in fact — but something had been extra weird and needy about the way he did it — something Sierra couldn't quite put her finger on at the time; she'd been so caught up with attacks from the Sorrows and the drama of going from Robbie to Anthony. And now she couldn't remember what it was he'd said that set her slightly on edge.

"What you guys up to?" Ricky asked.

Jerome shrugged. "Nothin'."

Ricky didn't even look at him, all eyes on Sierra. "Hey, do you think, do you mind if . . . maybe I could join you guys?"

"What's going on, Ricky?" Sierra asked, because something obviously was, and she was in no mood and had no time to bullshit around until he decided to tell her what it was.

"No, I just, you know," Ricky stammered, looking every which way but at who he was talking to.

"I don't know," Sierra said.

"I just wanted to ask, you know . . . and like . . . feel me?"

"We don't feel you, kid," Jerome said with some added bass in his voice. "Spit it out."

"I just want to, I want to, you know, I want to do what you guys do!"

That was it. That was what he'd said. *I want to be part of what you're part of, Sierra*. She had worried he'd somehow found out she was a shadowshaper, that he was trying to get in with her crew while they were fending off attacks from all sides. That he was somehow connected to those attacks. She'd dreaded the whole thing and walked away quickly enough to not give him a chance to respond, which kept her wondering. But mostly she figured it was probably his awkward way of trying to be sweet. He had just asked her out, after all. And then everything had gone to hell and she had barely thought about it at all.

But now he was back and still trying to be part of what she was part of, and she liked it even less now.

"Come here," Sierra said, beckoning with her chin.

"Huh?"

"Come here, I said." Sierra was leaning her back against the step, her arms using it as a rest on either side, her legs crossed in front of her. She looked perfectly relaxed, unimpressed.

"Um . . . Are you gonna —"

"Ricky, either come here or buzz off, man. We got stuff we dealing with today."

He bobbled his head a few times, weighing the situation, then stepped forward and leaned in, his head within reach of Sierra's grasp. "Hold him," she said, and in a flash, Big Jerome was up and behind Ricky, scooping him up under his flailing arms in some kind of overcomplicated double-suplex-type move and holding him fast.

"Hey!" Ricky yelled. "Get offa me!"

Sierra got up in his face. "Hush!" She put a hand to his forehead, closed her eyes. Dove.

It didn't take long. Where Shadow and Light powers showed up as bright or dark splotches amidst someone's inner soulworks — pretty much as one might imagine — Iron Housers just appeared like a hardened sheen over everything, a kind of spiritual calcification. Sierra had first noticed it when she'd peeked in on Anthony the night before in his bedroom.

Ricky was the House of Iron's spy. And he had been since at least last month, when they'd sent him to infiltrate Shadowhouse. He'd done a piss-poor job of it.

Sierrra shook her head. "This is just sad."

"They said, they said . . ."

"They said what? You know what? Never mind. I'm so unimpressed it's giving me a headache. You can put him down."

"You're not gonna do the *whoosh, whoosh* thing and delete his powers?" Jerome asked.

Sierra shrugged. "Why? So they can find another spy to come bother us? At least this way they're stuck with an incompetent one."

Jerome considered, then put Ricky down. "Good point."

"I'm right here, you know. I can hear you."

"Okay," Sierra said. "Run along, Ricky. You with a bad crowd right now, and you're gonna get hurt."

He shook his head, turned, ran off.

"That life advice was more than he deserved, if we're being honest," Jerome said. "But good call on not taking his powers."

Sierra stood, scowled. "And to think he tried to date me."

Jerome shook his head and they headed inside together.

"Um," Jerome said as he walked into the fourth-floor apartment. "Guys?"

Sierra came in behind him and ran to the bed. "What's happening?"

Tee and Izzy sat across from each other, their legs crossed in front of them, their hands barely touching. Their eyes were open, but it was clear they weren't seeing anything at all. They were barely breathing.

¿El trance de las Hierofantas, hm? Septima's scraggly voice whispered from behind Sierra and Jerome.

"Did you do something to them?" Sierra demanded.

¡Ay qué ridiculez! Absolutely not, Lucera. I merely am reporting to you what is happening, since you asked.

"The trance of the Hierophants? What is that?"

Very self-explanatory, no? It is what it sounds like.

Sierra pushed away the bristle of irritation with her great-great-aunt and leaned closer to her friends. Their breaths were shallow but steady. "They're going to be okay?"

Sí, Septima said. *¿Cómo no?*

"What are they doing, though?" Jerome asked. "What's happening?"

No se sabe, Septima declared with a shrug. *Only they know.*

"And I bet we don't know how long it'll last either," Sierra said, plopping down on the bed next to them, exasperated. "This is great."

"So we just . . . leave them alone?" Jerome asked.

Sierra made a face and leaned in close to Tee. "I guess?"

¿Café? Septima asked. *Juan brought me up the cafetera*

before he left, which was very thoughtful of him, you know.

"We got some at the bodega," Sierra said, taking up her position in front of the drawing-covered wall. "Thanks."

Five Hierophants. Sierra's eyes traveled over her own drawings. Fortress. The River. La Contessa Araña — her own great-great-great-grandmother — now properly positioned at the center of the mysterious and deceitful web she herself had created. The Reaper, the only Hierophant who remained a complete unknown factor so far. And Tee and Izzy.

Mort had gone from selling his services to the Sorrows like some supernatural mercenary to giving up all his powers. And giving them to two members of the very house he'd tried to take out the head of when working for the Sorrows. All in the span of a few months! Sierra wished she could ask him about what had happened since she'd beaten him senseless that night in Park Slope, but Mort remained as stubbornly unreachable as Tee and Izzy. He might never wake up, Sierra realized, with a twinge of regret. He'd been a creep, sure, but she had questions. And he'd come around, somewhat at least. And probably saved Tee's life, from what the others had said.

And there was the tangled web of spies and deceit spanning the three active houses. Dake, the Bloodhaüs spy, embedded with Iron House. And — Sierra drew Little Ricky's awkward, bewildered face, eyebrows raised, next to Old Crane's — now they knew who Iron House's spy was.

She sketched Juan next to her own face and wrote *Hound* beneath it. Then stood back. That sequence of lines running from herself to the foul creature at the center of this mess . . . it filled Sierra with equal parts pride and disgust. She was Lucera: bearer of the sacred lineage of powerful spirit workers. Rebel women who had defied those that would hold them back. But those that would hold them back were also part of Sierra's lineage.

She scowled. These were ugly truths she was just going to have to accept moving forward. Grandpa Lázaro was another complicated one — she drew his wrinkled old face beside Mama Carmen's. He'd brought shadowshaping to New York when he emigrated, along with Mama Carmen, and then jacked it up by trying to make it into an all boys' club and excluding Sierra, which damn near got everyone wiped out. He'd been a loving husband and father, by all accounts, and a halfway decent abuelo for about half of Sierra's life. He was so many different things, and Sierra was positive she barely knew a fraction of it.

But what had happened to all these legendary women? Sierra wondered. Even Mama Carmen, the closest Lucera to her, the only one she'd actually met. Of course, she'd had no idea what shadowshaping was when Mama Carmen had been alive, thanks to Lázaro's insistence on patriarchal shenanigans.

And then she'd barely had a full conversation with Mama Carmen when the elder spirit vanished out over the ocean, leaving Sierra with the confusing honor of being the new Lucera, whatever that meant, and a hundred thousand questions.

But Cantara Cebilín? María Cantara? Mama Carmen had mentioned them in passing, and Mami had those few pictures of Cantara Cebilín, but that was it. Who were these other Luceras and what had happened to them? When had they passed on the mantle to the next generation? What were their teachings and fears and loves and hates? What were they like in the quiet moments? On rainy days? What did they smell like? Do for fun?

The most infuriating part was that, besides those snippets from her mom and grandma, the only other info Sierra had on her ancestors was from a woman who had hated them, fought tooth and nail to destroy them and their legacy — Septima. And her versions of the family lore always smelled like American history textbooks: as self-serving as they were false.

But how would María Cantara or her daughter describe their own lives? How would they have told their own stories? The absence of those voices had become a gaping hole in the world Sierra was trying desperately to understand. It was starting to feel like a gaping hole within Sierra too. She was Lucera, and they had been too. But their teachings, their experiences, all they'd learned and wondered about: Gone. Just gone.

Sierra grabbed the *Almanac* off Lázaro's coffee table and flipped it open. This was where her great-great-grandma's stories should've been. Instead, there were pages and pages of cryptic, Eurocentric creepiness describing Doña Teresa's sick attempt at shoving the world around her into neat little easily manipulated boxes. Sierra resisted the urge to hock a loogie right into the ancient pages as she flipped through them.

Then, very suddenly, she stopped. Something was different. "Ah . . ." she said out loud to no one in particular.

"What's up?" Jerome asked, getting up from the couch, where he'd been playing games on his phone and humming to himself.

"Something . . . happening." There were cards where once there hadn't been. Across the yellowing paper, new images emerged like a slow-spreading stain. But Sierra couldn't make them out, not yet.

"What is that?" Jerome asked, peering over her shoulder.

"I don't know," Sierra said. "A . . . a new house, I guess. Come on." She crossed the room at a bound, shoved the *Almanac* into her shoulder bag, and grabbed her jacket.

"Where we going?"

"To find out what's happening," Sierra said, already out the door. "And stop it."

FORTY

"I guess what I'm trying to say is" — past the Jamaican spot, past the bodega, pull, pull, that unstoppable pull — "I don't know how to do this. I've never even had a boyfriend, let alone, like, you know . . . fallen for my best friend's big brother." *Fallen for. Big.* Past the gas station, now left, *left! LEFT!* And around the corner and all the way to the end of the block, and then right! Right! When you get there, until then, it's past the high-rises, past the row houses.

"And, you know, I'm not even saying . . . I don't totally know how I feel, to be honest, but then again, maybe that's not true. Hold up." *Past* the high-rises! Past the row houses! Pull! "I just . . . I'm afraid? So it's not that I don't know. I do. I do, Juan Santiago. I know how I feel."

Pull. Pull. Pull!

"You do?"

Pull.

"I do, and it feels like the first time I've really known. Sorry, we can keep walking."

Pastthehighrisespasttherowhouses!Pasttheparkedcarsthe smalldogwalkingpark!Pasttheemptybuilding!

"Juan! Slow down, man! I'm coming!"

Corner. Right around the corner. Right around the corner. Right around the corner.

"Hey, I know, I know you're trying to hold the thread. It's cool. And I know this isn't the time to really do all this? But, like — whoa, okay, I guess we're taking a right, cool. But yeah, when will be the time? Ya know? Like, when is shit not going to be exploding or flooding or attacking all around us? That's what it feels like . . . like, ever since this summer, practically, even though it really hasn't been *that* bad. But still."

Up, up, up the hill, past the bodega, past the coffee shop, past the dollar store toward the parkway, toward the parkway, pull!

"Still, I just want to say, in this moment, when we're alone. Or kinda alone? Out in the middle of Brooklyn but still, more alone than when we're with the crew, you know? I think what you did was amazing, and if I hadn't already fallen for you before, which, honestly, I totally had, well, I would've fallen for you then, for that, because that . . . I mean, who does that?"

Up the hill up the hill up the hill past the fire station past the library past the bodega up the hill toward the parkway pull!

"Thank you," Juan panted, and it felt insufficient. Like Bennie had just made a huge sandcastle, and Juan had turned one of those buckets upside down and made a little lump next to it.

"You're welcome," Bennie said, all the thrill washed out of her voice now.

Pull! Up the hill across the parkway veer to the right.

He'd blown it. *Thank you* was not what you say when

269

someone tells you they fell for you. Especially not this some-one. No. That was not right. Pull! Up the hill, across the parkway. "Wait!" Juan called at Bennie's back.

She stopped.

"Wait, wait. Let me . . . hold on."

Up the hill up the hill past the —

"Wait!" Juan yelled, and Bennie stepped back, startled.

"That wasn't for you. I'm still trying to . . . manage."

"No." Bennie made a show of looking sweet, not mad. "It's fine. I know you're in the middle of a lot."

Up the hill, across the parkway.

"But like you said: When are we ever supposed to, you know, stop? When do we ever get to be alone? I just . . . I just got out yesterday."

Pull! Up the hill, across the parkway.

"Right." Bennie shook her head, put a mittened hand on his face. "It's too quick. I'm moving too quick. I'm overwhelming you. I'm sorry."

"No!" *Too loud, Juan, too loud.* "Sorry, I mean: no. You're not overwhelming, B. You're, like, the only thing not over-whelming me."

Pull. Up the hill. Pull.

"This annoying Hound situation is definitely annoying me! Anthony lying to me but not my sister was annoying me. Waking up sure that I'm back in prison is overwhelming me. The whole world trying to destroy us yet again is over-whelming me."

Pull. Up the hill. Pull.

"But you, Bennaldra Matilda Jackson." Slow. Slow. Slow.

"You are the reason that even with all that, I am *not* overwhelmed."

Pull.

"Just deeply annoyed!"

"Juan?"

"Sorry. Let me try again." Deep breath. The pull fell back, vanished completely, and Juan looked at Bennie and knew peace. "Bennaldra. I know that it seems corny or superficial, but when I saw you all decked out for the parade, it felt like I was suddenly waking up, like someone had wiped the crap out of my eyes and for the first time ever I could see. It felt like music, the way music feels when a song takes me over and there's no wrong answer, only chords and notes and rhythm. In fact, the music did take me over, and you are a song to me, and that's the song we played that night at the Red Edge, it was for you, Bennie, all for you and no one else, and you're the only song I know, really, the best song I know, and you're nerdy and brilliant and beautiful, and you know the ins and outs of me and see me for all the things I am and I —"

Pull.

"And I want you, I choose you, I am with you, through and through, whatever happens next."

Bennie blinked, mouth hanging slightly open. Juan stepped in closer, so their frosty noses were right up against each other. "Can I?" he whispered, all smooth like.

She blinked and, instead of answering, closed the last little dots of space left between them and put her lips against his, and Juan felt her puffy jacket against his, and he pulled her closer and tilted her to get that angle just right, and then they stopped kissing but just stayed that way, face-to-face, close as could be, and smiled into each other's smiles.

"Thank you," Bennie said in a rough approximation of Juan's voice.

Juan laughed, squeezed her closer. "Look! You know what I got going on, okay! I'm sorry!"

"Best response ever, honestly."

"Uh-huh, almost as good as *It's fine*."

"Well . . ."

Pull. Pull. Pull. Pull.

Juan shook his head. "Oh boy . . ."

"Starting up again?"

"Mm."

Up the hill, across the parkway, pull!

"It's okay. We gotta make moves. I know."

Juan nodded. Didn't let go.

Up the hill. Across the parkway.

He closed his eyes. Kissed Bennie once more. Wondered why he hadn't been kissing Bennie his whole life, how had she been there all along, how had he not seen . . . but then, he hadn't been ready for her before. Hell, he was barely ready for her now. And maybe not seeing her in all her glory was his own quieter, wiser, subconscious self quietly protecting him from jacking up something really, really good. And the past two years of being on tour, hooking up with random, usually white, girls that he barely knew and couldn't care less about, well . . . he hadn't been ready for Bennie.

And now . . . he either was or he'd make himself be, whatever it took.

"Juan?"

"Let's go."

Up the hill they went, past a bodega, past a dollar store, past a bakery, across Eastern Parkway, and back down a hill, and all the while that pull, that taut, insistent yank that let him know which way, and Bennie tapping away on her phone, updating Sierra probably, and then they rounded a corner and stopped short.

"Oh God," Juan said, feeling all the grace and glory of the past few moments shatter and get whisked away in the chilly December breeze.

"Wasn't Izzy just —"

"Yeah."

Across a small park and another street, the detention center loomed.

FORTY-ONE

Slowly, molecule by molecule, their bodies fell away.

The point where the skin of their thumbs grazed up against each other became a touchstone, a homing beacon, the light they knew would lead them back to the physical.

Heh — the physical. Already, the notion of a body seemed so five minutes ago; that lumbering sheath: useless, a prison. Why inhabit flesh when the air itself beckoned, offered unlimited views, possibilities? Why stumble through the world inhibited by skin, confined by bone, when infinity awaited?

The answer was simple.

They dispersed — shed those bodies like old suits — released damn near everything except themselves and, though the difference was increasingly irrelevant, each other.

And then, after a beat and a breath, they rose.

They rose, and below them their bodies sat face-to-face on the bed, thumbs touching, and awaited their return. They rose, and below the room widened and revealed what could not be seen from the floor level: the coffee table, *Almanac* open on top of it, the Sorrow, her golden hue lighting the far corner she cowered in, the boxes of Lázaro's stuff, still waiting to be sorted through. Then came the prickly tingle of plaster, piping, that fuzzy thrill as darkness momentarily overtook them and then suddenly the sky opened up and the whole city with it.

Freedom.

The air was freedom. Unstoppable, irretractable, utterly chaotic, and endlessly spacious freedom. Freedom taken, not granted, uninhibited.

This was Mort's strange gift. The Hierophant powers flowed through each new inheritor in some ever-evolving type of lineage that was barely fathomable; the emptiness within Mort — which had allowed him to take in and remodulate other powers as his own — adapted into something else entirely with Tee and Izzy: air.

Air and the power to become it, to join it.

Air and all that entailed.

And all around: Brooklyn's rooftop kingdoms shimmered and rose and fell and dipped, turned, dove; here a glass tower, there a project, brownstones, firehouses, a school yard, hospital, more row houses, the whole world, all the way to the bay.

A simple spin revealed it all, but there was somewhere they had to be.

An urgent turning point approached. The whole web trembled with it, each line and filament crackled and sizzled the song of all that came.

But it was a broken song, unfinished. No one really knew what would happen next.

The city reeled beneath them, swept along like an ancient highway beneath soaring wings. The city, then the sliver of water that divided one from another, and then down and down and down as the buildings swam up larger and larger and each turning car and cyclist, each sign and pavement and post and layer of concrete and window and light.

There.

The web knew where, the spirits did too. They'd all gathered outside the tall walls of a dusty lot covered in crumpled old cars.

A clamp must've been instated; no spirits in, no spirits out.

But that was for simple ghosts.

Yes, there was a clamp in place, they felt it burn and bristle against them as they breached; it was no match for simple air. And then they were within, and down, down, down amidst the wreckages and stains, the slow-growing rust and rising filth and bright sun glinting off shattered windshields and rearviews.

Swoop.

There behind a tower of cars, the shadowshapers cowered for cover: Nydia, Robbie, Caleb. Across from them, the tall, well-dressed figure of Uncle Neville peered around the corner, gun in one hand, signaling his taxi gangster friends to hold back with the other.

Swoop.

Between towers, through the glassless window of a corrugated hatchback, the stale air within, out the other side, and there: streaming in from a far entrance through a rusted-out forest of school bus carcasses — the Bloodhaüs, crouched low for stealth. Their mostly shaved heads, their heavy weapons. Iconography that begged for another time to come hurtling back into view and make them feel powerful again. The same men from that faraway night in upstate New York, a whole lifetime ago, but really just a few months.

A culmination in the works, for there in the center of it all — *swoosh* — there in the dust field surrounded by trash, rust, decay, the King of Iron stood sparkling in the midday sunlight to all those who could see him.

One ghost had been granted entrance then. The shadow-shapers left without their favorite attack, the Iron House unimpeded.

Still — something else was in the works . . . the King of Iron's caw seared the air, echoed over the heinous jingle of his phantom form. The King was displeased. Probably had been since being thrashed the night before.

Swoop.

Undetected, they inhabited the dusty air among the House of Iron's encampment.

There: Fortress, their hulking form standing perfectly still, not even the rise and fall of breath, their humongous body decaying and regenerating endlessly within those thick folds of gear. And beside them, the River, a seven-foot tower of molding filth and hair and dinge and swamp.

The two corporeal Hierophants stood perfectly still, silent as stone, as the King of Iron raged.

And what did you fools think would happen? What was the endgame? What was the plan? You fatuous, nonsensical demons don't think, don't care, don't build!

Discomfort and shiftiness from the men and women of Iron House, who weren't used to dealing with Hierophants, let alone seeing them berated. And who witnessed and barely escaped the disaster at the warehouse.

You do nothing! For ages and ages, you do nothing at all! Adherent to a code you yourselves don't understand or respect. And then one day, when it's convenient or when some other fool Hiero inspires your petty wrath, you just show up and rage and destroy, flood and wreck, and bring your rust and decay and corruption and then lo! Years, decades of work — disintegrated and drowned.

There: Anthony, looking stoic and unmoved, impossible to read, as he should be. Good.

And there: the Sorcerer of Iron, Officer Grintly, beside his king, shifting his weight from one leg to the other, making eye contact with someone across the crowd from him.

There: the young one, Dake, sent by Lucera to spy, but whose own house even now crawled ever closer.

Answer me, fiends! Explain your actions! How can you call yourselves allies to the House of Iron when all you do is bring decay and more decay?

"We don't." The River's mucousy, gargled baritone.

Eh?

And there it was, and in it came; the change the whole trembling web had awaited, finally afoot. The world seemed to hold its breath, watching.

"We don't call ourselves allies to the House of Iron. Our only regret is not finishing what we started."

Oh? That's not the song you were singing just two days hence, eh?

"Something changed," the River droned.

What, then? What changed? I demand answers.

"This," the River said. And then the man beside the King, Grintly, drew something from his jacket, a blade of some kind — it glinted in the sun as he pulled it back and then jammed it straight into the midst of Old Crane's sparkling form.

The King's shrieks hurled outward, tore the sky, shredded through steel and dust in terrible jagged earthquakes.

Betrayed! he howled, rounding on his assassin, his own sorcerer, even as Dake made his way through the crowd of Iron Housers, drew another blade of the same caliber as Grintly's, lunged forward, plunging it through Old Crane's shimmering back. A horrific crowing and the endless dissonance of metal clattering against metal. Crane whirled again, swinging his long scepter in a feeble arc. Dake dodged easily, stepped back, ready to strike again.

Fentrath steel, Crane warbled through rattling gasps. *Only a Hierophant would have access to those blades.* He reared up to his full height, pointing his staff directly at the River and Fortress. Neither moved, neither spoke. Grintly approached from behind, but Crane spun, knocking the blade into the dirt. And then Dake was on him, bringing the steel down directly on the old king's head, once, twice, and a third time as the ghost clattered to the ground with gurgling howls.

For a few moments, no one moved, no one spoke. Then Dake glanced at Grintly as the murmurs of shock and dissent began to rise, and Grintly stepped forward. "For the Iron House to grow, to survive, we must begin anew. A new age has dawned while we slept and clung to the ancient ways. A new enemy has risen, the House of Shadow and Light. They hoard the Deck of Worlds and seek only our destruction, not mutual growth like the Sorrows once did. To meet this new threat, we must forge new alliances, be born anew."

"You murdered the King!" someone yelled. The crowd began to close around them. "Traitor!"

"Calm, Iron House!" Grintly protested. "To advance we

must shed our old skin. I did what I did in the name of survival! To survive we must adapt. We must grow. Today —"

"Traitor!"

"Break him!"

"Today!" Dake's voice, carrying over the din of the crowd. "Today we witness the birth of a new house: the House of Blood and Iron. We rise from the tattered remains of our two broken houses, of betrayal and the onslaught of shadows. Those who we have spoken to, those who will join us, step forward, brothers and sisters. Join us!"

Scattered fights broke out amongst the Iron Housers as some made moves to join Dake and Grintly. And then shouts came from the end of the lot. The Bloodhaüs stepped out of the shadows into the fray. Armed and fierce, they streamed forth and a strange silence fell over the dusty lot.

"Who will oppose us?" Dake crowed. "Who dares?"

A man stepped forward from the Iron House crowd, opened his mouth, and then Dake slashed the blade once across his chest and the man fell, bled out into the dust, twitched and then died, the ghost-killing Fentrath steel brokering no chance for his soul to emerge.

"Who else? Who else?" Drunk on his own power, on the success of his plan, Dake stalked back and forth before the cowering crowd. The Bloodhaüs soldiers silent and smug behind him. "If you will join us, step forward and our Sorcerer of Blood will initiate you into this new army, as the two houses fall around us and a new one arises. You will join the forces of triumph, and we will banish the shadows. Step forward, step forward, my brothers and sisters, and we will rise."

And one by one, they did.

Up, up, up, past the towers of crumpled cars and into the sky. The change had come, and it rippled along the taut cords of power, through each Hierophant, all the way back to the source. The world had tipped sideways once more, and the change touched everyone. It had been on the way, and the Deck had felt its inevitability and responded in kind, girding, strengthening, maneuvering. And now a whole new order would take shape, but how or what remained to be seen.

One thing was clear, though: This carnage-hungry new house had the upper hand and was ready to defend it ruthlessly. The House of Shadow and Light may have held on to the Dominant spot amongst houses, but that was probably only momentary, and possession of the Deck seemed about the only thing keeping it there.

Up, up, up, trembling and nearly undone by the sudden shifts amidst that vast web of power. Up and up, but they couldn't simply disappear and disperse now that all seemed lost. They couldn't abandon everything, everyone. There was too much at stake. As the world seemed to veer toward dissolving, they let themselves hover slowly down.

Below, the House of Shadow and Light crept along the edges of their hiding places, whispering and wondering. They should've run, but it was already too late. The trap had been sprung, all that was left was to see how it would all play out.

"Now!" Dake called as the last few members of the House of Blood and Iron were receiving their powers. This boy. He had been there on that dark night upstate, had helped coordinate the kidnapping and near murder of one of the neighborhood girls. He had looked so much younger then, just a few months ago. He'd been scared. He'd been there in the field the night they broke apart the Bloodhaüs. He'd been plotting and planning all along, and now he would reap unimaginable destruction as soon as he got the chance. If only they knew how to fully control their powers, if only they could kill. It would be a simple thing: air to deprive air. But it wasn't the answer to this. It wouldn't solve the problem of what had just happened, only exacerbate it. "All we need is the Deck of Worlds to complete our supremacy!" A terrible pause. "Good thing" — he stomped from one side of the lot to the other — "we have some unannounced visitors who might know something about that lurking around, don't we?"

FORTY-TWO

"Sierra!" Dake's jubilant voice called out. "Sierra Santiago!"

She cringed in the deepest parts of herself. This . . . this disaster. This trap. She'd walked right into it. She'd let all this happen, and now it was only going to get worse.

"Or should I say . . . Lucera?" Nervous laughter from the pathetic, disgusting men and women who had just trampled their leader to form a new house with a bunch of nazi scum. "Come out, come out, House of Shadow and Light!"

She wouldn't be paraded out there for everyone's enjoyment. She wouldn't let herself be put on display. Better to pull out while they could, before anything else happened.

"You have something I want!" Dake said, a new menace in his voice. "And I'm not planning on letting you keep it."

If Ms. R and her crew laid down some cover fire, they could probably make it out. There were enough barriers to hide behind, and even if they didn't have the spirits helping them, they could use their light and shadow powers and . . . hopefully . . . get away.

Somehow it all seemed impossible. Dake had been one step ahead all along, planning his own coup.

"All we ask is that you be as reasonable as the House of

Light was," Dake called. "No one's trying to destroy you! We just want what's ours. What's fair."

Fair. Sierra had to resist the urge to spit.

"And anyway," he went on, laughter tingeing his voice. "It seems like a reasonable trade."

Trade?

"You have something we want, and we, well —" Sounds of a scuffle and then the sheer clap of a fist meeting flesh. A voice grunted in pain. Anthony's voice. No. "We have something you want."

No. No. No. No.

This was all too much, but there was no time to think, no move to make. Nothing except sheer defeat and the buckling hunger for revenge. How could she have let herself get put into this position?

"You want me to waste him?" Ms. R asked. She'd crept up beside Sierra without a sound, and now Sierra had to suppress the urge to laugh and cry at the same time.

"Yes," she whispered. "But no. It'll turn into a gunfight that we might not win."

"Speak for yourself," Ms. R snorted.

"But either way, if he dies, he'll probably just get more powerful, and the last thing we need is that guy as a ghost."

Ms. R just stared at her for a few seconds, and Sierra realized that she'd been so enmeshed in her own world, she'd completely forgotten there were people out there that didn't parlay with strange magical powers or believe in spirits. Then Ms. R just shrugged and kept her Glock ready. "Suit yourself."

And anyway, it didn't matter, Sierra thought, stepping out from the shadows and pulling down her hood. Whatever happened next, however bad it got, she would make sure Dake paid the price in full.

"Ah," he said. "There you are." He stood in the middle of his brand-new, utterly despicable house. Someone had dragged away the body of the man Sierra had heard Dake slaughter; a trail of blood in the dust led off to some car towers. Beside him, two Bloodhaüsers were roughly helping Anthony pick himself up from the dust. Officer Grintly stood on the other side, his service pistol trained on Anthony's head.

"Make a slick move," Grintly said. "Please. I've been dying to off this kid since I found out he was a traitor."

"Tough talk from a guy who just killed his own king," Sierra said.

"Hey!" Grintly waved the gun around as if she'd forgotten about it and anything she said might cause it to go off.

Sierra managed to keep the shrieking terror she felt buried deep inside. The truth was: These men very well might kill Anthony right in front of her face, even if she did do what they asked. And if that happened, she would probably spend the rest of her life trying to figure out what she could've done differently to save him. She shook her head. "What do you want, Dake?"

"I only ask that you provide us with what we rightfully des —"

"I don't have the Deck. Do you really think I just walk around with it?"

"I didn't think you would, no," Dake sneered. "You weren't smart enough not to get yourself put in this position, but I do believe you were at least smart enough not to bring the Deck with you."

"Well," Sierra said as if that ended it, knowing it didn't, hating every second of Dake having the upper hand, of Anthony's life hanging by a thread.

"Well, indeed," Dake said, and then he nodded at a short, balding Bloodhaüser in a leather jacket standing off to the side. The man tapped some things into his phone.

"Was that guy using his cell phone supposed to convince me of something?" Sierra asked.

"Check your phone," Dake said. "It's probably on silent since you were sneaking around here."

It was damn near always on silent, Sierra thought, pulling it out, but that wasn't the point. The point was staring back at her very clearly as photo after photo showed up in her message box.

Uncle Neville, walking down some random street in the Stuy.

Two kids out trick-or-treating, whom Sierra immediately recognized as Nydia Ochoa's.

Carmela, Anthony's sister, leaving the rec center with a duffel bag over her shoulder.

An older black man and red-haired white woman walking down a street in Crown Heights, arm in arm — they had to be Caleb's mom and dad.

Ma Satie, Tee's grandmother, gazing out from a window.

The Jacksons, Bennie's parents, at church.

Sierra's heart beat faster with every picture. Some faraway part of her knew that that was exactly what Dake had designed this to do, and she steadied her breathing as much as she could, held the phone close to her body to keep her hands from visibly shaking.

Then the final two pictures came through, the ones she'd

known were coming: her father in his uniform, standing at the entrance to Woodhull Hospital where he worked security.

And then an image she'd never imagined she'd see under these circumstances: Gael, wearing his camo pants and a beige T-shirt, napping in his bunk in Tora Bora, muscular arms clasped behind his head, sunglasses on, a *Popular Mechanics* magazine halfway covering his face. No, no, no, no . . . But of course this fiend would have people placed in the military. And now he had them in the prison system too, thanks to his treachery with Grintly. But Gael . . . Gael . . .

"You . . ." She tried, she tried to keep her reaction in check, not to let him see how much he'd gotten to her. A thousand screams threatened to pour out of her. Instead, nothing came.

"Yes, the rules are explicit that we're not to take away heads of houses' powers or actually execute each other. But there is nothing in the rules about friends and family, you will see. You, though — you broke the rules when you took away Axella's powers. So as far as I'm concerned? All bets are off. It's open season. And then you sent your phantoms to tail our people, isn't that right?"

A chorus of angry jeers rose up from the Bloodhaüs.

"Invaded our privacy, kept us in check. Never offered to share the Deck. Even the House of Light, for all their treachery, gave other houses an opportunity to borrow the Deck when they became emergent. Do you people see this?"

More jeering and hoots.

"And now you want things to be fair? Ha. Should've thought of that when you were hunting us down and tormenting us. Now you'll see what fair looks like."

"What's your point, Dake?"

"You already know what my point is, Sierra. You have two days. I'm sure you can only begin to imagine the disgusting dark corners of the Internet that I'm in touch with. I don't have to dirty any of my own people's hands with the blood of your loved ones. All I have to do is post their information in the right place and let the gritty underworld do its thing."

Sierra pushed back another round of shuddering nausea. He would pay, he would pay, he would pay . . . one way or another, somehow . . . that was all she could cling on to.

"Oh, and you can have him back, now that I got your attention." Dake signaled the two men holding Anthony, and they shoved him forward. "But don't forget. Iron House is no more, of course." The guy with the phone raised it, clicked a picture of Anthony as he walked across the dusty lot toward Sierra. "So he's on the list too. Got it? Clear? Any questions?"

Anthony reached her, and they exchanged the slightest of nods before he turned and faced the House of Blood and Iron beside her. She was glad he'd opted against any dramatics. They could have their soppiness later; right now, they were still mid-battle.

Sierra slowed her breathing again. Narrowed her eyes. "You know what the other emergent house is, beside yours, right? The one you just brought one step closer to Dominance by eliminating the Iron House?"

"Hm?"

"Do you? Ah . . . you don't. You don't have the *Almanac*, do you? Well, I'll tell you, before we leave. Consider it a gift, as Old Crane used to say. It's not a house at all. It's the Reaper. All five cards. The Reaper."

There it was. That tiny twitch on his face. That was all she needed. The day, the horrible, horrible day, hadn't been a complete waste after all.

Dake recovered quickly. "All that means is we'll need to join together to face what comes next. So the sooner we get all this unpleasantness behind us and you hand over the Deck, the sooner we can see about fighting this common enemy that's obviously coming to get us. See? I can play well with others."

"Go to hell, Dake."

Sierra and Anthony kept their eyes on Dake as they walked backward toward the stacks of ruined cars where their friends waited.

Once, a long time ago, when we were all very young, and the echoes of this bombardment or that still echoed through the warm Caribbean breeze, a girl walked amidst the deep forest with Death at her side.

Her name was Cantara Cebilín Colibrí (but most people just called her Cebi) and she did what she wanted, just like her mother, María Cantara. And one day, she would take on the title of Lucera, just like her mother.

But until that day, she would wander, and the forest and the warriors and gardeners and healers and storytellers all around her would be her protectors and keep her safe. They would, and so would Death, of course.

No one else could see Death, and that was just fine with Cebi. He would appear beside her as she hacked her way through the forest, a towering figure in a black robe, and he would move silently amongst the trees and flowers, and Cebi would tell him about her day, about her fears and doubts, about the world around her.

There were so many spirits in El Yunque. They gathered around whenever Cebi and Death went off on their adventures. They followed behind in a shimmering parade — some were people once, some animals, some had been other kinds of creatures entirely. They hovered around the campsite, coming to visit on celebration nights, when people would play music or tell stories, and they would inhabit the melodies, bring the winding tales to life, dance around within the small stick-and-mud sculptures and beaded clothes.

María Cantara had taught Cebi how to send the spirits streaming through her body and into whatever she wanted to bring to life, just as Death had taught María Cantara. *This is our legacy*, she said, smiling. *This is our life.*

It was how they fought off the different armies that had threatened their forest sanctuary, how they'd beaten back the forces of La Contessa, Cebi's abuela, who lived in a palace not far away and was constantly trying to destroy their small community.

The spirits had always been Cebi's friends, her protectors along with everyone else, and she welcomed the illuminated shadows whenever they showed up.

Except now.

Today, on this strange, breezy afternoon, as she traipsed along through the forest with Death at her side, a spirit she had never seen before appeared in the clearing ahead. He limped, flinching with each tiny movement, and Cebi could tell that something was wrong with his skin, even from far away. She hesitated, but Death was beside her, and she knew he would never let anything bad happen to her.

Come, the spirit beckoned. *I bring news from the palace.*

As she approached, she could see the man's flesh was raw and exposed, the way her mother's was on half of her face. Except it was like that everywhere: bristling pink and white and bloody. He wore only a torn loincloth, and he trembled with fever, even in death.

A steadying skeletal hand landed on Cebi's shoulder. She looked up at the towering form, then turned her attention back to the spirit.

La Contessa, he wheezed, *she builds a new army, a new . . . system . . . tried to make me a part of it, one of the five . . . I refused. I could never . . . you must warn the others . . . El Tuerco remains loyal . . . he sent me . . . he says you must . . .*

fight . . . The spirit stumbled, coughed. Cebi stepped forward, hands raised to help him, but he flinched away.

I . . . cannot . . . I have done so much wrong in this world . . . I must . . . And without another word, he stumbled into the shadows of the trees.

Cebi glanced up at Death and then hurried back to the campsite to warn her parents.

There, amidst the small houses and bonfires, she found everyone already preparing for battle. All across the campsite, young and old alike squatted in front of each other, painting half skulls over their faces in honor of their leader, María Cantara.

In the middle of it all, a group of gruff mountain men who Cebi had never seen before were arguing with her father, Barancoa. It wasn't the kind of argument that ended in blows, but it wasn't a diplomatic one either. All the men carried machetes; some had rifles too.

You have allied with our enemy, Barancoa said solemnly. *The same armies who slaughtered our people. We cannot fight by their side.*

Do you think we had a choice? their leader demanded. *Our alliance is one made out of necessity. And we need your help. The Americans will rout us and destroy us all. If we defeat them, then we can band together and crush the Spanish and kick them out for good, eh?*

Barancoa had been just a boy when a Spanish noble had whisked him away from one of the few surviving Taíno townships and forced him to serve him hand and foot as he traveled across the island, brokering deals and signing treaties he would soon break. Barancoa had been eleven when their small caravan had stopped at a remote palace in El Yunque so the nobleman could make amends with a wicked and deranged sorceress. He had seen the whole world burst into flames as a young girl became an inferno.

And he had fallen unstoppably in love.

He had also never forgotten what the Spanish had done to his people. *I'm sorry*, he said. *The shadowshapers have vowed never to assist the Spanish, and these are vows that cannot be broken. We are against all empires everywhere. Punto.*

You are against empires, and yet you just want to cower in your mountain hideaway while the rest of us do the hard work of actually fighting against those empires, another man spat, and Cantara Cebilín felt her fists clenching. She hated him for speaking to her father that way, but she hated him even more because some part of her felt that he might have a point. What if the Americans did take over? Would they be any better than the Spanish? There was no way to know, not really, and there were no right answers.

Basta, a voice said, and then María Cantara stepped from the shadows of the camp and all the mountain men froze. There were rumors about this woman with half a face, this powerful spirit worker with her crew of warriors and storytellers, but few had ever seen her. *We sympathize with your struggle*, she said, placing a hand on her husband's shoulder. *And we respect the road you have chosen, even if we cannot share it with you.*

But — their leader began. María Cantara silenced him with a glance.

We can, however, distract and contain La Contessa for you. I have already ordered our forces to prepare for an all-out assault. The Americans, I understand, have been relying on her powers to some extent, and I know there have been reports of . . . *unusual happenings out in the battlefield, hm?*

Yes! a man said from the back of the group. *As we retreated from Coamo, I saw a terrible creature moving through the enemy forces — it walked like a man but taller and hunched over, with long hairy arms and great gnashing teeth.*

¡Ay, boberias! cried another man. *This is useless.*

It's true, said a third. *A man made completely of fire attacked our ranks at Mayagüez! There was no stopping that devil, and we barely made it out alive.*

The leader turned to María Cantara and Barancoa. *Whatever the truth is — we are in retreat and heading for Asomante, where we will dig in and prepare for a final battle.* He looked infinitely sad for a few seconds, like the whole terrible thrust of what was coming flashed before his weary eyes. *Anything you can do to hold off La Contessa's powers will help, I'm sure.*

I understand, María Cantara said. *We will do what we can.* She held Barancoa close as the soldiers turned and walked away through the trees.

Cebi ran up to her parents, told them about the spirit she had met in the woods. The two exchanged a serious glance. *We march at midnight,* María Cantara said.

Many years before you were born, I made a promise to Death, María Cantara told her daughter as she put the finishing touches of skull paint on her face. They had pushed through the forest up a steep mountainside toward the palace, and now waited, making final preparations as the rest of their troops caught up.

Cebi glanced to her left, where she knew Death could be found at any given moment. He floated along beside her as always. *Go on.*

I promised you to him, m'ija. La Contessa sent him to take my life, and I promised you to him instead. It was brash, and I was only a child at the time, even younger than you are today. Still. I should not have so quickly gambled away your life.

Well, you didn't really, did you?

María Cantara smiled in her crooked way, and Cebi felt like there was no way she could love her mother any more. She wanted to be just like her when she got older. Even though the night seemed so terrible, and only danger lay ahead, here she was reminiscing and smiling.

Correct. It's just, when I say it out loud, to your face, m'ija . . . you know. When you were born, Death showed up, as if to collect you. I told him that I had made no promises about when he could take you.

And Death comes for everyone, Cebi finished for her. *Eventually.*

I like to think that Death knew what I was thinking, all those years ago, like it was a little joke we were both in on. But the truth is, I believe there is a greater importance to that promise than even I can fully understand. I tell you all this to say: There will be a day when Death comes for you, and when that day comes, you are to go lovingly, without a fight. But that's only for Death, you understand? Until that day, you fight like hell.

What if . . . what if Death has already come for me? He had, after all, been with her all along, for as far back as she could remember.

Maybe he has, María Cantara said with a wink. *He*

certainly never came back to visit me after that day. But I know he watches over our family, over all of us. We wield his powers, after all. There is a part of him in all we do.

Cebi again peeked over at Death, who glided along silently, empty eyes on the dark forest ahead.

A smash of thunder echoed across the sky, and then the sound of laughter erupted all around them. A woman's voice, shrill and unkind. María Cantara turned quickly, grabbing her daughter by the shoulders and crouching down. A small tear glimmered at the edge of her one good eye. The ruined half of her face shone in the moonlight, tight scar tissue and glints of bone. Cebi loved that her mother never covered up the scar tissue, never acted ashamed or afraid of what others would think.

M'ija, she said in a choked whisper. *It is worse out there than we had thought and . . .* Her voice trailed off.

Maybe Cebi should never have told her what the flayed ghost had said. Then they could've just gone along like they would've, and maybe they wouldn't be where they were, with whatever was about to happen being about to happen.

Mami, she said, barely concealing the sob.

I'm so sorry that there wasn't more time for me to teach you what all this means. I pray that future generations who carry on our legacy always take the time to pass on our teachings. For now, I must leave you with only this parting gift until I see you again.

She placed her hand on her daughter's head. *Close your eyes, my love. And whatever you do, don't follow me. Live a long and beautiful life, m'ija. This is all I ask.*

What? Mami, I don't under —

Close your eyes. There isn't much time.

Cebi did as she was told. Her mom's palm was warm on her forehead. And then light erupted through her, a glorious, overpowering burst of unstoppable illumination that seemed to cleanse away every shadow and doubt.

Ven a los cuatro caminos, a los cuatro caminos ven, her mother sang softly, and Cantara Cebilín smelled fresh soil and garlic cooking not far away, and her whole body burned with the power of her mother's light, which was now her own light, which was the light of the whole world.

Lucera, her mother said. *My parting gift is a name, and a legacy. I love you.* She kissed Cebi's face, and then she turned and walked away, through the clearing and directly toward the portico of the palace up ahead, which was now illuminated with torchlights from a bustling horde.

Mami, Cebi whispered.

Her father broke from the trees and ran up to his wife. She paused; they embraced. More cackling shattered the thick summer night around them.

Stop her, Cebi demanded, grabbing Death by his robes. *They'll kill her.* Death did not move, though.

Alone once more, María Cantara marched right up to the waiting group of figures. An ancient woman in a ball gown stood on the balcony of the palace, watching. La Contessa. She nodded at someone in the crowd below. There was a sudden motion, the crack of a rifle, and María Cantara collapsed. Cantara Cebilín opened her mouth to scream, but nothing came out. A shimmering figure now moved among the torchlit masses. María Cantara's ghost. She marched straight through them and vanished into the palace.

Finally, the shriek erupted out of Cantara Cebilín's throat.

It felt like a snake was trying to free itself from inside her, like the scream would tear her in half, like the whole world had ended as her mother's body hit the earth. Around her, the shadowshaper army advanced through the trees, closing in on the bristling hordes.

The old woman had disappeared from the balcony, but now three figures burned like human torches in the midst of the palace horde. The Sorrows. They surged forward, scattering even their own troops to either side, and blasted head-on into the approaching shadowshapers. An explosion burst from the balcony where La Contessa had been standing, then something shrieked through the sky toward Cebi, and the trees nearby burst into flames.

Artillery fire. A young man in an American military uniform now stood where La Contessa had been. He grinned, surveying the dark forest to see if he could make out the damage his weapons had caused.

The shadowshapers surged forward, cutting to either side of the burning golden light of the Sorrows.

Lucera.

Cantara Cebilín had lost her mom and gained a new name in a matter of moments. New powers came with that name, powers she barely understood. But she knew there was a rage in her heart that wouldn't be calmed, and there was one power she did understand.

Come, she said without even so much as a glance at the towering figure beside her. *Tonight you feast.*

Interesting, Cantara Cebilín thought, walking amongst the shattered bodies at the foot of the ruined palace as the sun rose over the mountains. *Some of these men resisted Death's grasp like champions, while most merely crumbled as she smashed through their lines. What was it that had given certain members of La Contessa's band of mercenaries that extra strength?*

The American on the balcony had been one who resisted. He'd turned out to be crudely fused to his artillery unit somehow, an appalling kind of sorcery. He had died screaming for his parents, his superiors, his silly god, and none had come to save him, and finally, Cebi had 'shaped Death into the very contraption that the American was part of, and the thing had devoured him whole, reducing them both to a charred catastrophe of burnt flesh and collapsed metal.

Lucera, a man's voice said, and Cantara Cebilín turned, felt the sun on her face, the light within her churn. It was not who she had expected. Her shadowshapers still skirted along the edges of the battlefield, hunting for survivors. This was someone different: a tall stranger of indeterminate age with broad shoulders and a white beard. A weird light glinted in his eyes that she couldn't name but somehow recognized.

Who are you? she said, with some growl in her voice. *And why do you know my true name?*

They call me Aguacero, he said, but his lips didn't move. He was speaking as Death did, directly into her mind. *But once I was known as El Tuerco.*

She knew the name. The flayed spirit had said he was sent by him. And her mother had spoken of this man, but more than that, her old grandfather, Santo Colibrí, used to sing songs around the bonfire that told tales of their love for each other, and the spirits would bring the songs to life. He had been one of La Contessa's elite guards, but he'd remained loyal to Santo Colibrí and María Cantara throughout, passing along information about La Contessa's nefarious dealings when he could.

What manner of being are you, Aguacero? Because a natural human does not stand before me.

One edge of his mouth quirked upward. *I am a Hierophant. A creation of La Contessa. I am one of five — well, four really, because she has yet to find who will fill the role of the fifth. The other three have escaped your wrath, along with the Sorrows, and they've taken La Contessa's most powerful work of sorcery yet — a foul implement of manipulation she calls the Deck of Worlds. There is much to discuss.*

And La Contessa?

The old warrior shook his head. *Holed up within. That is all I know. But you won't be able to get her out, I can promise. Her sorceries there are too powerful, even for you, Lucera.*

Cantara Cebilín made a noise in the back of her throat and was about to argue when a yell came from the woods.

¡Puñeta, no puede ser! her abuelo chortled, stepping over bodies gingerly and opening his arms wide as he broke into a run. *¡El Tuerco!* The two men met amidst all that carnage and death, in the stillness of a brand-new day. They embraced, and then their lips found each other, and they fell into a long, passionate kiss. *It's been so long, my love,* Santo Colibrí sang in a melodious whisper.

Cantara Cebilín smiled, her first smile since everything had gone to hell just a few hours ago. She felt Death nearby, his immense and calming presence. She wondered when he would come to collect her for good; the thought made her feel peaceful somehow, like the faraway song of a very beautiful bird.

The surviving shadowshapers began gathering around her as Santo and the Hierophant Aguacero continued their embrace. *What will we do?* they asked, glancing at the palace ruins, the bloodied bodies. *What happens now?*

She looked at her father, whose eyes still gleamed with the sudden loss of his wife. He stared back at her, and he understood, she knew he understood what had happened. *Lucera*, he whispered. She loved him for understanding, for not being someone she had to explain things to.

The enemy has dispersed into the world, she said, addressing, for the first time, her people. *And we must too. All except for a select few, who will stay behind to keep this monster contained in her palace.*

That falls to us, Santo Colibrí said, stepping forward, hand in hand with Aguacero. *And your male lineage going forward. Send them to us, and we will raise them in this tradition, and teach them how to keep this sacred ground safe. We will fight the empire from our seat of power as you fight it out in the world, and together, we will survive, and one day thrive.*

And so it was decided. There were tearful good-byes, and then, as the sun rose into the sky, the shadowshapers left their ancestral home, the land their tradition had risen up within, and made their way toward San Juan, even as news of a treaty with the Americans and the end of one war was announced amidst the birth of another, much, much longer one.

PART FOUR

FORTY-THREE

"Bridge!" Juan yelled, and Culebra revved up as one and then burst forward into the new section they'd been practicing. Juan allowed a slight smile as his fingers danced up and down the fretboard through a frantic progression of harmonies. Sure, some evil young neo-fascist bag of dicks with super-powers was trying to kill all their loved ones, but hey, at least there was music.

"Harder," Juan called, and Kaz doubled down on the drums as Pulpo's bass line fell into a mean trilling rumble. There was music to make sense of this mess, and maybe it couldn't solve anything per se, or wipe out the new house of nazi bros, but it could help Juan broker some kind of peace with his own rage and fear. He stepped on his overdrive effects pedal and added a glimmering ninth note to each chord, crunching into an ever-rawer thrash, and immediately shad-ows flickered into existence at the edges of his vision. He blinked at them without losing hold of this new riff.

Maybe music could solve something.

The shadow spirits strutted along the walls in long rhyth-mic stomps, their tall torsos dipping low as their arms bent and straightened in time to the bass drum.

"Back to the head," Juan called, "but fiercer."

Heh. Telling Culebra to go fiercer was like unleashing a pit bull into a chicken pen. Kaz hammered down an epic *GUNG GUNG GUNG gung gung GUNG*–type riff that sounded like some giant kaiju was about to crush an entire city. Pulpo responded in kind, mirroring the drums and adding in vicious side riffs and slides. Juan nodded, keeping his own chords to just a few trebly long notes so he could get a feel for the new mood. At the edges of the room, the spirits strengthened, their dance grew wilder. Could they make moves in the physical world? That's what 'shaping was, wasn't it? Giving some kind of form to an otherwise ethereal being. Grandpa Lázaro had been a storyshaper, which meant that as he spoke, the spirits would give the stories life in the air around them. He used to regale little Juan with animal tales and sometimes tidbits from his childhood, and Juan would watch in awe as each scene would unfold like a floating 3-D movie.

And Izzy could 'shape with her raps, which was the most badass thing Juan had ever seen.

What if he could music 'shape? It only made sense: The spirits had always shown up when he performed; he'd just never known what to do with them. Or maybe that wasn't the problem. Maybe it was just that he'd never tried.

"Vamp on this," Juan said. Kaz and Anthony fell into a steady holding pattern, flavored with occasional cymbal crashes and bass runs. The spirits found their way to the far side of the wide-open practice area, directly across from Juan. "Just like that." There were four of them. They held the rhythm; their dance had fallen into its own kind of vamp, the way backup singers did that little two-step over and over sometimes as the band heated up around them.

Juan kept hitting long noted jangly chords and letting them ring out for a bar or two until the change, nodding his head in time, watching the shadows gather, move.

It was time to step up. It was time to 'shape. As jacked up as his grandfather had been, Juan still missed Lázaro, missed his sparkling stories and quick smile, even missed his calm ferocity and stern warnings. All he'd wanted was for Juan to carry on the shadowshaping legacy, but Juan had pretty much slacked, and then Sierra had picked it up, and it had turned out to be more her legacy to carry on anyway. But the truth was, it was part of both of them.

He'd been watching his own fingers again, but now he looked up, stared directly at the shadows. It was time. He nodded and hit the chord he'd just switched to with a single fierce downstroke, then raised his right hand over his head.

The spirits broke into a run toward him. The vamp gathered momentum. The first tall, loping shadow leapt forward toward Juan, and then the door of the rehearsal spot flew open, letting a surge of bright winter daylight in, and Izzy stepped out of the cold and waved with a big, goofy grin on her face.

"Whoa!" Kaz and Anthony both yelled, the song grinding to a halt. "The King has come!"

Juan just stood there, panting.

"Why'd you guys stop?" Izzy demanded, taking off her jacket. "That shit was bananas."

The spirits were gone. He had to remind himself that they'd really been there. They'd definitely really been there.

"You okay, Iz?" Kaz asked. "We missed you!"

"Man . . . never go to prison," Izzy said. "It's the devil's dickhole for real. I'd say I wouldn't wish it on my worst enemy, but honestly after yesterday that's not true, so, you know . . ."

"Whoa, what happened yesterday?" Kaz sat back down and fell into an easy kind of blues walkabout on his high hat.

"Long story," Izzy said, shaking her head. "Bottom line is, yeah, I'm okay. It's a lot going on. I'm just glad to be free and out in the world again and ready to rip shit to shreds on the mic. I wasn't just chilling there in lockup, you know, I was writing."

She made the rounds, giving everyone hugs and pounds, and then glanced at Juan.

"Look, y'all: I came by to run some raps with ya, but Sierra just called an emergency meeting. Got the text as I was coming in. Figured everyone's phone would prolly be on silent."

"Oh, damn," Anthony said, pulling out his. "Yep."

"We can walk over together," Izzy said. "Sorry, Kaz."

Kaz shrugged. "It's cool, I'll just get some practice in, since I'm not invited to y'all's little secret clubhouse meeting. Just don't hurt nobody while you plot to take over the world or whatever."

Juan laughed and packed up his gear. "Man . . . no promises."

"Soooo, I almost shadowshaped," Juan said as he, Izzy, and Anthony crunched through the newly fallen snow on Bedford Avenue, hands in pockets, breath rising in steamy gasps through scarves and up into the pale sky.

He'd been trying to say it for like five minutes while Anthony and Izzy rambled back and forth to each other about how trash Dake was. The words had been right there waiting for them, but somehow they wouldn't come out, and he was pretty sure whenever they did, Izzy would guffaw and Anthony would shake his head and Juan would probably crawl back into his little non-shadowshaping pit and disappear.

Instead, Izzy nodded approvingly and said, "Oh, cool, that's whassup."

"Nice," Anthony added.

"It's just, you know." Juan waved his hands in circles in front of him to indicate that he of all people should probably be, like, one of the greatest shadowshapers of them all, considering he'd had access to the ability and an amazing mentor for basically his whole life, yet he'd squandered it completely and ignored the spirits and their obvious overtures to get his attention, and so he was really going to have to deal with the shame of not knowing his own heritage that well, but he was definitely gonna get good at it this year, he swore.

Izzy nodded. "Makes sense."

"I feel you," Anthony added.

And that's what good friends were for, Juan reflected — understanding you without you really having to bother explaining yourself too clearly.

"Thing is," Izzy put in, somewhat ominously, "we really about to need your help for real, as you may have noticed. So you might wanna get on that."

"Yeah . . ." Juan said glumly. "I know."

They walked for a while with just the crinkly *splortch* beneath their boots as a soundtrack, past the horseman statue and the creepy men's shelter fortress, across Atlantic Avenue and into Bed-Stuy. "So what . . ." Juan said, nudging Izzy. "You're like a Hierophant now or something?"

"Bah." She shrugged him off. "I mean, yeah. But I'm still Izzy, y'all. Still the King."

"Can you still 'shape?"

She spat a cackle. "Shit, I hope so. Nah, I'm playin'. I definitely can. Tried this morning to make sure. I can just do . . . uh, other stuff too."

"Like what?" Anthony asked.

"Erm, I'm not sure if I'm supposed to say, exactly."

"You are like . . ." Juan bounced his head from side to side, trying to figure out how to phrase it. "You're still on our side, right?"

Izzy stopped in her tracks, forcing some hipsters who'd been too damn close on their heels anyway to dodge to either side and then look back with passive-aggressive grimaces. "Excuse me?"

"You're excused!" one of the hipsters yelled over their shoulder.

"No one was talking to you, Susan! Come back here!"

"Iz," Juan said. "Stay focused."

She rounded on him. "Right! It was you I was about to ream out, thanks for the reminder."

"Erm."

"Listen to me carefully, both of you clowns."

"Hey!" Anthony said.

"Who I am and what I seen —" She had some growl in her voice now. Juan had seen Izzy fussy and vexed, and for real mad a few times, but this . . . this was something different.

That weird light flickered through her eyes, and her whole body moved like some kind of giant Izzy-shaped snake as she accentuated each point with her hands. "It's not just that I *want* those dirty motherless bags of trash to pay for what they've done and how they've done it. It's that they're going to, and we're going to see personally to it, and when I say *we*, I mean Tee and me, and that's just plain facts right there. But also, I'm a shadowshaper till I die, kid. That's who I am and who Imma always be, no matter what. These houses are all some old heffa's playthings as far as I'm concerned, but shadow-shaping is who we is, you and me. It's in your blood through heritage, Juan, but it's in mine too now, and me and my spirits, we roll deep. So you can bet ya pint-sized guitar-hero ass we gonna turn their whole trash world on its head. Only question I have is how many of our guys are they gonna be able to take out before we end them." She paused, the mist of her breath rising and rising around them. "Feel me?"

They blinked and nodded. Izzy walked off.

"Damn," Anthony whispered as he and Juan hurried to catch up. "I wanna be a shadowshaper too."

FORTY-FOUR

"So, we hit him hard and hit 'em where it hurts, and then we hit 'em again before they have a chance to respond. And then we fall all the way back and see what's what," Robbie said, and then he nodded at Caleb, who stood on the other side of a very scratched-over sheet of butcher paper from him.

"And that's when we make an overture to the other two Hierophants in play, the River and Fortress," Caleb said. "They got no allegiance to this new house or Dake, not really. They got no allegiance to anything. So they'll flip once they see the wind is blowing another direction."

"Theoretically," Tee said.

"Theoretically," Caleb allowed. "And then they'll tip the balance back our way."

"And we're still the Dominant house," Robbie added. "Which is why they have shied away from a direct confrontation so far and why they will keep shying away from it. They know they can't win."

There was a pause and some shuffling as the House of Shadow and Light (minus María Santiago, who had more meetings) adjusted themselves and looked around uncomfortably.

"What?" Robbie asked.

"No, it's fine," Bennie said. "It's just . . ."

"It doesn't protect our people," Sierra said.

"We put a detail on 'em," Robbie said. "Just like we did on the Bloodhaüs, but for their protection. Ghost security."

"But they ain't 'shapers," Bennie said. "Without a shape, those spirits won't be able to do much to prevent an attack."

"We assign a 'shaper to each of 'em," Caleb said.

Sierra shook her head. "And they just follow 'em twenty-four-seven? For how long? This plan goes on for weeks, at least."

Caleb and Robbie both just smoldered for a few moments. Then Caleb said, "We don't have much of a choice," in that quiet way of his that meant he was actually really riled.

"I know," Sierra said. "I'm not trying to shoot y'all down, I just . . . I don't know what to do either." The panic that had been threatening to rise in her and come gushing out for the past twenty-four hours made another go at it. She forced it away. "Tee? Izzy?"

The two new Hierophants stood next to each other in the far corner, both with their arms crossed over their chests, both frowning severely. "We don't like it either," Tee said. "But we also don't know another way. Giving them the Deck is . . . not a good idea."

"I know," Sierra said quietly. "I know."

"Any word on Mina?" Robbie asked.

"Desmond Pocket and his crack team of young street lawyers are on it," Sierra said. "Says the charges are bullshit, of course, and should have her out soon. And Neville has cats on the inside looking out for her."

"Why don't we just make everyone a Shadow and Lighter?" Jerome said.

"Huh?" Juan asked.

"No, he's right," Bennie said. "Dake's whole thing is that he's being vile but still playing by the rules. That's why he can get away with it and still have those two Hierophants on his side, technically. So if Sierra or Caleb just initiates all the people into our house, they won't be nonparticipants anymore."

"I mean, we'll do your boys, Nydia, and whoever else wants it, but then he just goes to the next person down on the list," Sierra said. "And then what? We just keep initiating people? And who knows if they even want to be brought into this mess?"

"And what happens when he decides not to play by the rules anymore and takes them out anyway?" Robbie added. "And if he's really just throwing our folks' personal info to random online scumbags, he might be able to slide by on the technicality of it not being his people doing the deed."

Everyone got glum again.

"I mean . . . I hate to say this, but any chance he's bluffing?" Jerome asked.

The whole room said *no* at the same time.

"I just think, we gotta ask ourselves," Sierra said. "Are we really willing to lose a loved one over this? Are we prepared to go through what that's gonna mean — the sorrow, first of all, but also the guilt of knowing that we're partly responsible for their death."

"We're not," Bennie said. "None of us are. That's not right. You can't take that on and you can't put it on yourself either."

"No," Sierra said, pushing away the panic once again. And then again. "But our actions can still cause it, even if it's not our choice."

"Are you saying you want to hand over the Deck?" Caleb asked. He said it sincerely, not a challenge.

"It sounds like you are," Robbie said, when Sierra just closed her eyes and looked away.

Caleb sighed. "If you give Dake the Deck, he'll still do all the things he threatened. Maybe not the next day or the day after, but I can guarantee you that one by one, he will take our people out. Except no one will be able to stop him."

Nydia stepped forward and everyone got quiet. "Look," she said, very softly. Both her hands were clenched at her sides and her head was bowed forward just slightly, brow furrowed. "I don't know whether giving the Deck back is the move or not. All I know is this: Dake has to die." She looked around the room, locking eyes with each of them. "Do you understand me? He's threatening my —" Her voice cracked, and she stopped. Sierra prayed she wouldn't break down. Nydia took a breath. "He's threatening my boys; he's gotta die. So what I need for this discussion to be is one about how, exactly how, we are going to make that happen." She paused, and no one said anything for a few seconds. Then she added, "Preferably slowly."

"I mean, I'm with that," Caleb said. "My thing about the how is, we don't have enough intel to really figure that out yet. Right, Vincent?"

Vincent emerged from the shadowy corner of the apartment where the spirits tended to congregate. *He's eighteen years old. Real name, Dave Kallert-Picker. Attends Argyle Prep, a private school on the Upper West Side; commutes in from Long Island every morning. Parents are Leslie Jean Kallert and Ronald Picker, a lawyer and an architect. Only child.*

"Great," Robbie said. "So we stake out the house and —"

He's gone to ground, though, Vincent cut in. *Parents think he's on some ski trip for Christmas break, but we're pretty sure he's hiding out wherever their new meeting spot is, and we haven't been able to figure that out yet.*

"Then we sic Juan on him," Bennie said. "He the Hound, y'all. And he's a beast with it! No pun. But I'm sayin' . . ."

"Wherever Dake is, he's gonna be well protected," Caleb said. "Like, impenetrable-fortress-type well protected. He only has to stay that way for another day. We'll be playing right into his hands if we come for him, and guarantee it'll set off whatever crap he has planned for our loved ones. That's why Robbie and I were looking into taking other people out."

"So we're right back where we started." Sierra sighed.

"So we just get everyone the hell outta Dodge for a while," Juan said, sounding more nervous than Sierra had ever heard him. "Just tell 'em to take vacations and —"

"Gael on that list," Sierra tried to say gently. "Dake got people in Afghanistan. Sending someone to Florida isn't gonna keep 'em safe."

Sierra put her head in her hands. Her phone buzzed. A message from Dake popped up on the screen with about thirty other numbers cc'd besides Sierra's. She groaned.

"You mean on top of being a kid nazi and a murderer, this guy sends group texts too?" Jerome growled, looking over her shoulder. "Yeah, he gotta die."

"What's it say?" Nydia asked.

Sierra read out loud: "Come celebrate the advent of a brand-new house and the dawning of a new age for the Deck of Worlds: Unity and Freedom Party this Wednesday at sunset."

"That's the day he demanded we hand over the cards by," Bennie said.

"Reginald Meadows off the NJ Turnpike," Sierra continued.

"That's where we faced off with Bloodhaüs a few days ago," Tee said.

"Follow the streamers and flashing lights. All houses welcome, emergent, Dominant, and everything in between. It's time to join together as one as we face a new threat with unity and power! Special entertainment provided by . . ." Sierra's voice trailed off.

"What?" Juan asked. "What's wrong?"

"Culebra," Sierra finished. "Apparently you guys have a gig playing at our funeral."

FORTY-FIVE

Juan Santiago sat on his bed and strummed a single chord on the acoustic guitar his parents had given him when he turned eleven. It was a B7 — one of his favorites. He loved the way his fingers stacked on top of each other like a tower with one sticking out. He loved the slightly off-center jangle of it, that wily tritone. He loved how it described a rainy day without a single word.

He closed his eyes, strummed it again, now willing the spirits to gather, imagining them there in front him, those long loping strides, those gangly arms. He advanced his fingers up a few frets and then back down, making a hazy slow progression as his occasional strums veered into a more rhythmic strut, something like a blues, something like a dirge.

Around him, the spirits surely slid through the air in time to his tapping foot, the tinkling notes as his fingers danced into arpeggios along each string. He would bust into a new rhythm, and the spirits would move with him, and then he'd let them stream through and inhabit the song and take form.

He opened his eyes.

Nothing.

He stopped playing, just blinked into the emptiness of the air around him.

Where were they?

A knock snapped him out of his disappointed reverie. "Yeah?"

"It's Bennie," the muted voice called from the other side. "Can I come in?"

"Uh, yeah! Of course." Juan stood. Sat back down. Put his guitar on the bed as the door opened.

"Don't stop playing," Bennie said. "I came to listen."

"I . . . okay." He picked it back up, hit that A minor, and laid into a sultry kind of flamenco riff.

"Ooo la la," Bennie cooed, doing a little twirl with elaborate finger snaps and then plopping on the bed next to him. Soon, she'd draped herself across his shoulder and, still strumming, he lifted his left elbow to accept her into his embrace and then lowered it around her. Slowly, and with the flamenco roll sliding into a gentler samba, he eased them both down onto the pillows, and for a little while, they just lay there while he played.

"You asleep?" Juan asked.

"Mm-mmm."

"Can I, um, ask you something? And don't say that I ju —"

"You just did."

"Urk."

"Don't stop playing!" She snuggled closer, her legs tangled in his now, and Juan had to make an active effort to remember what chords were and how to strum. Right. That.

"Seriously, though. This is, ah, difficult to ask."

"I'm here. What is it? I won't laugh at you, I can almost promise."

"Comforting," Juan snorted. "Can you teach me how to shadowshape?"

She propped herself on one elbow so she could get a better look at him. She was smiling — not in a mean way. "Of course, Juan! I just assumed —"

"I know, I know. I should already know. I totally should. And, like, maybe I do, kinda? Just, like, not really. Yeah, I been around it my whole life, yada, yada, but I never really . . . and here we are."

"Mmm." She nodded sagely. "What happens when you try?"

"Well, earlier when we were rehearsing it seemed like it was about to work. Spirits showed up and everything. But then we got interrupted, and then I was trying again just now, and . . . nothing."

"Oh, I mean — keep playing, man. Just because we having a conversation doesn't mean you get a break."

"Okay, damn."

"I mean, thing is, sometimes it just be like that? Especially when you starting out. And sure they know you . . ." She made her voice all spooky. "*¡Juancito!* Right? But they don't know you as a 'shaper yet, just as like family or whatever. It might just take a few tries before they know to show up."

"Hmm . . . I guess so?"

"And maybe you haven't found your 'shaping skill yet."

"But, I mean!" He shrugged. "It's gotta be music? Right?"

She shrugged back. "Who knows? Not always that simple."

Juan cracked a mischievous grin. "Show me."

"Aw, man, right now?"

"Nothing complicated. I just wanna see the summoning part." And then: "Please?"

She rolled over so they lay beside each other on their backs, his arm her pillow, then raised her left hand. Immediately, the room felt fuller somehow, the air heavy. She was so smooth with it! "Boom, just like that," he whispered.

She gave a sly smile. "Eh, I just been practicing."

"I gotta get like you."

He could make out the shadows now — a tall one and a short one. Couldn't see their faces, but he was relieved that neither appeared to be Vincent. Woulda been kinda awkward to have a girl summon up her murdered brother while you were having cozy time with her. Juan leaned the guitar against his desk and watched.

They swooped forward together and leapt over the bed (Juan did everything he could not to flinch) and then vanished into Bennie's open hand. With her other arm, she slapped the wall and both shadows emerged onto it.

One spirit slid along to the light switch on the far end of the room, disappeared into it, and then the overheads dimmed to a romantic glow. "Nice," Juan whispered. The other stepped on long, shadowy legs toward the speaker system, vanished. Immediately, the whole thing lit up, digital numbers spinning through the radio dial, speakers churning out waves of static and ads. Then something else clicked and another light blinked to life on the main hub. "Bluetooth?" Juan marveled. "Damn." The other shadow reemerged out of the light switch and sped back across the room to where Bennie's phone sat on the desk. Soon, a sweet piano melody spilled out from the speakers, and then a smooth lo-fi beat rose up around it amidst the whisper of a record player crackle and someone humming in the background. "What's this?"

Bennie smiled, eyes closed. "The new DJ Taza jam. Just dropped Friday."

"Mmmm!"

"This dude just puts out a new underground hit every few weeks, mixing in ol' Cubano jams and putting ancient rhythms together with hip new ones, and every time it's like a whole other thing. Young genius, man."

"Isn't he, like, old, though?"

"I just meant, younger than old white guys that call themselves geniuses, but yeah, he's in his thirties, I think."

"Ah."

For a few minutes, the song pulsed around them, calmed all Juan's aching muscles and washed away the endless pulse of fear that had been with him since yesterday, the knowledge that someone was coming for his loved ones and he wasn't even remotely prepared to stop them. For a few minutes, it was just his own heartbeat, the thump and clatter of DJ Taza's beats, and Bennie in his arms.

And then he imagined his dad at work, and some random creep from the Internet showing up with a gun. Before the man even raised his arm to shoot, Juan was picturing Gael doing some training exercise and a fellow soldier unstrapping his sidepiece, taking aim. Both guns went off at once, but the sound of Sierra's screams drowned out their ear-shattering claps.

Juan sat up, gasping.

Bennie was already sitting straight up, and when he looked into her wide-open eyes, he knew she'd slid into the same pit of terror that he had. He was wrapped around her before he'd decided to, and together they slid back down into the bed, holding tight as the drumbeat and piano wove their sad tapestry through the air around them.

FORTY-SIX

"Is there anything you can do?" Nydia asked.

Tee and Izzy looked at each other, then back down at the two wide-eyed boys with big, terrific fros staring up at them. "We'll figure something out," Tee promised.

They stood outside the Santiago brownstone. The December afternoon had turned weirdly warm as everyone skulked off to settle their affairs and worry after the emergency meeting, and Uncle Neville had rolled up in his Caddy with the boys in the back just as Nydia pulled Tee aside for a discreet word.

Now Tee and Izzy took in the gently waving air around Nydia's sons, Virgilio and Timba, aged seven and nine respectively. Protection, protection, protection ... what would it look like? The two Hierophants wondered, sorting through different possibilities and trying to discern the limits of their own powers. Nydia stood back, giving them space. Over on the street, Neville sat in the front seat of his idling Cadillac with his eyes closed and a jazz tune simmering out of the radio.

A shield, perhaps. A spirit shield. Mmm. It would block negative energy but probably not a bullet or a knife. A cloaking mechanism of some kind, then? They walked a small circle around the boys, squinting and cocking their heads. A deflection device.

We could pass them the Hierophant powers, Tee thought, half jokingly.

Ha, Izzy replied. *If only . . .*

Which summed it up pretty well. Being a Hierophant was simultaneously the most incredible and empowering and unnerving experience that Tee had ever had. As soon as it had clicked into place, she'd felt desperately in love with that tingling sense of wonder that ricocheted through her even now, and also absolutely ready for it to all be over. She had understood Mort's strange fatigue and entire off-kilter way of carrying himself in a whole new light, and she hoped he'd wake up soon and be able to explain a thing or two to them.

What about a confusion solution? Izzy suggested, always rhyming, even when she didn't mean to be.

I like, I like. They circled again, making funny faces at the boys to keep them giggling. It worked, mostly: Little Virgilio followed them with his eyes, a goofy grin plastered across his dark brown face. Timba looked a little warier but kept a half smile on as he watched them.

Tee and Izzy began waving their hands up and down, feeling the slight vibrations of pressure against their fingers as they went. Virgilio mimicked their motions with an enthusiastic cackle. Tee smiled, but the sadness of what they were doing swirled within her.

It was just a little shift in the energy field, that was all. A twist. Their fingers found purchase in those pulsing waves around the two boys, and then Tee and Izzy stopped, nodded, and stepped once to the left in perfect sequence with each other.

Imminent tragedy aside, God, it was cool having a mind-melded, ultra-powerful lover!

The energy field shifted with them; they both felt it like a wave of warm air shoving past them. And then it was done.

Tee turned to a perplexed-looking Nydia, and the three of them stepped a little away from the boys. "This is what'll happen: Anyone coming at them will see them, or think they do, and attack with whatever they have, but they will miss. Wherever they're seeing Virgilio and Timba, it won't be where they really are. Understand?"

Nydia bounced her head around. "Kinda. Will it really stop them from being hurt?"

"It'll give them time to get away," Izzy said. "And they'll be almost impossible to catch."

"But," Tee added, "that'll only work for a direct attack, right? So . . . sorry to be grim, but —"

"It's fine," Nydia said.

"— if someone uses an explosive device, for instance, or something else that doesn't require much precision, this won't help much."

Nydia frowned, nodded. "I appreciate you guys. A lot."

Tee shrugged. "It's the least we can do."

"Anyway," Izzy added, "you fine as hell."

Tee rolled her eyes. "Sorry. She right, though."

"It's cool." Nydia shrugged. "I know. I mean, thanks."

They shared a good chuckle in spite of the lingering dread and then said their good-byes, and Tee and Izzy strutted off down the street, yanked forward by this strange new instinct neither of them could name, this sudden knowledge and ferocity.

They would find somewhere safe and settle in and, once again, leave their bodies behind like clothes on the bedroom floor after a rugged, delicious night. And they would soar, as one, as none, up through the Brooklyn skies and out over the rooftops, past the steel and bustle of Manhattan and into the wilds of Jersey, over highway and railroad, and then across the ranging, dingy field, beneath passing planes and away from the rumble of faraway traffic. And they knew what they'd find there, amidst work crews setting up a large stage and sound system. They could feel it as sure as they could sense the slightest trembles along the stretched-out fabric of the web they now formed a part of. They knew as surely as they knew their own names and knew their love for each other was meant to not only be but last.

There, rising from the marshes and tall, waving grass, they would find a wall, a force field — one designed by the power-wielders of the brand-new House of Blood and Iron, one very like what had surrounded the car graveyard yesterday, designed to keep spirits out and protect those within from the skills of the shadowshapers. They would find it, and they would feel their way along its sloping invisible face bit by bit, testing, probing, sensing.

They would find a chink, a way to bring the whole thing down.

And then they would smile, an inward kind of smile, unseeable but deeply true, and whisk off into the dimming skies.

FORTY-SEVEN

Sierra sat with her legs crossed, facing the marker-covered paper on the wall, and sighed. She'd clicked off the lights and turned a desktop lamp to face the wall, so the whole thing was lit up. On a pillow in front of her, the Deck of Worlds let out its eerie glow. It was definitely brighter now, though Sierra had no idea why or how. She shook her head at it, frowning. Looked back up at the spirals and arrows she'd drawn the day before. Just a big mess, really. Barely made sense at all. And there was so much that she didn't know. That no one knew.

How could they have gotten so hemmed in?

She picked up the top card on the Deck, turned it over. A half-naked muscular man sat on the Iron Throne draped in animal carcasses. The Emperor of Blood and Iron. His head was bowed and partly obscured by a cowl made from the head skin of a warthog. His crimson-stained hands gripped the armrests of his throne like he was stressed.

Sierra grabbed a lighter off the coffee table and flicked it to life beneath the card. The flame just simmered there, the card undamaged.

She scowled at it. Got up, went to the kitchen, and came

back with a pair of scissors. They didn't even dent the thing. She rolled her eyes and put it back.

Stinking magic cards.

Then she blinked. Picked up the top one again, squinted at it.

That was strange.

She leapt up, clicked off the desk lamp.

Now the only light in the apartment came from the gray afternoon sky outside and the far end of the room, where Septima was tending to a still-unconscious Mort. And the Deck. But not the card in Sierra's hand.

She put it back, picked up another — one from the new emergent house, the Silver Hound. It wasn't glowing either. So what was?

The next card was the River, also not glowing. She remembered when she'd first seen that picture of a pleasant stream of water rolling through the countryside; she'd wondered if that Hierophant might be delightful somehow, an ally. Fat chance. She'd glimpsed the River standing there with Dake yesterday, and he was as foul and seedy as any Deck denizen to date.

The next card was the Reaper, and it was definitely glowing. How had she not noticed that before? She must've always looked at the individual cards with lights on; the glow was soft enough to be indistinguishable under the glare of any other light.

"Hey," Anthony said from the doorway, and Sierra jumped, dropping the card.

"Whoa!"

He hurried over. "Sorry, sorry! You okay?"

Sierra put the card back on top of the Deck, shook her

head, blinking. "Yeah, I . . ." She looked up at him. "Yeah. As much as . . . you know . . ."

"Yeah."

"Just trying to sort through this some more . . . But, I'm . . . I'm happy to see you."

Seeing Anthony was both a horrific reminder of all that was about to go wrong and a soothing balm amidst everything that had already gone wrong. Sierra tried to balance the two, couldn't, then just gave up and kissed him.

"Mmm!" He knelt down to more easily wrap around her, then heaved her up with a grunt.

"Lift with your legs! Lift with your legs! I'm heavy!"

"I am!" Anthony said. "And no, you're not!" He straightened all the way and pulled her close. "Or really, yes, you are, and it's delicious."

"Why, thank you."

"And anyway, I been working out."

She wiggled her eyebrows. "So I see." Sierra closed her eyes and counted to ten, enjoying the feel of Anthony's strength holding her up, the exquisite warmth of those arms enwrapping her, his breath on her neck. Then she exhaled and nodded. "Okay."

"Time to get to work?"

"Mmhmm. More play later, please."

He set her down gently. "You can bet on it."

She smiled up at him.

"Oh," he said. "And I wanted to ask you something . . ."

"Yes," Sierra said, bapping his arm. "But first, kneel, please."

"Are you gonna —" He lowered himself into a squat, then

got on his knees. "That's what I was gonna ask you!"

"Good. I don't think it'll get us far in terms of getting you off the kill list, to be honest, but it should happen anyway. If you're down?"

He nodded enthusiastically. "Been down."

"Sir Anthony," Sierra announced Britishly. "Sir Anthony . . . ?"

"Malachi."

"Ooh, I like that! That should be your stage name, not Pulpo."

"I'll let Juan know so he can ignore me."

Sierra snorted, then got serious again and closed her eyes ceremoniously. "Sir Anthony Malachi King."

"This is the second time we're doing this in a week," Anthony said.

She peeked one eye open. "Are you over it?"

He shook his head with a concerned frown. "Opposite. I am worried, though. But that's all happening regardless. This? This is the good part."

Beaming, Sierra raised one shoulder and dipped her head so her ear touched it. "I think so too. Shadowshaping is . . . forget everything else. Shadowshaping is it. And I know, I mean, obviously, I would say that, right? But, like, for real, shadowshaping has changed my life, saved my life, made me who I am, and even though when we first started talking, I wanted to keep you as far away from all this as I could . . ."

"Hoo yeah," Anthony said. "I remember that."

"Right. But that way back in October when the Deck was really just first starting to make an appearance on our scene, and everything was terrible, and everyone was trying to kill us."

330

"As opposed to now, when the Deck has been around for a few months, and everything is terrible, and everyone is trying to kill us."

"Fair point," Sierra allowed. "I guess I realized that this is my life one way or another, and anyone who's gonna be a part of it better know about it and understand. And anyway, the Deck is *not* shadowshaping, and I finally get that. What we got is different. And it's better. Hold on." She raised her right hand and put her left on his forehead. This was so much better than anointing him with some obnoxious card. This was hers — her magic, her world, and it was about to be his too. She smiled inwardly for a moment, taking in Anthony's closed eyes, his slight smile. She just wanted to close the distance between them and wrap around him, but there would be time for all that later, there had to be.

"Come forward," she whispered. Before she could say *spirits*, Anthony scooched a couple inches toward her on his knees, and Sierra rolled her eyes. "Not you, homey."

"Oh!" he whispered, squinting his eyes open just a little to see who else was in the room. "My bad!"

Spirits emerged from the darkness around them. The Black Hoodies first, then others that Sierra recognized from her adventures.

"I called you forth to bear witness to our newest shadowshaper," Sierra said. "And I call forth those ancestors of Anthony Malachi King who wish to stand with him as he steps forward into his destiny." At first, nothing happened. Sierra was about to shrug and keep it moving — it had been worth a try anyway. But then a glowing form appeared behind Anthony, then two more. Then five more. Sierra widened her eyes. "You didn't tell me you had a whole-ass *crew* walking with you, man."

Anthony smiled, eyes still closed, shrugged his big shoulders. "I didn't know!"

Six of the eight appeared to be women, three of them elderly, and it made a strange kind of sense. Sierra hadn't known how to put it into words, but something about the way Anthony carried himself spoke of a man who walked with powerful female energies around him.

"Welcome," Sierra said, and the cadre of shadow spirits nodded, and one snapped an impressive salute.

Then a shimmering face emerged from the shadows beside her own, and she narrowed her eyes. "Oh, now you show up!"

Grandpa Lázaro lowered his old wrinkled head, a gesture Sierra had no idea how to respond to.

She turned back to Anthony. "Dude been dead for three months and not a peep. Now we initiating the first boy into shadowshaping since he died, and he wanna make an appearance. I see you, Abuelo."

"Everything okay?" Anthony asked, eyes still closed.

"Yeah, yeah, yeah," Sierra said. "Pay me no mind. Family stuff. Let's do this."

She put her hand back on his forehead, taking a breath to center herself.

Lucera. The name seemed to reach her from somewhere far away. Her name. Her inheritance of power. How many times had the other Luceras who came before her stood in the middle of a terrible storm, placed their hands on a loved one's head, and increased their embattled house by one more soul? The power rose in her now, the swirl of shadow and light, and then the fierce blend of the two, and beyond that, something older, fiercer even. Shadowshaping. She let it slide down her arm, pool in her palm at the point where it touched Anthony's head.

"Ooh," he whispered. "I feel that."

"Shh!"

Then she released.

FORTY-EIGHT

"You look different, Doudou." Ma Satie's withered face glared up from her rocking chair.

"No, Mamie."

The old woman sucked her teeth. "What you mean, *no*? You don't look different? How you know, eh? You in front of a mirror?"

Tee shook her head. Izzy had already snuck in through the bedroom window, and Tee was anxious to get to her. It felt like every moment without her was a violent one, an empty one. She definitely didn't want to get stuck being interrogated by Ma Satie, who always somehow knew everything, every damn thing, no matter what. But also: She had work to do and that took precedence over everything else. "I just mean . . ."

"Think hard now before you make an excuse, Doudou. Because whatever it is, you know I'll break it."

Of course she would. Tee almost rolled her eyes but managed to stop herself. Finally, she rallied, looked her grandmother right in her withered old face. "I look different because I am different."

"Ahhhh . . . now we're getting somewhere, eh! Sit with your grandmother, Trejean."

This wasn't going to be easy. Nothing was easy. Tee sat. Outside, it had begun to snow again, the gentle flakes cascading slowly past the orange haze of streetlights as the sky grew dark.

"It look good on you," Ma Satie croaked.

"What's that, Mamie?"

Ma Satie leaned over, put a warm crinkly hand on Tee's shoulder. Her breath smelled like milk and her voice shifted to a shrill whisper. "Power."

Tee closed her eyes and nodded. "Yes," she said softly.

"I mean, you 'ave always been powerful, Doudou. But this different, mm."

"Yes."

"It's a great danger, that circles near?"

"Yes." Tee felt tears; she let them come. "Yes, Mamie." She opened her eyes, took in the lines running down her grandma's face, the dangles of her flesh along her neck that quivered as the old woman nodded.

"Alright," she said. "Do what you 'ave to do, eh."

It didn't take long. She'd already gotten the hang of it from their first run with Nydia's boys. Now Ma Satie's bright energy waves seemed to leap out at Tee as soon as she looked for them. A fierce kind of light surrounded the elder, and Tee thought about how much of a life she'd lived before Tee even existed, how many messes she'd survived, how many loves she'd lost. "Close your eyes, please."

To her surprise, Ma Satie didn't snap back or even sigh. She just did what she was told, head slightly bowed. It caused a sudden eruption of emotion to surge through Tee. This frail matriarch who had survived so much — at least two abusive husbands and one war, not to mention the death of her only son — and now some random teenage asshole was threatening her with his grimy Internet army. It was all so infuriating. But Tee had to focus. She could tumble into that well of rage forever, and what good would it do? She had to put that away, at least for the moment, and concentrate on keeping the people she loved safe.

Her fingers found that gentle buzzing purchase against Ma Satie's energy field, and then Tee dragged her hands a few inches to the left.

"Ooh!" Ma Satie exclaimed. "Ooh!"

"You okay, Mamie?"

"Aha, oh, yes! Ah, Doudou. You really come into your own, ha."

"Yes, Mamie."

"Good, love, good."

Tee stood. Kissed her grandma's wrinkled little forehead. "I love you, Mamie."

"Mm, love you too, Doudou."

She started to walk away.

"And, Trejean?"

Stopped. Scrunched her face. Waited for it. The moment she'd wondered about for years now. Here it came. "Yes, Mamie?"

"Tell that boy you always have sneaking around these parts not to be such a stranger, eh?"

Tee rolled her eyes. Didn't know whether to laugh or cry. How could elders understand so much and so little at the same time? she wondered. "I don't know what you're talking about, Mamie."

"Aha, I'm sure."

Tee shook her head and walked into her room, closing the door behind her and then silently sliding the deadbolt she'd installed into place.

Izzy was watching her from the bed. Tee hadn't turned around, but she knew. She knew a lot of things these days, more and more it seemed, and it was still as exhilarating and exhausting as it had been when she'd first woken up. She knew the whole web of connections, spiraling back to that hideous old countess, trembled in a state of ongoing anticipation and anxiety in a way it never had before. She knew whatever was going to happen next, it would all depend on how everything played out in the next two days. She knew a great many forces were at play now, and all of them — from the spirit world, to the other Hierophants, to various other entities who hadn't made themselves known yet — all of them watched and waited, poised, breathing heavily in the shadows, some ferocious, some terrified, all warbling semi-blindly through a world on the brink of utter catastrophe.

She released a long breath. All of it mattered so much, but right now, in this sacred and tiny and dark moment, none of it mattered. None of it could. It had to fade, because in another few hours it would launch heavily into prominence, and then, whatever happened, she and Izzy would be dealing with all that mess first and foremost, and not much else. And that meant that now, it all had to fade away. Just for a little while. She was still blinking away some tears from her moment with Ma Satie, and now they threatened to come again, full force. Outside, the snow kept falling, and it was fully night now, and Izzy awaited her on the bed, sitting perfectly still, breathing heavily, sending away the very same thoughts and demons that Tee was.

Tee turned. Took in Izzy's watching face, her wide eyes and long jawline. She'd already changed into some of Tee's pj's — the pair that hadn't fit Tee since she was thirteen that Izzy had dug up from deep in some closet — and her long brown arms rested on her knees, and her chin rested on her arms, and goddamn, she was a sight to behold, and just like Ma Satie, she'd been through so, so much, but also nowhere near as much and such different storms.

Tee wanted to burst across the room and wrap all the way around her girlfriend and send them both collapsing onto the bed in a mess of kisses and loving. She felt Izzy wanting it too, felt the heat rising off her from across the room. Instead, Tee walked. She breathed deeply and stepped slowly, saw Izzy crack a half smile when she realized Tee was making her wait, playing her patience.

Tee reached her, reached out to her, took her rising body into her arms, and held her.

This is a lot, they said.

So much.

This can't go on forever, not like this.

No.

But tonight, this is what we are.

Yes.

Hold me.

Yes.

They eased slowly down onto the bed, together, as one. They loved.

FORTY-NINE

"Again," Sierra said, trying to hide her smile.

"Aw, man!" Anthony fake grumbled.

"You love it," Sierra chortled. "You know you love it."

"Yeah, yeah, yeah. You just like watching me mess up." He stood beside the now completely rearranged butcher paper on the wall and raised a hand over his head.

"True. Now which one you gonna 'shape into?"

"Which one's even left?"

It was a fair point. He'd sent all the little drawings she'd made of the House of Iron scattering across the paper into a mess of quirky lines and broken faces. She'd told him not to mess with the Hierophants section because she was still trying to figure that stuff out, which meant . . . "Mess up the Bloodhaüs. They're irrelevant now anyway."

Sierra had tacked a new sheet on and sketched what they knew of the House of Blood and Iron onto it earlier that morning. She'd been staring at the whole damn mess since then and felt like it was making less sense with every passing hour.

"Bet," Anthony said. He breathed in deep, put an adorably focused frown on his face, and then wiggled his eyebrows.

Sierra shook her head. "Good grief, man. So dramatic."

"Hey! I'm concentrating!" A shadow stretched toward him from the corner, broke into a run. Dove and disappeared into his raised hand. "Whooo!" Anthony yelled as that shivery feeling Sierra knew well probably swirled through him. She snorked. He smacked the paper right over the crossed-out image of Axella. The woman's mousy face exploded into a splatter of dashes and dots.

¡Desgraciado! Septima called from across the room. *Este no tiene esperanza.*

"What'd she say?" Anthony asked. "She impressed?"

"Oh, definitely." Sierra laughed. "¡Oye, cállate, vieja!" The Sorrow had been harassing him in Spanish since they'd started practice, basically the shimmering Puerto Rican–spirit version of those old guys who heckled the Muppets all the time.

Anthony sighed. "I'm a disgraceful shadowshaper, aren't I?"

"No, man, you're just new. It's cool. And anyway, we gotta see what happens when you try with other mediums. It's probably gonna be music, because that's where your heart is. I just start people off on drawings cuz it's basic — the ABCs of shadowshaping."

"And happens to be what you do best."

"I mean . . ."

Anthony raised one hand and smacked the paper in one fluid motion. It happened so fast, Sierra barely caught the shadow spirit sprinting across the room, and then more lines exploded across the paper as a few more Bloodhaüsers shattered. Sierra burst out laughing. Everything was so awful, the laughter just seemed to roll up on her out of nowhere. She couldn't remember the last time she'd really belted out a hearty cackle.

Anthony smiled, encouraged, and did it again, now sending

the last remnants of Bloodhaüs into a cataclysmic splatter. Watching her enemies get wiped away, even just cartoon versions of them, was the art therapy Sierra hadn't realized she'd needed all this time. "Yes!" she cheered. "Do it again!"

Anthony raised his hand, prepared the other one to slap; another spirit rushed toward him. And then Sierra blinked. Something clicked inside her. "Wait!"

"Huh?" Anthony turned, just as the spirit slid into his raised hand and vanished. "What is it? Whooha, icy brain freeze but in my arm!"

"They just . . . What if we could . . ." Sierra didn't have full sentences yet; the ideas were still half-formed. But they were growing.

"What if we could . . ." Anthony nudged.

"What if we . . ." She started pacing. Pulled out a Sharpie without thinking about it, popped the cap. "What if . . ."

Pieces came together, flew back apart.

Anthony leaned against the wall with one hand, and the splotchy lines danced to life around his finger — that spirit finally coming through. They didn't scatter, though — maybe he'd been hitting too hard all this time.

"Hey, does this have anything to do with what you were onto when I walked in?"

Sierra stopped pacing. "Huh?"

"With the cards? You had the lights out and —"

"Shit! Right! I . . ." She rummaged around on the coffee table, snatched up the Deck, and started shuffling through it. "Maybe it does. Turn off the light again."

He bent down and clicked the knob at the base of the desk lamp.

The Deck did its eerie glowing thing. "You see, right?" Sierra asked.

"Yeah. It always does that. Creepy-ass Deck."

"Does it, though?" Sierra said, the excitement growing within her. "Or is it just these?" She spread the Deck in her hands and sure enough, the Reaper cards were the only ones glowing. Anthony's eyes went wide.

"Whoa."

Ay, pero sí pero claro, Septima insisted, appearing behind Anthony and then sweeping in to inspect the Deck more carefully. *The Reaper is the most powerful Hierophant. The most elusive. Nobody knows who he is, or where he is. Even what he is. But it is his light that powers the Deck. Eso ya se sabe.*

Sierra snatched the cards away from Septima's glare. "*You* might've known all along, but the rest of us haven't had access to the Deck until Mina got it away from you, and you decided not to mention that fact."

Buuuueno, Septima drawled.

"What does it mean?"

"What does what mean?" María Santiago said, opening the door and standing silhouetted melodramatically in the blast of light from the hallway. Sierra cringed a little. She still felt pretty terrible about sneaking the Sorrow into Lázaro's apartment and having to keep her there even after her mom rightfully freaked out about it. Nothing was easy, nothing made sense.

"The Deck," Sierra said. "I'd always thought the whole Deck was glowing but turns out —"

"Déjame ver," María said, shoving Septima out of the way. "Hi, Anthony."

342

"Hey, Mrs. Santiago."

"— it's just the Reaper card glowing," Sierra said. "That's why the glow is stronger now, because the Reaper has taken up a whole ascendant house's worth of cards."

María took the Deck out of Sierra's hands and shuffled through some of the cards, glowering. "This poison," she muttered.

It's true, the Sorrow muttered from the corner, where she'd remained after being pushed there by María. *It is poison.*

Sierra, María, and Anthony all turned their curious faces to Septima. "That's not how you felt for the past however many hundred years when you and your sisters hoarded the Deck and used it to play all the rival houses off each other," Sierra said.

It's true, it's true, Septima mewed. *I don't deny it. I have benefited from its power, of course. And now . . . from here, from this side, even still amongst the Dominant house, but in the midst of this, yet another war, endless war, I see it now. That's what the Deck does, it tears people apart. You think it's working for you because you use it to crush your enemies one by one —* she pounded a crinkled, shining fist into her palm — *and watch them turn against each other and scatter before you, like pathetic insects.*

"Uh . . ." Anthony said.

Pero the Deck is what makes us hungry. The Deck is what makes us greedy. The Deck is both the mechanism and the motivation. The power and the positioning. We are nothing without it, because it has created us in its image, but in doing it so, it makes us empty, husks, tazas vacías. She shook her ancient head.

Sierra was barely listening. The Sorrow had finally come around, that was all that mattered. As the others talked, Sierra turned back to the mess of lines around the only remaining figures on the wallpaper: the House of Shadow and Light, the lineage of Luceras, the Hierophants. And in the middle of it all, La Contessa, her web still stretching outward into the chaos. The source. The power hub.

"Shit," Sierra whispered.

Language, Septima chided.

María threw her arms up. "Thank you! I've been trying to get this girl to speak with some respect ever since she turned twelve."

You have to be firm with the children, but there's only so much we can do.

"Shit," Sierra said again, louder this time.

"*Sierra!*" both María and Septima hissed at the same time.

"What is it?" Anthony asked, stepping up beside her and gazing at the paper. "Do you know what to do?"

Sierra narrowed her eyes, scanned the figures in front of her, the splattered lines. "Yes."

Anthony made little get-on-with-it hand rolls. "And?"

"We're going to give them exactly what they're asking for."

FIFTY

Juan watched the world pass out the window of the revamped Access-A-Ride van. The gray day seemed to grimace back at him: traffic and smokestacks and ugly clouds across an ugly sky. Occasional glimpses of the Manhattan skyscrapers behind them. Crisscrossing highways all around. Blah.

"We getting close," Rohan advised from the driver's seat. "Just FYI and all that."

"What the hell are we doing?" Juan said. "None of this makes sense."

"It doesn't," Robbie said. "But we don't have much of a choice."

Juan had never particularly liked Robbie. He didn't hate him or anything, and he definitely trusted him. But the guy just rubbed him wrong. He was too polite about everything, and him basically ghosting on Sierra once they'd found each other and started dating? That was the last straw. It was cool that he stuck around after getting curbed for Pulpo, but that only meant he merited tolerating, not actually being nice to.

But today wasn't the day for snappiness or infighting. Juan swallowed his retort and scowled back out the window. "Sierra said what again?"

"She said we'll know what to do," Anthony said. "And when to do it."

"Mad cryptic," Juan said. "Mad, mad cryptic."

Bennie put her hand on his leg and squeezed, and that was about the only good thing to happen all day, and things were obviously about to get much, much worse.

"Are we even gonna be able to 'shape?" Juan asked, trying not to sound terrified. "Didn't y'all say there was like a no-spirit barrier around the lot the other day? What if —"

"We don't know," Caleb said.

"And where is Sierra in all this?" Juan asked.

"Wouldn't say," Pulpo said.

"And you're cool with that?"

He shrugged, maddeningly chill about all this but also probably losing his shit in a massive way on the inside. "Not much we can do about it, but yeah, I trust Sierra. She'll probably make some grand appearance right when we need her and wreck shit."

Juan allowed himself a slight smirk. That would be in line with how she did things. He still didn't like it.

"Look," Caleb said, turning around from the passenger seat. "I don't like it either, kid, but it's what we got, and Anthony's right: Your sister knows what she's doing. In a way, it's simple. All we have to do is show up and act normal, meaning be irritable and ornery about everything because shit isn't going our way, which is easy because we are and it's not, and then, you know, do what's gotta be done."

"See, that's the part I'm unclear on," Juan said. They pulled off the highway and wound through some dusty back-roads amidst vacant lots and random abandoned gas stations.

Smoke poured out of power plants in the distance, further graying the already gloomy skies. "What does that *mean*?"

Anthony shook his head, looking more and more spooked as they approached. Up ahead, the stage light towers and platform appeared over the tall grass. Already, a crowd had shown up, tons of people milling about, waiting for whatever horrific shitshow was about to go down. "All she said was, we'll know when the time comes, and when it does: Fight like hell."

FIFTY-ONE

"Think this is close enough?" Neville asked, putting the Cadillac in park and stretching an arm across the front seat so he could turn back and see Tee and Izzy.

"It's hard to say," Tee said at the same time as Izzy said, "Tough to say, really."

They glanced at each other, but neither one laughed.

Nydia did, though. "Oh, man. Hierophant status really is some shit, huh?"

They both nodded, because the fact was, it was, it really was, and that was all there was to it.

Neville shook his head, made a face, craned his neck to make sure he could see Tee's eyes, then glanced into Izzy's. "I know y'all got some extra shit going on," he said, sounding like the dead-serious Uncle Neville they'd first seen come fully to light that night of their upstate run-in with the Bloodhaüs. Neville was always about that life, no question, but he was usually as quick with a laugh and avuncular chuckle as anything else; you just kind of assumed he'd literally kill anyone that got in his way, because he probably would. But it was rare you actually saw the killer look flash past his eyes, and this was one of those times. "But I'm telling you right now: The only, and I mean *only*, reason I'm not getting out of this car right now and putting a bullet through the skull of this corny little nazi I keep hearing about, is because I have been assured that that's not the move right at this moment by Nydia here, and she is technically the boss."

Tee and Izzy nodded solmenly.

"And," Neville allowed, "I've been tasked with something even more important than killing a fool, and that's keeping you two safe. Or at least, your bodies safe, while the rest of y'all goes fluttering off to do whatever it is you gotta do and all that, right?"

Another nod.

"Alright, cool. I'm just gonna let you know that whatever happens, Uncle Neville gonna keep you safe. Not if, not but, not anything except that's what it is. I don't know if that makes you feel any better about all the hell going on, but I hope so."

It did actually. They felt the slightest warm sense of ease enter their bones as he spoke, because, quite simply, they knew his words to be true. No one would touch them while Neville was on vigilance duty, and that was that.

"Additionally," he said, now with a slight smile. "I got Reza and one of her peoples, Bri, set up out in the weeds with a high-powered rifle and a steady bead on the surrounding area, just in case they try to throw more at us than I feel like handling at the moment. Uncle Neville's getting old, you know."

Tee and Izzy smiled. It was a tiny, fleeting thing, but it was an honest one, and they knew it'd give Neville a little bit of peace to know his humor had hit home. He looked up at Nydia, who was watching him lovingly. "You good, sweet thing?"

"Never been better," she said, and kissed him on the lips. "Just kidding."

"Didn't think so," he said.

"But I will be once this shit is over." She popped the door. Shot a final glance at Tee and Izzy. "Be careful, girls. And make sure you know how to get back so you can make it in time whenever whatever's gonna happen happens."

"Stay safe," Tee said.

"Safe is for suckas," Izzy said. "Just don't die or get grievously injured."

Tee rolled her eyes. She had a point, though. None of them were going to be safe for the next few hours, so why bother pretending?

Nydia shook her head and conceded the point. Then she stepped out of the car, blew another kiss at Neville, swung a messenger bag over her shoulder, and headed out through the weeds.

"Alright," Neville said, catching Tee's eyes in the rearview. "What's next?"

FIFTY-TWO

Sierra, ten cuidado, Septima called from behind. *Está mojado.*

"She doesn't listen," María huffed. "I told her to bring an umbrella. Did she?"

Claro que no.

"I think I liked it better when you two were fighting," Sierra grumbled over her shoulder.

"What?" María asked just as Septima said *¿Qué dijiste?*

Sierra rolled her eyes. "Never mind!"

Not bringing an umbrella to a rain forest had been a pretty newbie mistake, but that wasn't the point. And anyway, it wasn't really raining so much as aggressively misting. The air seemed alive with heat and water particles flying in every direction and sudden gusts of warm tropical breezes carrying the thick flowery must of some nearby river. It was, in short, the best reprieve ever from nasty-ass December in Brooklyn.

Puñeta, Septima cursed. *Pero esa muchacha se va a caer.*

At least, it would be if those two ladies would ever shut up and let her enjoy it. "I'm not going to fall," Sierra called. "I'm fi —" *Of course* in that moment her foot would slip on a smooth rock surface and she'd have to catch herself on a nearby tree, scratching her palms a little. Of course.

"Sierra!" María called with unnecessary urgency. "Are you okay? Be careful!"

Que te dije, Septima admonished, clearly over the moon about her own foresight. *Que carajo te dije.*

"Guys, I'm fine!" Sierra said. "I'm totally fine. You both gotta chill."

The whole past twenty-four hours had been like the Halloween special of some terrible bilingual sitcom. First it was the rush to get last-minute tickets and speed off to the airport (after a quick stop at Tee's), and Septima and María fussed like two old hens the whole way while Neville zipped in and out of traffic on Atlantic Ave and Sierra stared out the window, trying not to think about all the hell headed their way.

At JFK, Sierra had broken it to Septima that they were going to have to put her in a carry-on, since she had some solid parts amidst all that woo-woo ethereal mess, and it wouldn't do to have a weird floating head and hands accompany them through security. "It'll be fine," María had told the Sorrow in her conciliatory, time-to-put-your-big-girl-pants-on voice. "And at least we're not putting you in one of the checked bags."

Septima sighed.

"And we'll get you a nice cafecito when we arrive, okay? Bet it's been a while since you've had an actual Puerto Rican coffee *brewed* in Puerto Rico itself, hm?"

Sierra had watched in a kind of awe. When did these two bitter enemies reconcile? She couldn't remember the moment, but it was kind of adorable to see her mom go into extra-mom mode over an ancient spirit. And then, as always, Sierra had remembered all the awful things Septima had done and tempered her excitement some.

They'd crashed in a cheap airport hotel that night and then set off to El Yunque at dawn. The bus dropped them at a depot on a winding mountain forest road, and they'd been trooping through the dark green fronds and dangling vines in the early morning gray for an hour, following María's vague recollections from her childhood visits to Tío Angelo's place.

Now Sierra stopped to catch her breath on the hill they'd been hiking up for the past hour. It was still early, sure, but she had no idea how long anything was going to take, and things were probably going to happen fast in Jersey once they started. "Are you *sure* this is the right way, Mami?"

"How many times do I have to tell you . . ." María panted from a few feet back.

"I'm just saying, it was a long time ago . . ."

Sierra, don't sass your mother.

"You know, I've had just about enough of —"

Yeah, yeah, yeah, the Sorrow said, floating up ahead and then turning to face them. Her flowy essence cast its golden sheen across the forest greens, sparkled into a rainbow through the prism of the morning dewdrops. *Escucha por favor.*

"What's up?" María asked, coming to a stop beside her daughter.

I just . . . I want to say something. Septima glanced around (as if there was anyone else for miles, Sierra thought). *It's that: I am sorry. I am so, so sorry. I have been a terrible, terrible person for most of my life and the long extended period of my afterlife existence. I have taken advantage, I have killed, manipulated, maimed. I have hurt people, and that in itself is unforgivable, but worse estill, I have hurt my family.* She sniffled. *Mi familia. It really hit me the other day, when Sierra was talking about the ancestors, and how they protect her, and I thought, but not me. Me? I almost killed her. Several times. What kind of an —*

"Ya," Sierra said sharply. "Enough. I hear you."

"And I accept," María said. "I don't speak for Sierra. She decides about her own forgiveness. But I believe you, Tía Septima, and I accept. I have seen how you have come to care for my daughter, for us, and it is genuine. And that's what matters most, more than the past. The future. For what it's worth."

It's worth the whole world, Septima said, closing for an awkward hug.

Sierra hadn't decided how she felt about the whole thing. There were too many angles and she was too busy trying to make sure they did what they came here to do to figure out forgiveness.

She looked away, not wanting to interrupt the reconciliation but not really wanting to take part in it either, and something bright caught her eye up ahead.

LOS ANGELOS BAR & CAFETERIA a sign read in brightly painted red letters. Beyond it, fans spun lazily in an open-air wooden structure. A tall, wide, hairy-faced man watched them stonily from the entrance.

Sierra recognized him from their family photo album.

"Tío Angelo!" she called. The last time she'd been to Puerto Rico, she'd been a kid, seven or something, and she barely remembered anything except that hot wet air and the scruff of Tío Angelo's big beard when he hugged her.

That solemn face broke into a wide, unruly smile as soon as she said his name, and Tío Angelo, looking like some kind of revolutionary Boricua Santa Claus, burst into a raucous chuckle. "Sierra! You've grown up! And María! Wow!" Then he squinted, frowning. "What the hell is that golden glowing thing?"

"Ah . . ." Sierra said. "Uh-oh."

Tío Angelo drew a long machete. "Is that a Sorrow, María? You've brought a Sorrow to my house? I don't think so, mi amor."

***

Inside Los Angelos, beer ads and saint statues decorated the walls. At the far end, an impressive wooden bar stood before a cabinet of various liquors. "Look," he said gruffly, "there's a lot neither of us understand about what's happened on each other's ends. I respect that." Outside, the rain came down in earnest; it pounded on the tin roof overhead and ricocheted off plants and flowers, wetting the tables at the edge of the bar. Sierra tried to ignore the flickering golden glow that was Septima, waiting silently and somewhat pathetically out in the elements. "And María has been updating me with the basics of what's happened, which I appreciate."

Sierra looked at her mom. "You never told me that."

"Just the basics," María said. "I wrote to him after everything that went down on Halloween, kind of hinting at what was happening, and turned out he knew more than I'd realized about all this."

"Pero, por supuesto, nena." Tío Angelo released a cigar-stained chuckle.

"I have learned that there is no such thing as *of course* when it comes to spirit legacies in families," María said. "Look at Rosa. Or me, for instance."

Angelo nodded. "Mm . . . true, true." He turned a furrowed brow to Sierra. "And I must say, my deepest congratulations, Lucera. It gives me great hope and joy to know that the legacy continues, and I see that it shines within you very brightly."

"Thank you," Sierra said, trying not to hurry him along, needing desperately to hurry him along. "And —"

"But the point remains. I cannot help you as long as that monstrosity is with you."

"She —" Sierra started, but Angelo cut her off again.

"Do you know why I live here, in this remote corner of the world, Sierra?"

This sounded like a rhetorical question or a test, and Sierra had time for neither. "No?"

"Because the mother of that creature you brought here still lurks within the shadows of those ruins. And it is the tradition of our family to keep her contained. It is our role. Has been passed on for generations, just like the role of Lucera, hm? It's not that she's trying to escape. No. She doesn't need to, of course, because her web stretches out into the world and her foul stench pervades along with it, including and especially in the form of the Sorrows."

"Yes," Sierra said. "And we've come to end all that."

"And furthermore," Angelo continued without even pretending to listen. "It is to protect the realm from those who would come to see her, pilgrims so to speak, who want to embellish their foul powers. Just two months back, in fact, we caught three of those ones who call themselves the Bloodhaüs, trying to reach out and find themselves face-to-face with La Contessa herself, and probably in some quest to destroy you."

"Oh?" Sierra hadn't heard about any of this.

He scoffed. "Now they rot beneath the earth."

"Oh. Wow. But, Tío —"

"This is the role we have always played and —"

Sierra slammed her hand on the wooden table they sat at. "Tío!"

Finally, he stopped talking and looked her in the eye. Bullheaded men only understood brute force. It was a shame so many of them ran the world, Sierra thought briefly. How much further would we have progressed if — whatever. She rounded on her uncle, letting that flicker of her shadow and light magic seep out around her to remind him of exactly who he was talking to. "Maybe you've fallen so in love with your tragic traditions that you're terrified of what might happen if you didn't have to uphold them anymore, hm?"

Angelo blinked at her.

"Or the idea that you might have to do something else with your life. I thank you for all you've done to combat the influence of La Contessa. I really do. And we've come here to destroy her and end this forever. All of us. And —" She placed some glowing cards on the table, facedown. "We brought these to help us do it."

Tío Angelo's eyes widened. "Oh."

"She has a point, Papá," a voice said from the far end of the bar. Sierra looked up. A young man, maybe twenty-five, stood just under the awning in soaking-wet jeans.

"Ay díos mío," María exclaimed, running over to him. "Is that Angelito?"

Los Angelos, the bar was called, Sierra realized. Plural, not possessive. Of course, because Spanish. She hadn't thought about it, though, and she'd forgotten completely that Tío Angelo had a son.

"Hey, Tía María," he said, laughing and accepting her cheek kiss. "And look, Papa, if they brought the cards, they mean business. And if this Sorrow is with them, then it's here to help. That's it. You know I hate the Sorrows as much as you do, but Sierra, our new Lucera — she crushed the House of Light, La Contessa's own daughters. Damn near wiped them out. If she trusts this creature, or thinks she needs her help anyway, who are we to say she's wrong?"

Tío Angelo grumbled something and blinked a few times, rocking his head back and forth.

Angelito turned to Sierra. "Look, cuz, don't worry about it. If the old man won't take you, I will."

FIFTY-THREE

That thickness. That heavy shroud. A chill swept through the air, but it still felt heavy over the crowd, like a muggy day. The gray sky, the gray, gray sky. The bustle below.

Up, up, up and over and around. The force field they'd explored yesterday formed a kind of egg around the event. Invisible to the normal eye, invincible to even the tougher power players on the scene. It had to be the Hierophants holding it together. Fortress and the River — it smelled of their filth: very old, ill-maintained and ill-mannered, weighty with whole epochs of discontent and malnourished, slippery dimness. A crawling, festering kind of power. Almost unstoppable. Almost.

The Hierophant Air was something altogether new. They probed the intricacies of this invisible wall, as they had yesterday, slid their amorphous, barely there matter into its cracks and crevices, the fault lines of its thick fabric. And then they expanded, filling them, filling them, braiding through the tiny seams, growing and growing, and seeping farther, deeper, colliding against molecules and then rupturing them, collapsing cross-stitches and clumsily fused together notches, disfiguring half-broken moldings.

A tremble: The Hierophant Air felt it bristle through the

steadily decimating lining of the force field. They paused the work, breathing in and out, expanding and contracting, reenergizing and aware, suddenly, deeply, acutely aware, and ready.

Another shudder, more bristling. They knew now, the other two Hierophants. They felt the disruption in their beings, the unraveling of what they'd made.

Good. It was bound to happen.

Down below, the two towering figures on either side of the crowd leapt into action, hustling with gigantic, pounding steps toward their respective power points to find out what went wrong.

It was too late, though, deliciously too late. And they were too obtuse to realize how they were about to become the keys to the final unraveling of their creation.

The Hierophant Air chortled as they sprang back into action, blasting full-throttle through the newly widened ravines they'd carved through the near-catastrophic shield wall.

They split into two streams of current, shrieked through tunnels down either end of the shield, and then each sped into a breathless, unstoppable torpedo blast of air directly into the power centers that Fortress and the River had hurried to check on.

For a moment, there was nothing, just the December wind shushing past and the murmur of the crowd. Then, with a ferocious tremble that few if any could actually feel except the Hierophants, the shield split entirely and disintegrated into nothing.

"My friends!" Dake's voice blasted out over the loudspeakers. "My friends! My brothers and sisters!" A cheer went up. The event was beginning. The web trembled and spasmed. "Welcome!"

Wherever Sierra was, she better hurry.

FIFTY-FOUR

"Go ahead," Dake said, glancing back at Juan with a nasty grin on his face. "You can play beneath me while I talk, boys."

Juan didn't like the way this white kid said *boys*. Or *beneath me while I talk*. Or anything else, for that matter. Dake spoke like someone who had worms just waiting to pour out of his mouth at any given moment. And it didn't help that he was wearing a fur coat and a metallic crown. Culebra was usually the most freakily adorned at any event, but now they were all just in puffy jackets and scarves to stay warm, and this Hitler Youth–loser was dressed like some world wrestler's busted nephew.

"What do you call it?" Dake said slyly, like he was in on some joke no one else got. "Vamping?"

"Uh, sure," Juan said.

"Don't act surprised that I know a thing or two about music!"

Juan shrugged. "I wasn't." He definitely was.

"I used to be in love with a musical theater fanatic, you know."

"That is somehow unsurprising to me."

"She didn't . . . never mind." Dake shook his head, momentarily lost, then gathered himself, snapped his head back to the roaring audience as Juan rolled his eyes and signaled Kaz — poor Kaz, who had no idea what the hell was going on but gamely showed up to this ludicrous, satanic gig anyway — to get things started.

"Friends!" Dake boomed.

Kaz ripped into a fierce march, alternating between his snare and toms.

"Yeah, just like that," Dake said creepily. "Alright now."

Juan already hated this dude, but he had the stage presence of a lecherous gynecologist doing karaoke at a high school, and that just amped the hate all the way to twenty.

"We have gathered today for unity!" Cheers. "For one-ness!" Cheers, even though that meant the same thing as unity but whatever. "For victory!" Cheers.

Pulpo climbed the scale, smacking low notes with his thumb and plucking octaves with his pointer, as Kaz circled back to the one. They landed on it together, and Pulpo launched into a double-time walking bass line amidst Kaz's sparkling cymbals.

"We have a new enemy in our midst, and it's not one of the houses. It's not the now-defeated Iron House or even the treach-erous, soon-to-fall House of Shadow and Light."

Boos from the crowd. Juan rolled his eyes, chiming into the thunderous progression with some wistful arpeggios. Who the hell were all these wannabes anyway? Dake had invited every house vying for power in the tristate area, sup-posedly, which from the look of things amounted to about a hundred very random, mostly white people of all ages and no particular fashion sense. Some were dressed in all-green jumpers, others had on pointed hats. A few wore capes and cowls, trying to look as edgy and grim as possible. But many were just indescribably plain: collared shirts and V-necks, slacks, some business attire, some army jackets. How did this cross section of mediocrity stumble onto the magic of the Deck? Juan wondered.

Did it really matter, though? It did not. All that mattered was that Dake ended up incapacitated when all this was over. Preferably permanently.

"Are we happy to be here?" Dake yelled, choking up on the mic and getting too close to it in a way that spoke of someone with too many rock-star dreams deferred. "Are we ready to change the world?"

Juan obliged the moment by transitioning from the overlapping tinkled notes to full, thrasher power chords, and Pulpo responded in kind, doubling down on his already heavy riff.

"Yeah! I like that!" Dake said punchably. "Okay, look, everyone. As most of you have heard, I gave Lucera and her Shadow and Lighters a few days to do what is right and hand over the Deck to the people! Because we, the people, are who deserve the Deck! Am I right?" The crowd seemed to agree. "Because it's ours! Am I right? Yeah! It belongs to the people, and we, we are the people. We deserve the Deck! We will use it to change the world for the better, and finally, finally, those of us who wield it can take control as we're supposed to, yes?" Wild cheers. Wild, terrifying cheers. "Because we're the greatest nation on earth! What's to stop us once we have the Deck, hm?"

Juan looked out across the many angry, enthralled faces. Any moment, their rage and ecstasy could boil over and they could just swarm over the stage and tear him to pieces.

"And anyway," Dake yelled, "that time period is up! And so let's have it! I know there are members of her house with us today, in fact, some of them are right here onstage providing the musical entertainment! Give it up for Culebra!"

Butchered the name, somehow managed to make it rhyme with *cholera*, but that was no surprise. People cheered, which was a surprise. Juan severely hoped Sierra knew what the hell she was doing so this nightmare would be over soon.

"But I don't . . . Hmm . . ." Dake made a show of gazing out into the crowd, one hand blocking the nonexistent sunlight out of his eyes. "I don't see this Lucera-slash-Sierra character they love so hard."

Juan decided Dake could mention his sister being loved hard exactly one more time before the whole play-nice thing would be over and he'd have to beat the paste out of him. Judging from Pulpo's face, he'd at least have a tag-team buddy in that endeavor.

"I guess she decided not to show up!" Dake said, amidst hisses and jeers from the crowd. "I guess we'll wait a little bit for her and see if she decides to make an appearance, huh? And until then, please enjoy this lovely entertainment from the band."

Dake turned around just as Juan was amping up the song. The guy looked completely different, his face suddenly shrouded in rage. "She better hand over that Deck," Dake snarled in Juan's ear. "Or you know what'll happen."

"I can't hear you!" Juan lied, playing harder. "The music is too loud!"

Dake shook his head and stormed to the back of the stage, where his over-the-top Iron Throne awaited. He eased languidly into it and watched Culebra burn through their spontaneous power anthem.

Juan was just gearing up for a solo when someone tall came running up the back steps to the stage. Juan abruptly stopped playing. Juan had thought Sierra's drawing of the River had been, you know, a caricature. She hadn't seen the guy herself either, after all, and was just going from what the others told her. But . . . the man — was it a man or some kind of horrible deadlike creature? Juan didn't know — the thing that came barreling up the stairs, it looked exactly as horrific as Sierra's rendering. Long, long fingers and a long, scraggly beard and drenched black clothes and a greenish pale face, mouth hanging open with water constantly dribbling out and eyes with no pupils and ugh!

The River hustled over to Dake, who sat up immediately. They traded words, frantic ones from the look of it, and then Dake yelled at someone behind the stage — a short bald guy who came running up with a laptop in hand. Juan played a few cursory chords so no one would notice he was barely paying attention. Pulpo seemed to understand, glancing between Juan and Dake and then dropping some overly fancy, show-offy riffs on the bass.

The computer guy was at it now, sitting on the floor beside the Iron Throne and clacking away frantically, Dake looking over his shoulder. Juan knew exactly what that asshole was doing. The crew had said Dake was connected to all kinds of fiends on the nasty end of the web, that that was who he was planning to set loose on the shadowshapers' loved ones. And whatever had just happened, it clearly violated Dake's sense of safety and the bullshit deal he thought he'd made. Which meant that this little freak was probably disseminating every-one's personal information on message boards all over creepy nazi forums.

Right now.

Still strumming, Juan started backing up toward the throne. He figured he could take that computer out with one well-placed swing of his Stratocaster. After that, well, he'd probably get trounced and thrashed, sure, but the Blood and Iron tech guy would be shit out of luck and their families safe, for the moment anyway.

He got a little closer, trying to weigh how fast he'd have to run to make it in time to cause maximum damage. Was this part of Sierra's plan? She'd said they'd have to fight like hell, that they'd know when, but Juan had no idea if this was that? Shit.

That satanic River demon had vanished, which was good in a way but also terrifying, because — where the hell was he?

He was gonna do it. He stopped playing. Fingers found the metal nub where his strap was secured to the guitar, got ready to slide the fabric over it. And then another tall figure flickered past behind the stage, but this one wasn't solid: It was a shadow. Juan blinked. There was Bennie, halfway up the stage stairs, swinging her hands nonchalantly in a way that Juan realized wasn't nonchalant at all: She was directing spirits. The tall shadow swooped through Bennie and then flashed forward across the stage, and then sparks flew up from the computer guy's laptop, and he leapt away screaming, as Dake jumped to his feet and glanced around.

And then the air changed ever so slightly in that way Juan knew meant that spirits weren't just nearby, but everywhere, and sure enough, those tall walking shadows began pouring in from all sides.

They'd breached the spirit barrier! Somehow!

And then a voice came over the loudspeakers, booming out over Culebra's wild vamp. Sierra's voice.

"You wanted the Deck of Worlds?" she yelled with a triumphant kind of chuckle. Juan signaled Culebra to stop playing, then glanced at Bennie. She'd turned her attention to the sound board, and he could see she was still concentrating, techshaping. She was amazing. *"You wanted the cards for the people?"* Sierra's voice taunted. *"Well, here you go!"*

Out in the audience, everyone was looking around, trying to figure out what the hell was going on. He could tell their interest was piqued. They *did* want the cards, all to themselves, in fact. Of course they did. They just hadn't expected to get them today. They'd expected to grumbly accept the dominance of yet another cutthroat house and hope to get close enough in its favor to one day backstab the right person and get their hands on the Deck so they could be the ones throwing massive ridiculous parties in the middle of the New Jersey wilds.

"Hey!" someone yelled into the sudden silence. Juan thought it might've been Jerome. A poof of thick rectangles of paper went shooting up into the air from one corner of the audience, and the cards fluttered down over bulging eyes and outstretched hands.

At the opposite end, another voice yelled, "Hey!" — Nydia maybe — and the same thing happened. Then a third time, right in the middle of the audience.

For a smooth couple seconds, utter silence took over. Then,

like someone had flicked a switch, the whole crowd exploded into a frenzy of grasps, yells, lunges, and then, inevitably, punches and kicks.

"Holy shit," Juan whispered. Shadows stomped forward from where they'd been lingering at the edges of the audience.

This was it.

Juan looked at Pulpo, who stood beside him with a slight smirk on his face. "You ready to shadowshape like the lives of your loved ones depend on it because they do, my good brother?"

"Hell yeah!" Pulpo nodded, signaling Kaz, and Juan kicked the overdrive pedal, and both of them leaned into a wide stance and let loose.

FIFTY-FIVE

"So what's it like?" Angelito asked as he whacked through some more thick underbrush. Their strange procession snaked along through the jungle behind them: María and Septima trudging along in the middle, then Tío Angelo and one of his nephews on rear guard.

"What's that?" Sierra asked.

"Being Lucera and all."

Whack! Whack! Whack!

"Oh, ha . . . I mean . . ." What indeed? She'd been Lucera since June, six months now, and still hadn't really figured out how to put it into words. She'd tried with Anthony, clacking away as honestly as possible about what it all meant on the Olivetti Nydia had gifted her for her birthday. But she didn't think it really made much sense, just a bunch of aggy thoughts and feels. Truth was, no one knew how it felt, not really, cuz no one else was Lucera. And Mama Carmen had barely held on long enough to pass along the mantle and then been gone completely and so . . . Sierra was left to figure it all out for herself.

Angelito glanced back at her and chuckled. "That's a whole lot of stuff that just passed across your face, cuz."

Whack!

"Yeah . . . because it's completely impossible to explain. And we've been at war basically since I became Lucera, and dealing with the damn Deck, so I don't even feel like . . . I've barely gotten to *be* Lucera, because I've had to be a wartime Lucera the whole time." For a flickering moment, Sierra wondered what life would've been like if the Deck had never shown up, if the other houses hadn't decided to team up to topple her, if she'd just been able to be happy and shadowshaping with her friends for the past six months. They could've made so much art, gotten so much closer to their spirits, who knew what else? The thought opened up a sadness inside her so deep she didn't know what to do.

Whack! Whack!

"Yeah, I know what you mean," Angelito said with a sad laugh. "I mean, not exactly, because yeah, what you said. But Papa's been training me to be part of this elite guardia since I could walk, basically. I studied IT at San Juan University, and he nearly lost his damn mind the whole four years I was away." He gave an eye-rolling nod toward where his father was still grumpily eyeing Septima. "I mean, he's right to be on it. And yeah, it's our lineage, our duty, I get that. But you weren't wrong, you know, what you said back there."

"Er . . ." Sierra made a face. "I feel kinda bad about that. It was a real outsider-coming-in-to-tell-folks-on-the-ground-what's-what kinda move."

"Yeah," Angelito said. "But like I said . . . it wasn't wrong. We will have to figure out how to live our lives when all this is over. I just don't think it ever occurred to him that it *could* be over one day. Without the cards, it's pretty much impossible to get anywhere near the place, and the House of Light had always had the Deck, so . . . Ah!"

"Ah?" Sierra looked up, followed Angelito's pointing finger to a hill sloping up above the treetops ahead. It was almost not there, the vegetation had overwhelmed it so much, but there amidst the curling tree branches and dangling vines, the peeling plaster walls of La Contessa's ancient palace could be seen. A single tower rose up over the domed ceiling of the main hold. Sierra shuddered. "Ah."

Once grand, the entranceway now festered and molded, crumbled and peeled. This had been a courtyard, Sierra realized. Now the forest had taken it over mostly, burst through the concrete and plaster, shattered elaborate statues and fountains in a slow-motion rampage over the course of decades.

"She's not going to let you boys in," Sierra said when they paused at the front door. "You know this, so let's not argue, yeah? But once she's distracted, ah, come through swinging, please?"

Angelito nodded, flashed his wily smile. "Será un placer."

Even Tío Angelo looked pretty giddy about the prospect of finally facing his lifelong foe. "Just promise me," he warned, eyeing Septima.

"Yes, yes. First sign of anything off from this one, we'll shut it all down, I swear."

Septima bowed to Angelo. *I just want to say*, she started.

"Uh-uh," Sierra cut her off. "We don't have time for all that now. Let's move." She and María headed into the shadows of the entranceway.

Sorry! Septima called over her shoulder. *Lo siento tanto.*

"Yeah, yeah, yeah," Sierra mumbled to herself. "She's sorry."

"Sierra," María warned as they opened the front door and stood on the threshold.

"Look, Mami." She turned, looked her mom in the eye. "I love you. I wish it hadn't come to all this. And I'm terrified that you're here, that you'll get hurt. But I also know it's important that you be here. That you have to be here for this moment, whatever happens."

María looked misty-eyed for a moment, then shook it away and nodded sternly. "I believe in you, m'ija." They hugged. Septima hovered up to them, sending her golden haze across the dusty linoleum floors and a once elegant, now dilapidated coatrack.

Let's do this, the Sorrow said shakily.

The front room was gigantic, something like an amphitheater. It spiraled upward into the dome shape that had been visible through the trees, and moldy, mostly scratched-over frescoes decorated the walls all the way to the top. The far end was all shadowy, but . . . Sierra squinted . . . something was moving over there. The shadows themselves seemed to come to life, but it wasn't spirits, Sierra realized. It was that whatever was moving was huge.

"Mmmmm, Luceraaa," a creaking, languid voice said. "Por fin."

It wasn't a spirit voice like Septima's; La Contessa Araña was still a flesh-and-blood thing. Sierra shuddered. From somewhere — far away, though — another voice called: *Luceraaa.* No: a chorus of voices. The same spirit song she had heard back in June when she'd first become Lucera.

Sierra stepped forward, held the cards she carried up. "We have come, Contessa. And we have the Deck."

"You have *some* of the Deck, mmm . . ." the ancient voice mewed. It sounded like she was chewing on something wet and drippy. "The rest is . . . in play, I see. There has been a haze over my web for a few days now, as often happens in times of change, eh? I cannot see as clearly now, but a shift is coming, a great shift. New alignments, new Hierophants. All is chaos. That's why you have finally come, Lucera . . . you are afraid. You wish, like I once did, to bring order to a world that is swinging against you."

"Yes," Sierra said. "The tides have turned. We need your help."

"Fffffffinally." La Contessa Araña seethed. "If only my own daughters had been smarter. If they had brought the Deck to the source, even part, along with you, Lucera — if they had convinced you to join them finally once and for all — they could've probably attained dominance, wiped out their enemies, consolidated power instead of being wiped out. Now . . . now that you have done what's right, Lucera, all that is obsolete. We will annihilate these new houses, we will destroy and reign as we once did, and I will reign with you, and the family legacy will be complete again, after so many generations."

Madre mía, Septima called, swooping forward. *It's me, Septima.*

"Septima, stop," Sierra whispered.

The Sorrow spun in front of her and María, her back to the giant writhing shadow. *I will bring her what you have brought, and I will destroy her with it!* Septima hissed. *Quick, give me.*

"Septima," Sierra said again.

Don't you see? Septima pleaded. *It's the only way. It's my destiny. I will atone for all I have done.*

"What's that?" La Contessa shrieked. The darkness seemed to come alive around them, long shadows stretching through the dank vastness of the palace.

"Septima, shut up!"

Fool! Septima spat, then she spun around and broke toward the far wall.

"What the hell is she doing?" María gasped.

For a terrible moment, they just watched as Septima's golden light traversed the dim hall. It was beautiful in the worst way. Then two tall shapes at the far end that Sierra had thought were pillars lifted and came down with sharp crunches, and a huge form emerged from the darkness. La Contessa looked like some horrible configuration of flesh, all dripping and bulging through the tattered remains of an elegant ball gown. Her shriveled, hideous face squinted out at them with several pairs of eyes that shone from the folds of her gigantic forehead. Spider legs sprouted from a bulbous protrusion behind her; they stretched up and outward into the darkness.

"¡Traicionera de puta!" the monstrosity screeched, and then one of her legs twitched and came shooting out of the darkness, stabbing through Septima's golden shroud.

The Sorrow let out a horrific shriek and then was simply gone. Darkness fell over the room and all Sierra heard was the thick and mucousy rattle of her horrific great-great-great-grandmother breathing in and out.

"Okay," Sierra said, taking her mom's hand in her own and squeezing. "Run."

FIFTY-SIX

Spirits surged through Juan as he strummed.

Beside him, spirits surged through Pulpo as he plucked. It suddenly seemed so simple, shadowshaping, like Juan had been doing it his whole life. Which, maybe, in some strange, small way, he had.

The music surged. Kaz had been going berserk on the drums since hitting the four count — like, only a true music savant like Juan could even distinguish where the one was, the whole sequence was so ludicrous — and Juan and Pulpo had just been hammering away at the same chord sequence in rising and falling riffs.

And the spirits had known exactly what to do, it seemed. As soon as the song had started, they'd turned their shimmering faces to the stage and galloped toward it on those long shadow legs, right in time to Kaz's maniacal beat.

And then, one by one, they'd leapt forward from either side, and one by one they'd surged directly into Juan and Pulpo, then busted back out again, now somehow solider, fiercer. Each newly rebirthed spirit had thrashed into the rollicking, battling crowd, scattering people to either side like some miniature tornado blast.

"Is this what we're supposed to be doing?" Pulpo asked, leaning over to get close to Juan's ear.

Juan scanned the place. People were beating the crap out of each other everywhere. It was like one of those videos that go viral on the Internet of some all-out brawl erupting at a fast-food joint or whatever — just utter chaos. It would've been hilarious if it wasn't real people getting their faces bashed in and being tossed into stampeding crowds.

Those cards, though. They all wanted to get their hands on those cards. And as soon as they did, they'd use them to subjugate each other.

Sierra — wherever she was — had had a lot more cards tossed into the mix than there really were in the Deck. Every once in a while, someone would emerge from the mire with one in his hands, then gape at it and start to complain that it wasn't even — and then get his ass beat before he could finish the sentence as the writhing, roiling pile of whupass rolled ever forward.

Juan nodded. "Yep. Chaos is the plan. We doing it."

"That's for damn sure." Down below, a guy shoved someone into another guy, and the shoved guy ducked so when the first guy went to punch him, he ended up knocking the guy behind him's teeth out, and then middle guy leapt up from his crouch and caught a face full of knuckles from a woman who'd run up behind the first guy. Then the woman kicked him in the chest, crumpling him, and snatched something from his hand: one of the cards.

"Good grief," Juan said as another spirit came running up, blitzed through him, and then stormed out, smashing directly into the lady and knocking her on her ass. The card went flying, and the throng of people hurled into each other over where it landed.

"STOP!" Dake's voice burst over the mayhem and music. Juan whirled around, still playing. This guy. The young fascist stood on the throne, arms stretched to either side. He was still wearing that ridiculous fur, but now it seemed to crawl and seethe around him, a thing alive.

Ugh. That blood magic was still a thing, Juan realized, just now it was combined with the Iron House powers, and who knew how all that would play out?

For a few seconds, it seemed to work. The melee paused as everyone looked up. It was all the time Dake needed. Immediately, his throne extended upward, iron spikes and pistons stretching beneath it with a wrenching squeal.

"Master!" a skinhead called from the front of the crowd. "I have the card! I have the card of the Emperor of Blood and —"

He didn't get the next word out, because someone sucker punched him into a crowd of people who immediately pounced on the knocked-out nazi.

"Bring me that card!" Dake yelled.

Juan and Pulpo exchanged a glance and then focused on that exact spot, where bodies writhed on top of each other, bones cracked, and people screamed. Shadows all over the field turned suddenly and began converging.

Juan saw Nydia and Jerome both working their way there from opposite sides of the crowd. But then an impossibly tall figure emerged from under the stage and Juan leapt back with a yelp.

The River. He launched into the crowd and foul, muddy water seemed to gush up from the ground around him. Nearby, a huge figure in filthy black fatigues and a gas mask elbowed people out of their way as they surged through the human tangle.

Shit.

The shadows weren't close enough. Already, the River and Fortress had tossed swinging, screaming bodies to the side like they were digging through the trash. A shadow spirit slammed into Fortress, and the Hierophant batted it aside like a mere annoyance. The River stood, the card raised above his head, way out of reach of anyone, and stepped gingerly back toward the stage, ascended it with one spooky, horrific lunge, and then seemed to almost float past Juan and Pulpo to where Dake sat upon his raised throne. A heavy, foul stench filled their air in the Hierophant's wake. He held the card up to Dake, who reached out and took it from him with a triumphant cackle.

Everyone watched in awe; even Kaz stopped playing.

The throne grew outward in several directions, reinforced and newly ferocious with spears shoving toward the sky and either side. Then Dake himself started expanding: iron appendages draped in gnarled, bloodstained fur unfolded from his back like horrific wings. He shrieked in pain, legs and arms lengthening as metallic shards shoved underneath his skin and then poked out at odd angles amidst splatters of blood. Gleaming, crimson tusks wrenched themselves out of his cheeks.

"Holy shit," someone in the audience said, summing up everyone's general mood perfectly. "What the —"

"THE HOUSE OF BLOOD AND IRON IS DOMINANT!" the newly crowned emperor bellowed. "And now a great slaughter will commence!"

Juan glanced at Pulpo, then both of them dropped their instruments and ran.

FIFTY-SEVEN

Sierra and María Santiago sprinted through a shadowy passageway that led out into a wide corridor, then threw themselves against a wall to catch their breath. They could hear the sounds of that horrible, disgusting creature cackling and howling and banging through the palace not too far away. It didn't seem to be coming up too close behind them, but Sierra was pretty sure the damn thing could just drop out of nowhere at any given moment. She kept her eyes on the shadows around them, ready to run.

"What the hell?" María panted.

Sierra didn't have a response. She just shook her head, coughed into her hand, tried to slow her breathing.

"Where do we . . . ?"

Luuuuuuuuuuuuuu, came that faraway call.

They both perked up, glanced around. "You heard it, right?" María asked.

Ceraaaaaaaa!

"Yeah, but where from?"

They took a few steps into the corridor. Someone had ripped the faces off all the dusty, age-old portraits along the walls. The carpeting was moldy and covered in bird shit or . . . something shit . . .

Luuuuuuuuuuuuuu . . .

It sounded like it was coming from somewhere up high, way above them, and deeper into the palace.

Ceraaaaaaaaaaaaaaaaaaaa!

Sierra pointed her chin toward the far end of the corridor, where a marble staircase wound up into the shadows. María nodded.

"¡Nietas desgraciadas!" La Contessa shrieked, clattering down at them through an explosion of broken, rotting wood and plaster.

"Ah!" Sierra shoved her mom out of the way and rolled a few times to stay clear of the collapsing ceiling. She was on her feet, pulling María up. La Contessa clearly hadn't counted on the extra crossbeams and deluge of plaster that would rain down after her. She shoved one hairy spider leg out from the rubble and then another, as she coughed, sputtered, giggled amidst the cloud of dust.

Sierra and María didn't bother waiting to see what happened next. They turned and barreled down the corridor. The sounds of buckling wood and more cackling meant that she'd freed herself, and then came the clackity click of all those legs scattering along the floor and, Sierra realized with horror as she glanced back over her shoulder, the walls.

La Contessa surged forward in a skittering, spiraling blur across the defaced portraits and up into shadows of the ceiling and then launched back down, a single strand of web trailing her, those long, pale arms reaching for Sierra and María.

"Go!" Sierra yelled. "Go!"

They made it to the stairwell and dashed up, jumping over La Contessa's long, sectioned legs that slid between the bannister posts to trip them up.

"¡No se vayan!" La Contessa sang in her terrible shriek. "Ya voy . . ."

A stitch opened up in Sierra's side as they reached the second-floor landing. They couldn't stop, though. They couldn't even hesitate a moment. Already, the sounds of those skittering legs grew louder from the stairwell.

"I don't . . . I don't know how much more I can go for," María panted as they started up the next flight.

"I know," Sierra said. "But we . . . we have to, Mami . . . please."

Luuuuuuuuuuuuuuuuuu, came that distant spirit song, but it didn't sound so distant anymore. And it was definitely coming from somewhere up above them.

Ceraaaaaaaaaaaaa!

"Come on!" Sierra said, pulling her mom along. La Contessa clattered onto the second-floor landing. Sierra peered over the bannister, saw those many red eyes glaring up at her, that scrunched-up, gnarled face, those dangling dollops of skin and rows of teeth. La Contessa smiled. Sierra ran.

"We're so close!"

Luuuuuuuuuuuuuuuuuu . . .

"One more flight!" They pounded up through the darkness and dust.

Ceraaaaaaaaaaaaa!

Sierra could hear more voices now — tons of them. It sounded like many, many women talking over each other. But they didn't seem scared or urgent at all, just talking and talking endlessly . . . who could be having a regular conversation at a time like this? And why weren't they even listening to each other?

It didn't matter. There was no time to worry about that.

The stairwell narrowed, then narrowed some more, finally became just a rickety ladder.

Luuuuuuuuuuuuu . . .

"¡Vengan acá, mis nietas!" crooned La Contessa.

Ceraaaaaaaaaaaaa! And more voices, louder voices, talking and talking.

"Go!" María yelled, getting out of Sierra's way. There wasn't time to argue — Sierra hand-over-handed it up the ladder, pushed against the trapdoor at the top with everything she had, shoving it out of the way, and then glanced back. For a second, Sierra thought her mom was about to pull some horrible heroic-type move and allow herself to get captured. But no, María was climbing as fast as she could up the ladder, her expression stricken with fear, eyes wide, lips tight. Then a face appeared behind her: La Contessa's red eyes and open mouth, long fingers spread wide, poised to close around María's ankle.

LUUUUUUUUUCERAAAAAAAAAA!!

So many voices! And they all sounded the same! And they were all speaking Spanish! It was deafening.

Sierra lunged upward into the darkness and then turned back, reached down, and grabbed her mom's outstretched arm and heaved her up, up, waiting all the while for a sudden wrenching that would rip her away. Instead, they rolled onto a wooden floor and then slammed the trapdoor shut behind them.

And then everything became suddenly silent.

FIFTY-EIGHT

Down, down, down into the fray, as bodies tangled and thrusted and collapsed, broken, into the mud. Down amongst kicking, stomping boots, open mouths, grasping hands, mud and more mud, the rising, dark tide of the River, coating everyone in filth. Down and then forward in a flush of wind, and the Hierophant Air swooped along past more crackling, colliding bodies right up to the towering figure of the River himself as he lunged at a group of combatants encircling him.

No, not just combatants. Nydia and Jerome. Friends.

Up above, the monstrosity that Dake had become fluttered in uneven, clumsy circles, still figuring out how to work those corruptions of wings.

The River howled, stumbling back a few steps as a burst of light issued forth from Nydia. Then a flash of green and red smashed into his face, wrapping around it and searing a sharp, suddenly fleshless strip across the Hierophant's forehead. Jerome let out a crow of victory, but already the River had recovered and raised both hands, sending black water streaming through the already burbling mud at their feet. Nydia yelled, sent a blast of shadow outward, but the River dodged easily, snatched the librarian's slender wrist in his gigantic, crusty hand. Immediately, Nydia started coughing and dark water poured out of her mouth in spurts.

Jerome hurled a blast of light and then shadow at the River, yelling and swinging his arms wildly, but the towering man swatted them off even as another red-and-green shape slashed across his face, shredding more skin away.

The Hierophant Air swooped low along the churning mud, then burst upward in an explosion of wind so sharp it shoved the River backward, both hands extended to either side to keep balance.

Nydia fell away, coughing, and Jerome ran to her side.

The River, already recovered, scanned the empty space in front of him, empty eyes twitching. Then he stopped and smirked.

They had been seen.

"Get down!" someone yelled, and everyone ducked as Dake's tangle of humanity, iron, and animal swooped clumsily overhead.

"Run!"

Nydia and Jerome had already disappeared into the crowd. The River glared up at Dake, watched as he dove toward the crowd, those long wings of bone, metal, and fur flapping mechanically.

"Take cover!" people yelled. "Get away!"

The River spun back around to find his new nemesis, the Hierophant Air, but it was too late: They'd already slid close to his face, stretched across it, felt the tiny pinpricks of flesh boiling up and suffocating beneath their embrace. The River snatched at them with his huge hands, scratched his own face with those long, broken fingernails, came up empty and bleeding. Fell to his knees, arms flailing.

Farther off, Dake fluttered back up into the sky, now with two people gripped in his monstrous talons.

Not just two people: Juan and Anthony. Friends.

The Hierophant Air released their grip on the River, who collapsed into his own mud, gasping. They blitzed through the crowd, an impossible wind, and then up into the sky after the Emperor of Blood and Iron.

FIFTY-NINE

Silence.

Silence and a gentle breeze. The smell of mold and filth replaced by the fresh, musty scent of soil, and beyond that something rich and pungent — garlic! Sierra hadn't had that combination of scents in her nose since Mama Carmen's spirit had made her Lucera and then vanished as light filled Sierra's whole body, bright light, and then the gentle aroma of soil and cooking garlic had reached her, along with —

An ancient, familiar voice broke the silence with a song: *Ven a los cuatro caminos, a los cuatro caminos ven.* Sierra and María stood up, looked around. They were in the cupola at the top of the tower. Open windows on all sides revealed the thick clouds over the forest below, mostly shrouded mountains in the distance. The room was empty, but Sierra could just make out a weathered map painted on the floor beneath her combat boots.

Donde los poderes se unen se vuelven al uno.

A shimmering form appeared before them, an elderly woman with brown skin. Half her face was just raw flesh pulled tight over her barely concealed skull. María Cantara, Sierra knew without having to ask. In her cheekbones, her wide eyes — the lineage was unmistakable. She smiled as she finished the verse and bowed her head slightly.

Welcome, my daughters, I have waited so long for all three of you.

María blinked. "¡Tatarabuela! It's . . . but . . . three?"

Sierra nodded once at the spirit.

"Sierra? What's going on?"

"You've been here all along, haven't you?" Sierra said.

The ancient spirit cocked her head. *Of course. Clouding her vision, you know. Among other things.*

"How did you . . ." Sierra didn't know how to put it. "It was such a long time, to be trapped."

Ah . . . She gave a soft chuckle. *How did I keep from losing my mind up here all alone, for all this time, with only my rotten mother who'd trapped me here in the first place to keep me company? You see, my vision hasn't been clouded, not at all. I have seen, even in my imprisonment, I have seen. And so I have recited as I saw. I watch, I watch, and I recite.*

"Recited what?" María asked. "To whom?"

The stories of our people, of course. Our legacy, m'ija. Yours and mine, and this young one here, hers too, of course. And so many more.

"The voices," Sierra said, feeling a surge of something like sadness, something like joy well up inside. "They were all you."

Mmm. María Cantara nodded. *They stay, you know. The stories. Keep me company, so to speak, but they're good for much more than keeping an old spirit's mind intact.*

"Why haven't you destroyed the web?" María asked.

Ah, there is only one force strong enough to destroy the Deck of Worlds and all its rotten power. For a moment, an infinite sadness took over her withered face. *And I did not have access to it, you know. Not until now, of course.*

"The Reaper." Sierra smiled, taking out the cards and placing them on the floor in front of her great-great-grandmother. "Three," she said.

"You two keep saying that," María groaned. "I'd love it if someone would let me in on what you're talking about."

My dear, dear daughter. María Cantara sighed, gazing at the softly glowing stack of cards. *At long last. Rise. Rise and take part in this final chapter of our struggle, m'ija.*

Sierra stepped back, still smiling, and took her mom's hand in hers. A hooded glowing spirit emerged from the cards, then pulled back the cowl to reveal a solemn face, half of it painted with an elaborate skull design. "Cantara Cebilín Colibrí," Sierra whispered.

The spirit nodded, then turned blinking eyes to her mother, María Cantara. *Mami,* she whispered. They embraced.

Are you ready, m'ija?

Another nod, and then words filled the air once more: *Once, a very, very long time ago, when the stars seemed so close and the trees and soil still sang songs of that first act of creation . . . So he stayed, and when María Cantara turned back to the darkening woods around them, she felt the icy presence of Death like a gentle breeze beside her. . . . Santo Colibrí watched in horror and admiration as his daughter seemed to catch fire within a blast of heavenly light while arrows and spears shrieked through the air. . . .*

Sierra turned in circles, eyes wide, as the voice of her great-great-grandmother told stories of her lineage that danced around her. She turned to her mom. "Are you ready, Mami?"

María blinked away tears. "Sí, m'ija. Let's end this forever."

They turned to the trapdoor, each grabbing a handle, and pulled it open.

SIXTY

The wind whipped against Juan's face as Dake dragged them higher and higher into the sky in flitting fits and jolts. Those metallic claws dug into his shoulders, he was positive they were drawing blood if not puncturing through tendon and bone too, and he was also pretty sure he was going to die.

Beside him, Pulpo had stopped screaming around the same time Juan had and was just blinking at the open sky around them.

Dake was just trying to get high enough to be sure they wouldn't have a chance when he let go. Fine. Juan would at least make things as difficult as possible for him. He reached up with the arm that hadn't been pinioned at the shoulder and grabbed one of Dake's monstrous claws, wrapping his fingers around a metal rod and getting a pretty good grip on it at that.

"Pulpo!" he called, indicating for him to do the same. Pulpo just blinked and took in air in tiny, horrifying hiccups that Juan could've recognized anywhere: a panic attack. He'd somehow managed to keep the panic at bay all through prison and now it had risen up at the worst possible time.

It hardly mattered, though. Grabbing on wasn't going to do much at the end of the day, not really.

Juan stopped trying to tell Pulpo what to do and felt a strange calmness seep into him. He was with his best friend, and they'd done their best. That was all there was to it. They might've even helped save the shadowshapers. Who knew?

"I'm here," Juan said. "I'm here with you."

Pulpo's eyes found his, and the gulping gasps slowed down just a notch. Didn't mean the panic attack was over, Juan knew, but it was something.

Suddenly, the air around them filled with spirits.

Juan looked around. They were beautiful, those streaming shadows charging up into the air alongside him — beautiful and useless. He had no instrument, nothing to 'shape with. And even if he could, what good would it do? He could maybe take out Dake, or at least distract him, and then what? Get dropped anyway and smash like a potato across the greater New Jersey swampland. Great.

The whole spirits-can-lift-you-up thing sounded pretty, but it only worked when you were Lucera, as far as he understood it. They couldn't just go around levitating random shadowshapers.

Juancito, a voice said, then many voices: *Juancito. Lucha. Fight. Why?*

Lucha, Juancito, lucha.

Pulpo was looking around too now, and his breathing seemed almost normal. The spirits had distracted him, caught him off guard, and somehow yanked the singeing edges of his mind away from that ongoing fire.

Alright, Juan thought, somewhat irritably. *Imma fight. At least I can mess up this freak's day a little bit before I die.*

He swung his legs back and forth, ignoring the wrenching

pain it opened up in his already throbbing shoulder, and then kicked them all the way up into the tangle of iron and fur and bone that was Dake now, turning Juan almost totally upside down. Then he started kicking.

The claw digging into his shoulder released very suddenly — maybe Dake was hoping Juan would plummet but no such luck! Juan took the opportunity to adjust his position and start ripping chunks of skin and fur away from wherever he could grab it.

Pulpo, Juan noticed, had started doing the same.

Dake screeched and veered sharply toward the ground.

SIXTY-ONE

Words swirled around Sierra as she and her mom crouched side by side before the opening in the floor and raised their left hands.

There were so many spirits in El Yunque. They gathered around whenever Cebi and Death went off on their adventures.

Out of the darkness below, a shape stirred, then lunged, the light catching those glowing red eyes and the glint of carapace. Then four legs wrenched their way up onto the lip of the opening, blocking out everything else. Sierra and María stepped back, waited.

"Foolish, foolish children," La Contessa snarled with a hint of laughter in her voice. "Don't they even realize —" As soon as her face appeared, Sierra and María clambered over her legs and shoved both their right hands onto it. They clasped each other's left hands over their heads. La Contessa Araña's skin was clammy and loose, like it might chafe off her skull at any moment.

A smooth bristle of chilly energy flushed through Sierra's arm.

Cantara Cebilín: the Reaper.

"¿Y esto?" La Contessa growled. Sierra glanced at her mom, met her gaze, and then looked back down and released with everything she had. Around them, the whole history of the shadowshapers, of each Lucera, hung in the air, ready.

Cebi did as she was told. Her mom's palm was warm on her forehead. And then light erupted through her. . . . Cantara Cebilín sat at her spot by the window, watching the avenida slowly pass by. She sipped her cafecito and took in the warm afternoon sun.

The stories caught fire around them, surged past their ears with a murderous whoosh, and linked with Cantara's spirit, 'shaped, and then burrowed into La Contessa's screaming face.

Sierra Santiago headed quickly down Lafayette, pulling out her phone as she walked. If she couldn't get wisdom from the women in her family, she'd find it elsewhere.

That moment! Just six months ago, and it felt like a whole lifetime. With wide, ancient eyes, the spirits had been watching all along. They watched and they fought alongside their living counterparts, to make this world a better, safer one for their children, and they carried the shadowshaper legacy across that tangled web of power, straight back to its source: María Cantara, who waited patiently in her tower in the woods.

Sierra's own story intertwined with those of her ancestors, became something gigantic within her.

"You can't!" La Contessa wailed. "You caaaan't!" Powered by Death herself, the stories sizzled across the ancient spider creature's skin, shredded through her like buzz saws, blitzed in and out and back in again. "Noo!" she howled, and then she trembled, and her red eyes began to mist over with gray as her many legs went slack, and then she simply slid down, away from the opening, and plummeted.

Sierra and María stood, still watching in awe as La Contessa Araña went crashing through one stairwell and then another before landing in a shattered, dusty heap on the first floor, a long streak of black blood exploding outward upon impact.

It is done, María Cantara whispered.

Sierra and María collapsed on the floor panting as the stories danced circles around them.

SIXTY-TWO

Surging through the sky toward Dake, the Hierophant Air felt a tremble and then a sudden, resounding lurch in the fabric of the world.

It was over.

It would all come crashing down now.

It was just a matter of where the pieces would land; who would survive the crash.

Dake's trajectory stopped midflight. He'd been dipping and diving, trying to shake the two boys who were mercilessly shredding him from below. Now a chunk of his wing went spinning off into the sky. Then a flap of fur.

Dake screamed.

Below, others were screaming as their powers faded.

It wouldn't be instantaneous, but it wouldn't take long either.

They had to get back to their bodies; one task remained.

As Dake began to plummet, his flailing, collapsing wings utterly useless, Juan and Anthony leapt to either side. The Hierophant Air whooshed them closer together and then swept beneath them and hovered, slowing their fall, slowing their fall, easing them toward the ground with the last of their waning strength. The boys blinked at each other, seemed to understand.

A thud marked the collision of Dake with the hard surface of the stage. His body already broken from the sudden rupture of all those unnatural structures within himself, now it burst into a splatter of blood and near-flattened flesh as dark waters enveloped everything in a burbling deluge.

Nearby, the River fell to his knees, water gushing forth from all his orifices. He collapsed, his filthy robes emptying out in seconds as the mud overtook him. Fortress thrashed to either side at nothing at all, like their mind had somehow gone before any of the rest of them. Then they were on their knees, flailing, flailing, suffocating as the power that had kept them going long past their expiration date seeped unendingly away and away and away.

But now something was moving, shifting, where Dake had fallen. A thick translucent arm emerged from the mire. That fool's cursed spirit.

And the Hierophant Air didn't have any time left.

"Drop me," Anthony said. "I got this." He had felt the whooshing presence of Air around him, the sudden cushion. And anyway, there was no more time.

"Yeah," Juan said. "We got this." Juan was merely boasting through terror, but the boy Anthony's grim determination spoke of a moment long waiting in the wings.

Below, a trembling spirit fought its way out of the newly birthed swamp. Dake's wretched phantom, now part man, part beast, all monster, shimmering and enraged.

Anthony slid his hand into his pocket as Air released him. It glinted in the pale moonlight as he fell.

The phantom Dake looked up with a snarl just in time to see Anthony plummeting through the air, blade raised over his head, and then it was too late. Anthony brought both his hands down as he landed, slicing through Dake's glowing form and then splashing into knee-deep dark water. He slashed and stabbed over and over as swamp thrashed around him and the last tattered shreds of Dake vanished in the breeze.

Juan landed with a splash of his own a few seconds later, gaped at what his friend had done. "The knife . . . from the . . ."

Anthony smiled, eyebrows raised. "Palmed that shit when they knocked me down."

"Genius!" Juan yelled, and they began sloshing their way to safety.

Safety.

The Hierophant Air fluttered through the crowd, desperate as this last gasp at life, at existence, flickered toward nothingness. Any wrong move was certain death, and even the right ones might not do it. Scattered along the ground: the Deck of Worlds. All the houses were gone now, all the suits wiped out. All that remained was the grinning face of Death on each card.

Beyond the stumbling, cawing crowd, through the tall grass, the Cadillac awaited. Air flushed toward it, away from the crowd.

Up ahead, two men huffed and puffed, jogging toward the car.

The car where their bodies were.

It was over then, probably. Neville was nowhere to be seen.

Ka-blam! A shot rang out, sending one of the men sprawling as a splash of blood splattered outward into the gray sky.

The other whirled around, terrified, and then a tall blur burst out of the weeds and collided into him.

Uncle Neville.

Fading, fading, with barely anything left at all, the Hierophant Air surged forward, past the tangle of limbs, Uncle Neville on top letting loose one downward punch after another, and into the back seat of the car, and there they were, those two beautiful bodies that knew each other so well, that loved each other so hard, that now would never be the same again, and the Hierophant Air streamed along their skin and found that familiar seat of warmth and flesh within, and then Tee opened her eyes with a gasp and turned immediately to Izzy, who was blinking and coughing and shaking her head, and they pulled each other close, both alive, through the fire and wind and impossible world, still there, still very much there.

SIXTY-THREE

My daughters, María Cantara whispered softly.

Sierra was the first to get to her feet. She helped her mom up, and together, they took in the room around them, the forest beyond it, the two spirits facing them.

"You've kept all the stories," Sierra said, squeezing her mom's hand. "All our stories."

I have, m'ija.

"I . . . I thought they were gone forever."

We couldn't let that happen.

Sierra scrunched up her face. "Are you going to do like Mama Carmen did and disappear now that we've finally found you?"

Cantara Cebilín laughed softly. *No, mi amor. Your grandmother had to go into hiding amidst the ocean. She was already halfway into a new realm when you reached her, and there was no turning back. That was different. She was always hardheaded, that one. Never did anything halfway for very long.*

"That's for sure," María said.

Sierra laughed. Suddenly it was all so . . . normal

somehow — there they were hanging out with their long-dead abuelas, and it made perfect sense.

Carmen made the mistake of thinking if she ignored the Deck and its evils, it would just go away. This is why the burden fell to you, Sierra. I'm sorry it did, but I see you were up to the challenge.

"Barely," Sierra said. "And I gotta see how my friends made out. There's a whole other war going on in Jersey."

They are safe, María Cantara said, and Sierra felt some of her tired muscles unclench. *They fought hard, and they are safe. And another story will be added to our history.*

Sierra looked again at the map sprawling across the floor. "This is El Yunque, isn't it?"

Mmhmm.

Cantara Cebilín stepped forward, a slight smile on her face, and pointed toward the center of the map, where a tiny version of the palace could be seen. *The palace was built at an ancient junction of two trade routes, and this tower marked the middle point.*

"The crossroads!" Sierra said. "Like from the song."

"*Ven a los cuatro caminos, a los cuatro caminos ven,*" María sang softly. "Mama Carmen used to sing it to me when I was little."

This is the original crossroads that the song refers to, María Cantara said. *There have been many others over time, of course, but this was the first.*

There was so much history, so much lore, so much magic, Sierra realized, somewhere between reeling and swooning. And it all could've been lost. . . .

"Sierra?" a gruff voice called from somewhere below. "María?"

"Tío Angelo!" María yelled back. "We're up here! The tower! We're coming down."

"¿Están bien? Gah! What the hell is this . . . ¿Qué puñeta es esto? ¡Angelito, mira! ¡Se acabó la fea esa por fin!"

"Can you come home with us?" Sierra asked.

Cantara Cebilín stepped over to María Cantara and they stood beside each other, smiling as sunlight poured in around them and lit up the room, the map, the whole world. *We can do anything we want*, María Cantara said, *now that the Deck is destroyed and La Contessa gone for good. We are as free as the wind, m'ija. As free as the wind.*

Once, not so very long ago, when the streets of San Juan still blazed with piano riffs that danced lovingly against a deep and ancient tumbao, and young poets still dreamed of revolution, Death came collecting.

Way out in the depths of El Yunque, three shimmering specters made their way through the trees toward the ruins of a once glorious palace. They came from opposite directions on the island, united at the gates of their old home. Together, they floated past warning signs and barbed-wire fences, beyond spirit wards powerful enough to keep even Death at bay; and then silently they glided deep within the crumbling walls to where something gigantic seethed amidst the shadows.

Mother, the Sorrows said as one. *You are not well*.

This was quite an understatement. La Contessa had recently completed her transformation into the spiderform after an agonizing span of decades, as bones and flesh rended and grew and sizzled and burst. She was haggard, exhausted, and still throbbed with intense pain. Plus, *that dead woman in the tower*, as she now referred to the daughter she had murdered, was still siphoning away at her power.

Mother, what can we do?

The old woman shook her huge, shriveled head, sending her great jowls swishing back and forth like sails. She blinked all eight eyes thoughtfully and scowled, revealing hideous and hairy fangs.

The Sorrows collectively took a small swoop backward from their beloved mother. *Let us destroy her, Mother. Together, we can do it.*

We have grown strong, said Septima.

— *wise*, added Veinalda.

— in our time away, finished Angelina.

Now we have come home, they said together. *Let us join forces and —*

NO! La Contessa Araña croaked mustily. *You silly children. Even together, we will be destroyed. Your dead sister has been gathering her strength all this time. I don't know how, but . . . it doesn't matter. She has. And ours is on the decline, do you not see? Are you so busy trying to be me that you ignore what is in front of you? Our power is on the wane. The Deck of Worlds crumbles as these petulant shadow-worshipping devils run amok in the world. And great change is afoot . . . No. You will not destroy her. Nor will you stay here . . .*

Together, the Sorrows sighed. *Mother . . .*

Enough. She silenced them with a wave of one of her long, hairy arms. She had endured the quiet of the palace crumbling gradually around her as her cursed daughter's ghost rambled on and on and on. Now the Sorrows would endure her quiet because, as happened at least once a day now, the memory of that last night of her freedom surfaced and made an echoing calamity within her mind.

María Cantara had simply walked into her own death and then, freed of her mortal body, had kept walking straight past all that carnage and up into the tower before anyone could stop her. La Contessa's tower. The center of her power. Almost immediately, the enemy had unleashed hell on her forces, but La Contessa knew what had to be done. That shadow monster was up to something and whatever it was must be contained instantly, otherwise, all was lost.

As explosions erupted outside and the screams of the dying echoed through the courtyard, La Contessa grabbed a vial of a spider essence she'd been working on for years and then scaled the outer wall of the tower. The threat would be kept at bay. The ghost of her daughter would not escape. More than that: She would use this moment as an opportunity. Already, the essence was taking effect — she felt her fingers grow long and sticky as she climbed, felt the noxious grind of transformation begin to churn within her.

María Cantara wouldn't escape this time. That was the most important thing. The urgency still pulsed through La Contessa, all these decades later. She wound the invisible strands of her power around and around the tower. She had siphoned energy from the Hierophants, her own daughters. Sure, it had weakened her troops, but resources had to be delegated. The carnage below was a single battle. Up there in the tower, she was about to win the war, for once and for all.

Around and around and around she went until there was no escape, no hope for escape, and the tower was impenetrable to any spiritual power, even Death.

When that was done, she flung her strands outward, far out into the world. Tingling and shining with the sorcery of the Deck of Worlds, the strands became a web — a vast, interconnected network of information, power, ritual. She linked her strands to the Sorrows, to the Hierophants, to the Deck itself. And of course, to her own seething, transforming abdomen.

When she was done, the battle was well underway down below. Her troops would probably be routed, yes, but the palace was safe, and anyway, she was tired. She crawled through a window into the tower stairwell. Up above, her prey was trapped, utterly trapped, and for the first time since María Cantara had been born, La Contessa had the upper hand.

Surely she did, she thought, as she folded her long arms and legs into herself and became a trembling ball in a shadowy nook on the underside of the stairs. But a murmur slid into her wincing mind as she drifted off to sleep. It was so quiet — barely audible beneath the din of battle, but it was definitely there, tinkling down from the top room in the tower above: a single laughing voice, speaking to no one at all in the middle of the night.

Bah! La Contessa sputtered, trying to shake away the memory.

Except it wasn't a memory, not really, because the voice had kept up its incessant babbling all through the decades, on and on and on, and even now, an endless rattle of barely intelligible jibber-jabber, until La Contessa was unsure if she had been the one to imprison her dead daughter or the other way around. They were prisoners of each other, it seemed, trapped forever in an ongoing duel, like the sun and the moon.

You will take the Deck of Worlds and relocate to New York City, La Contessa said to her startled daughters.

But —

THERE ARE NO BUTS. The shadowshapers are heading there next, and once they arrive, they will endeavor to set up a new power base within its boroughs. You must counteract their work. You must bring Lucera over to our side. She will join you, or she will be destroyed. If she replaces herself with a new Lucera, then that is who you will bring into the fold. The Sorrows must be complete once more for us to regain dominance.

All three sisters bowed. *Yes, Contessa.*

But before you go, you must handle another order of

business. *The Deck too is still incomplete. There are five Hierophants, you know. I have resisted filling the final slot, because I do not trust Death, but we are too weak to continue without his help. I am . . . depleted. That creature of darkness has sapped so much of my light, dear children. As long as the final Hierophant remains vacant, the Deck will be incomplete, and I will eventually waste away. You must give this role to Death. He is the only one strong enough to withstand this duty, to fill the role of the Reaper. Do you understand?*

Yes, Contessa.

Meet him somewhere away from here. If we let him within the boundaries of this palace, he will destroy me and free María Cantara's cursed spirit. She shook her head. This is what it had all come to. *Now go.*

The Sorrows bowed. They hovered away amidst the never-ending murmur of their long-dead sister.

—————

Up in the tower, María Cantara walked a slow circle around the room and gazed out the window, along the strands of thread leading off into the world. There, in his wooden house not too far away, Angelo read from his book of shadowshaper folktales to his young nieces, María and Rosa. She spoke the scene aloud, added it to the ever-growing fabric of stories that filled the room around her.

Farther off, in the bustling city of San Juan, Carmen and her husband, Lázaro, packed their suitcases and talked quietly about the future. Who would join them? What did this new life have in store for them? They held hands, then held each other, shook their heads at the hugeness of what was to come.

A few blocks away, Cantara Cebilín sat at her spot by the window, watching the avenida slowly pass by. She sipped her cafecito and took in the warm afternoon sun, the bombastic strains of a new salsa hit coming from the restaurant around the corner, the wild cackle of bochinche from the other viejas on the block.

She didn't have to look up to know that Death now sat across the small fold-out table from her, in the shadows of her apartment.

That morning, Carmen and Lázaro had told her they were moving to the mainland. *Brooklyn*, they'd said, a little apologetically, as if that would make it alright somehow. But it was alright any old how. It didn't matter where. It was time for them to go, and Cantara Cebilín knew it as well as they did. And she knew, even then, that it would be time for her to go pretty soon too. She was, after all, very old, and she'd lived a very long, very beautiful life. She had had lovers and she'd even loved some of them. She'd woken up some days, some years even, as a man, and lived that way, and other days, other years, as a woman. And sometimes as neither, and she'd lived that way too. And no one, but no one, could tell her otherwise or make her feel any way about it except ecstatic to be exactly who she was in that very moment.

She'd fought hard and outmaneuvered the Sorrows at every turn, mastering the Deck of Worlds and beating them at their own game, time and time again. She hadn't acquired the Deck itself, but she managed to keep Shadowhouse on top and deprived the House of Light of any real power beyond possession, thanks to La Contessa's shortsightedness all those years back. And she'd helped a new group of young warriors rise who were inspired by those long-ago mountain men's desperate struggle against the Yankee invaders.

After Láz had left to pick up the girls from Tío Angelo's spot out in El Yunque where they'd been staying, Cantara Cebilín had led her daughter into the bedroom. Carmen had known this was coming; there was no teary conversation the way there had been when María Cantara had performed the ritual on that desperate, fiery night. Carmen sat on the bed, waiting expectantly for what was about to happen, barely able to contain her own excitement.

Good, Cantara Cebilín thought. She loved how excited her daughter was about the tradition, about the power she wielded and all that was yet to come. She wanted to give a grand speech the way María Cantara had, to pass on some wise and prophetic wisdom, but she found there was nothing to say when she searched herself.

That Lázaro is a real piece of shit, she blurted out instead. *Keep an eye on him.*

Carmen had rolled her eyes. *Ay, Mami, por favor . . .*

Alright, alright. Cantara Cebilín sighed, putting her palm against her daughter's forehead. *Ya tú sabes.*

And now, hours later, Death sat across from her, grinning that never-ending Death grin. She pulled a filterless Conejo from her pack, offered him one. Death just stared at her. *Suit yourself.* She shrugged, lighting hers.

It's time, isn't it, she said, after a few minutes of smoke and salsa and bochinche and seagulls and car horns had passed.

Don't answer that, I know. She grinned her own eerie rictus, which she'd been told many times had a certain creepy mystique to it. She enjoyed that. *It was a good little ploy, my mami's, no?*

It was; didn't matter whether Death thought so or not. It definitely was. Still . . . something was different than she'd thought it would be. Something she couldn't place. This wasn't the peaceful send-off she'd been expecting. It felt more like the beginning of a whole new mission. Typical. She'd spent her life fighting one rugged battle or another, why should her death be any different?

Once, a very long time ago, Death's icy whisper trilled within Cantara Cebilín, *I told your mother, María, that I would gift her my powers.*

And you did, Cantara Cebilín said, taking a deep drag and exhaling it into the shadows of her apartment.

And I did, Death agreed. *Do you know what she said to me when I told her that?*

This sounded like the windup to a great joke, and Cantara Cebilín did not want to ruin it, whatever it was. *What?* she asked.

The voice that came next inside her head was not Death's; it was her mother's when she'd been just a girl of twelve or thirteen. *I can take any life I want?* she'd asked, full of all that childish earnestness and curiosity.

For a good few moments, Cantara Cebilín and Death laughed together. Then she lit another cigarette. *Ah, Mami . . . that was a good one. What did you tell her?*

The truth, Death said inside Cantara Cebilín. *That my power is much greater than that, as she would see, and that it was well worth the price she'd paid.*

Cantara Cebilín felt a sadness well up within her. *Her face,* she said.

Mm, Death agreed. *And her innocence.*

Cantara Cebilín unleashed her grim smile again. *Was my mother ever really innocent?*

Mm, Death agreed. *That was taken away by La Contessa before María Cantara ever had a chance.*

What is your power, if it's not to take any life you want?

Death stared at her for a few moments. *You don't know by now?*

Well, I —

My power is not about death, Cantara Cebilín. It is about life. The movement of life, mm? And what is life, if not movement?

Shadowshaping, she whispered.

Death nodded. *Everyone sees the movement of Death in what I do, what we do, hm. What they don't see is the movement of life. Life moves through the spirit, through the shadowshaper by way of the spirit, through the art by way of the shadowshaper. You see? Life moves through it all. Life is what powers it, much as a creature of the light, Lucera, is what powers a whole realm of shadow, yes? They are all one. This silly opposites game you mortals play all the time, it's such a tragedy really.*

Cantara Cebilín gave a dry laugh. *I know what you mean, man.*

Death stood, the tip of his cowl almost hitting the low ceiling. *Are you ready?*

She stood too, barely coming up to his chest, grabbed her

pack of Conejos, and glanced around the room. *Yes, old friend. Where is it we're going this time?*

To see the Sorrows. Your grandmother has finally decided to fill the final Hierophant card. They reached out to me, acting as her emissaries.

Cantara Cebilín groaned. *Will this bitch never give up?*

Not until she's stopped, no. But that job doesn't fall to us. Not yet anyway. For now, it is only for us to say one thing to La Contessa's request.

And what's that? Cantara Cebilín asked, stepping forward into Death just as Death stepped forward into her. Gradually, lovingly, they became one.

Yes.

EPILOGUE

SIXTY-FOUR

Nothing will ever be the same. That was the simple truth of it, Tee thought, running her fingers in circles over Izzy's forehead.

Izzy nuzzled deeper into Tee's embrace. *I know, babe*, she thought. *And I think that's okay.* They were wearing matching tuxedo tops and ball gowns, and they both had dapper little top hats poking off at an angle.

It is, Tee assured her. *I'm just taking it all in. It's a lot. It's a whole lot.*

"You two alright back there?" Ms. R's friend Bri asked from the front seat. She had impeccable makeup and a smile that promised it would never lie. "Looking mighty solemn."

"They alright," Ms. R assured her, looking warmer and more amiable than they'd ever seen her in a forest-green suit and Stetson hat. "That's just their faces. Plus, they been through a lot."

"No wonder you guys all get along so well," Bri mock pouted. "Grim face of dead-ass chicks." She turned around in the seat, flashed a devilish grin. "You know she thinks you guys are the bee's knees, right?"

"Bri," Ms. R groaned.

"Really?" Tee and Izzy said at the same time. They'd been doing that a lot recently. It probably wasn't going to stop anytime soon.

"She's always talking about how you're so mature for your age and whatever weird spiritual woo-woo crap y'all are going through, she hopes it'll be over soon."

"Bri!" Ms. R growled.

"Ah, it is over, isn't it?"

"Very," Tee said, finally smiling.

"Extremely," Izzy concurred.

"Well, I'm glad! Because it's Christmas! Heyyy!" Bri opened the window and yelled into the frosty air. "Merry Christmas, bitches!"

Ms. R rolled her eyes in the rearview and smiled at Tee and Izzy. "I'm glad too," she said quietly. "And look, Charo doesn't invite just anybody to the Christmas party."

"I can imagine," Tee said. "We appreciate it."

"Well, I told him about the ordeal . . . more or less, you know . . . and he wanted to do something special for the crew."

"We appreciate it," Izzy said. She settled back against Tee's shoulder. *I don't know what's going to happen*, she thought. *But I know I love you.*

Tee smiled down at her. *I love you too.*

Even though we can't leave our bodies anymore and become air together?

Especially *because we can't leave our bodies anymore and become air together.*

Izzy kissed her neck. *Good*, she thought. *Me too.*

SIXTY-FIVE

"It's in E-flat minor, you dick," Juan chided.

"It's not!" Pulpo said. "Listen."

Juan listened as the corny bachata band wound around toward the chorus one more time. Culebra's own Yoda, a big ol' Cubano dude named Gordo, was sitting in on keys and kept doing weird chord modulations and winking like he was in on some wicked divine joke. Which, to be fair, he definitely was.

"There!" Juan said triumphantly. "That was the five, and now we're in the one and . . . shit."

Pulpo made a little explosion motion with his hands. "Boom."

"Point is . . ."

"Uh-huh."

Around them, the party swirled, full tilt and rambunctious. Juan had never imagined a taxi company would have such a lit holiday party, but then again, the Medianoche was unambiguously a front for more nefarious operations, so that probably explained it.

"Why does Gordo take these corny gigs anyway?" Juan said, still salty about being proved wrong.

"Uh, he says it keeps his chops on point. Plus, he gets paid? And I think he likes it. Look how much fun he's having!"

The other guys in the band were busy trying to look like Dominican guapos, but Gordo was living his best life, bouncing up and down as they made their way into the bridge. The spirits were having a blast too, Juan noticed. They circled the stage, longstepping and two-stepping and sidestepping in time to the thundering timbales.

"The fact is," Juan said, glancing at his best friend, "now that we're both shadowshapers . . ."

"Culebra show's gonna be a whole new level of lit," Pulpo finished. They dapped, chuckling and shaking their heads. Juan had no idea how yet, but everything was definitely about to get really, really weird and cool.

"I know you hate dancing," a voice said behind them. "But . . ." Juan closed his eyes. He'd been waiting to see Bennie all night; he'd been thinking about seeing Bennie all night. He'd been pretending not to be thinking about seeing Bennie all night. He hadn't seen Bennie face-to-face since the whole mess in Jersey — there had been a brief checkup in the ER (at Caleb's insistence) and then dealing with family stuff and one thing and another — and sure they'd Skyped, uh, every single night usually for a couple hours, but like, it wasn't the same, and anyway: He stood and turned, and there she was, wearing a dark purple dress with no sleeves and bright red makeup and looking somehow totally at ease even though both of their worlds had come inches away from total collapse just a few days ago.

Juan felt his mouth drop open.

"Yeah?" Bennie said. "Like that?"

He nodded. "I do hate dancing. But for you, I make an exception."

They both bowed formally to Pulpo and then made their way to the dance floor, giggling like schoolkids.

SIXTY-SIX

Once, very, very recently, when Brooklyn still seethed in an epic struggle between what had been for a long, long time and what was brand-new and undeservedly self-confident, when movements rose and fell with a series of zeroes and ones, and fresh forms of music still awaited to be born amidst the churning avenues and colliding peoples, a girl and her family gathered together to celebrate a hard-earned victory.

Sierra Santiago, the fourth Lucera, sat between her mom and dad at a table loaded with piles of chicharrones, arroz con gandules, amarillitos, tostones, and about six different kinds of delicious sauces. A cafetera full of Bustelo sat steaming in the middle. In short, she was in heaven. Out on the dance floor, Juan Santiago tried desperately to keep time with Bennie, both of them laughing so hard they could barely breathe.

Neville and Nydia slow-danced nearby, even though the song was extra fast and spunky, they held each other tight in their own beautiful little world: two who had survived and made it through together, and no Dominican hypercaffeinated bachata bounce would stop them from having their moment. Virgilio and Timba played some goofy game on a tablet, giggling, while Tee and Izzy kept an eye on them from across the table, their hands wrapped in each other like an old married couple. Mort sat beside them, chatting amiably with Tee like they were old friends. He'd woken up when the whole Deck collapsed, wandered downstairs for a cup of coffee, and scared Dominic Santiago half to death.

Farther off, Caleb, Robbie, and Jerome talked excitedly about their plans for building a Brooklyn shadowshaping club for little kids, and all the games they would play, all the new ways to 'shape they'd discover, all the possibilities that lay ahead.

"Oh," Dominic said, glancing at his phone and then putting it away quickly. "Oh, oh!"

"*Oh* what?" Sierra demanded. "What are you being sneaky about?"

"Oh, nothing," Dominic said, utterly unconvincingly. "What do you mean?" He kept glaring at something just over Sierra's head, so finally she rolled her eyes and turned around and then screamed, because there was Gael, swooping toward her like some gigantic well-dressed bird of prey and then wrapping her up in his arms and squeezing with all his might until Sierra could barely breathe.

"What the!" Sierra gasped. "How the!"

Gael shrugged. "I got leave! It's Christmas or whatever, hey!"

He leaned down and kissed María on the cheek and then hugged Dominic, making it explicitly clear to Sierra that she'd been the only one *not* in on this brilliant move. "Wow, you guys," she gaped, sitting back down as Gael headed over to the dance floor to embarrass Juan in front of his new girlfriend. "How did you . . . I'm impressed."

María lifted one shoulder and wiggled her eyebrows to

make sure Sierra knew that, yes, she was pretty pleased with herself for keeping that secret. "I still got some tricks up my sleeve, Sierra."

"Hey," Anthony's sonorous, delicious voice said. "Can I . . . ?"

"Dance?" Sierra said, popping up a little too enthusiastically.

"Ha, yes, definitely that, but also I wanted to bring over —"

A smiling face appeared behind him.

"Carmela!" Sierra yelled, hugging her.

"Hi, Sierra!" The girl looked really excited to see her, as if they hadn't been about to knock each other out a few days earlier. Then she got solemn. "I just wanted to . . . I just wanted to say thank you. Anthony told me about shadowshaping and everything, and . . . yeah."

He rolled his eyes and made bunny ear quotations with both hands. "Right, I *told* you! By which she means she read all the whole beautiful story of your shadowshaping life that you typed out for me while I was in prison! Little spy!"

"Shouldn'ta left it out on the table if it was so private!" Carmela protested. "If I'd realized it was letters, I wouldn't have read it, for real! I thought it was a story he was writing, but then I realized it was too pretty for him to have written it, and then I made him tell me everything, and, and . . ."

Anthony rubbed his eyes, laughing.

"And I want to be like you when I grow up!"

"*I'm* not even grown up yet." Sierra didn't know what to say, so she hugged her again. "And anyway, I'm just glad you're still alive," she whispered, letting go.

"But, I mean, I wanna be like you," Carmela said, breathless, amazed, full of so much life. "What you are . . ."

"A shadowshaper?" Sierra asked. "Ha! I'm sure we can —"

"Lucera!" she said, laughing. "I want to be a Lucera too! Can I? Like . . . is that a . . ."

Sierra's face must've registered all the shock she felt, because almost immediately, Carmela's eyes went wide, and she looked like she was about to back-step.

"Of course you can!" Sierra said, shaking off everything else. "I've . . . we've just never . . . there've never been two before! And it's always just been in the family but . . ." She shook away the last lingering uncertainties, as well she should've. "Of course you can, sis. It's a brand-new day. We make the rules now. We just gotta figure out how."

"And now," Anthony said, "yes, I would like this dance, if you don't mind."

Over by the band, the shimmering images of Vincent, Alice, Little Tolula, and the rest of the Black Hoodies watched approvingly.

Beside them, we mingled with the other spirits, some dancing, some chatting, some just watching, our wide, ancient eyes taking in the beauty of the world we fought so hard to bring to life.

And thinking of all we had survived, all the many moments that we had fought through to arrive at this one, we watched, with love and victory in our hearts, as Anthony King offered the crook of his elbow, and Sierra Santiago slid her arm into it, and together they walked onto the dance floor, our stories tucked safely within their thoughts, and the future stretched ahead like a beautiful song.

ACKNOWLEDGMENTS

What a journey it's been! I'm so grateful first and foremost to all the readers who have read and been moved by Sierra's story, who have seen themselves in her and her friends, who have connected to this magic. I write for you.

A gigantic thank-you to all the editors who've worked with me along this marvelous shadowshaping adventure, starting with Cheryl Klein, who pulled book one from the slush pile (literally! snail mail!) and believed in it from the beginning. The torch went then to Nick Thomas and Weslie Turner and then on to Jody Corbett, and I'm so grateful to all of you for seeing these books through to fruition.

Thank you to the whole team at Scholastic, all of whom have been amazing throughout this process, especially Arthur A. Levine, Lizette Serrano, Emily Heddleson, Tracy van Straaten, Rachel Feld, Isa Caban, Shannon Pender, Amy Goppert, Melissa Schirmer, and Erik Ryle.

A very special thank-you to Christopher Stengel, who designed all the amazing Shadowshaper Cypher covers, and Zephorah Nuré, who embodies Sierra so perfectly on each one.

Thank you to Tim Paul, who created the Shadowshaper map of Brooklyn. And thank you to the brilliant Nilah Magruder, who drew the Deck of Worlds, and always brings my words to life with such excellence.

To Eddie Schneider and Joshua Bilmes and the whole JABberwocky Lit crew: You are wonderful. Thank you.

Many thanks to Leslie Shipman at the Shipman Agency and Lia Chan at ICM.

Thank you Renée Ahdieh and Roshani Chokshi for giving notes on the initial draft! To Tracy Deonn Walker for coming through in the clutch with thoughts about the ending! And a huge thank-you to Adriana M. Martínez Figueroa for her thoughtful consultations about the story and characters and advice on Puerto Rican curse-outs!

Brittany Nicole Williams was by my side and had my back throughout the process of this book coming into existence and, like my whole life, it wouldn't be what it is without her. But most especially: Before even the first word had been written, it was Brittany who mentioned how she imagined Septima ending up a crotchety old vieja in Sierra's attic — a thread that, once pulled, ended up revealing so many of the secrets of *Shadowshaper Legacy*. Thank you!

Thanks always to my amazing family: Dora, Marc, Malka, Lou, Calyx, and Paz. Thanks to Iya Lisa and Iya Ramona and Iyalocha Tima, Patrice, Emani, Darrell, April, and my whole Ile Omi Toki family for their support; also thanks to Oba Nelson "Poppy" Rodriguez, Baba Malik, Mama Akissi, Mama Joan, Tina, and Jud and all the wonderful folks of Ile Ase. And thank you, Sam, Lauren, Jalisa, and Sorahya and fam. Thank you, Sam Reynolds, Jason Reynolds, Jacqueline Woodson, Akwaeke Emezi, Jalisa Roberts, Lauren Chanel Allen, John Jennings, and Sorahya Moore and fam.

Baba Craig Ramos: We miss you and love you and carry you with us everywhere we go. Rest easy, Tío. Ibae bayen tonu.

I give thanks to all those who came before us and lit the way. I give thanks to all my ancestors; to Yemonja, Mother of Waters; gbogbo Orisa, and Olodumare.

ABOUT THE AUTHOR

Daniel José Older is the critically acclaimed and *New York Times* bestselling author of *Shadowshaper* and *Shadowhouse Fall*, as well as the novellas *Ghost Girl in the Corner* and *Dead Light March*, all part of the Shadowshaper Cypher series. He is also the author of the middle-grade series Dactyl Hill Squad, *Stars Wars: Last Shot*, *The Book of Lost Saints*, the Bone Street Rumba adult urban fantasy series, and the short story collection *Salsa Nocturna*. He won the International Latino Book Award and was shortlisted for the Kirkus Prize in Young Readers' Literature, the World Fantasy Award, the Andre Norton Award, the Locus Award, and the Mythopoeic Award.

Daniel splits his time between Brooklyn and New Orleans. You can find his thoughts on writing, read dispatches from his decade-long career as a New York City paramedic, and hear his music at his website, danieljoseolder.net, and follow him on social media at @djolder.